CITY OF THE DEAD
IS A "SHOCKER"
—Time

"Brutal and uncompromising!"
—San Francisco Examiner-Chronicle

"Thoroughly engrossing . . . one of the best storytellers around"
—Chicago News

"The toughest, most harrowing, most gruesome novel in a long, long time"
—Publishers Weekly

"Truth lies at the core of City of the Dead!"
—Los Angeles Times

"The chiller of the season!"
—Philadelphia Inquirer

Books by Herbert Lieberman

City of the Dead
Crawlspace

Published by POCKET BOOKS

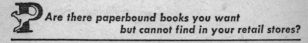

**Are there paperbound books you want
but cannot find in your retail stores?**

You can get any title in print in **POCKET BOOK** editions. Simply send retail price, local sales tax, if any, plus 35¢ per book to cover mailing and handling costs, to:

MAIL SERVICE DEPARTMENT
POCKET BOOKS • A Division of Simon & Schuster, Inc.
1230 Avenue of the Americas • New York, New York 10020

Please send check or money order. We cannot be responsible for cash.   *Catalogue sent free on request.*

Titles in this series are also available at discounts in quantity lots for industrial or sales-promotional use. For details write our Special Products Department: Department AR, POCKET BOOKS, 1230 Avenue of the Americas, New York, New York 10020.

Herbert Lieberman

CITY
OF
THE
DEAD

A KANGAROO BOOK
PUBLISHED BY POCKET BOOKS NEW YORK

CITY OF THE DEAD

Simon and Schuster edition published 1976

POCKET BOOK edition published August, 1977

All of the characters in this book are fictitious,
and any resemblance to actual persons, living or
dead, is purely coincidental.

This POCKET BOOK edition includes every word contained in
the original, higher-priced edition. It is printed from brand-
new plates made from completely reset, clear, easy-to-read type.
POCKET BOOK editions are published by
POCKET BOOKS,
a Simon & Schuster Division of
GULF & WESTERN CORPORATION
1230 Avenue of the Americas,
New York, N.Y. 10020.
Trademarks registered in the United States
and other countries.

ISBN: 0-671-80877-X.
Library of Congress Catalog Card Number: 76-4969.
This POCKET BOOK edition is published by arrangement
with Simon & Schuster, Inc. Copyright, ©, 1976, by Herbert
Lieberman. All rights reserved. This book, or portions
thereof, may not be reproduced by any means without permission of the original publisher: Simon & Schuster, Inc.,
1230 Avenue of the Americas, New York, N.Y. 10020.

Printed in the U.S.A.

ACKNOWLEDGMENT

I would like to express my gratitude to Dr. Yong-Myun Rho, Deputy Chief Medical Examiner, City of New York, who served so graciously as technical adviser on this book.

FOR
JOSÉ QUINTERO

The psychiatrist knows all and does nothing.
The surgeon knows nothing and does all.
The dermatologist knows nothing and does nothing.
The pathologist knows everything, but a day too late.

———OLD ADAGE

The woes of Mahatma are known to Mahatma alone.

———ANONYMOUS

CITY OF THE DEAD

FRIDAY, APRIL 12. 8:15 A.M. THE FDR DRIVE.

The wail of sirens. Police cars screaming northward. Ambulances following in hot pursuit. Up ahead, the gray spidery latticework of the Queensboro Bridge. Across the water, the candy-striped chimneys of the Con Ed Ravenswood plant belching smoke skyward. Just beyond that, the ugly sprawl of the Queens skyline. Barges and tugs push sluggishly upriver. Gulls wheel and shriek overhead.

A blur of motion as the patrol cars plunge into the 90th Street overpass, whoosh through the dark wet shade, then burst into the sunlight on the other side. Startled, drivers veer off to the side, scurrying to get out of the way.

A left at 96th Street and west to Madison. From there, north and on up into Harlem—108th, 116th—then left at 126th into the huddled, dingy street of squalid, front-stoop tenements. This is the 6th Homicide zone—an area famed for the highest murder rate in the city of New York. Traffic clogs the trash-lined street. Ragtag schoolchildren, satchels of books, greasy bags of lunch, squealing and darting round the stoops, ecstatic with the unexpected excitement.

Up ahead, patrol cars nose their way in through waves of milling people—a soft wall reluctantly yielding before the wailing sirens, the rotating dome lights, and the black stub-nosed police vans.

The lead car wheels into an area cordoned off by ropes. the wail of its sirens slowly dying. The police forensic unit is already there, rear-receiving doors flung open. A dozen patrolmen struggle to hold back the surging crowd.

A tall, gray-haired man climbs out of the rear seat of the lead car, confronted suddenly by a wall of black faces —sullen, anxious, resentful.

"All right—step back—move back—move it on back."

1

"Come on—let the man through."

"This way, Chief."

The crowd pauses, holds back a bit, as the tall, powerfully built man limps past. Then slowly it closes behind him. An ominous silence descends over the place. You can almost touch the resentment.

Inside 315 West 126th Street—a dingy hallway tattooed with street graffiti. *Shaz 135—Cool Fezito 116—Mamasuck 139*. The stench of fried fish and urine. Frightened eyes peering out the cracks of partially opened doorways; faces peering down over the crumbling banisters two stories above. The man they call the Chief ascends the stairs moving slowly up past and through the hushed crowd from one flight to the next.

"All right—let the man through."

"This way, Chief. Right up here."

"Who you shovin', man?"

"Move it on, buster—move it on."

"All right—everyone back inside. Go on back to bed. Have some breakfast. How about it?"

The Chief is led down a choking, fetid corridor—raw garbage littering the floor, doors all shut, defaced by more graffiti; ushered finally to one apartment door that is open.

Inside, the place is already swarming with police and detectives. The periodic white flash of police cameras exploding; lab technicians on their knees dusting for prints; the intent and purposeful rasp of pencils as police artists scrawl diagrams onto sketch pads.

The Chief inches his way forward into what is obviously a bedroom. A soiled, bare mattress is flung across the floor. Over the mattress a single naked light bulb depends from a frayed electric cord. On a sheet of greasy paper beside the bed lies an uneaten piece of moldering fried fish.

"Mornin', Chief."

"All right, what d'ya got here, Flynn?"

"A goddamned mess." Detective Sergeant Edward Flynn glowers about the squalid room. "That's what I got here."

"Spare me the huffing and puffing, will you?"

"Huffin' and puffin', my ass. Nine o'clock in the mornin' and already I'm up to my eyeballs—six homicides, a pack of long-haired freaks walkin' picket around the station house, and I've just had about a dozen Maalox."

"I'm not interested in your problems, Flynn. I've got enough of my own. All right, where is it?"

"In the toilet," Flynn sulks. "Follow your nose. You can't miss it."

Two beefy, strapping patrolmen step aside. The tall, gray-haired man enters an abhorrent little privy—a communal end-of-the-hall toilet in an end-of-the-line apartment—a dank, foul-smelling cubicle with peeling paint and a punched-out window to which lethal shards of glass still cling. Its main feature is a slimy porcelain tub with curved, incongruously elegant legs. The tub is half-filled with water, and in the water sits a handsome young black—late twenties—eyes open, jaw clamped tight, the mouth twisted into a hideous grin that makes him appear to be laughing at the ceiling. The handle of an ice pick projects from the center of his chest. Blood seeping from the wound has turned the tepid water around him to a pale rose.

The tall, gray-haired man mutters something, stoops painfully to his knee, and a moment later, with the flash bulbs popping and exploding all about him, he proceeds to examine the wound in the center of the chest. The pick has gone straight through the sternum, right up to the hilt.

"Beautiful, Flynn."

"I knew you'd appreciate it."

Still stooped there painfully beside the tub, the Chief jots notes hurriedly onto a pad. He notes the degree of rigor mortis in order to affix a time of death; examines the throat area for ligature marks; checks the whites of the eyes for traces of petechial hemorrhage.

Putting the note pad away in his inside pocket, his eye catches a small cut on the inside surface of the young man's left wrist, another on the inside of the right thumb.

"Defense cuts," the Chief murmurs to himself.

"Poor bastard didn't have a chance," remarks the detective hovering above him.

The Chief rises painfully to his feet. "All yours. When you're finished, call my office. Have them wrap it up and send it down to me. Make sure they bind the hands. I want to examine those fingernails later today."

Even as he moves out amid the flashing of police cameras, the lab technicians of the forensic unit are moving into the vile little privy, already on their knees before the wet, grinning figure in the tub, dusting the handle of the ice pick in his chest for prints.

Out in the hallway again, the crowd mutters and yields begrudgingly before the tall, gray-haired man.

"All right—go on home—it's all over now."

"Step back—let the man through."

Two cops with a canvas bag move up past the Chief.

"Got time for one more?" asks Morello, Lieutenant of Detectives.

"Where is it?"

"Just a few blocks down—113th Street."

"Okay," the Chief sighs. "Let's get over there." He turns for a moment, staring back at the small, truculent figure of Detective Flynn scribbling into a pad. "Call me this afternoon, Flynn. I should have the serology reports by then. You go get this bastard now. And Flynn—get off the Maalox. It's constipating."

Then out on the street again, and even as the patrol car inches its way through the mobs, the sound of fists pounding on the right rear fender reverberates through the vehicle. The grim, silent occupants do not even bother to look back.

8:45 A.M. 113th Street between Seventh and Eighth Avenues. More clogged traffic. More police vans. More wailing patrol cars with rotating dome lights. More police cordons and megaphones. Outside, up on the rooftops, six stories up, the heads of patrolmen peer down onto the choked and littered street.

Six flights up on a filthy landing, near a door leading to the roof, more detectives, more lab men, more flashing bulbs.

"Watcha got?" the Chief says.

The sergeant in charge reads from identification cards found in a cheap red vinyl wallet. "Rosales, Barbara. Nineteen. Hooker. They know her around here."

Once again this morning the Chief stoops down— this time to the torn and crumpled form of a rather coarse and plain-looking Spanish girl with bad skin.

"Junkie, too," the Chief says, permitting the still-limp arm with the needle tracks to fall back down onto the cold floor of the stairwell.

"Probably turning a trick up here," says Morello, looking around. "Picked the wrong John this time."

"Hazard of the profession." The Chief kneels, makes a series of mental notes while examining the body.

The girl is half sitting, half lying on her side, right shoulder propped against the wall, obscene graffiti figures scrawled on the moldy plaster above her. A huge wad of Kleenex has been stuffed down her mouth all the way into the windpipe. A single shredded edge of the stuff dangles out of the corner of her mouth. A pair of cheap black rayon panties have been yanked down below the knees, which are badly bruised and bleeding, showing how and in what position the girl struggled. Great white splotches of dried semen are all about the inside of the thighs and pubic area, and extruding from between the buttocks, an unfinished half pint of Southern Comfort, the neck of the bottle rammed up hard into the rectum.

"Okay." The Chief, completing his survey, rises to his feet. "When you finish up here, wrap it up and send it down to me."

"Hey, Doc," says a burly Italian patrolman, stooped over the body, "what's all the funny little puncture marks around her face?"

"Rat bites," the Chief says, turning to his driver. "All right, let's get out of here."

As he is leaving, the burly Italian cop tugs the unfinished bottle of Southern Comfort down from its snug berth and holds the mouth of it up to his partner. "Hey, Fazello—how about a shot?"

Loud, raucous laughter cascades down the narrow stairway, following the descending figure of the tall, gray-haired man.

Back in the patrol car again, tooling down the FDR Drive. The Chief sits hunched far back in the rear seat. Long, cramped legs sprawled out sideways for comfort, he watches the wide brown swatch of the East River slide backward past the window, unraveling like a filthy carpet. His face wears a perpetual scowl. He seems a harsh, vindictive sort. Not one of your enlightened liberals. He'd known too many murderers. He abhorred violence and mourned the passing of the electric chair. He was suffused with a kind of Old Testament eye-for-an-eye morality.

Though now in his sixties, his job had turned him gray at twenty-nine.

April again. Burgeoning spring. Tax time and the month of suicides. Gone now are February and March, season of drowned men, when the ice on the frozen rivers melt, yielding up the winter's harvest of junkies, itinerants, and prostitutes. Soon to come are July and August—the jack-knife months. Heat and homicide. Bullet holes, knife wounds, fatal garrotings, a grisly procession vomited out of the steamy ghettos of the inner city. Followed by September—early fall—season of wilting vegetation, self-guilt, and inexplicable loss. Battered babies with the subdural hematomas and the petechial hemorrhages. Then October—benign, quiescent; the oven pavements of the city cooling while death hangs back a little while, prostrate from all the carnage. Only to rush headlong into November and December. The holiday season. Thanksgiving and the Prince of Peace. Suicides come forth again.

Like so many other thriving enterprises, Paul Konig's is a cyclical business. He has his slack season and his busy season. Salad days and dog days. His good times, which, he knows, always proclaim the certainty of the approaching bad. He is, after all, subject to the same pressures and uncertainties as any other businessman, but his trade is unique. He is a forensic pathologist. Chief Medical Examiner, City of New York.

≈≈ 2 ≈≈

9:15 A.M. OFFICE OF THE CHIEF MEDICAL EXAMINER.
Konig at his desk. Crystals of doughnut sugar melting on his lips. The bitter morning taste of paper-container coffee and the first cigar, muzzy on his palate. Stacks of reports are strewn before him. A calendar agenda with that day, April 12, circled in red—an 11 A.M. lecture and laboratory at the University; a 2 P.M. call at the Crim-

inal Courts Building. There is, in addition to the regular avalanche of correspondence he carries on with pathologists all over the world, the usual assortment of invitations to address conferences, teaching offers for prestigious university seats, letters from coroners, doctors, and medical missionaries halfway round the world petitioning his advice on some tiny, arcane point of pathology. Sensing the absurdity of it all, he would answer each letter himself, feeling that doctors, just like clergymen, had an obligation to at least pretend to a wisdom they didn't really possess. For his part, the longer he practiced and studied, the deeper and more inescapable grew his conviction that he knew nothing. Nothing that really mattered.

On his desk, too, are the department's budget, which has to be completed for the City's fiscal planners; a number of bills, including a mortgage payment for a beach house in Montauk; and a stack of recent protocols, death reports: "This is the body of a well-developed, well-nourished white male, approximate age 26, height 5′ 9″—" Finally, separate from all the rest, is an envelope marked "Personal." He picks that up first, his fingers trembling ruefully on the flap before he tears it open. In it he finds a birthday card—an outlandish caricature of a large, shaggy bear in a doctor's robe with a stethoscope around its neck. It's signed with a big, untidy scrawl of red letters—"Dear Daddy, Sorry, Sorry, Sorry. Love."

Once again he lights the dead cold ashes of his cigar from a Bunsen burner, ponders the card, then reaches for a pot of coffee bubbling on a cooking ring behind him. Then he is reading and riffling through his reports. A short time later he's moving around the office with a sprinkling can, watering the jungle of pots and planters lining the long wall of windows—the begonias and the azaleas, the narcissus, the hyacinths he is forcing, the huge lantana, the spider plants, the long, muddy rows of spiny succulents, and the fabulous green-pink profusion of wandering Jew. His movements have a precise rhythm—several steps and a splash, several steps and a splash. On he goes from one pot to the next, cigar screwed into the center of his mouth, pausing only to flick off a wilted blossom or a dead leaf. He moves slowly and easily through the impeccably ordered chaos of his office, through the controlled disarray, past a brain floating in a tank of formalin, a table stacked with innumerable tissue slides, a slope of mortuary records stacked on the floor and reaching to the ceiling—the threatened landslide of the past fifteen years. It all has an order and rhythm perceptible only to him.

Halfway through the thrice-weekly ritual of the sprinkling can, the phone rings. Picking it up, he hears Carver's throaty voice through the receiver at the same moment that he hears her speaking just outside his door in the anteroom.

"You've got your lab at the University at eleven and you're due at court by two."

"I know. So what?"

"You asked me to remind you, so I'm reminding you."

"So you reminded me. Good for you."

"The Skardon people are here now. Wanna see them?"

He sighs dismally. "I s'pose this is as good a time as any."

"Up on the Thruway." Konig again ignites the cold ashes of his expired cigar. "Just north of Pelham—about a mile south of the exit." Over the flame of his lighter Konig's eyes search the harried faces of two people—a man and a woman—seated opposite him. "About thirty feet from the road, in some bushes. Have any idea what she was doing there?"

"Where?" the man snaps. "In the bushes?"

"No. On the Thruway."

"Coming home from school. She was coming home for spring vacation."

The woman whimpers softly into a handkerchief. Red, teary, sleepless eyes show above the expensive fabric. Cambric, Konig observes and says, "Hitchhiking?"

"I s'pose so." The man nods impatiently. "She always hitched. Said it saved money. What the hell she had to save money for, I don't—"

The woman sobs out loud. The man glares at her. "For Chrissake, Emily, will you quit the goddamned whining. We don't even know yet if this girl is actually—"

Konig makes a grunting sound. "You say she's been missing about three days?"

"That's right," Mr. J. Phelps Skardon says. "Started out Tuesday afternoon right after classes."

Probing outward from beneath the craggy, beetled brow, Konig's eyes continue their careful appraisal of the Skardons. Upper middle class. White Protestant. Undoubtedly wealthy. Family wealth, he imagines. Never lifted a goddamned finger for it. Skardon, Konig surmises, is a professional. A lawyer, undoubtedly, from the way the man questioned him at the start of the interview, his manner brusque, impatient, behaving as if being called down to identify what might be the remains of his daughter was an embarrassment, an inconvenience. His attitude toward Konig, the civil-servant doctor, is vaguely contemptuous.

Mrs. Skardon is a small, pretty woman. Her eyes seem puzzled and terribly frightened. Neurasthenic, Konig imagines, the victim of innumerable psychogenic disorders—palpitations, cold sweats, insomnia, chronic constipation—all generated no doubt from twenty-five years of marriage to a bully. Konig can see the bully now, barely repressed inside the man, but already beginning to show in the beet-red flush in full bloom above the collar of his shirt and in the somewhat cyanotic lips. Mr. J. Phelps Skardon would die in roughly two years, Konig estimates, the victim of a stroke.

"Any idea what she was wearing when she left school?" he asks.

"Now how the hell would I know that?" Skardon lashes out, then sees something flicker in the cool, steady gaze of the pathologist that makes him sit back a bit, subdued, miffed, a little contrite. "We don't know what she was wearing. What was this other girl wearing?"

"Not very much," Konig says. The woman moans and Konig rises. "Well, I s'pose we ought to go and have a look."

The Skardons rise too, he bounding up, she somewhat more tentatively.

"You stay here," the man bawls at her.

"But I want—"

"No need for it." Skardon cuts off all further discussion. "This'll just take a minute."

A small, feckless puff of air falls from Mrs. Skardon's lips, a word unspoken, and she sinks back into her seat. Konig can still hear her whimpering as the door closes behind them.

Silently they walk from Konig's office across a reception area to a small room at the back of the building. There is nothing there but a long, rectangular plate-glass window beyond which lies a wide, gray dumbwaiter shaft. Konig presses a button beside the window. Instantly, a motor whines; the steel cables beyond the glass begin to move upward, and then from the floor somewhere below them, a dumbwaiter platform rises, bearing the waxen, yellow cadaver of a young girl. The motor turns off and the platform stops behind the glass before them.

For a long while they don't speak. Then Skardon, his eyes riveted on the figure behind the glass, suddenly says, "Was she raped?" His face has gone white, the color of parchment.

"Several times." Konig eyes him coolly. "We found three distinct semen types inside her." He gazes for a moment at the badly battered features of a girl approximately seventeen years of age, face twisted in the rictus of violent and painful death. She had clearly once been a pretty, vital child, in her first year of college, with a privileged background and the world just beginning to open before her. She'd been beaten viciously.

Gaping through the plate glass at the body, J. Phelps Skardon's face twists with hate. "Were they niggers?"

"Beg pardon?"

"The animals who did this to my daughter. Were they niggers? This is their kind of thing."

Konig watches the man steadily. He appears to be on the verge of apoplexy. "I'm afraid I couldn't say. I can tell you the type semen. Hence the blood type. But I'm afraid science has yet to find any physiological difference between black and white semen."

Skardon hangs there, leaning against the green wall, stupefied. His features wear an expression of betrayal.

Konig sighs wearily. "From what I have to go on, there's no way of saying who her assailants were. Anyway, it's all now in the hands of the Bureau of Detectives."

Locked in awkward silence, Konig walks the Skardons back to the First Avenue exit. At the door they stand about, shuffling their feet, avoiding one another's eyes. No one speaks. At last, grunting, truculent to the very end, J. Phelps Skardon barges down the front steps, leaving the poor, tremulous, craven Mrs. Skardon to fumble along behind.

Suddenly, not knowing why, and stunned at his own anger, Konig cries out after the two figures just stooping to enter a cab. "Why in God's name did you permit her to hitchhike?"

Skardon turns and stares back at him. It is at that moment that the man begins to cry.

Almost 10 A.M. now, and along with April sunshine pouring through the front door comes a torrent of troubled, querulous humanity—pathologists, policemen, lab technicians, reporters, and, of course, mourners. The mourners are always easiest to spot. They wear their apprehension and their grief like carnations in their lapels.

Ambulances and police vans are pulled up at the sides and the back of the building. Patrol cars are everywhere around the place. Gurney carts roll out; canvas sacks roll in. "The meat delivery," the police call it.

Inside, the noise all along the green corridors is deafening. Clatter and gonging of metal doors. The incomprehensible garble of a PA system with the susurrant static and crackle of loose wires summoning people from one place to another.

Konig weaves through this torrent, limping a little from the ache in his leg. Sciatica. APC's and Valium. Nothing else for it but to wait it out. He greets several of his colleagues on their way down to the autopsy rooms—the deputy medical examiners—Pearsall the amiable, Bonertz the melancholy, Delaney the bigot-prig (will work only on white corpses), and then, of course, shifty-eyed Carl Strang, pompous and grandiloquent, who watches the Chief closely and covets his job.

There are a number of other men—Indians, Orientals, Slavs—good men who have come halfway around the world to study with the Chief. There are also newly appointed associates, officious and bumbling, anxious to please, and medical students sporting rumpled gowns with stethoscopes conspicuously placed for highest visibility—badge of rank sort of thing. The Chief smiles inwardly to think of the usefulness of a stethoscope at a morgue.

Konig descends now to the autopsy rooms, going down a steel spiral stairway into green glowing light. Down out of long green corridors he drops. Aquarium green. Municipal green. Bureaucratic green. Green moist tiles—freezing in winter, sweating in summer. Down into a soft green diffusion—the netherworld of First Avenue. Past the Acheron of a dozy guard, across the Styx of the iron anteroom gate, moaning open, clanging shut behind him.

The gong of heavy steel doors reverberating through cavernous green-tiled tunnels.

Down he goes, still descending, yet another short flight of stairs, the slow, slurred click of his slightly limping tread pinging off the ceilings and walls. Another gate squeals open, gongs shut behind him, and he is now in the deeper green of the subbasement level. The air is heavy with the thick, fumy vapors of formaldehyde.

There is a curious smell to an autopsy room. Death and asafetida. Formalin and fright. Once you've smelled it, you never forget it. The odor—almost forty years' worth —so much a part of Konig's being that he is no longer aware of it. It imbues his clothing, his skin, his hair. His car smells of it and his closets at home. When his wife was alive, she wouldn't permit him to come near her until he'd showered.

Konig now enters a gray cool area filled with the high-pitched electrical whir of refrigerator motors. Already lined up on his left, a number of stainless-steel trolleys, each bearing a lumpen, belted canvas sack—a grim succession of the night's harvest of victims. There is a whole wall of refrigerator compartments running from floor to ceiling, temporary repositories for the unclaimed, the anonymous, the unwanted. Known often just by numbers, the stiff, formal impersonality of two and three digits, here the dead lie, all left to the cold impartiality of separate drawers. All awaiting the pathologist's blade.

Konig drops down a final three steps, pushes open swinging doors and enters a bright white glow. Here, green-robed attendants shuttle back and forth on padded feet—hooded acolytes in some ancient druidical rite. Konig moves past steel pans of cirrhotic livers, a diseased lung gurgling in a tub of formalin. Each time Konig makes this descent, each time he enters this abattoir, this charnel house fuming with the ever-thickening waves of stench, his whole being is suffused with the curious, yet somehow entirely befitting notion that he has once again come home.

Already the place is a hive of activity—twelve tables going all at once. Cadavers naked, flayed open, sectioned. Unreal-looking things. The organs opened, exposed, give the appearance of wax fruits.

A great din and hum of human enterprise animates this autopsy room. It could be the production loft of a prosperous dress manufacturer, the tailors all bent and busy over their tables.

Here are the pathologists, cutting, weighing, evaluating; and the police stenographers, scribbling dictation from them onto their pads. The young medical students hovering around the various tables, asking questions. The scrubbers—dieners they call them—sewing up the cadavers with large needles and black thread after the pathologists have finished. A strange breed of men, these. One there in particular, a small, dark, recently naturalized Albanian with furtive eyes and scarcely any English, Konig watches uneasily, knowing him to be one who liked to handle young female cadavers, liked to undress them, prepare them for cutting. Then would linger over the flayed carcass, long after the autopsy was completed and everyone else had gone, ostensibly sewing it up.

And then, of course, the cadavers, twelve of them lined up on steel tables—the objects of the quest. Here, a black man, throat slashed from ear to ear, laryngeal cartilage glinting from the gaping wound, flashes a death grin. On the table beside him, an ancient, wizened little lady, with dainty hands and feet, somewhat beyond eighty. Body shrunken, oddly childlike, face blue with cyanosis, the sparse, frizzled pubic hair of a child, she seems to be gazing upward at heaven. She'd been hammered to death and robbed of sixty cents in a welfare hotel room the night before.

A little farther down, a bedraggled itinerant with a huge halo of gray hair encircling the face of a saint. He'd been martyred in a doorway on Canal Street. Then two homicides—undoubtedly two of Flynn's half dozen of the night before—three gunshot wounds, a stabbing through the throat and a fatal garroting. Then a beautiful young girl, with the features and lineaments of a fashion model, dead of barbiturates at twenty-two. After her, a drowned black prostitute who'd been in the water several days, her hair separated from the scalp so that it could be lifted off like a cap. White froth bubbles from her nose and the body is swollen from distention of the tissues with gas.

There are few things that can be hidden from the pathologist. But at that point there's no longer any need to hide. The reasons for hiding have all been eliminated. The only questions that remain are academic. The pathologist stands before the flayed and naked corpse like an old shaman reading auguries in the viscera of sacrificial sheep.

"Emboli in left coronary artery."

"Aortic incompetence. Ascending aorta dilated with longitudinal rugae on the intima."

"Liver enlarged with gross fatty change."

"Testes, 30 grams."

"Rectal lesions—rectum markedly dilated, containing fresh semen."

No further need for shame or disguise. Shame seems such an empty gesture at this point. It is all written there clearly for the pathologist to read, as if the organs were a kind of papyrus upon which the foolish hieroglyphics of our lives are scrawled.

Beneath the cool white glare of overhead fluorescents, Konig pauses to watch Arthur Grimsby, a young assistant, remove the calvaria of what was once a male Caucasian, approximate age forty to forty-five, blood type O+. A jeweler shot to death in his shop on Delancey Street.

The saw buzzes and particles of hair and bone whir off its blade in a pretty lariat.

"Neat," Konig murmurs as young Grimsby's hand severs the medulla and cranial nerves preparatory to removal of the brain.

Already the Chief's gray, avid eyes have spied the point of entrance of the bullet. It is at the forehead and just beneath the hairline. Long before Grimsby, he has spied the point of exit at the back of the head, as well as the route the bullet has taken in between. He has a fairly good idea from the powder burns on the skin at what distance the pistol was fired, and from the angle at which the bullet entered the skull, something of the position in which the jeweler met his end.

Grimsby extracts several fragments of the bullet with a prong, plucking them out and holding them up to the light like rare gems, for all to see.

"Neat," Konig murmurs again. "Careful you don't mess those bullet tracks."

The Chief always pauses for the children. He doesn't want to, he simply has to. It is a compulsion of his, a rather sick one he has concluded, since he knows that there is literally nothing more he can learn from contemplating such pathetic spectacles. He has seen so many in his day. They all tell the same dismal story. But, still, in nearly forty years of practice, of seeing the most grisly testimony to man's inexhaustible genius for cruelty, he has never quite been able to steel himself to the sight of a battered child. When the job is done well, as so frequently it is, it is truly an awesome sight to contemplate.

The one he is looking at now, mauled and beaten beyond recognition, is a toddler. No more than two or so, and the facial features have literally been erased by the use of some heavy, blunt instrument.

Seeing the ragged, broken little shape on the table, Konig suddenly has a vision of his own daughter, Lolly—Lolly as a child at the seashore, toddling toward him with a shovel and a sand pail upon which enamel dolphins gambol; Lolly in the mountains, a brash little girl astride a dun mare; Lolly on her first trip abroad, a sere and yellowed photograph, frayed with age, showing a smiling ten-year-old perched on the taffrail of a French passenger liner.

McCloskey, the youngest man on the staff, is now working up the little cadaver. The Chief hovers there behind him, a little self-consciously, and watches. Several times the young pathologist pauses from the painstakingly meticulous work, a lapidarist laboring in miniature, and gazes up at the frosted ceiling windows.

"Pretty, isn't it?" Konig murmurs over the shoulder of the young man.

"Lousy," McCloskey replies. His back still to the Chief, he bends once more to his task. "Nearly a hundred separate contusions. Liver ruptured. Face a pulp. Nearly every bone broken—even the fingers."

"By all means the fingers," Konig says, a touch of spiteful levity in his voice. "They never forget the fingers. That's often the most painful. Particularly in young children. Parents claim the kid fell out of his crib." Konig chuckles.

"Spare me any reference to the parents, please." McCloskey's powerful frame swells. "If I ever set eyes on them—get my hands on them—"

"Mama's probably preggers right now with the next." Konig laughs again and wonders why it makes him feel better. "I'll finish up for you."

McCloskey flushes. "If you don't mind, sir, I'll finish this one myself."

Konig passes up an embolism, talks a young assistant through a very delicate arterial survey, then pauses for a moment to watch Deputy Chief Medical Examiner Carl Strang work up the remains of what was once a dignified Lebanese gentleman. Strang is inserting a syringe into the corner of the cadaver's eye, then very deftly draws off a few cc's of vitreous humor.

"Get me a spec report on this," he snaps at a young assistant. "Tell them I need it quick— Oh, hello, Paul."

The smile, the lethal smile, flashes, then the pointedly assessing glance. "You all right?"

"I'm fine."

"You look a little peaked."

"Been up and running since five." He studies Strang's sharply chiseled face. "I have a feeling I'm going to be called up before the grand jury."

"Oh?"

"The Robinson business."

"They're not going to prosecute, Paul."

"They're not?"

"Too sticky—too political."

Konig tastes the bitterness rising in his gorge. "Carl, tell me something—Blaylock didn't talk with you at any time before you did the Robinson job?"

"Certainly not."

"And you still feel your conclusion of asphyxiation by hanging will stand up?"

"I have no doubt of it." The Strang smile is more radiant than ever.

It's just one smile too many for the Chief. Suddenly he lashes out. "But why in God's name couldn't you at least have done a tissue study?"

"No need to. The abrasions were superficial."

"Superficial? Around the head—superficial?" Konig's voice grows harsher. Several Indian doctors in the area turn. "Oh, forget it." His voice drops and he gazes down now at the dignified-looking Lebanese gentleman on the table. "What's the story on this?"

"Diabetic—pancreatic lesions—insulin tracks—"

"Look at the chancre scar on his belly."

"It's old—at least ten years."

"Exactly why I'd do a lumbar—he's a syphilitic."

The impertinent smile wavers on Strang's features as the Chief turns abruptly and strides from the room.

Now 10:30 A.M. and a procession of assorted mankind all with vested interests marches in and out of Konig's door. First, an insurance adjuster clamoring for a verdict of suicide on a death certificate. Konig is no friend to the insurance companies, with their actuarial tables and their wheedling, obsequious adjusters. Always quick to extract their annual tithe at premium time, but squirming desperately, dragging their feet, trying to weasel out when their day comes to pay off. He is determined to make it hard for the man.

Next a young pathologist, just out of residency and full of the kind of gushing idealism Konig knows will shortly disappear. Then a Messianic salesman from a medical supply house, hawking expensive machinery, evangelizing "the new technology." "Revolutionary," he calls it. "It will change everything." It is nearly eleven o'clock when Konig permits several brochures to be pressed upon him, with promises to read them that night, all the while easing the man gently toward the door.

Then at last he slips with a sigh into his jacket and makes ready to stroll the short distance across First Avenue to the University lecture hall where his students await him.

≈≈ 3 ≈≈

11:00 A.M. PATHOLOGY LABORATORY,
NEW YORK UNIVERSITY SCHOOL OF MEDICINE.

"There are very few amenities observed in the autopsy room, ladies and gentlemen." Konig stands bathed in a cone of white light at the center of an amphitheater on the ground floor of the University Medical School. The course he is teaching is Forensic Medicine 320. He has taught it now for nearly a quarter of a century to a generation of medical students, most of whom had little aptitude or interest in the subject, having had their eyes on more lucrative specializations, and there only because the University made it obligatory for them to be there—at least for a year.

One hundred and fifty youthful, intent faces peer down on Konig now as he whips back, magicianlike, the sheet covering the waxen cadaver of a rather handsome middle-aged man.

"Everything is reduced to its most basic and elemental," Konig continues, "and unlike the diagnostician, who deals in the luxury of hypotheses, the pathologist deals only in final truth. The cause of death is all that is at issue here." His eyes sweep up and down the length of the cadaver as he speaks, encompassing in one glance a multitude of detail.

"All we know about this pleasant-looking gentleman," Konig continues, "is that he was forty-five years of age with no prior history of cardiovascular disease. There is no history of hypertension, seizures, or convulsions. He was not diabetic and he was on no medications. He had an annual checkup, the last of which took place three weeks ago, was pronounced fit as a fiddle by his internist, and the last time his wife spoke with him, two days ago, he was in a cheerful frame of mind." Smiling, Konig gazes around at the bright young faces of his audience, then nods to an assistant. "Well, ladies and gentlemen, I believe we are now ready to begin."

With a nine-inch-long scalpel, Konig makes three lightning-swift incisions. Two proceeding from each tip of the scapulae, bisecting at a point above the sternum, and from that point plunging straight downward to the pubic symphysis. The three deft slashes form a large letter Y—sort of a cosmic-joke-of-a-Y to denote a man already marked by fatal destiny. Like the Y that stands for YOU.

Several more slashes of his blade and Konig flays open the neck and chest. With bone cutters, he severs the cartilage joining ribs to sternum, tears asunder a series of small clavicle joints, and then, with a queasy ripping sound, yanks away the whole front of the chest. In no more than a minute, the livid, rigored thing on the table has been split apart like a chicken with all its internal organs gleaming brightly there in place like a bowl of fruit.

Blood has begun to seep into the small trenches lining the table and collects there in tepid little pools. Konig swings his scalpel round through the inside of the lower jaw, disconnecting the tongue. He tugs sharply downward on the muscle, releasing the larynx behind it, then pulls it out through the yawning neck. Another stroke severs the gullet and two or three more free the heart and lungs. Next he hauls the whole grisly concatenation of things out, holding them up by the windpipe for all his audience to see— once more the cosmic magician producing rabbits from a hat.

There's an audible gasp of admiration and some scattered applause as he drops the whole business into a steel bowl held out to him by an assistant.

The bowl is now held under the tap, the spigot turned on, and while the stream of water is played over the organs, Konig commences his examination of them. He cuts into larynx and tongue in order to detect signs of vomiting or hemorrhage. He rotates the heart in his hand, exposing its chambers, rinsing out the blood, testing each valve for signs of defect. Lastly, he takes a pair of scissors and snips his way up the arteries, searching there for plaque and emboli, as well as in the blood vessels of the heart itself.

"Nothing remarkable here," he proclaims.

Returning to the body, he proceeds to remove the viscera, examining each organ in the same meticulous fashion. He draws off a sample of gastric contents into a small jar, as well as a sample of urine by merely pressing the bladder. He then turns these over to his assistant. "A little something for the toxicology lab, just in case of foul play."

A few more deft motions and he has lifted out spleen and liver, sliced them up like a fresh loaf of bread, and dropped sections into several nearby cardboard buckets used for storage and transport of internal organs. "Still looks good," he cries out.

The steel sink is now nearly full of organs submerged in roseate water. Konig is now ready for the *coup de grâce* —a single sweep of the blade across the top of the head that opens the scalp from ear to ear. Several additional slashes and the scalp becomes a pair of flaps which he yanks down over the man's face in much the same way one might pull off a pair of gloves.

With the saw blade he then cuts around the skull slightly above ear level and at last lifts off the calvaria—the skullcap—like the lid of a cookie jar. Gleaming there in the cold white light are the membrane sacs containing the brain. Slashing these open, he then works his rubbered fingers under the frontal lobes of the brain, at last lifting it out, whole and intact, from the base of the skull. It is only a matter of moments until he separates the medulla oblongata from the spinal cord, then lets the entire brain slither into a steel bowl, examining it closely as he sluices water over it from the spigot.

"All appears quite normal, ladies and gentlemen. This is a bit of a riddle," he announces, although it is really no great riddle to him. The diffuse hemorrhage at the base of the brain has told him all he needs to know. He proceeds to slice the brain into neat sections. "Ah—I beg your pardon. Not so much of a riddle, after all."

He holds up a section of cortex dripping with blood. "Ruptured saccular aneurysm in the circle of Willis—a blowout, ladies and gentlemen. No more, no less."

With small knives he carefully dissects out the damaged section of artery at the base of the brain, pointing out the weakness in the wall, a small point of fatal rupture about the size of a pea. "A tiny but lethal flaw in an otherwise very capable machine." He casts a smiling glance around his audience. "Thus fate makes monkeys of us all."

≈≈ 4 ≈≈

11:45 A.M. MEDICAL EXAMINER'S OFFICE.

The warm, redemptive sun of April streams across Konig's back as he chats wearily on the phone with the Deputy Mayor.

"I'm perfectly aware of that."

"You are? Well, I certainly hope you are because you're damned well going to have to be there."

"I want to be. Wouldn't have it any other way."

"I'm glad you feel that way, Paul," the Deputy Mayor whines in slightly crazed nasalities. "The Mayor doesn't want—repeat, does not want—any further embarrassment. He's had embarrassment enough. When barely a quarter

of the year's gone by and you've already got seven suicides in the Tombs, and now another—you know things
are getting pretty hairy. I've had the Governor's office, the
ACLU, the NAACP, the B'nai B'rith, the Board of Corrections, a half-dozen assorted civil rights groups, and a
charming fraternal organization calling themselves the
Savage Skulls all eager to see me. Breaking down my door.
Serving me with ultimatums and subpoenas. Shouting obscenities up and down the halls."

"Well," Konig says, his mind on some aspect of the
curious little defense cuts he'd seen on the thumb and
wrist of the young black man up in Harlem that morning,
"that's unfortunate."

"Unfortunate?" There's a sputtering sound, then laughter full of choking rage. "Goddamned right, unfortunate."

"What would you like me to say? I fully realize your
concern. I'm sorry. But I'm still going to stand with a verdict of asphyxiation by hanging."

"Why won't you say which of your people did the autopsy?"

"It's of no consequence who did the autopsy. Suffice
it to say, the conclusion of this department is self-inflicted
death by hanging, and I'll stand behind that."

"I'm asking you, Paul, as the sensible man I've known
for twenty-five years—who conducted the Robinson autopsy? It was Strang, wasn't it?"

"Sorry, Maury. You're wasting your breath. That's
privileged information, and I will not disclose it. Not to
you, and not to the Mayor."

Konig flinches and pulls his ear from the receiver as it
starts to hiss and sputter a stream of invective. "Fine—
fine. You love martyrdom. You always have. My friend,
Saint Paul the martyr. Well, you will be martyred, because, my dear fellow, now that permission's been granted
to exhume the body and reautopsy this Robinson boy, I
think you should know there are several people out for
your ass."

"I know just who."

"Good. Then you know this is no minor-league stuff,
and if there's the slightest thing fishy—repeat, *the slightest
thing*—you're going to be hauled before the grand jury so
fast it'll make your head spin. If you think you can bull-
shit your way out of this one the way you do, Paul—the

way we all know you do—with a lot of fast-talking technical arglebargle, I'm here to tell you you're sadly—"

"I told you—I'm perfectly willing to go before the grand jury."

"I know you are, goddamn it," Deputy Mayor Benjamin sighs wearily. "How well I know that you are. Christ on the cross. Waiting for the spikes and the crown of thorns. Well, don't worry, Calvary's coming. You'll get it, too. And you'll love every minute of it. Goodbye."

No sooner has Konig, fuming with rage, slammed down the phone and taken up his notes in preparation for his court appearance that afternoon than it rings again.

Muttering, he lets it go on ringing, waiting for Carver to pick it up outside. But she doesn't. Then it occurs to him that it is noontime and she's already gone to lunch.

He resolves not to answer the phone but to go on with his notes. The ring persists for ten or a dozen times, its jarring regularity taking on something of an almost human malevolence. Konig grits his teeth, determined to outlast it. But it is a war of wills and he is losing.

"Christ," he snaps and snatches up the receiver. "Konig here," he snarls, but hears nothing. "Hello. Medical Examiner's Office. Konig here. Who's this?" Still no sound other than a faint, distant ringing through the wires. "Hello—hello."

He is about to fling the receiver back on the cradle when his arm freezes and he can feel the scalp beneath his gun-metal-gray hair begin to tingle. Then he hears something like a sigh—a long, rather weary exhalation of air—and in that moment he knows who is on the other end.

"Hello—Lolly?"

Another sigh.

"Lolly—Lolly—is it you?"

He waits. No response, only a rather agitated breathing. There's no mistake in his mind now. He knows—is absolutely certain—it's she. She's trying to reach him from somewhere out there in the great wilderness of the city.

"Lolly—Lolly, dear—don't be frightened," he says, terrified that she'll hang up. "Say hello. Please say hello. I miss you so much."

He waits, but he hears nothing—only the breathing.

"Lolly—I got your card this morning. It was funny."
He picks up the card and looks at the shaggy comic bear

in doctor's clothing. "I guess I do look a bit like that. Not quite so shaggy though—I shaved my beard. Idiotic to grow one in the first place at my age. Anyway—glad you remembered. You didn't have to, but all the same, I'm happy you did. You all right?"

No answer, but there's the breathing. It seems to have slackened and evened out a bit. He can almost hear her listening with her breath. That was enough for him. "Can't you say anything? Maybe just hello—just so I can hear your voice. I'd love to hear your voice, dear. That would be the best birthday present."

He waits. Still nothing.

"Lolly, if you won't talk to me, won't you at least write? Mail a letter from the Grand Central Post Office. It can't be traced. All I want is to know you're all right. That isn't so unreasonable, is it? If you need money, I'll send it to you. General Delivery. Care of a mail drop. Anything. Anything you want? Clothing? Food? Please, dear—just tell me you're okay. That's all I want. I won't interfere with your life. I've done enough of that already. I know that now. I've had a lot of time to think, a lot of time to myself, and I know I was wrong. I've been wrong right along. I'm stubborn. A stupid, stubborn, pigheaded fool who believes he knows the right way for everybody. God, what an ass I am."

Suddenly he's laughing. "You know what I've been thinking?" He laughs again, but it's a rather forced laugh. "These past few weeks I've been having this persistent memory of you when you were just a few weeks old. I used to hold you on my knee and play with you and you would always cry and Mother tried to tell me that it was because my voice was too loud, and that it frightened you. But being the stubborn, stupid ass I am, I didn't believe her, and I kept playing with you and you kept right on crying. Lolly—" Something catches in his throat and he starts coughing violently. "I feel so rotten about you." He coughs. "So goddamn sorry." Coughs again. "Sorry—so sorry." Coughing. Coughing. His voice trails off in a singsong lament.

"Your mother," he runs on blindly now, having to speak, terrified she might hang up the moment he stops, "your mother, God rest her—your mother," and suddenly for a moment he sees his child out there in some squalid flat with a naked light bulb, amid the sour gray linen of yes-

terday's unmade beds. He can see her huddled before the
phone somewhere out there in the jungle of the city—the
slight, pretty, sensitive face with the large, startled eyes
—her mother's eyes—listening to his cough-choked voice.
He imagines her in some grimy tenement district with its
angry outcasts, its prowling predatory creatures. Cold,
prideful, and frightened, how ill equipped she was to sur-
vive there—a fawn in leopard country.

"Lolly—Lolly," he hurries on, "it's five months now.
Can't we bury this thing? The house is so lonely with
you and Mother gone. I'm thinking of selling it. Taking
an apartment. It's too much for me to keep up. Too big.
I prowl around it at night like a lunatic. Talking to the
shadows. I can't live there anymore. It's full of ghosts.
Can't we see each other?"

He waits for some sign of relenting, but none comes.
"Please, Lolly. I'm begging you. I'm not ashamed to
beg—" The thing catches in his throat and again he
starts to cough. The breathing on the other end suddenly
stops. For a horrible moment he thinks she's gone. Left
him there dangling.

"Lolly—are you there? Lolly, don't go." He waits and
the breathing resumes once more as if in answer to his
question. "Lolly, I've had an idea. You know this month
I'm making the final payment on the place out at the
beach." He talks rapidly now, speech spilling from him, a
little out of breath, just trying to keep her there. "I've
been thinking, dear—I've been thinking—you know, now
that Mother's gone—no reason why you shouldn't have
the house now. I mean, it was always meant for you
anyway. That's why Mother and I bought it in the first
place. No reason why you have to wait for me to die to
get it." He laughs oafishly. "I know how you love the place
and now you can live out there. Right on the ocean,
where you've always wanted to be. I'm having the whole
place repainted next month. Putting in a stone patio
overlooking the water. Everything's paid off. You could
have it just for the taxes. I mean, I'll pay the taxes—
but it's your place. All yours. I'll sign it over today if
you'd like. Just give me the word and it's yours. You can
live there by yourself or with anyone you want. Even that
friend of yours—" His voice lowers automatically, as if
he fears being overheard. "I won't interfere, Lolly. I promise. I'll never interfere again. We've had some bad times,

darling. But that's all behind us. All I want now is for us to be friends again, and—"

He is about to go on, but in the next moment he hears a click, heartless and emphatic, then a rather high, distant ringing through the wires.

"Lolly—Lolly—Lolly—" He is shouting, as if he can bring her back by the sheer force and authority of his voice. But she's gone, swallowed up once more out there in the great vortex of the city. Suddenly he's angry, something amounting to rage erupting inside him. Or is it hate? He doesn't know if it's Lolly or himself who's the object of it. He has degraded himself on the phone, pleaded like a feckless old man to someone who would not even deign to speak with him. Perhaps it wasn't even she, but a perfect stranger. A wrong number or some creep who'd inadvertently blundered onto the line, gotten interested in his story and let him go on pouring his heart out. But, of course, he knows that isn't so. He knows he's spoken to his daughter, found her for a precious few moments only to lose her once again to that eerie, impenetrable anonymity in which she chose now to live.

He flings the phone back on the cradle, and not knowing exactly where he is going, he starts up. But in the next moment he falls back, slumping in his seat, his legs waxen and trembling. He has the feeling that if he could cry he would feel better. He sits there for a while and tries to cry, but he can't. Nothing will come. He's not the sort of man to cry. At least not outwardly. He wasn't even able to cry when Ida died. Instead, he played poker —all night.

Suddenly he starts to shake. Very shortly he is shaking all over, and now he sits there in the noontime silence of a deserted office building, shaking, in a cold sweat, waiting patiently until whatever the emotion raging through him like a tide recedes.

Several moments later he has regained a modicum of composure—the demeanor of the pure professional with which he has faced the world for nearly four decades. But he feels spent and weary. Somewhere deep within him is the ache of longtime grief.

In the next moment he reaches down into the bottom right-hand drawer of the desk and withdraws from it a stethoscope. Unbuttoning his shirtfront, he screws the plugs firmly into his ears and listens. What he hears from the catacombs and tunnels just beneath his skin is the fatal ticking of his own life. For high up in the apex of his heart he can hear, quite distinctly, the steady, remorseless hissing of a badly damaged mitral valve, like the sound of air escaping from a slowly flattening tire.

A short time later he has barged across the hall to Haggard's office. The Chief Detective, Bureau of Identification, like everyone else at that hour, is out to lunch. Konig fumes with indignation. What right has Haggard to be out? What right has the Deputy Mayor to talk to him that way? What right has Lolly— He's seething with his sense of betrayal and hurt.

Haggard's desk is a mess. A mountain of clutterment. Sheaves of records of missing persons. Mug shots. Fingerprints. Death certificates. Notes to himself.

"Ortega, Luisa—8 years old—ht. 4′ 3″—wt. 72 lbs. Vanished Jan. 3, 1972. Last seen vicinity of—"

"Barthelmy, Miguel—37 years—ht. 5′ 8″—wt. 160 lbs. Vanished on or about— Wife claims— Presumed dead.

"Jackson, LeRoy—"

Above the desk on a cork pegboard, a gallery of faces. Mug shots, prints of thumbs and index fingers. A whole diaspora of the lost and wandering; a museum of the displaced and murdered. The faces all have a rather ghostly quality, like faded old daguerreotypes of people long since dead.

Muttering, Konig rifles through the papers on the desktop. Then, finding a scratch pad, he hastily scrawls the words: "She's called again." He tears the sheet off, clips it to her birthday card, and props it up on the desk lamp where the detective will be sure to find it.

In the next moment he is gone.

∾ 5 ∾

12:15 P.M. A BENCH ON THE EAST RIVER PROMENADE.
The bright new sun of early spring. Joggers plodding
northward on the river walk; a pair of miscegenate
lovers making tumultuous love on a nearby bench; an
old derelict on yet another bench, asleep and mumbling
epithets beneath yesterday's *Daily News*.

Konig eats lunch from a paper bag brought from home
and erratically packed. A hard-boiled egg. A raw tomato.
A raw carrot. All seasoned from a cellophane envelope
of low-sodium salt and washed down with a paper container of tepid black coffee.

Tugs and barges slip up and down the brown pasty
water. Gulls wheel in wide arcs overhead as Konig sits
fuming over his barely touched bag of lunch. He might
have been with the others eating expensive and barely
digestible Italian food at Adolpho's, drinking bad wine and
listening to Strang hold forth amid a court of jesters and
sycophants. He had little stomach for that. Funny the way
men quickly smell which way the wind is blowing. Junior
and associate medical examiners already sensing which
way the power will fall and gravitating toward it like iron
filings in a magnetic field. It was, of course, Konig's
choice. It was for him to name his successor. Strang was
absolutely the worst man for the job. Though a capable
enough pathologist, he was, however, a superb politician,
an out-front man who loved to talk to the media and to
press hands. He knew how to raise money and to smile
when the Mayor was nearby. There were far better, more
devoted, pathologists on Konig's staff, but Strang was
the departmental superstar, upstaging everyone, always
knowing how to catch the Mayor's eye, a prodigious
generator of "earnestly concerned" memos, invariably
and "regrettably" incriminating colleagues of whom he
was either jealous or wary. Yes, it was Konig's choice, but

already there were powerful supporters eager to lend their weight to Strang's succession.

Perhaps that is why Konig found himself more and more taking solitary lunch hours. Taking comfort in his solitude. Seeking quiet and respite from the turmoil of his days. Still, it seemed churlish now after almost forty years to complain about the course his life had taken. After all, it had been his own choice. He, the brilliant resident cardiologist, a boy in his twenties with the whole world before him, suddenly veering sharply from a safe and comfortable path into the uncharted wilderness of a rare and poorly remunerated specialty—forensic pathology. Two of Bahnhoff's lectures audited casually with very little in mind other than a vague, desultory curiosity, then suddenly the whole world upside down. Bahnhoff, like Spillsbury with whom he'd studied, was a genius. An ascetic and a scholar, he lived only for his work, and like Spillsbury, he was driven by a ruthless passion for the truth. He did not care what means were necessary to get it. That was the man who taught Konig. People who boasted that they knew Bahnhoff (liars most of them—Bahnhoff, though world-renowned, permitted few people near him) claimed Konig was exactly like the master. Eerily so. Konig for a time even began affecting a slight German accent and started smoking the same kind of cigars. He had the same painstakingly methodical approach as the master, the same awesome memory coupled with the same uncanny intuition. Working with Bahnhoff, they all claimed, was for Konig a kind of Faustian contract. He gave up his soul, became the head of the department, and a kind of legend in his own life. But now, it seemed, the devil was waiting in the wings.

Now, nearly forty years later, sitting on a bench, the odor of low tide and river sewerage in his nostrils, the taste of ashes in his mouth, Konig feels a curious bitterness. Why? he asks himself.

What was it for? Why had it ever been? He had such a promising career before him. "The million-dollar-a-year cardiologist," they used to call him. To have taken such a course, the seedy, unheroic vocation of a civil-servant physician. His life spent in a series of shabby, barely respectable offices, served by surly, resentful clerks. All about him a scrap heap of old instruments that had fallen into desuetude; brand-new, utterly useless instruments that had arrived there mysteriously, that no one had ever ordered. And then, of course, the cheap, decrepit office furniture, the nameless litter and debris, the peeling walls and ceilings of his life.

Ida once said laughingly (but his decision had disappointed her) that it was his "natural morbidity, a fatal attraction for the grotesque. '. . . half in love with easeful Death,' " she had said, quoting the ode. And there was indeed something to that, some nagging little grain of truth. No matter how much he squirmed and wriggled, tried to avert his eyes from that disconcerting fact, it was nevertheless there. Always nagging.

It could have been so much easier, he thought, gumming dispiritedly the dry, tasteless egg yolk in his mouth. He could have been like his old classmate Nachtigal, the Park Avenue dermatologist with a clientele of movie stars and anxious politicians, spending his days curing dandruff and removing unsightly wens, transplanting hair from the back of the head to the front, dispensing cortisone for everything from acne to alopecia and hawking cheap shampoos on the side. The cunning little elixir bottles all marked with magical, arcane figures—xx34–2 (p) — (3xy). All the cheap, fraudulent claptrap of the high priest mumbling cryptic numerals over the man with the falling hair, the lady with the hirsute lip.

He could have done that. He could have been, like Bernard Nachtigal, a millionaire three times over. What fatal flaw then, what idiotic perversity, led him on this fatal downward trajectory to the morgue?

12:45. Too early for the court; too late to go back to the office. Konig crumples his soiled, half-eaten bag of lunch and tosses it into a reticulated trash can chained to the bench. The sleeping derelict mumbles, his head lolls on his shoulder, a sour, greenish chyme leaks onto his chin as Konig limps past.

He has decided he will walk to court. Three miles at least to the Criminal Courts Building, 100 Centre Street. Sciatica be damned. Walking will, of course, only make it worse, but he knows he cannot sit still in a cab for any length of time. That under no circumstances will he face the assorted indignities of the mass-transit system. He refuses to be carted about in the great black funeral hearse of a limousine the City has provided for him, with its impressive bronze shield that can make life easy even in the chaos of the city streets. So he will walk, the weather being fine, and besides, he has business en route.

Consciously and with great deliberation he tells himself that he will walk all the way downtown on the river promenade. But he knows, even as he proclaims this weighty resolution to himself, that at a certain point, he will veer sharply west into the dense, teeming little neighborhoods of the East Village and the Lower East Side—Avenues B and A, Houston, Essex, Hester Streets—then cut south to Little Italy and Canal, and on through the narrow, winding little beehive streets of Chinatown, working south through a maze of lofts and warehouses, truck plazas, dingy storefronts, hardwares, plumbing contractors, electrical repair shops with dead geraniums wilting in the windows, neighborhood butcher shops with the flayed carcasses of pigs and rabbits hanging from steel hooks, blood oozing from their tiny pink nostrils.

He had taken that route many times in the past five months. Always choosing to walk, no matter how weary, rather than ride. Drawn there irresistibly, as if on some invisible leash. Prowling streets. Eyes searching out shadowy alleys, doorways reeking of urine, trying to pierce the dirty brown brick of turn-of-the-century tenement buildings fallen on hard times. Wanting to see past the people on the stoops to the dark, noisome halls beyond, where malicious strangers often lurked, and on into the tiny, inhuman cubicles with the trapped, hapless occupants huddled in the dark, fetid corners. Somewhere in that squalid maze, he is certain, his lost child cowers.

He is moving now as if through a dream on a tide of churning humanity—stray dogs, squalling urchins, the immense and suffocating stench of outdoor fish stalls, *bodegas*, and costermongers. A grayish, greasy curtain billows outward from an open ground-floor window, carrying with it the smell of fried fish and moldy upholstery. Konig glances up, seeing a fat, antiquated lady with a wen on her nose drowsing at the sill on great beefy arms, head nodding on her chest. A sleeping sibyl. Perhaps he might take himself to her, present votive offerings, seek oracular guidance. "Where should I go? What must I do? How can I get back to where I was?"

He often thought that if he could give himself up to magic and the local wizards, to beads and talismans, all would go well. He would go to an astrologer, chew macrobiotic foods, contemplate Zens koans—anything. If only he could get past this corrosive cynicism, shrive himself of the hubris of forty years of weights and measurements to reach some blessed little green oasis of hope, he might yet save himself.

In Chinatown he pauses to look in a window full of pressed ducks hung on wire nooses, heads lolling grotesquely sidewards; then another window crammed with jars and canisters of dried herbs behind which a wizened septuagenarian mandarin in a black skullcap smiles quietly back at him.

He turns, dispirited, and lurches quickly on.

≈≈ **6** ≈≈

1:45 P.M. MANHATTAN CRIMINAL COURTS BUILDING.

Seedy, decrepit halls, reeking of refuse and bureaucratic neglect; a causeway of vagabonds and mendicants, victims and offenders, rubbish and court magistrates.

Konig is fifteen minutes early. He limps into one of the judges' lounges which he, as a lofty municipal officer, is entitled to use. The place is empty, the only trace of magistrates being the lingering fog of expensive cigars, the smell of cracked and ancient leather in a room where the soiled, bird-spattered windows have not been opened for decades.

Wincing, Konig hoists his aching leg onto a camel hassock and pops a Valium. Court makes him nervous; interrogation causes queasiness in him. Question and answer, innuendo, recrimination and threat, the beady eye of the prosecutor, the muffled sob of grieving litigants. After years of civil courts and grand juries, Konig still arrives at court like a novitiate, struck with awe and wonder at all the casuistry and outright lying, the wheedling, oily words of clever men, the near certainty that justice won't be served.

Just enough time now for him to study his notes, review his protocol in preparation for the inquisition. Printed in medical and forensic journals, translated into a dozen languages, Konig's protocols are world-renowned. He has filled three volumes with them and they have been the subject of lengthy transoceanic correspondences carried on with an international community of scholars and specialists —people who come to him for the final word—for he is, in his chosen field, the court of last resort.

Written in the style of Professor Virchow, Prosector of the Dead House of the Berlin Charité Hospital during the last half of the nineteenth century, Konig's protocols are marvels of precision and lucidity. They are without literary pretensions, neither eloquent nor graceful; merely a recitation of naked, unembellished facts, dreary when taken individually, but staggering in their remorseless cumulative drive toward final truth.

Konig's eyes now begin to scan his protocol.

CASE BENJAMIN WILTON

This is the body of a generally well-developed white male. Appears to be that of man twenty years of age, height 1.65 meters. Gunshot wound of head. Death in eighteen hours from edema of lungs. On autopsy, entrance of bullet is found to be above left eyebrow. The track of it runs from left frontal lobe to right occipital lobe of brain. Extensive edema of the lungs. Numerous unrelated manifestations: dilations of aortic arch; endocarditis mitralis; herpes zoster; chylification of intestines.

B.W. aged 21. Occupation at time of death: car salesman, but known trafficker in addictive drugs. No signs of drug use or addiction present on body. Shot through the head with small handmade pistol, caliber .38, above middle of left eyebrow. Unconscious on arrival at hospital—6 P.M.—Jan. 3, 1974. Breathing stertorous; pulse scarcely perceptible; blood pressure 60 systolic over 30 diastolic; urine passed involuntarily; loud tracheal rales; heart sounds barely audible; no albumin or sugar in urine; left pupil larger than right. Periodic exudation of grayish-white matter from the wound. At midnight, pulse had risen somewhat; respiration still stertorous though a little easier. Early the following morning the man's condition showed marked deterioration. He died at noon.

Postmortem examination (occupying two hours and three-quarters) Jan. 4, 1974.

EXTERNAL EXAMINATION

1. Body generally pale in color. Flanks, scrotum, and glans of a uniform reddish-purple.
2. On turning the body over, a large quantity of yellowish-brown fluid containing dark-brown particles escapes from the mouth.
3. Rigor mortis marked in extremities and muscles of the neck. Slight cadaveric odor perceptible.
4. Hair of head abundant, curly, dark brown. Beard full; hair on right side of head stained red; much matted together and roots covered with dry, clotted blood.
5. On the forehead, directly above middle of left eyebrow, a small, blackish bullet hole, 9 millimeters in diameter, with a narrow rim of reddish-brown abraded skin surrounded by a halo of powder tattoos to a radius of 10 centimeters.
6. Eyelashes dark brown; pupils round; irises pale grayish-blue. Front teeth perfect, of brownish cast. Molar teeth defective and carious. Teeth tightly clamped.
7. Eyelids partially closed; corneas firm and transparent. Nostrils filled with large quantities of dried blood.
8. Hands large; nails long and bluish, edges compacted with thick black dirt. Neck not easily movable. Abdomen somewhat scaphoid.
9. Penis small, much contracted; very little prepuce; no cicatrix of any kind perceptible. What remains of the prepuce dark red and rather dried. Scrotum small and wrinkled. Some appearance of blood externally on both sides.
10. The parts about the anus much soiled with brown excrement. The anus closed.

A fly buzzes somewhere in the room. Konig's head snaps up as if he'd been abruptly summoned. Something like the sensation of a long needle passing up the length of his spine transfixes him to his seat. He feels a cold tingling at his scalp and suddenly he is filled with a creeping sense of prescience.

"Come on, Lolly. Come on, honey. Walk to Daddy."

"Paul, how can you expect the child to walk? She's barely ready to crawl."

"She'll walk—she'll walk for me. Just watch her."

The fly buzzes through the finger loop of the shade and proceeds to dance up the frayed length of the attached string. Konig's eyes fasten on the fly's progress as if hypnotized, but it's not the fly he sees; he's staring at something quite far beyond it.

INTERNAL EXAMINATION

11. Scalp opened by intermastoid incision from one ear across to the other. Skullcap removed. The bones difficult to saw through. Six to 8 millimeters thick.

12. Left frontal sinus filled with pulpy matter . . . dark-red clots, right frontal sinus. Vessels much distended with blood . . .

"Come on, Lolly. It's this way."

"No, it isn't, Daddy. I'm sure we came the other way. Through that little copse behind the church . . ."

. . . debris in aperture of skull. Much destruction and hemorrhage along the track of the bullet wound.

"It's four strokes then raise your head. Four strokes, raise your head. Four strokes—"

"I know, but I keep getting water in my mouth."

"That's too damned bad. We're going to keep right on doing this until . . ."

. . . the head being raised and drawn forward, a .38-caliber deformed lead bullet is recovered from area just below right ear. Brain being removed, its base seen to be infiltrated with blood.

"Compravao, compravi, comprava, compravamo, compravate, compravano."

"Good. . . . Now the past absolute."

"But, Daddy, we're not up to the past absolute."

"So what? There's no law against being a little ahead of the rest. Come on now—comprai, comprasti, com-pro . . ."

13. . . . continuous incision carried from chin to pubic symphysis. Sternum removed.

14. Heart approximately the size of a man's closed fist. Very rigid . . . *"Lolly, your mother and I have decided . . ."* About 40 cubic centimeters dark-red blood small buffy clot escaping from right auricle. . . . *"to separate. Just temporarily, mind you. Sort of a vacation from each other."* . . . Mitral ostium so narrowed as to admit only the tip of the ring finger. . . .

The fly buzzes through a shaft of sunlight, circles several times around Konig's head and lights on his lapel, suddenly quiet there and rubbing its forelegs together. Konig is peering through a gray, shadowy hallway, the place reeks of wet plaster and urine; his eyes move beyond walls and beams to a squalid little cubicle . . .

15. Large quantities of thick bloody froth escape from left bronchus.

16. Tongue retracted behind jaws, covered with dirty brown coating . . . some bloody mucus in pharynx. *Lolly on her knees, cowering in the clammy shadows, whimpers softly to herself. A large black figure, moving, sliding, insinuating itself toward the cringing figure. . . .* Glottis open. Larynx and air passages filled with thick frothy fluid containing yellowish-brown flakes. *The shadow of a cleaver whooshes sickeningly through a series of overhead circles above her.*

17. Spleen, 120 grams. Splenic pulp—brownish-red. Left kidney, 130 grams. Bladder normally distended. Urine clear, amounting to approximately 80 cubic centimeters. *Lolly whimpers, a small bleating sound, like that of a trapped, wounded animal, knowing*

it's to be devoured. Her hands rise above her head as if to protect herself.

18. Liver, 1,500 grams. Gall bladder filled with somewhat ropy but otherwise clear dark-green bile.

"Oh, Daddy. Daddy."
"Come on, honey. You can do it."

19. Stomach distended. Contains about 150 cubic centimeters of greenish thick fluid.
    Lolly on her knees praying before her executioner.
20. Upper part of duodenum contains a whitish fluid. Greenish-yellow bile flows freely from orifice of common bile. Pancreas pale, normal.
    The cleaver reaches the apogee of its climb . . .
21. Upper part of intestine contains grayish fluid resembling gruel, slightly colored with bile.
    . . . and starts its swift, irreversible descent.
    Lowest part of ileum contains quantity of very fluid feces. Large intestine from ileocecal valve full of thick, pulpy feces.
    Lolly's scream rips through the air like a switchblade. A vision of her head drifts before his eyes —disembodied—severed from the torso—eyes open, showing large areas of white, pupils rolled upward beneath the lids . . . one side of her face bloody and contused.

Konig is on his feet, whirling through the room, caught and turning through the mote-filled shaft of sunlight, as if pursuing some fleeting image. He doesn't realize he's been on his feet for several moments, cold, clammy sweat soaking through the armpits of his shirt, and whirling . . . whirling.

The door swings open. A myopic, dwarfish clerk pokes his head into the room, a little aghast at seeing Konig's demented pirouetting. Konig halts abruptly and they stare at each other.

"Well, what the hell do you want?"

Still gaping at him through bottle-thick lenses, the clerk gulps. "They're ready for you now, Chief."

"That is correct."

"And you are a duly licensed physician and surgeon?"

"That is correct."

"In what state?"

"State of New York."

The dull, mechanical litany of the *voir dire* drones on.

"How long have you been licensed to practice medicine?"

"Since 1935."

"And you are presently engaged in the practice of your profession?"

"Yes. I am Chief Medical Examiner, City of New York."

Sun streaming through tall, soot-streaked windows into the drowsy, stuporous air of the courtroom. The judge, slouched over the bench, appears to be dozing behind his spectacles. The jurors, bored and distracted, suffocating in the dusty, airless space, dream of home and release. Their gazes seesaw slowly back and forth from witness to attorney, keeping precise time with the cadence of the ensuing dialogue.

A tiny, wizened court reporter, his feet barely touching the floor, taps incessantly on the keys of a small recording machine. Traffic noises throb upward from the street below. From somewhere south and west of them, somewhere in the vicinity of the river, fire engines and police sirens wail out a message of disaster. But here, inside the courtroom, the relentless nasalities of the prosecuting attorney drone on through the waning afternoon.

Q. "So that, in summary, Doctor, it is your carefully considered opinion that the bullets were fired from a hand gun—caliber thirty-eight—situated somewhere to Benjamin Wilton's left side?"

A. "That is correct."

Q. "And that there were two points of impact?"

A. "Yes. One over the left breast, which was superficial, grazing. The other bullet struck over the median center of the left eyebrow and lodged below the right ear. That was not superficial."

Q. "And, Doctor, you have testified, have you not, that the murder weapon was fired at a distance of fifteen to eighteen inches from the victim's head?"

A. "Ballistics tests and powder burns found at the point of entry suggest such a distance."

Q. "And that the bullet penetrated the skull at a downward angle of roughly fifty degrees?"

A. "Ballistics tests and the track of the missile within the
victim's brain suggest such an angle."

Q. "And because of that angle of penetration, and given
the victim's known height of five feet five inches, it
is then your carefully considered opinion that the victim's assailant would have to be a man nearly a whole
foot taller?"

A. "That, of course, is somewhat more difficult to fix
with any certainty. But if the victim wasn't sitting at
the time of the attack—and since no chair was
found in the immediate vicinity of the body, I must
conclude that he was standing, or at least on his feet
—then the distance at which the gun was fired and
the angle of penetration suggest to me the assailant's
height to be somewhere in the neighborhood of six
feet three and six feet five inches."

Q. "A tall man you would say?"

A. "Yes, sir."

Q. "Somewhere in the neighborhood of the young man
seated beside—"

DEFENSE: "Objection, your Honor."

JUDGE: "Sustained. Will prosecution please refrain from
such leading questions?"

Q. "Your witness, Counsel."

Someone in the back of the court is snoring. The shaft
of sunlight streaming through the window has slanted
several points eastward. The drugged, somnolent air has
grown thicker and closer; purple shadows have begun to
gather in the far corners of the room.

Konig's head is pounding. It is this part of it that he
hates—the part that makes him physically ill—when they
try to twist his words, all of which he has chosen and
measured so carefully, and then distort them to their own
purposes.

But although the process makes him physically sick,
so that he lives in dread anticipation of courtroom ap-
pearances, he is, nevertheless, known in the trade as a
formidable witness; in the parlance of lawyers, "a cool
cookie." He doesn't stumble. No one has ever suspected
or even had a hint of this vulnerability in the man. He
has never shown it. The façade that he brings to court is

supremely composed. Glacially aloof. The exterior is serene while the interior churns with rage.

Q. ". . . so then, is it not noteworthy, Dr. Konig, that you've been scrupulously careful to give only rough approximations of such critical data as . . ."

Konig knows what is coming next. The legal mind is quite predictable, incapable of any great surprises.

Q. ". . . the assailant's height? Aren't your approximations only hypothetical? Wouldn't you have to concede—"
A. "Yes. That is correct. I believe I stressed the point that estimation of the assailant's height would be difficult to fix with any certainty. I offer only approximations. That's all forensic science is capable of at this time. We're not gods . . ."
Q. "I would certainly agree with you there."

Mild laughter throughout the courtroom. At that moment Konig's eyes happen to fall on the alleged assailant, a surly young thug with a previous arrest record and a known history of violence. Like the others in the court, he, too, appears to be enjoying counsel's little joke on Konig by smirking widely. The judge stirs himself from private ruminations long enough to gavel the court to silence and call for order. Konig continues, seemingly unfazed.

A. ". . . but I would also respectfully point out to the court that these approximations are presented within fairly narrow parameters, so that their value as information is not inconsiderable."
Q. "But still you would have to agree—"
JUDGE: "The bench recognizes the intent of counsel's line of questioning here and requests that he refrain from attempting to disparage what the bench deems pertinent and highly expert medical testimony."

Konig enjoys a small twinge of vindication. He has been up against this counsel before and they have old scores to settle. Now, without seeming pompous or immodest, Konig has scored a few points for the integrity and forthrightness of the Medical Examiner's Office, while the counsel has come off seeming sly and somewhat captious at best.

Q. "But it seems clear now from your testimony that cause of death cannot be attributed to damage inflicted by the single bullet wound."

A. "Yes, sir. That is correct. I've been very careful to specify that the victim lived for eighteen hours after he was hospitalized, and that the mechanism of death resulted not from damage incurred by the brain but from the lungs, and, strictly speaking, from suffocation."

Q. "Is that unusual?"

A. "Not at all. Not with this kind of wound. In fact, fairly common. Often injuries to the head caused by contusions will bring on fatal edema of the lung."

Q. "And is that the case here?"

A. "Yes, sir, it is."

Q. "So that the bullet wound to young Wilton's brain was not in itself the cause of death?"

A. "Not in itself, but it was certainly *the* contributive factor."

Q. "And if I may backtrack a moment, Doctor, you do not entirely eliminate the possibility of suicide?"

A. "I don't eliminate it. I only say that given the angle of the bullet's penetration over the left brow, the fact that the gun was fired from the victim's left side, where it was also subsequently found, given the distance at which the gun was held, the powder burns, and given the victim's preference for right-handedness—"

Q. "How do you know the victim was right-handed?"

A. "Well, sir, for one thing, we did a series of microradiographs of Wilton's dentition. The prevailing direction of toothbrush strokes in the enamel was that of a right-handed person. For another thing, it was documented in medical records sent us by the family physician."

A mild stir of approval through the courtroom, and the counsel momentarily flustered.

Q. "Let me understand this. Are you saying the victim could not have fired with his right hand?"

A. "I don't say he couldn't have. I say it's extremely unlikely. It's easier to understand if you turn your right
index finger into an imaginary gun and bring your
right hand over to your left eye at such an angle that
the bullet would come out below your right ear." With
his own finger, Konig demonstrates his point. "It's an
extremely awkward angle, as you can see. Then, if
you keep that same position and pull your hand fifteen to eighteen inches away, pointing it downward at
the rather steep angle of fifty degrees, as this weapon
had been pointed, I think you'll find it almost impossible."

Konig, attempting to further demonstrate the improba-
bility of the position, elicits another stir of delight from
the court. Obviously, he has impressed the spectators.
Not, however, the counsel, who is smiling wickedly.

Q. "But surely, you don't eliminate, do you, Doctor, the
possibility that the victim could have shot himself with
his left hand?"
A. "You're not serious, are you?"
Q. "I ask the questions here, Doctor, and I most certainly
am serious."
A. "You mean that after a lifetime of being right-handed,
the victim suddenly for this special occasion decided
to become left-handed?"
Q. "Why not? You yourself stated that the gun was found
at Wilton's left side. Wouldn't that suggest that he'd
used his left hand?"
A. "I have never, in forty years' experience, heard of a
right-handed person suddenly becoming left-handed
in order to commit suicide."
Q. "But you haven't answered my question, Doctor. I
have asked you if it is possible for a right-handed
person to shoot himself with his left hand—"
A. "I cannot recall in all my—"
Q. "Doctor, just answer the question. Is it possible? Yes
or no?"

There's a palpable suspension of movement while the
court, eyes fixed on Konig, waits. Even the incessant
coughing, clearing of throats, snuffling of noses, are all
held in merciful abeyance while the man on the witness
stand weighs the question.

Even as he ponders, Konig's eyes fall once more on the alleged assailant—the young thug—his attitude now a mixture of swagger and bravado at finding himself the object of so much fuss. Suddenly their eyes meet and for a fraction of a second Konig sees that nasty little smirk flicker there once again—something both defiant and mocking. A jeering taunt born of a child's sense of indestructibility. A fatal error, that smirk, for in that moment, Konig feels a rush of hate for the boy and a furious need to get him.

A. "Yes, sir, it is possible. But not in this case. Because in this case, the victim's left hand was found clutching the first wound over his left breast. Since Wilton lost consciousness immediately after being shot in the head, it is certain that at the precise moment of his losing consciousness, his left hand was very busily occupied trying to staunch the flow of blood from his breast. If I follow your line of reasoning, Mr. Counsel, and assume that Wilton did in fact commit suicide, the only possibility is that he shot himself over the left eyebrow with his left hand, then dropped the gun and grabbed his bleeding breast with the same hand. That would be impossible since we all know that he lost consciousness directly after incurring the head wound and, as a result of massive brain injury to the motor centers, was instantly paralyzed, and undoubtedly never moved a muscle again thereafter. So if he couldn't have used his right hand, as I have demonstrated, because of the angle of the shot, or his left hand because it was found clutching his left breast, then it follows that someone else must have fired the shot."

Konig smiles graciously in the direction of the young assailant. The boy blanches and at the same moment the smirk begins to quickly fade. The Chief rises and steps down from the stand, nodding cordially, first to the judge and then to counsel, whose mouth has fallen open and is working uselessly. Striding out of the court, he has a sense of enormous satisfaction.

Once again the Chief has won. His reputation as a formidable witness remains intact. The media will report the incident glowingly. Congratulations and kudos will redound to the Medical Examiner's Office. What does it matter that Konig deliberately misled the court. Fudged a bit. That business of the left hand, coming out of left field the way it did, leaving the defense in total disarray. That, he knows, was not exactly so. Assuming Wilton had shot himself with the left hand, a simple involuntary spasm might have brought that same left hand back over the left breast after Wilton had dropped the gun and lapsed into total unconsciousness, despite the motor paralysis he'd suffered subsequent to the second shot.

But that was not the way it happened, and Konig knew it. The sly, unctuous, pettifogging attorney with the fancy but preposterous left-hand theory knew it too. So did the judge and the whole court know it. But the system being what it is, all are powerless to do anything. All except Konig, who was not powerless.

With his deepest instincts, the Chief knows the smiling young jackal in the court to be guilty of heinous murder. From his years of pounding about police courts and morgues, he knows everything there is to know about this boy. Past and future. He might even hazard a guess as to when that same dangerously childish fantasy life will no doubt earn the boy a place in one of the morgue's large refrigerated lockers—but not before many other innocent people die. And this, Konig cannot—will not—permit. So what does it matter that he fudged a bit? He'd done it before and he would do it again. Unhesitatingly, if he thought he was right. And this wasn't actually an outright lie. It could very well have been exactly the way Konig said it had been. It very probably was. Of that Konig is convinced. His sense of justice tells him so, and that, after all, is enough for him. He'd gotten the bastard.

"She did or she didn't?"

"I said she did."

"I know, but a minute ago you said she didn't."

"I said she hung up a minute after she heard the clicking."

"No, you didn't, Paul. You said she hung up right after the clicking. Right after is not a minute after. A minute after right after is fifty-nine seconds."

4:15 P.M. OFFICE OF THE CHIEF MEDICAL EXAMINER, DIVISION OF MISSING PERSONS.

Konig sits opposite a tall, sinewy man, late fifties, with red leathery skin, a craggily handsome pockmarked face, and the small, vivid blue eyes of a china doll. The man wears sleeve garters and a shoulder holster. With his boyish face and flocculent, cotton-candy hair, he gives the impression of a man gone prematurely white overnight.

"What the hell's the difference?" Konig bellows.

"Plenty, my friend, plenty. And stop shouting at me."

A shaft of dust-blown sunlight streams through the window at Francis Xavier Haggard's back, slants across his litter-strewn desk, and falls on a 6″ x 9″ white form headed DD13. The form trembles ever so slightly in Haggard's long, bony, curiously artistic hand—the hand of a sculptor or a musician, certainly not the hand of a detective.

"She knows the calls are being traced." Konig's face flushes a violent red. "Sounds like a goddamned drum when that thing starts banging."

"But still she keeps right on calling—right?"

"Right. But I want that thing off my phone. Here, as well as at home."

"Fine. Take it off. But when that goes, I go, too—right? I'm off the case—right?"

44

"I don't want you off the case. I want you on."

"Oh, no, pal. It doesn't work that way. My way or no way."

"It's been your way for five months."

"Fine. It may have to be my way another five months."

"Oh, no. No, sir."

"Fine. Do it your way. I'm off the case."

Konig flings his hands upward in despair. "That tracer is no goddamned good. It inhibits her. She won't even talk to me with—"

"A minute ago you said she knew there was a tracer on that phone—right?"

"Sure, but—"

"Never mind the 'buts.' You said it—right?"

"Well, you'd have to be one helluva God-awful idiot not to—"

"So obviously it doesn't matter to her whether the line's bugged or not—right?"

"Will you please stop with that 'right' thing every other minute?"

"She calls, doesn't she? Lemme see—she's called"— Haggard's long, bony fingers moves like fate down the black-ruled lines of the DD13: Konig, Lauren. Age 22. Sex female. Caucasian. Ht. 5' 6". Wt. 118. . . . Last seen— "six times the past three months—right? So bug or no bug, she keeps calling—right?"

"Sure. Then hangs up the minute the goddamned clicking starts."

"That doesn't mean anything. I've seen enough of this kind of stuff in my time to know this kid's calling for a reason. She needs to hear a friendly voice. And this card—" Haggard plucks up Lolly's birthday card and examines it. "You know, you do look a little like this goddamned bear."

"Christ!" Konig bolts up, winces at the sharp pain in his leg, then starts prowling up and down the room. "I want results. I want something to happen."

"Sure you do. Sure you do. So do I. But I told you this wasn't gonna be easy. No Social Security. No work record. An assumed name. If she keeps still, minds her own business, what the hell are we supposed to go on?"

"I don't care what the hell you're supposed to go on."

"There are eight million people in this city—eighteen thousand kids each year on the lam."

"I don't care if there are ten—fifteen—fifty million. Spare me the statistics. I want my kid back."

The small blue china doll's eyes fix on Konig very steadily. "And that's another thing, Paul. Your kid isn't a kid anymore—"

"My kid—"

"You gotta start to accept that. She's over eighteen now. Leaving home's not a criminal offense when you're over eighteen. As far as the law's concerned, technically she isn't even a missing person."

"Well, if she's not"—Konig's face is now a dangerous purple—"if she's not, I wish to hell you'd tell me exactly what she is then. A girl gone five months from her home, without once notifying family or giving whereabouts—"

The detective rolls a pen slowly back and forth across his desk beneath the palm of his hand. "You know what she is? I'll tell you what she is—I'll be glad to. She's a young lady, twenty-two years of age, who lost her mother, the best friend she ever had, and it knocked her for a loop. So she wakes up one morning, withdraws twenty-five hundred dollars, all her personal savings, from the bank and decides she's had enough of home. As far as this department is concerned, she's breaking no laws. A solid citizen—right? Listen, I got refrigerators downstairs full of kids from ten on up who come to the Big Apple from as far west as Texas, California, with parents out there screaming for some kind of lead, some kind of positive identification. What I'm doing for you, I'm not doing as a detective. I'm doing it as a friend, a good, personal friend of over twenty-five years. And when I say that I want that tracing device on your phone—"

"It's no goddamned good," Konig half shouts, half pleads. "She's not calling from her bedroom or the phone down the hall."

"That's right. She's calling from some phone booth outside."

"Then she may as well be calling from the moon. We're never going to find her."

"Come on, Paul—for Chrissake." Haggard flings the birthday card down on the desktop. "That isn't postmarked the moon. Grand Central Station isn't the goddamned moon. That kid's right here. In this city. Around the corner, for all I know."

"If she's not calling from some fixed address, some permanent base of operations, what the hell do we need this disgusting little tracing device for?"

"Because," the detective groans wearily, "it gives us a pattern of her movements."

"When you're lucky enough to get a reading, before she rings off."

"I tell you, this kid wants us to find her. How come she calls you here, knowing all the while we got a tracer on your phone?"

The question brings Konig up sharply. His fingers plow his hair exasperatedly.

"Answer me, Paul. How come? You can't answer because you know it's true. She wants us to get a reading on her."

"Baloney."

"We got two, didn't we?"

"Two out of six—quite a pattern."

"One, a phone booth at First Avenue and East Houston. Another, a luncheonette on Astor Place. That's a pattern, isn't it?"

"The East Village from First Avenue and East Houston to Astor Place?" Konig laughs scornfully. "It might as well be Bulgaria."

"Okay. It is pretty feeble. But it's a pattern. The next reading we get we can triangulate—narrow down. And I gotta feeling this kid's gonna be calling more often now the warm weather's coming. I gotta feeling she's getting a little homesick out there. And the more she calls, the better our chances to zero in. We got descriptions— DD13's and DD26's—out in every borough and precinct, every station house knows 'Konig, Lauren. Age twenty-two.' They got pictures of her on the walls. You happen to be luckier than most. They know it's the Chief's kid. They're keeping it very quiet, but they're all out there looking. So I say the tracing device stays."

"It goes," Konig shouts and flings a fist in the air. "And you can goddamn well go too."

"Fine. Delighted. As of now, this minute, I'm off the case."

"Fine with me too. I can do a helluva lot better by myself."

"Help yourself, pal."

"Thanks. I will." Konig whirls around and starts out.

"A pleasure to do business with you. Happy birthday."

The door slams. A picture slides on the shuddering wall, shatters in a heap on the floor. Moments after Konig's departure, the dusty, warm air is still reverberating from the sharp concussion.

Haggard sits quietly in the warm, slanting sunbeams of the dying afternoon, the steely blue eyes still pondering the tidy 6″ x 9″ form.

Konig, Lauren. Age 22. . . . Ht 5′ 6″. . . . Medium build. Hair light brown. Eyes blue. Light complected. Freckles on nose and cheeks. Two vaccination marks upper left arm.

Scars: Thin white pencil-line scar above right eyebrow. Appendectomy scar, approximately thirteen years old.

Distinguishing marks: Small, dark mole, left cheekbone. Raspberry mole, right scapula. May have scar on back of left hand from . . .

In the next moment he swivels round in his chair and reaches into the inside pocket of his jacket draped across the top of a dusty file cabinet. From the pocket he withdraws a crumpled yellow sheet of paper, a police teletype, dated that day.

SUBJECT—DD26. Apr. 12, 1974. Female, white, age 22–25, resembling attached photo, your description, DD26, Dec. 14, 1973, observed walking small dog, black-and-white markings, vicinity Houston and Varick Streets. Believed residing loft-warehouse residence—324 Varick—under assumed name Emily Winslow. First called our attention by local residents that neighborhood complaining of activities of quasi paramilitary group operating in area and describing themselves as the "New World Militia"—NWM. Subject has been observed several times in company of members of this group. Though not suspected of any criminal activity, subject under surveillance past three days as per your instructions. Now checking work records, Social Security, and FBI files—Emily Winslow.

Kindly advise.

Sgt. Leo Wershba
17 Precinct
NYPD

The detective's eyes linger for several moments over the crumpled sheet of teletype. After a moment longer, he crushes the paper slowly in his fist. The squealing swivel action of his chair rotates him a full 180 degrees until once more the sun is at his back, and he is facing his desk, reaching for the phone.

≈ **8** ≈

4:45 P.M. TOXICOLOGY LAB.

Alembics. Beakers. Flasks. Bubbling distillers. Cardboard tubs of brain and liver, kidney and stomach. Plastic bags of blood and urine; jars of feces, vomitus, gastric remains. Envelopes of hair, fingernails, mucosa, nail scrapings. The high whir of electric blenders liquefying brains and livers soon to pass through boiling alembics and gas chromatographs, the distillates then to be analyzed for traces of alcohol, morphia, barbiturates, hypnotics, amphetamines, hydrocyanic acid gases, potassium cyanide, ethyl chloride, phosgene, cyclopropane, ethylene, Avertin; all the common phenol derivative acids—nitric, muriatic, sulfuric, oxalic, carbolic; the metallic poisons—arsenicals, lead arsenate, calcium arsenate, acetoarsenite of copper, arsensic trioxide, known as ratsbane. Bichloride of mercury. Lead. Antimony. Phosphorus. Bismuth. Thallium. Strychnine. Nicotine. The belladonnas, or the "three dream sisters"—atropine, scopolamine, hyoscine. The opium derivatives—morphine, heroin, codeine, papaverine, paregoric, laudanum. The hypnotics—chloral hydrate and paraldehyde, and the barbituric acid group—barbital, Nembutal, Amytal, Ipral, phenobarbital, Seconal. The "flying drugs"—speed, Benzedrine, Dexedrine, caffeine. The hallucinatory, lysergic acid. Then marijuana (hashish), the alkaloid, cocaine—and most deadly of all, aconite, known also as monkshood or wolfsbane.

Konig sits opposite Dr. Ozokawa, the Chief Toxicologist, in a miasmic fog of uric acid fumes wafting fitfully out of the chromatography laboratory next door, where several hundred beakers of the urine of expired people boil through various stages of analysis. The ammoniacal level in the air is so high that it causes tearing of the eyes and a burning sensation in the nostrils.

Hunched over, in shirt sleeves, Konig and Ozokawa sit in this poisonous air corroborating toxicological data with autopsy findings. They sit like old friends trading bits of gossip—Ozokawa's strychnine for Konig's convulsions; Ozokawa's hyoscine for Konig's dilated pupils; Ozokawa's cyanide for Konig's mouth froth; Ozokawa's arsenic for Konig's ulceration of the small intestine; Ozokawa's barbiturates for Konig's cyanosis and respiratory arrest.

They chat easily of the facial discolorations found in strychnine, aniline, and nitrobenzene poisonings; of the cherry-red flush of carbon monoxide and cyanide poisoning; of the dilated pupils of scopolamine, the pinpoint pupils of heroin, the emaciation of metal poisonings, the ghastly burns of corrosive acids, the peach-pit odor of cyanide, the garlic odor of oxalic acid.

Ozokawa's voice drones on through the dying afternoon, his clipped, percussive pronunciation struggling for clarity. "Evans, Rebecca. Age nineteen. DOA. Morphine, two milligrams in blood, urine, brain, and vomitus. Whittaker, Otis. Age thirteen. DOA. Morphine, three milligrams in urine, brain, and feces. Perriguex, Willi. Age fourteen months. Lead—" Ozokawa glances up from the small white 6″ x 9″ file card, sun flashing through his lenses. "You find no external signs of abuse on the child?"

"None." Konig shakes his head. "Straight lead poisoning."

Ozokawa nods his great glabrous dome of a head, then continues. "Peruda, Miguel. Age twenty-three. Dexedrine, Benzedrine, I suspect also lysergic acid, though it was not detectable."

Konig makes note of that on his pad. "Must have been on the ceiling most of the time."

Ozokawa's head nods sleepily.

"Kowalski, Peter. Age eighteen. DOA. Alcohol in blood and urine, .3 percent. Amytal, seven grams. Cooper, Margaret. Age forty-one. Lysol infusion—self-administered." Ozokawa grimaces and makes a queasy face. The noise of horns and traffic drift up from below. "Campbell, Eugene. Age twenty-nine. Oh, here's an interesting one. At first it

looked like acute alcoholic poisoning. Nearly .5 percent
ethyl alcohol in the blood and urine—phenomenal. Then
we came up with acetoarsenite of copper."

"Paris green—pretty fancy."

"Caught it in the kidneys and bone tissue."

"Hair and nails?"

"All over."

"Thought something was funny about those ileocecal
ulcerations."

"Soon as I read your report I tested for arsenic. Somebody slipped him something."

Konig grunts and makes a notation on his pad to call
Flynn. "Go on."

"Oh, yes. Let me see now . . ." Ozokawa's drowsy eyes
move up and down his list. "The chap whose car rolled
over the embankment and exploded—"

"Oh—Doblicki."

"Yes, your human torch."

"Not too much left to work with there, I'm afraid."

"Serology was able to get us a blood sample. About
four cubic centimeters. Levels of .4 percent of ethyl alcohol—"

"Surprised he was able to get behind the wheel and
drive, little less get the goddamned car over the embankment. What were the CO levels?"

"None."

There is a pause in which the Chief's eyes rise slowly
to Ozokawa's. "None?"

Baffled, Ozokawa looks down at the card again. "Troopers' report says they found liquor bottles in the wreck.
Tests show the man was certainly drunk."

"I know he was drunk, and I don't care what the goddamned troopers say." Konig's voice rises. "But you can't
die in a fire without having CO levels in the blood ap-
preciably elevated. Unless, of course—"

Ozokawa's bilish eyes seem perplexed.

"—you weren't breathing at the time."

"I'm almost certain, but I can go back and check. There
was no appreciable CO in the blood."

"There wasn't any soot or cinders in the larynx or trachea either." Konig's on his feet now, nearly shouting,
barging from the room.

Baffled, Ozokawa rises, trailing after him. "Where are
you going?"

"To try and get that body back."

"Where is it?"

"New Jersey. Someone out there claimed it. I've got to see it again." Suddenly he laughs harshly. "The bastards nearly got away with it. That guy Doblicki was dead before he ever got into the goddamned car."

≈≈ **9** ≈≈

"You mean you've known about this all along?"

"For at least three years."

"And you've done nothing about it?"

"Done? What should I have done? Torn the office apart? Ferreted out the man? Had a public departmental hanging for you and *The New York Times?*"

5:15 P.M. KONIG'S OFFICE.

Gathering shadows. The day drawing to a close. The Chief's voice ringing on the thick, dusty air. "Answer me, Carl. What should I have done?"

Strang sits cross-legged, glacial, unflinching, across the desk, the high slope of dusty mortuary records behind him. "When did you find out?"

"I told you. About three years ago. And goddamn it, don't take that smug, stuffed-ass tone with me." Konig flings a wad of papers across the desk. "Why do you go on with this innocent, babe-in-the-woods routine, Carl? Like some goddamned Boy Scout. You know this racket as well as I do. The phony friend routine. The phone petition for pauper's burial. The phony put-up by some sleazy mortician looking for an unclaimed stiff he can bury at City expense. Five hundred clear for him and maybe kick back fifty, seventy-five bucks—"

"For some scab working right here," Strang snarls. "In this department. Supplying the guy with a monthly list of unclaimed bodies. That's what bothers me. Don't you see what you've got here, Paul? It's a body-snatching operation. Going on right under our noses. The City's being

bilked for thousands and we're in complicity with these
morticians. If the papers ever got hold of this—"

"If they do—" Quiet settles over the room. Konig's
voice is suddenly very calm. "If they do, I'll have a pretty
good idea who their source of information was. It wouldn't
be the first time, would it, Carl?"

"Now just a min—"

"Not the first time your outraged sense of propriety
would've prodded you into sending private little memo-
randa to the newspapers or to the Mayor's office."

Strang flinches. The hooded lids flicker and a bright
flush creeps upward above his collar to his throat. "I'm
afraid it's out of my hands, Paul."

"What do you mean—out of your hands?"

"I mean this man marched in here this morning—"
Flustered, Strang struggles to regain his composure. "Came
all the way from Salt Lake City. Wanted to claim his
cousin's body."

"His cousin?"

"Kaiser."

"The one they found last week in a doorway?"

"Right. He was a lush. A bum. Drifting from one flophouse to the next. Who'd have thought anyone would've
bothered to claim the remains?"

"This man, the fellow from Salt Lake City. What's his
name?"

"Wilde."

"That's right—Wilde. How'd he find out?"

"About Kaiser? Says he saw the notice published in a
local obit. How the hell those things get into the papers
twenty-two hundred miles away— Anyway, he got right
on the phone the minute he read it. Hopped the first
plane out and came right over from the airport. Still
had his suitcase with him."

The Chief's eyes narrow shrewdly behind the lenses of
his spectacles. Nodding, he listens to Strang's story with
disquieting calm.

"Said this Kaiser—his cousin—had been missing forty
years," Strang rushes on. "Just got up one morning and
walked out on his wife, his family, his job. Said they gave
up looking for him years ago. Just assumed he was dead,
until they saw that notice. He said all he wanted now was
to take the body back and bury it in the family plot in
Salt Lake City. Then when I told him somebody else, a

'friend,' had already claimed the body, went through the routine procedure for burying mendicants at City expense, the guy almost went through the roof. Kaiser was no mendicant. Apparently the family's pretty well heeled and they want the body. Demanded I call up the 'friend' right then and there. Find out who he was—"

"And so of course you called the name listed on the petitioner's application"—Konig leans backward in his chair, the tips of his fingers arching together to form a bridge—"and had the so-called 'friend' tell you he never knew anyone by the name of Kaiser."

"Right. That's right, Paul. And I can tell you right now, this man Wilde's no pushover, no fool. He's not going to be bullied and conned."

"We've never bullied or conned people. We've always tried—"

"I didn't say we did. I was only saying that this man is not going to sit still for any kind of run-around. He was red in the face when he left here and on his way to the DA's office."

"You probably gave him the address."

Silence settles over the moiled and troubled air.

"I'm sorry you feel that way."

"I'm sorry, too." Konig's voice lowers with contrition. "I apologize. I had no business saying that. I've had a lousy day and—"

"Tell me something," Strang cuts him short. "Do you at least intend to find out who it is here leaking information to these morticians?"

Konig's eyes lower once more to the tiny figures and ruled lines of the departmental fiscal budget. "I already know who it is."

Eyes still lowered, nevertheless he can sense Strang sitting there, open-mouthed, gaping at him. He turns his pencil once more to the budgetary sheets, shortly hearing Strang rise and the sharp, percussive click of his feet striding swiftly from the office.

2 full-time Deputy Chief Medical	
Examiners	$40,500
2 Associate Medical Examiners	$33,000
Recommended promotion of two	
Assistant to Associate Medical Examiners at increments of	$13,000

The phone rings. Konig jumps. His pencil snaps, and while the phone continues to ring, he carves large, fierce circles over the face of the budget with the shattered edges of the pencil.

"Hello."

"Hello—Chief? That you there?"

"No. I'm home. You're talking to a recording. What the hell do you want, Flynn?"

"Listen. You gotta get down here."

"No way. It's after six. I'm not—"

"You gotta. We turned up a graveyard. Regular butcher shop. Arms. Legs. Balls. The works."

"Forget it. I'm on my way home."

"You can't," Flynn gasps breathlessly. "I mean you just can't. The place is right down at the river's edge. The tide's risin'. I'm afraid we're gonna lose half the goddamned stuff. Somebody who knows somethin' has gotta look at this stuff right here before we can move it. Don'tcha have someone up there you can send?"

"Everyone's left. It's after six. What the hell do you think this is here—an all-night car wash?"

A stand-off pause. Both men listen to each other breathing. Finally Konig breaks the silence. "How far down's the stuff?"

"Not far. Two, three feet. Might've been deeper once, but the tide's been workin' on it pretty regular. We're findin' it all over the place and I'm just afraid we're gonna lose—"

"Okay—okay," the Chief sighs. "Where the hell are you?"

"Coenties Slip. Right off Water Street—on the river."

"Okay. Send a car."

"It's probably out front there right now," Flynn's voice smirks. "I sent it about twenty minutes ago. Pick me up on the corner of South and Cuyler's. We'll go in together."

6:45 P.M. COENTIES SLIP AND SOUTH STREET.

"The guy's out walkin' his dog, see? Right along the river. 'Bout six A.M. The dog's runnin' around off the leash, see? And the guy's just suckin' up the breeze. Enjoyin' the sunrise—"

"Skip the poetry, will you, Flynn? Just get on with the details."

Flynn seems momentarily injured by the Chief's impatience, but he continues. "Anyway, the guy whistles for Rover. The dog starts runnin' toward him, see? Tail waggin'. All full of piss and vinegar. Only he's got a goddamn hand in his mouth."

"A hand?"

"Yeah—a human hand."

Konig and Flynn are speeding down Coenties Slip toward the river. The car streaks in past Jeanette Park and the Seamen's Church. At the Heliport they turn left and start to nose into milling crowds streaming toward a brilliantly illuminated area up ahead. The siren on the patrol car whoops frantically and a path clears, falls away before them.

They wheel into a large cleared circle, a police cordon of patrol cars, vans, sawhorses, badly harried foot patrolmen. A soft, pale purple has fallen over the day with a kind of tangible weight. The bright beacons and guide lights from the Heliport have begun to shimmer and flash on the brown pasty surface of the river.

Somewhere between the Heliport and the Old Slip, the police have set up a number of temporary floodlights. Also, the klieg lights of a TV mobile camera crew have just begun to bore through the twilight indigo dusk.

Just at the edge of the river, where the water slaps and lollops at the shoreline, a dozen men in rubber hip waders, armed with lantern helmets and shovels, move calf-deep through the mucky water like a flock of crows foraging a meadow. It is into this glaring circle of illumination that Flynn and Konig come.

"Watcha got?" the Chief says to a beefy young Irish cop with a high flush who appears to be directing the operation.

"Shoulder loin. Top round. Ground chuck. Ribs. Filet mignon. Fricassee. You name it, we got it."

A burst of laughter and crude joking. Konig scowls and barges over to another area where several patrolmen appear to be standing guard over a number of ill-shapen parcels strewn about the place and wrapped in clear plastic bags.

"Here's a little goody for you, Chief." Eyes glinting wickedly, Flynn holds out one of the bags to Konig. In it is contained a severed hand, the fingernails of which have been lacquered a bright, lurid purple.

Unimpressed, Konig scowls first at the hand, then at Flynn. "All right—let's have a look."

"Help yourself, Chief." The beefy young cop slings down before Konig a package containing what appears on first glance to be a large section of quartered beef. A few of the others laugh and shuffle nervously.

The Chief kneels down, the same sciatic agony of the morning shooting rockets from his back down into his leg. He opens the bag, and beneath the white glare of klieg lights and the puttering drone of an ascending helicopter from the nearby terminal, he studies the contents.

There before him, spilling out of the bag, are the remains of a badly hacked thoracic section. A great deal of the outer flesh has been stripped from it, but even in that light, and with the most cursory glance, Konig can see several stab wounds on its surface, one of which, he is certain, has penetrated the pericardium.

"That's fairly recent," he says, making a mental note of the degree of putrefaction. Slowly he rises and moves down the line from one parcel to the next. Here is a leg minus the foot; there a forearm; after that a thigh encased in a covering of mud and slime, the arteries and smaller blood vessels sheared off and dangling like disconnected wires. The next parcel contains a pelvic section. Then come several packages containing gobbets of flesh and innards hacked indiscriminately out of various parts of the anatomy. In addition, there are a number of smaller parts, odds and ends, toes and ears, a full set of male genitals, the split testes gleaming gray-white, like broken eggs.

More plastic bags are hauled up from the river and stacked with the others. Konig, in turn, examines these. They are a chaos and tangle of unrelated bits and pieces. He has no idea how many bodies are represented by all those parts. But already his cool professional eye has picked up a pattern of regularity. Great quantities of flesh had been stripped from all the parts; the blood had been drained from the bodies; and there are no heads. The massive stripping of flesh had been done to make the job of identification difficult. The absence of heads would make it nigh onto impossible.

"Never seen nothin' like it," murmurs an older Italian cop standing behind Konig, shaking his head in disbelief.

"No heads?" Konig snaps.

"Not yet. We're still lookin'."

The Chief rises wearily, still pondering the plastic parcels, rates of calcification at the epiphyses, formation of pelvic bones, size of sacral bones, while police cameras flash all about him and batteries of technicians scavenge meticulously over the surrounding area.

A number of detectives and patrolmen hover about, staring, speechless at the incomprehensibility of it all. The Chief knows their thoughts. He can read them as if they were writ on parchment. The marvel and mystery of it all, these broken bits and pieces lying there beneath cold white light like shattered toys, once a part of life. Once walked and talked. Incomprehensible.

"You boys got all this stuff tagged?" Konig asks.

"Tagged and pinpointed for location," replies the beefy young cop.

"It all come from the same general area?"

"From out there." One of the other cops points to a place where the men in hip waders and lantern helmets stumble through the shallow water. "Some of it's uncovered at low tide."

"Trouble is the goddamned tide's comin' in now," Flynn says. "We're gonna lose half the stuff."

"You probably lost half already. What time's high tide?" Konig asks.

"About eight P.M."

"Be a good idea to get the place cleaned out before too much more of it gets washed away."

"We're doin' our best, Chief," says the Irish cop. "We've had the place cordoned off and a dozen guys diggin' down there since this mornin'. I figure we got it pretty well cleaned now. There ain't too much more to dig."

"There's more," Konig remarks casually, his eyes scanning the bloody parcels. "You boys hit a graveyard."

Flynn gazes at him questioningly.

"Number one," Konig continues, more to himself than to those assembled, "those remains don't all come from the same body. Offhand, I'd say you've got parts from two or three different bodies there. Number two, all these parts have been buried about the same length of time." He prods a splintered edge of femur protruding from one of the bags. "The putrefaction in this thigh, for instance, is about the same as in that thoracic section. It's a young leg, too, judging from the degree of calcification. I'd say it belonged to a young male, early twenties—"

"What about them balls, Doc?" one of the young cops joshes.

"Pretty well hung, ay, Whitey?" More laughter and rude joking.

"And number three," Konig goes on mechanically, computerlike, gathering data, collating, filing in his head, scarcely hearing any of the raucous, irreverent banter of the weary men around him. "The person who did the dismembering had some sophistication—not a great deal, but he knew his anatomy and where to cut. Used a hacksaw. You can see the teeth marks in that femur—"

"We got the saw too," says Flynn.

Jarred for the first time out of his quiet ruminations, Konig glances up. "Where?"

Flynn smirks broadly. "Come on with me."

Together they walk back up through the cordons and the milling crowds, drawn there by the excitement of television crews working under bright lights. They trudge down along the shoreline, past the bustling Heliport, like two old friends taking an after-dinner stroll along the water. From where they are they can see an endless stream of car lights flowing over the Brooklyn Bridge, and traffic pouring toward the Battery Tunnel. Far out over the water, the lights from Brooklyn Heights all the way down to the Erie Basin are flickering magically.

"Where the hell you taking me now?" Konig snarls, pain shooting down his leg.

"Right up ahead, where you see the lights."

They trudge along the shoreline to a drab tiny shack squatting like a toadstool at the edge of the water. A dim orange light glows from within, and at the front several patrolmen hover at the doorway, smoking and chatting quietly.

As Flynn and the Chief appear through the thick velvet dusk, the cigarettes are quickly extinguished and the men step aside from the door.

"How the hell'd you find this place?" Konig stoops beneath the strangely shallow lintel of the doorway and enters.

"Rover, the little dog who found the hand." Flynn's smile is full of self-congratulation. "After he had a whiff of that hand, there was no stoppin' him. Just turned him loose at the river and he led us right here to the front door."

Several detectives prowl about in the dim light. The police photographers and lab technicians still swarm about the place like ants.

It is a low, vile turn-of-the-century shanty they've come to, full of the smell of mildew and rutting cats. One room with a rotting wood floor, the sort of place used for storage by fishermen in more tranquil times but in modern times fallen quickly into disuse—a haven for derelicts and squatters. Discarded beer cans and Thunderbird wine bottles are strewn all about. Two lean, mangy cats mew and wind their way through the fetid rubbish on the floor. There are several rusty, broken beds covered with thin, sheetless, urine-sodden pallets, tufts of mattress filling spewing out of gaping fissures. Old, yellowing copies of the *Daily News* have been stuffed into the punched-out windows for protection against wind and rain. Several open cans of beans and corn, half empty, lie forlornly on the floor, festooned with a green, fuzzy, faintly luminescent mold.

"Fragrant, ay," says one of the cops.

"Like a shithouse," remarks Flynn, a handkerchief pressed to his nose.

"Probably was." Konig glowers into the rank shadows. "No toilet. No running water."

"You got the biggest toilet in the world running right outside your front door." Detective Morello, emerging from a shadowy corner, waves in the direction of the East River outside. "Hi, Chief."

"They haul you down here, too, Morello?"

"He ain't goin' home to the wife and kiddies tonight," Flynn jeers. "Not while I gotta work."

With the tip of his shoe Konig pokes almost coyly at some rubbish on the ground. "Who owns the place?"

"We're checking the Bureau of Records for the deed now," Morello says.

"Whoever owned it"—Flynn waves his arm through a curtain of spider webs—"wasn't a very good housekeeper."

"My guess is it belongs to the City." Morello scribbles elaborately into a pad. "Anyway, it's a derelict. Looks like squatters and winos holed up here for the winter. Pulled out at the first crack of warm weather."

Konig peers gloomily about. "How do you figure this is where those pretty packages down on the beach came from?"

Flynn smirks and gestures in the direction of a dark corner of the shack. "Come on over here."

Reaching there, Konig peers down the beam of Flynn's flashlight into an old porcelain tub plucked out of the junk heap of some abandoned and demolished building and borne here to serve no discernible purpose other than possibly ornamentation. Its sides are splashed liberally with dried blood. Within the tub itself there are shards of bone, tufts of hair, clots of gore.

"The workbench," Flynn says.

"The tools are over here," Morello calls from the other side of the shack.

They walk back to a small, rickety bridge table covered with a variety of junk—odds and ends, cheap brummagem—harmless enough, but among it all there are an ax, an adz, chisels, a tire iron.

"There's your hacksaw." Flynn points proudly down at a rusty old saw, the blade of which is crusted with dried blood. The Chief's eyes quickly take in the size and configuration of the teeth, matching them in his mind with the imprint of those he saw shortly before on the bones beside the river. "Got any prints?"

"I don't know what we got," Morello says. "As soon as we get all this stuff back to the lab, we'll see what we got."

"Any leads?"

"Couple of people in the neighborhood claim they seen

a Salvation Army officer goin' in and out of here from time to time."

"Salvation Army officer?" Konig gapes back at Flynn. The detective shrugs wearily. "That's what they claim."

Outside once again on the beach, a television crew is making its noisy conspicuous way toward the shack. The thudding, concussive beat of helicopter rotors stirs the air overhead. Down on the river, the men in hip waders and lantern helmets slog in from the muddy water, where the tide has become too high and too swift to work, with any safety. Konig and Flynn are standing again in the large circle of white light where men busy at a variety of tasks bustle about amid the growing accumulation of grisly plastic bags.

"Never seen nothin' like it." The old Italian cop still stands dazed and stuporous above the place, shaking his head incomprehensibly back and forth. "Thirty years on the force—never seen nothin' like it."

"Okay." Konig snaps his note pad closed and takes a final glance at the long, neat row of carefully tagged parcels. "Soon as you finish here, wrap it all up and get it to me." He turns and starts to limp toward his waiting car.

"Hey, Chief," Flynn cries out behind him. Konig turns to see the detective waving at him the plastic bag containing the hand with the purple-lacquered fingernails. "Say bye-bye to the little lady."

"Never mind the hands, Flynn. Get me the goddamned heads." Konig scowls and ducks into the car.

≋ | | ≋

"Postcards. Pictures. Pencils. Pretty views."
7:50 P.M. AN ITALIAN RESTAURANT ON MINETTA LANE.

Konig sits in a steamy little *trattoria*—white trelliswork about the doors, artificial flowers woven into the lattice-work, and on the walls cheap views of Pompeii and the Bay of Naples.

There is an open garden in the back with a splashing fountain and an arbor hung with paper lanterns, where young couples full of earnest talk lean heads toward one another and dine in the mild spring evening.

Konig sits by himself at a corner table, ruminative, and sequestered from the noise outside. A plate of cooling, untouched food sits before him while, elbows on table, he muses over a glass of white wine.

"Postcards. Pictures. Pencils. Pretty views."

Twilight on a long strip of deserted beach. The lone figure of a fisherman in shorts and skivvy, hip-high in boiling spume, leans forward into a gusty breeze casting a surf pole with lead lures far out over the breaker line. Behind him sits a pensively pretty young girl, fifteen or sixteen, watching intently the high, arching trajectory of plug and line paying out over the onrushing waves, then reeled in slowly, then repeated. Suddenly the line shudders and goes taut.

"Postcards. Pictures. Pencils. Pretty views."

"Hurry, Lolly. Fast. I've got him."

The girl scrambles to her feet. Stumbles forward.

"Tension. More tension, damnit."

"Daddy, I can't. I can't."

"Tension—more tension, for God's sake. You're losing him. You're—"

"Wanna buy a postcard?"

Konig glances upward over the rim of his wineglass. "Beg pardon?"

"Wanna buy a postcard or a picture?"

"A picture?"

"Pictures—views of Greenwich Village. New York City."

Konig stares idiotically into the face of a young girl.

"Got some real pretty views. Washington Square. The Arch. The Mews."

"No," Konig mumbles and turns back to the solace of his wineglass.

"Empire State Building. George Washington Bridge. Grant's Tomb."

"No—no thank you."

"How about some pencils?"

"No. I think not." He turns away, a curt dismissive movement, but still she stands there hovering above him.

"Food's gettin' cold."

"Beg pardon."

"I said your food's gettin' cold."

"Oh." Konig grumbles, stubs out his cigar, takes up his fork and makes ready to eat. But then, the next moment, slightly flustered, he puts the fork down. "I'm not quite ready to eat."

"Mind if I sit?"

Stunned, Konig glances up to see the girl smiling rather impudently down upon him. "You mean here? Sit here?"

"Isn't that a veal cutlet?" the girl murmurs, slipping into the seat opposite him.

"Hey, wait a min—"

"Gonna be ice-cold if you don't eat it soon. And that salad—"

"Would you please mind hauling yourself right back up and—"

"Lettuce startin' to wilt right there in the bowl. It's a shame."

"Look here, you weren't invited to—"

"Just lemme freshen that salad up with some of this oil and vinegar."

Konig stares around helplessly for the head waiter. Though the room is full of laughing, chattering people, no one seems to notice his predicament.

"Hey—wait a minute." Konig snatches a flask of vinegar from the girl but she has already irrigated his salad with a thick oily dressing. "Now what the hell did you do that for? You've flooded the goddamned thing."

"Sorry. Just tryin' to perk it up a bit."

"Well, who asked you to? If I'd wanted it perked up, I would've perked it up myself. And I don't want any pencils or postcards. Now will you please—"

"Wouldn't you like"—once again the impudent, rather provocative little smile—"a twist of lemon on that veal and—"

"Would you leave here?" Konig's voice grows louder. He searches about desperately for the head waiter.

"If you don't want that veal—"

He spies the maître d', starts to stand and gesture toward him.

"—I'd be glad to eat it for you."

For the first time, Konig turns and peers squarely into the girl's face. It is a small gaminelike face, haggardly pretty. She can be no more than fifteen or sixteen but there is already something blatantly sexual in her mocking glance, in the tightness of her faded jeans and sweater. It is all a kind of bold, unabashed self-proclaiming. Still, beyond the playful impudence in the eyes, the little flashes of defiance, the frank sexuality, there is also a note of fright and quite possibly desperation. The desperation becomes more discernible as the peppery little Neapolitan maître d' comes, puffing and sputtering, quickly toward them.

Konig sees a small note of pleading in the girl's eyes and in the next moment he observes in those same eyes a set of blue-gray pupils that are unmistakably constricted.

As the maître d' marches up to them, her voice rises. She laughs and chatters with a kind of desperate cheer. "So I told this silly little—"

"All right—get out," the little Neapolitan with the large mustaches fumes down at her. "Go on. Get the hell out."

The girl peers dismally down at the plate of cold cutlets.

"I'm awful sorry, sir." He snatches the girl's arm. "How many times I tell you I don't want you here? This ain't that kind of place. Now I'm gonna call a cop." He starts to tug the girl to her feet. "Awful sorry, sir."

There's great confusion while the tugging goes on. Plates and silver clatter. The wineglass nearly topples. Konig makes a desperate lunge and catches it. "That's all right." He is painfully aware that everyone in the room has stopped eating and is watching them. "Perfectly all right. Let her stay."

"Stay?" The Italian gapes at him. "You want her to stay?"

"Yes—it's okay." Mortified by the scene they've created, Konig hears his voice coming at him from great distances. The Italian's expression bristles with disapproval. "It's all right," Konig goes on a little frantically. "She's with me. I'll have another glass of wine, please." He makes a gesture, dismissing the man.

Baffled and muttering, the Italian moves off, and suddenly Konig and the girl are all alone. Sighing and flustered, he watches her cut and fork pieces of the cutlet into her mouth.

"Nothin' wrong with this cutlet," she says.

"Good. I hope you enjoy it."

"Thanks," the girl replies, staring dismally down at her plate.

"Forget it. Just finish up and go."

There's something famished, almost savage, about the way the girl screws her eyes downward to the plate and chews, her fork darting quickly between cutlet and salad. She chews quickly, too, swallowing large, unmasticated chunks of food, hunched over her plate protectively, like a hungry dog, fearing that she must get it all down fast before someone whisks it away.

Returning with Konig's fresh glass of wine, the waiter scowls down at the girl. Unable to forgive her for cadging food, he mutters and goes off.

When she's finished the cutlet and salad, she starts with the bread and butter.

"Want something to drink?" Konig growls. "Milk? Soda?"

"Nope." The girl hiccoughs, wipes her butter-smeared mouth with a napkin, then pulls a half-smoked cigarette from the cuff of her jeans. She leans forward to the table candle, lighting the cigarette, her face glowing suddenly in the guttering flame.

"Sorry I don't have one for you." She inhales the smoke deeply.

"That's all right. I don't use them."

She sits back now in her seat. Content. Hugely satisfied, she gazes around the room now at the young, effusively chatty couples, all involved in themselves. Then suddenly she's looking at him again, first sideways, then directly, head-on, the eyes once more impudent and suggestive. No longer a trace there of that momentary desperation and pleading. She gazes boldly at him, but it is all rather bogus. Postures and attitudes learned from cheap television serials and trashy films.

"Aren't you gonna eat?"

"No. I'm not hungry."

"Sorry about all that fuss." She glances at the waiter, still smoldering at her from a corner of the room. "He's such a bastard anyway. Pardon the language."

"That's all right. Forget it."

"Wanna buy some postcards?"

"No. Thank you."

She pushes a stack of cards toward him. "Look at 'em."

"No, I said I—"

"Go on—just look at 'em."

"Oh, God." He sighs and snatches up the cards, flicking idly through them. Views of the George Washington Bridge. Statue of Liberty. Empire State Building. Shea Stadium. Fulton Fish Market. Then suddenly a glossy, postcard-sized photograph of a girl naked on a bed, legs up and parted. Then another, same girl, on her stomach, buttocks up, thrust assertively outward.

Konig glances at the girl now smiling wickedly opposite him, two columns of smoke wafting from her nostrils. "If you like those you can have them for twenty dollars."

"Oh?" Konig feels her leg brush his under the table. "I'm afraid not." He flicks to views of the meat market and Times Square by night.

"If that's too much I could maybe let you have it a little cheaper—like eighteen?"

"No, I really don't think so."

"Fifteen?"

"It's not the price." Konig laughs, feeling a little foolish. "I'm a little past that."

"Oh, come on now, Daddy," she taunts him softly. "You'll do just fine. Leave it to me. Make you happy. Make you feel real good."

In spite of efforts to be stern, Konig grows giddy. The thought of his weary old bones in bed with that child, feigning passion, struggling to be amorous, is laughable.

"Betchya good." The girl laughs. "Betchya real good."

Konig smiles in spite of himself. "You must be all of fifteen."

"I'm nineteen."

"Oh, come on."

"I am. I'm nineteen."

"You're nineteen like I'm twenty-two. Where you from anyway? Texas? I'll bet Texas, with that drawl."

"Not Texas," the girl sulks. "Close though."

"Oklahoma," Konig says, seeing something register in her eyes. "It is Oklahoma, isn't it?"

"That's my business."

"I recognize that accent. Spent enough time in the Army down there. What's the big secret anyway?"

"No big secret. I just don't care to say." The girl scowls, cross-armed and adamant. "Come on, Daddy. Let you have those cards for fifteen. Special to you. Three ways. Straight, French, and Greek."

"That's all I need," Konig groans. "I'd probably expire."

"Don't talk that way. You're not as old as all that."

"I'm older. I could be your grandfather."

"Bet you're hell in bed. I can tell just by lookin' at you. I like older men anyway. Used to know an old buck back in Tulsa—" Her voice breaks off abruptly as she sees triumph glow in Konig's eye. "Aren't you smart though. Stop lookin' so smug. Ain't been in Tulsa for years."

"What's your name?"

"Heather."

"Heather?"

"Heather Harwell."

Konig gives her a long, dubious gaze.

"Now what's wrong with that?" the girl protests.

Suddenly a huge belly laugh from Konig. Several people turn and stare at them. The peppery little Neapolitan glowers in their direction.

"Heather Harwell." He chuckles more quietly. "Boy, you really can pick 'em."

"What's so funny?"

"Sounds like the name of a comic strip. The Adventures of Heather Harwell. Girl Postcard Hawker, Infant Hooker."

"Shhh." The girl stares anxiously around.

"What's your real name?"

The girl sits stony and tight-lipped.

"Your family in Tulsa?"

"Boy, you ask a lot of questions."

"Heather Harwell's not your name. No one from Tulsa is named Heather Harwell. They all have names like Minnie Turl."

"It's my professional name."

"Your professional name?" Konig hoots. "You mean the name you hustle under?"

"Shhh." She tries to silence him again. "For pity sake, will you quit screaming that out? It's the name I model under. I'm a model."

"For dirty postcards?" Konig laughs cruelly.

Defiance blazes in her eyes. "For fashion magazines. I've been in *Vogue* and *Harper's*—"

"Oh, come on."

"Well, I have. And maybe someday I'll be in television commercials. I've got a friend says he knows people who can help me."

"I'll bet he does. But just for now it's dirty pictures."

"That's not my regular line," the girl snaps. "And besides, they're not dirty. Dirtiness is—"

"—in the eye of the beholder," Konig taunts her cruelly. "I see."

"Come on, Poppy. Let's not fuss. Come home with Heather."

"Your folks know anything about what you do up here?" Konig sees something like fear register in the girl's eyes. "I bet they don't even know where you are."

"Come on, Daddy-o. Heather's pad is right around the corner. Twelve fifty—special to you."

"Answer me." Konig suddenly bears down hard. "Your family doesn't know you're here."

She starts to get up, but he pushes her roughly back down in her seat. "You're a runaway, aren't you?"

"How come you ask so many questions?"

"How long have you been on the lam?"

"You some kind of cop?"

"I'm no cop." Konig feels something like rage mounting in him. "When's the last time you spoke with your parents?"

The girl flushes violently. "Leave me alone."

Just then the maître d', scowling and indignant, steams up to them and flings the check on the table.

"I didn't ask for that yet," Konig snaps, and the little Neapolitan retreats before the Chief's glowering visage.

Konig turns back to the girl. "Answer me."

"Answer you what?" All at once she is coy and provocative, fingering the fabric of his sleeve. "I've never heard such a silly lot of questions. First of all, I'm nineteen years of age. What the law calls a consenting adult. I'm not a runaway. In order to be a runaway, you gotta have something to run away from. Either a home or a family. I most distinctly have neither, having lost all of my family in an air crash."

"I'm sorry," Konig mumbles, momentarily buffaloed by the sweet, almost childish candor of the girl. Then his trained, somewhat jaded eye suddenly detects the treacherous little actress-liar at work there behind the furrowed brow, the long, lugubrious face of mock tragedy.

"That's all right." The girl suffers on with histrionic

bravery. "You were sincerely concerned. And I'm touched. Now come on home with Heather, honey. Ten dollars. A sawbuck. Rock-bottom. Special to you 'cause I like you. But don't let the word get around. Come on." She tugs at his sleeve. "Let Heather make you happy. Show you heaven."

Konig gazes at her for a long moment, sighs wearily and laughs. "Okay, let's go."

For a while she gazes at him dumbly, not quite believing. Then comprehension comes upon her. Her face lights; her eyes dazzle. "You really mean it?"

"Absolutely. Why not? Do me good."

"Wait here." She bounces up.

"Where you going?"

"Little girls' room—for a tinkle." She scurries off, then scurries back. "You won't run off?"

"Course not. I'll be right here." Konig removes several bills from a billfold. "Hurry up."

She turns, starts off, then turns again, smiling. "You won't regret it."

"I know—I know," he growls. "Hurry up."

Konig counts off a number of bills, leaves them atop the check, all the while eying the small white vinyl wallet the girl has left there trustingly with her cards and pencils. In a moment he has the wallet and is riffling through it, flicking past a wad of old photos stuck behind dirty yellow plastic windows—pictures of a raddled old frame house with a windmill in the front yard, a fat dozy mongrel dog with sweet eyes, one of Heather in a bathing suit, then one behind the wheel of an old Plymouth convertible with a ruined top, then several shots of Heather with an assortment of young men, all of them of the greasy-frisette, tattooed-bicep variety. Then suddenly he finds what he's looking for—a driver's license issued in the name of Molly Sully, Box 382, RFD, Tulsa, Oklahoma. Date of birth: 3/5/58.

He tucks the license carefully back into the plastic sleeve and returns the wallet to its place.

Then suddenly Heather Harwell, nee Molly Sully, is there again, smiling, face scrubbed, mouth red with a fresh coating of lipstick somewhat untidily applied. "Okay, Poppy—let's fly."

≈≈ 12 ≈≈

8:40 P.M. A THIRD-FLOOR LOFT IN A WAREHOUSE ON
VARICK STREET.

Francis Xavier Haggard stands cross-armed and pen-
sive before a high, crumbling plaster wall, studying the
curious motto scrawled there.

The letters, sprayed on graffiti-style in tall, wavery
blood-red letters, cover the full length of the wall and run
from nearly floor to ceiling. A spray can of Red Devil
paint lies on its side, empty and discarded, at the foot of
the wall beneath the motto.

THE DAY OF THE MUFFLED OAR IS COMING

Haggard's pebbly blue eyes fasten thoughtfully on the
words, trying to decipher their cryptic, somewhat portentous message. He appears to be a man deep in reverie.

Behind him two young people hover silently in an open
doorway. One, a short, stocky, powerfully built Greek man
by the name of Tsacrios, mid-twenties, darkly handsome,
with tempestuous curly hair and sullen eyes; the other, a
lithesome black girl called Cynthia, with the bone structure and lineaments of a fashion model. Leaning against
the jamb, she wears a man's silk paisley robe cinctured
tightly around the waist with a tasseled sash, and, quite
apparent, nothing else beneath. Their faces convey a
mixture of distrust and fear.

The detective turns from the wall, then commences his
slow leonine prowl through the awful chaos of the loft.
The place gives the impression of a violent ransacking,
drawers ripped out, feminine apparel strewn across the
floor, broken furniture, shattered lamps, ceramic crockery
and ashtrays hurled violently against the wall, in some
places punctured plaster.

There are two small army cots where people have re-

71

cently lain. Onto these the contents of dozens of tubes of
vibrantly colored acrylic paints have been squirted,
dripped, and oozed, creating on the tumbled sheets and
blankets a violent lunatic pattern. Mingled into this
frenzy are the remains of dozens of fine horsehair brushes,
all shattered and broken, then stretchers and canvas, battered and slashed irretrievably.

Haggard moves farther into the loft, stooping beneath
joists and pipes beaded with cold dripping water, ducking
to avoid naked hanging light bulbs. His prowl moves him
toward the gloomy shadows in the rear of the loft. Here
he finds curtained off, without the grace of a door, a dismal but clean little privy revealing someone's recent pathetic efforts to beautify it by attempting to cover up a
soot-blackened window with a pretty bamboo shade.

Outside of that is a tiny, makeshift alcove containing a
small electric stove and a zinc-plated sink with a wood
plank shelf above it lined with jars of instant coffee, pea-
nut butter, jam, powdered milk, a soap cleanser, Ritz
crackers, and two biscuit tins. Beneath the sink lies the
crumpled, maggoty body of a small black-and-white mongrel dog, muzzle sticky with blood.

Stooping and weaving his way beneath joists and pipes,
Haggard completes his slow circumambulation of the loft,
arriving once more at the heap of nameless debris in the
center of the loft. With the two young people still watching him from the doorway, he pokes with the tip of his
shoe through the wreckage, a graveyard junk heap of
paintings, dozens of them, in shreds and tatters, as if the
stretchers had been smashed brutally and each canvas
very deliberately punched through, then ground under
heel.

The violence in evidence there has a maniacal look
about it. The devastation is total, absolute. But it is still
possible to describe the shape and content of many of the
paintings, all of which appear to have a distinctly nautical
motif—seas and skies, both tranquil and stormy, beaches,
sand dunes, driftwood, marine flora, storm-weathered
shacks, nets, dead fish washed up on the shore, the
wrecked hulls of old beached scows, barnacle-encrusted,
shattered, peeling, tumid bellies turned upward toward
the sun.

One there in all this frenzied heap catches Haggard's
eye. A lone figure at twilight, a man in shorts and skivvy,

standing hip-high in boiling surf, caught just at that moment when his great surf pole, brought back as far as it will go, quivers in the space of that second just before it will be hurled forward like a lash. There's something in that lone figure on the beach consigned to what appears a perpetual twilight, something about the powerful shoulders, that intransigent, ramrod carriage with the sea wind beating inland against him, fluttering his garments, something in that figure that the detective recognizes. The bottom left-hand corner of the painting is signed in a tiny, unassertive orthography—Emily Winslow.

"I hope you get the bastard."

A voice shatters Haggard's inward ruminations. He turns to the stocky young Greek in the open doorway with the pretty black girl hovering just behind him.

"When you get him I'd appreciate your letting me know. Unofficially, of course, just before you pick him up. I'd like to have a few moments alone with Warren. See the poor little mutt back there?"

"Yeah. I saw him." Haggard gazes ruefully at the young man with the round, cherubic face of a Quattrocento prince. Pulling the crumpled DD13 out of his inside pocket he walks toward him. "You're sure now this is the girl we're talking about?"

The two young people glance at the photograph on the police form.

"That's her all right," says Tsacrios. "Looks a little younger there. But that's her all right—isn't it, Cyn?"

"That's her. No mistake. We never called her Lauren though. We called her Emily."

"Emily Winslow?" Haggard stares down at the girl.

"That's right," the girl replies, a little rattled by the intensity of his gaze.

"How long she live here?"

The young man scratches the back of his head. "Oh, maybe three, four months. She looked like the kinda chick moved around a lot. Know what I mean?"

Haggard gazes at him quizzically.

"Like she never unpacked her things," the girl adds by way of explanation. "Never seemed settled. Like she was always ready to move on at a moment's notice."

"Frightened, scared like a rabbit, you know," Tsacrios offers sympathetically. "Sweet kid though. Kind of person who looks like she had a lotta hard luck."

The detective nods, then pauses. "And you say you heard all this ruckus going on last night—"

"Around seven-thirty, eight o'clock. Somewhere like that. Right, Cyn?"

"Yeah—somewhere like that." The pretty black girl stares at Haggard with almost hypnotic fascination. "Some awful ruckus."

"Why'n't you call the cops?"

"Oh, man—hey—cops—" The young Greek half turns, thumps his forehead with the palm of his hand, then turns back. "Like if we called cops every time that kinda thing went on—"

"It went on often?"

"Often? Hey, man—like every other night. He used to beat up on her."

"He hit her?"

"Sure he hit her. Banged her around plenty. Right, Cyn?"

The girl gazes wide-eyed around the shattered desolation of the room. "Man, it was awful. I mean, like the screaming and crying."

"You don't know his last name, do you? This"—he glances downward at his notes—"Warren?"

"That's all I know. She used to call him Warren. Right, Cyn?"

"That's right—Warren. Some of those other cats who used to come around here—like his friends. They used to call him something like Keedro."

"Keedro?" Haggard jots the name down. "Sounds Spanish."

"No, man." Tsacrios shakes his head emphatically. "He was no Spanish. I know Spanish. This guy was no Spanish. He was more like Midwestern. Fair—blond. Lots of hard r's. Funny little steel-rimmed glasses. Wasn't from anywhere around here."

"How old?"

"Late twenties, early thirties, wouldn't you say, Cyn?"

"Yeah—thirty, maybe thirty-one or -two. Nice-looking. Very refined, sort of. Like I mean I can see what she saw in him. But those eyes, man—"

"What about them?"

"Crazy." The girl shudders and ties the robe sash more tightly around her. "Crazy. Scare you to look into them eyes, right, Tony? And that voice. Quiet, man. So quiet. So gentle, right, Tony?"

"Yeah. Very gentle. Only he liked to beat up on chicks. Get the picture?"

"Yeah." Haggard scribbles in his notebook. "I get the picture. Where'd she meet this guy anyway?"

Tsacrios glances at the black girl. "Who knows? Probably one of the coffeehouses. She used to spend some time over there at night This creep Warren used to haunt those joints. Sit around there all night snowing the dumb little uptown chicks with a lot of fancy talk about the 'people's revolution'—*Angst, Schmerz,* and *Weltanschauung.* You know, the bit. Then he'd screw 'em and take their money."

Haggard lifts his light-gray Borsalino and scratches the back of his head. Something gnaws and nibbles at him. Something in the story that doesn't jibe for him. When at last he speaks, he speaks out loud, but more to himself than to the two young people watching him. "I don't get it. This girl—Lauren—Emily—she was fairly sophisticated. I don't see her swallowing that kind of routine."

"Right. You're right." The black girl nods eagerly. "But like I say, he had something. And when he was around, like she was stoned. Didn't think straight."

"Or maybe she was scared of him," Haggard dreams on out loud, "but didn't know how to get rid of him."

"Could be." Tsacrios shrugs. "Like I say, he liked to beat up on the chicks. Did somethin' for him. Once he came downstairs while I was out, started to mess around with Cynthia here. She pushed him and he was gettin' ready to bust her when I walked in."

Haggard smiles, seeing the sudden animation in the young Greek's eyes.

"I grabbed him by the collar and threw him out the front door. Told him if I ever found him down there again I'd bust his ass. Never said a word. Not a peep out of him. Just went and that was that. Like I say, without those flunkies around, he was nothin'. Right outta the funnies."

"Didn't seem too funny to me," says Cynthia. "Especially the heater. Like I never found that too funny at all."

Haggard's brow cocks. "He carried a gun?"

"Gun?" the young man snorts, does his half turn and thumps his forehead. "Guns, mister. Plural guns. *Mucho* guns. That was all part of the image. Always had one strapped on under his jacket. Sit quiet just holding a gun and thinking. Never said a word. Just sat there. You wondered what he was thinking. When all his pals were up here stomping around in berets and combat boots waving guns and doing their number about the Fascist pigs and corporate enemies, this guy'd just sit there quietlike and think."

"Who were these pals?"

"Creeps." Cynthia makes a face of revulsion. "Loafers and hangers-on. The free-lunch crowd. Just sit around all day with their guns and talk about the 'people's war.' But not even smart—good—talk. Just dumb. Real dumb. Like crazy."

"Couple of them came up here once with dynamite," Tsacrios mutters.

"Dynamite?"

"Yeah, man—like I'm tellin' you. Sticks of dynamite."

Once more Haggard's small, beady eyes glide over the graffiti-scrawled wall: THE DAY OF THE MUFFLED OAR IS COMING.

"This Warren," he says after a moment, "he have some kind of job? Do anything for a living?"

"Used to call himself an editor." Tsacrios laughs scornfully.

"An editor?"

"Yeah. Some kind of underground press or something. But I never seen no paper he ever put out. Did you, Cyn?"

The girl shrugs. "Creepy cat. But like I say, I can see what she saw there. He had something. A kind of excitement. And like when he spoke—" The girl breaks off, unable to find the precise word. "I don't know— Very quiet —his eyes kinda slow—like you could almost believe him."

"If you didn't listen too carefully." The young Greek scowls. "If you thought about it for a little while, then it got to be pretty stupid. But this kid, this Emily—what's her real name again?"

"It doesn't matter," Haggard says. "Keep talking."

"Well anyway, this chick—he had her completely snowed. Took all her money."

"Where'd she get her money?" The detective seizes on the word.

"From the paintings, man." Tsacrios strides across the littered floor to the mound of wrecked, battered canvases and glares down at them. "That's why I'd like to get my hands on him."

"You mean she was selling this stuff?" Haggard asks.

"Selling? Man, she was just beginning to hit. All over the place. Had a gallery. Clients. People with money interested in her. That's why he hadda go bust this all up." Tsacrios kneels down by the wreckage, prodding it tenderly with a finger, an expression of irretrievable loss on his face. "Now ain't that a shame? Pretty things. He just couldn't stand it. She was painting good. Real good. And he and that phony underground rag of his were a total bust. Used to call her painting 'bourgeois.' Every other word out of this creep's mouth was 'bourgeois.' Said the people who bought her paintings were 'bourgeois' and they got the money to buy the paintings from robbing 'the people.' So, of course, he felt justified in taking whatever money she made from painting to return to 'the people.' "

"I don't figure 'the people' ever saw too much of it," Cynthia says.

Haggard nods. "You said something about a gallery?"

"Sure, she had a gallery uptown."

"Know which one?"

"Nope. East Side someplace. Pretty posh. You know which one, Cyn?"

The girl shakes her head, gazing at Haggard forlornly.

"Don't worry about that," the detective says. "I'll find the gallery. What I'm concerned about now is where he took her. You don't have any ideas, do you?"

He glances back and forth from one to the other, his fierce eagle glance causing them uneasiness.

"All I know," says the girl at last, "is that wherever it was, she didn't want to go there. He dragged her outta here."

"Him and his pals?"

"Yeah. He come over here last night with three of them. We heard all this screaming and fighting. Things crashing on the floor."

"You didn't go up?"

"No, man." The Greek does his half turn. "Like I told you, when you hear that kind of stuff six, seven nights a week, after a while you stop hearin' it. And anyway"—he looks away, eyes lowered and ashamed—"there were three, four of them. And they're real creeps. Guns and everything."

"Can't say I blame you." Haggard snaps his notebook shut.

Tsacrios glances at the girl a moment, abashed, a little contrite. "She wanted me to go up and try and stop them. You live long enough you learn to keep your nose out of where it don't belong. But if I ever see him again, minus the flunkies—"

"Sure," says Haggard. "I understand. Got a phone I can use?"

"Downstairs in the studio," Tsacrios mutters.

"Studio?"

"Yeah—I got a loft below. I'm a sculptor."

Downstairs, a few moments later, Haggard stands in another loft with the exact same long-high-wide configuration of the demolished studio above. This, too, is an artist's studio but it looks more like the back room of an auto-body shop. Strewn about the place in various stages of dismemberment are the remains of what must be at least a dozen fatal collisions—smashed fenders, demolished hoods, detached doors, rusty universals and drive shafts, grillworks—rewelded and tortured into writhing shapes, tall, spikelike trees, brittle sea flora, long, spiny pincushion shapes, and delicate weblike filigree, all wrought of chrome and hammered steel.

"Right back there"—the young Greek waves vaguely at the shadows in the rear—"on the wall." He leads the bewildered detective through a maze of devastation—ghastly wreckage, acetylene torches, riveting guns, welding masks, long, white rubber hoses depending like vines from the ceiling, screwed into huge green metal tanks of pure oxygen.

"Help yourself." Tsacrios propels Haggard forward into the shadows, then at a point turns and leaves him, weary and perplexed, beside a wall phone.

In a matter of moments, he has dialed the 17th Precinct and is speaking directly to the desk sergeant. "Hello—Wershba?—I'm down here on Varick Street. Yeah, you were right. This is the place all right, but the girl's blown." Swiftly he describes the situation and everything he's seen here. "What I need quick is a rundown on everything you've got on this New World Militia bunch. I want names, prior arrest records, fingerprints—anything you got. Particularly some guy by the name of Warren. No, no surname. All I got is Warren. Caucasian. Medium height. Sandy hair. Mid-twenties to early thirties. Glasses. Active in revolutionary activities. Might be Middle Western. See what the Feds have. Also, any of these other guys you can lay hands on—pull 'em in for questioning. There's an awful mess here and, frankly, it looks bad. This Warren character has taken the girl. Yeah—sometime last night. We'll need a couple of lab guys down here right away. See what kind of prints they can lift off all this mess. Also, I want a rundown on every art gallery—that's right, Wershba—art gallery. Art—a—r—t. All galleries, midtown area, East Side, that know of or that have ever dealt with an artist called Emily Winslow. And, Wershba—listen to me. Listen hard. Not a word to anyone. This is the Chief's kid. That's right—Konig's daughter. So don't blab it around. He's not to know a thing till we've got something more definite. From what I've seen up here, and from everything I just heard, I got a sick feeling in the pit of my stomach."

In the center of the studio area once again, Haggard stands dwarfed and mute before a 1953 Oldsmobile grillwork that has been unraveled by means of blowtorches and refashioned into what appears to be a chromium hatrack. A small white tag identifies it as KINETIC APOCALYPSE #3. He lifts his Borsalino again and scratches the back of his head. "What's that supposed to mean?"

"What's what supposed to mean?" Tsacrios glances up from a struggle with the cork of a half-gallon bottle of Chianti.

"Kinetic Apocalypse Number Three."

"Oh, that." The cork is liberated with a triumphant pop. "Don't mean nothin' really—just a nude of Cynthia."

Haggard glances back and forth from the lithe, willowy beauty of the black girl to the thorny, lethal-looking chrome and shrugs. "Okay—if you say so."

The young Greek extends a glass of wine toward him. "How about it?"

"Thanks." The detective smiles wistfully. "Another time. Haven't had my dinner yet. Guess I'll mosey over to the local coffeehouse."

≈ 13 ≈

"This is as far as I go."

The pert, sullen face glances up at him in the dim orange glow of the streetlight. "But you said—"

"Never mind what I said. This is where we part."

9:15 P.M. SOMEWHERE IN THE WEST VILLAGE.

Konig and the girl stand in the dank, wavery shadows of a partially gutted tenement destined for imminent demolition. A tattered police order instructs all remaining occupants to vacate the premises by a certain date. Above them the sporadic lights of the last few remaining tenants —the obdurate and those with no place to go—flicker forlornly in the hazy April night.

"But you said—"

"I know what I said." Konig grows curt, gruff, a little nasty. "But this is it."

Surprise and hurt mingle in the girl's eyes. A child denied a long-awaited present.

It is now fifteen minutes since Konig paid the bill at the little Italian restaurant on Minetta Lane, then started walking west toward the girl's apartment over near the river. Now having reached there, he has what he's come for. An address. In that time they've laughed and chatted. Been easy with each other. She'd been happy, secretly smug and congratulating herself on what an easy thing it had been to win him over. She'd been thinking of herself as shrewd and him as foolish. But not unkind. She doesn't think he will try to hurt her as some of the others have.

Now, suddenly, the momentary laughter is all gone. He is stern, harsh, censorious. There is something even a little menacing about the way he looks at her. As if he were furious with her.

"Ah, come on now." She pushes up against him in the shadows, her child's lips eagerly seeking his old man's

80

mouth. The obscenity of it offends him and he pushes her off.

"Come on, Poppy. Don't be scared."

"I'm not scared, and stop calling me that disgusting name. I'm not your poppy." He looks up at the gutted, squalid thing, the tangle of brick and rusting iron crouching above them. "You live in this?"

The girl seems suddenly grief-stricken, at a loss, unable to fathom all the sudden rejection.

"Go upstairs now," Konig says more softly, a bit of the edge off his voice.

She stares at him helplessly, fright and puzzlement in her eyes. Then she turns.

Watching her go, Konig calls after her. "How long have you been on drugs?"

She turns back, mouth open, trying to form words.

"How long you been on junk?" Konig's manner grows more harsh and insistent. "Answer me."

"Are you a cop?"

"Answer me, I said."

"You're a cop. I knew it." She starts toward him imploringly. "Oh—hey, listen—I—"

"No, you listen to me." He hold her off at arm's length. "I'm not a cop."

"Then how d'ya know?"

"I don't have to be a cop. All I have to do is look in your eyes."

Suddenly the girl starts to tremble. He shakes her violently.

"Now listen to me. You keep on that stuff and you're going to wind up in a garbage can." He gazes upward at the crumbling brick and plaster, the punched-out windows, the graffiti scrawl of myrmidon street kids. "As a matter of fact, you're more than halfway there right now." He crams twenty dollars into her tiny cold fist. "Go upstairs."

The girl gapes down at the bill, her shoulders slumped wearily in defeat. He senses the struggle going on within her. She'd like to fling the bill back in his face, but he knows she won't. He can see the need already too great upon her. The girl, he knows, won't have her money long. Even now he can sense the avid burning eyes of the junk pusher crouching behind the brick wall with his precious little packets of forgetfulness, just waiting for him to go.

"Take this, too." Konig produces a small white professional card from his billfold. "When you're ready to try and break out, come and see me. I'll do what I can to help you."

9:20. Konig limping back crosstown, some huge, vague, unspecified rage smoldering within him. No destination. Uncertain where his faltering tread impels him. Bone-weary, yet determined not to go home. No reason to. Dreading the empty house and its haunted shadows. Un-aware of the pain shrieking down his leg, he hobbles through the green-red gridlike maze of traffic patterns blinking up and down Sixth Avenue, then starts up West 4th, unaware that at that very moment behind the yellow plate-glass storefront window he is passing, beyond which flicker the tawdry lights of cheap reproduction Tiffany lamps, Francis Xavier Haggard sits hunched and miserable over a cup of bitter-as-rue espresso, trying to assemble, make some sense of the odds and ends, the bits of trivia hailing down upon him in badly fragmented English from the lips of an excitable young Armenian waiter gesticulating above him.

Konig drifts across the moist, hazy April night, moving beneath bright white street lamps ringed with gauzy, spectral halations, past a flowing tide of young, laughing, ani-mated faces. All the world is young here, making him feel suddenly ancient. Some obscene, discarded, castoff thing. Full of curious envy and contempt and sick at heart. Their vitality taunts him. He searches those faces, all restless, eager, seeking life on the littered pavements. Searching, yet unaware that he is searching, seeking out one face. Suddenly, the small, frightened features of Heather Har-well, nee Molly Sully, of Tulsa, Oklahoma, waver momen-tarily before his eyes. He wonders, now that he's dis-patched her, why the need to have been so cruel about it. The final, heartless brutality of his rejection of her, he realizes now, afforded him some odd, unsavory pleasure. Then the need to humiliate her further with the twenty-dollar bill, proffered for nothing—no services rendered—with almost regal contempt. The faintly oily odor of her hair, mingled with that of cheap spray, still clings to him, and the memory of small, frail, pathetically childlike bones crushing up against him in the dark—not for lust, it sud-denly occurs to him, but rather the small child's need for protective warmth against the night—suddenly saddens him.

Up Broadway and over to St. Marks Place, he shambles through the gaudy night, pausing from time to time outside the yellow-orange windows of saloons and coffeehouses, small bistros and bookstalls, little Japanese gift shops reeking with incense, hung with paper lanterns, stuffed with fake jade, cheap brummagem, past endless pizza parlors, tiny hole-in-the-wall Greek restaurants, the smell of singed lamb, oily pilaf, sausages frying on vendors' griddles, a hundred different smells licking outward from open doorways like a moist, sour tongue. And everywhere the young. A flood tide of the young—students, lovers, painters, poets manqué, bearded teenagers plotting a better world in cheap all-night cafeterias, drug-crazed junkies hovering like lean, hungry jackals in shadowy doorways, pondering desperate solutions to desperate problems. Konig's eyes sweep and scan these youthful faces.

Oh, Lolly, Come home, dear. Please come home now.

"Evening, Chief."

Konig looks up into the smiling rubicund visage of the night guard.

"Working late tonight, are you, Doc?"

Konig gazes around like a stranger. A little startled to find himself there. "Oh, no—nothing, Scanlon. Just some paper work. Won't be long."

"Take your time. I'll be here if you need me."

The pleasant lilt of a Gaelic chuckle fades behind him; the echo of his own footsteps clatters through the long, empty green corridors, and once more Paul Konig has entered the green, comforting gloom of the world he knows best.

≈ 14 ≈

Full-time Deputy Chief Medical Examiner
$40,500
5 full-time Associate Medical Examiners
$33,000/$165,000

10:00 P.M. KONIG'S OFFICE.

Silence. Only the ticking of the old Regulator wall clock, the gurgling of the coffeepot, the quiet hiss of the Bunsen burner sighing beneath it. Konig's pen scratches across the large municipal ledger sheets of the office annual budget.

8 full-time Assistant Medical Examiners
$10,500/$84,000

Goddamn Strang anyway. He and Blaylock. Both of them oughta be sacked—hang 'em both.

Chief Toxicologist, full time $19,500

No goddamned tissue study—no mention of ecchymosis in the protocol.

Hematologist, full time, 4 Assistants and—

Ought to send him up to Yonkers. Serve him right. They'd eat him alive. Carslin and those smart-ass ACLU boys. And me having to take all that goddamned guff from Benjamin. Flexing his muscles. Threatening me with the grand jury. Chief Deputy Mayor and all that crap. Knew him when he was chasing ambulances. "The Mayor doesn't want—repeat, does not want—any further embarrassment." Well, screw the Mayor. And the Chief Deputy Mayor. Screw them all.

84

12 Scrubbers / Mortuary $7,500 / $90,000

Calcification at the pubic symphysis. That pelvic section on the river today. No spring chicken. Course, it'd been submerged a while.

3 full-time Van Drivers

Need two new vans. Be lucky if I get one to replace these goddamned antiques. Goddamn Strang lecturing me about my duties, my responsibilities. Insufferable prig. Stuffed ass. Sucking around for my job. Asking about my health all the time. Watching me. Keeping score on me. As if I didn't know about that silly goddamned racket. Stupid ass— No CO levels in the blood. No cinders in the larynx or the trachea. Fools. Fools. Hope they get that body back for me.

1 new Prince-Hauser Autoclave. $16,500
1 new Barschach Gas Chromatograph $12,500

That smug bastard in court today. Suicide? Christ, O Mighty. Can you imagine the gall? Suicide—with a straight face, mind you. All solemn and pompous. Next time that young gorilla kills, it ought to be— Oh, Lolly, Lolly— Something about that hand with the fingernail polish. Odd. Was it left or right? Can't remember. Funny. Postcards. Pictures. Pretty views.

Konig laughs out loud. Looks up startled to hear the sound of his own laughter rattling through the quiet night around him.

Silly goddamn kid. Postcards and dirty pictures. Coked to the gills on hash. Gonna be a big, famous model. Be dead in a year if she's lucky— Oh, Christ, Lolly. Don't study medicine for me. Do it for yourself. Only for yourself. If there's something else you want to do, do it. But do it for yourself—

Suddenly he rises from his desk as if summoned, and not knowing exactly why, he starts from the office. Footsteps reverberating down the empty hall. The door of his office still open behind him, a plane of pale-yellow light spilling across the darkened corridor.

Something about that goddamned hand.

His feet, that slurred tread, the ache shooting down the

thigh into the calf, a long, cold, thin blade of pain. Down he goes. Down Stairway D, spiraling ever downward into the green world of the mortuary below, turned gray and penumbrous now with only the scant illumination of a few dim night lights. No matter though for Konig. He knows the way by heart. Could find the place in his sleep. Peaceful there now with everyone gone. He almost prefers it. Just like old Bahnhoff. His own world. All to himself. Everyone but him an intruder. No noise now. No confusion. No questions and answers. Bumbling attendants and meddlesome colleagues. The place quiet, immaculate. Scrubbed clean of the day's carnage. White tile and stainless steel. Gurney carts, minus their dismal, sacked cargoes, all lined up in neat, long rows. Shiny, efficient, expectant. Awaiting the morning flood of mayhem.

A single bare bulb illuminates the place, casting huge cavelike shadows across the walls. The only sound the soft, high whir of refrigerator motors cooling cadavers. Konig opens one of the body boxes and peers in. There in the dark chill, wisps of icy vapor rising from it, is the body of the young Spanish girl found in the Harlem stairwell that morning. Yesterday she was alive. Tomorrow she'll be on the tables bright and early in the morning.

Konig moves on. The next, a badly decomposed cadaver found up in the Bronx Zoo that afternoon. Not much left —a separate skull and mandible. Torso and extremities clad in a white short-sleeved shirt, a pair of dark-blue denim trousers, dark leather belt, heavy metal buckle. Numerous live and dead worms and extensive green and white mold cover the body surface, now largely mummified. Despite refrigeration, there is heavy cadaveric odor. This too will go on the tables tomorrow morning.

Next, the body of an adult Negro female. Well developed. Well nourished. Approximate age thirty. About 5′ 5″. Weight 122 pounds. Eyes open, staring into the icy darkness of her vault. The conjunctivae are pale; the corneas, clouded; the irides, brown with evidences of *tache noire*. Somewhere on her retinae is imprinted the image of her executioner—the last thing she ever saw. A long, gaping knife wound runs from just below the sternum to the pubic symphysis, virtually gutting her. A sizable amount of small intestine bulges outward from the wound, a strange flowerlike excrescence, like a red anemone blooming there between her breasts.

Next, the young man found that morning soaking in a bathtub with an ice pick in his chest. The pick is gone now, off to the police laboratory. And the youth lies there, handsome and curiously vital-looking even in death. A young black king dreaming. On the verge of waking to go forth.

The next locker is the one he's been looking for. Contained within it as well as in the next three lockers are the neatly packaged remains that were exhumed from the muddy shoreline near Coenties Slip that afternoon. There are the legs and arms, the pelvic and thoracic sections, the packages of feet and genitals, jawbones and ears, gobbets of flesh. All neatly packaged in plastic and meticulously labeled, ready for the exhausting and largely fruitless business of identification.

And there among all the other packages, in a separate receptacle of its own, what he has been looking for, what has been on his mind for several hours without his actually even knowing it, the hand with the luridly enameled fuchsia fingernails. It lies on its side in the plastic bag, waxen and rigored—frozen by refrigeration into an exquisitely sculptured gesture. Rather like the plaster hand of a supplicant broken from a piece of religious statuary.

Konig lifts the package from the freezer and gazes down once more at the garishly painted thing. He takes it out of its container, holding it in his hand, turning it in the light. There has been, he now sees, an attempt to mutilate the fingerprints on the hand by abrading them on a file or against a hard surface, thus making the job of identification more difficult. Not unusual. He's seen that one before. But there is something else about the hand. Something far more interesting suddenly occurs to him, what he's been mulling about all evening, ever since he first saw the hand dredged up, still dripping mud and slime from the river. And that is the fact that what he, and what everyone else down there at the time, had blithely assumed was the hand of a woman, he now feels might very well be the hand of a man.

Suddenly he turns, glancing upward as he does so at some vague, indeterminate point above him. A footstep rings softly on the metal steps of Stairway D. He listens a moment more, then turns back to the hand, dismissing as implausible the notion of anyone coming down there at that time of night.

Then suddenly another step. A pause. Then a series of two or three more steps, tentative and stealthy.

In the next moment he has returned the wrapped hand to its place in the locker and slipped noiselessly through the swinging doors of the autopsy room.

Several moments pass while he waits there in the great, gloomy, formalin-sodden shadows. From where he stands just behind one of the doors, he has an excellent vantage of the wall lockers through a small glass window cut into the center of the door. Listening to the uneasy, slightly wheezing sound of his own breathing, Konig waits. He waits for what seems an extraordinary length of time. Until it seems to him that he's imagined everything, that he will wait there forever, listening to the vague creaks and groans of metal stairs contracting and expanding, settling into their fastenings.

Several times he peers through the glass window, seeing nothing but the long, impassive wall of gray lockers. He's quite ready to forsake the whole thing, but something tells him to wait. For besides the revelation of the dismembered hand, there's yet another piece of business down here remaining to be settled.

In the next moment, within that small pane of window glass is framed the face of a man. It is an old, tired face, deeply lined, full of apprehension, a little appalled, yet a little excited at finding itself in such an unlikely place so late at night. It's not an unpleasant face either, but rather kindly and avuncular. The face of an elderly Italian man whom Konig himself hired more than twenty years ago.

Moving with the stealthy tread of a small mouse venturing out of its hole, the man creeps toward the wall lockers, pausing several times, glancing nervously around before he reaches his destination. Once there his eyes scan wildly up and down the numerical labels on each drawer. Then he goes about systematically correlating locker numbers with names and entering them on a clipboard.

Shortly, he pauses before a locker. With a simple motion he reaches up, pulls out a drawer, and the body of Barbara Rosales rolls out once more into the dim light.

Konig watches the man hovering there above the sheeted cadaver. The man appears to be studying the face of the dead girl, a mixture of pity and awe in his eyes. Then, with a slow, tremulous gesture, he draws the sheet downward, revealing the badly battered, unclad body.

It is at that point that Konig steps out of the darkened autopsy room. "All right, Angelo."

The head whirls, and the man freezes there, crouching, winded, his face gone the sickish color of raw mushrooms.

They stand there regarding each other for a moment. Then Konig speaks. "Go to my office now, Angelo, and wait there for me."

"Stop crying," Konig shouts, red in the face, at the slumped, disheveled figure seated opposite him. "For Chrissake—stop crying. That's not going to help anything."

Angelo Perriconi slumps deeper into his seat, as if he were trying to osmose himself into the wood and vanish. His face is hidden behind trembling hands and he sobs like a baby, pausing only from time to time to wipe his running nose across his sleeve. "Oh, my God, my God."

"Forget about God, Angelo. What the hell do you think you were doing down there?"

Muffled wails issue from behind the old man's hands.

"Answer me. What the hell do you think—"

"*Dio mio, Dio mio.* Now I gonna lose my job. Now I gonna lose everything—"

"Will you stop that goddamned bawling and—"

"What I gonna do?"

"Listen to me. I'll tell you what you're—"

"What I gonna do?"

"Listen to me." Konig's thunder is so loud that the frenzied little man halts abruptly and gapes up at him.

"I'll tell you what you're going to do, Angelo. First of all you're going to give me the name of every mortician in this city to whom you've ever sold the names of unclaimed bodies."

"Unclaimed bodies?" The man half rises out of his seat. "I never—I never—"

"Come on, Angelo. Cut the crap. I've known about your little sideline for years—"

"Oh, no, Chief. I swear—I never—"

"Angelo!" Konig bellows, his fist smashing into the center of the desk; papers fly, glasses rattle, pencils roll.

"Oh, no, Chief. No. I never—I swear—I never—" The little man hiding behind his hands again, shaking like a leaf, is reduced to inconsolable sobbing.

"Angelo"—Konig starts again, more reasonably, more restrained—"you're going to give me those names or else

I'm going to file a formal report of what I saw downstairs tonight."

"Oh, no. No—please, Chief. No, don't do dat."

"If I file such a report," Konig hammers on remorselessly, "it won't be a private matter. Your wife, your family, everyone, will hear about it."

The old man whines behind his hands. "I givva those names, they gonna breaka my legs."

"Angelo, I want those names."

"They breaka my head—they gonna kill me."

"No one's going to kill you."

"Dio mio, Dio mio." The man wails like a mourning spirit.

"Listen to me, Angelo."

"Ma che vergogna, ma che disgrazia."

"Listen to me." Konig's voice shatters once more through the office. Cringing from the sound, the man slumps deeper into a sour heap in his chair, and while he continues to whimper softly to himself, shaking his head incredulously back and forth, Konig stands above him like the wrath of God and speaks. "Now, this is what we're going to do. Number one, you're not going to be fired. You will resign for purposes of health. I'll certify that. You're only one year from retirement. I'm pretty certain I can get you your full pension."

The little Italian starts to protest but Konig waves him to silence.

"Number two, you're going to give me that list of names—"

Angelo Perriconi resumes his loud wailing.

"Shut up, Angelo. Let me finish. You're going to give me that list and no one is ever going to know that you gave me the list. Your resignation has come about for reasons of health—right?" Konig peers down hard at him. "Right, Angelo?"

The man snivels and shakes his head.

Konig continues. "So no one will connect your resignation with this goddamned body-snatching racket. You understand?"

Whimpering, sniveling, the man nods his head and Konig continues. "Actually, I blame myself as much as you for this whole thing. I've known for about three years that you've been selling names and taking kickbacks from shady people. I figured you needed the extra money. I know you've got kids, a big family. I know there's a boy in college. I suppose I looked the other way, hoping you'd quit yourself. I was wrong. I should've stopped you the moment I learned about it. Oh, will you stop that goddamned sniveling."

The little Italian jumps, like a child recoiling from a blow, making Konig feel more angry with himself, more desolate. Averting his gaze from the little man's shame, Konig's eyes search desperately around the room, lighting finally on the coffeepot. "Want some coffee?"

Angelo shakes his head and slumps deeper into his seat.

"As it is now," Konig goes on ruefully, "I'm pretty sure we've got a full-fledged scandal on our hands. The newspapers will pounce on this like vultures. They won't let go. Leave that to me. I'll handle that."

"My wife—my kids— Whadda hell they gonna say?"

"They're going to say nothing because they'll never know."

The sobbing comes abruptly to a halt and the slumped, piteous figure turns a startled face toward Konig.

"I certainly don't propose to tell them," Konig goes on. "Do you?"

Still puzzled, not quite certain of the drift of thought here, the man shakes his head negatively.

"Do you, Angelo?"

"No, sir."

"Good. Then it's our secret. Right?"

Again the baffled man shakes his head, but a ray of hope has begun to creep into his features.

"Our secret—right, Angelo?"

"Right." The man sobs huskily, humiliation and defeat carried in the slump of his shoulders.

"Now go home, Angelo. You're tired."

The man gazes up at Konig with red, teary eyes, mouth struggling to form words. But Konig, knowing all the arguments and all the old evasions, places his large index finger firmly against the little Italian's lips. "Go home, I said."

Once again in the solitude of his office, Konig, rattled and exhausted, settles wearily down to the municipal ledger sheets, the innumerable lines and columns, interminable figures, debits and credits, the shaving here in order to pad there, the small duplicities, the shabby fudging in order to wangle a piece of new equipment. The whole silly mosaic of evasions and petty frauds to be completed by the end of next week, delivered to City Hall, and there somehow to make sense to the jaded eye of the City Comptroller.

At approximately 11 P.M., eyes burning, the ache of his leg having spread up into the small of his back, Konig flings his pencils down and makes ready to go home. Stacking the ledgers neatly in the center of his desk, he reaches behind him and flicks off the Bunsen burner under the coffeepot. He is ready to go. But something still gnaws at him. Some bit of uncompleted business.

In the next moment he falls back in his chair, reaches for the phone and is dialing information, long-distance operator, Tulsa, Oklahoma.

Shortly, there is a high-pitched ringing on the wires, a number of gongs and bells, voices of unseen people caught momentarily in the lines stretching across the darkened continent. Fathers, uncles, sisters, brothers, enemies, and friends. Then a phone picked up thirteen hundred miles away and suddenly the receiver flooded with a roar of voices and twanging guitars.

"Will you turn that goddamn thing lower," a woman's voice shouts from the other end.

Konig shouts back. "Hello—"

"Wait a minute, f'Chrissake—will you?"

Konig hangs there amid a pause of mutterings and movements coming to him from Tulsa, Oklahoma. Then suddenly silence, as if a radio or TV has been rudely snapped off.

"Hello—"

"Hello—Mrs. Sully?"

"Hello—"

"Hello. Is this the Sully residence?"

"That's right." The woman's voice has grown strident, somewhat testy.

"Sorry to bother you at this hour."

"What hour?"

Konig glances at his watch, laughs a little awkwardly. "Oh, it's a few hours earlier there, isn't it?"

"Depends where you're calling from. Who is this?"

"This is Dr. Konig in New York City. I'm calling about your daughter."

"Who?"

"Your daughter. Do you have a daughter—about sixteen or seventeen—name of Heather—er, Molly. Actually, it is Molly, isn't it?"

There's a pause in which they listen to each other breathing.

"Hello—hello—Mrs. Sully?"

"Wait a minute, would ya, please? Tim—" Konig can hear the note of alarm in her voice as she cries out, "Tim."

Another pause as Konig waits, hearing something like agitated whispering on the other end. Then suddenly a gruff, beery masculine voice.

"Hullo."

"Hello—Mr. Sully?"

"Speaking."

"This is Dr. Konig in New York City. You have a daughter Molly?"

"Thas right."

"Well, this may all sound strange to you. Incredible, really—" Konig laughs a little idiotically. "Has she been missing?"

There's another pause while he can actually hear the other man pondering the question. "Left here eighteen months ago. Ain't heard from her since."

"I knew it." Konig's heart lightens and he rushes on eagerly. "I knew it. Listen—I saw her tonight."

"You saw her?"

"Had dinner with her. Quite by accident. I mean, I looked up and there she was—selling postcards in a restaurant in Greenwich Village. I knew she was a runaway. I knew it. Just knew it. Had that feeling. But listen, don't worry. She's all right. She's not in any immediate danger. But I'm afraid she's going to get into a great deal of trouble. I'll talk to you more about that when you get here. I know where she is—where you can find her. If you get the first plane out tomorrow—"

"Who'd ya say this was again?"

"Konig—Dr. Paul Konig. I'm the Medical Examiner for the City here. Listen, I have the address. If you want her picked up, I can—"

"I don't want the address."

"She's not using her own name, but—" Konig's voice trails off. "Beg pardon?"

"I said I don't want the address. I don't give a good goddamn where she is."

Konig frowns into the black mouthpiece of the phone. "Oh?" He hovers there a moment, quite at a loss. "But your daughter—"

"She ain't no daughter of mine. Walked outta here eighteen months ago with a lotta fancy notions. Far as I'm concerned—"

"Tim—Tim—" Once more the agitated, pleading whispers come hissing through the wires. "Tim—"

"She don't ever set foot in—"

"Tim—"

"Shut up, Alice. You hear that, mister? You ever see that little bitch again, you tell her for me—"

Konig hears the sound of muffled sobbing on the other end.

"—I'll bust her fuckin' head she ever comes suckin' around here again."

≈ 15 ≈

SATURDAY, APRIL 13. 12:45 A.M. RIVERDALE, NEW YORK. A big old Tudor set high on a hill above the Hudson River. Inside, in the huge living room with its lofty, beamed ceilings and its musty, heavily curtained silences, Paul Konig stands before tall French windows. From where he stands, he can look out over a stone patio and a moon-flooded garden that creeps up to its edge, and beyond that to a steep, grassy declivity tumbling downward to the river. Beyond the great black void of the river, he can see the cliffs of the Palisades rising squat and gibbous on the other side, and atop them, a dim, sluggish pulse of lights denoting early-morning traffic on the Palisades Parkway.

"Paul—we need more champagne."

"Coming, Ida. It's coming. For God's sake, give me a minute. I only have two hands."

Beyond the stone patio, shadows drift and flicker back and forth in the moon-flooded garden.

"Isn't she lovely?"

"Image of her mother."

"Fortunately for her."

Laughter rippling up through the branches of beech and poplar swaying above the garden. The air heavy with the scent of lilac and honeysuckle, hyacinths around a goldfish pond. Laughter echoing now through the great tomblike silence of a house long vacant.

"Aren't you proud of her today?"

"Of course I am. Of course I'm proud of her."

"What's she going to do now she's finished school?"

"God only knows. Watch out for that cork—bang— there it goes. Get a glass. Quick."

More ghostly laughter echoing through the immense silences of the house.

"Got some funny notion she wants to go abroad for a few years and paint."

"Doesn't sound funny to me."

"You finance her then. I won't. I've footed bills for twenty years. I'm tired. Now's her turn."

"But I imagine you'd feel a little different about financing her through, oh, let's say for instance—medical school."

"Don't be so goddamned smug, Chester. We all have ideas about what our kids should do."

"Just ideas, Paul. Seldom ever works out the clever way we plan it for them."

"Well, I don't want her to go to medical school to please me. She can do what she goddamned pleases. I've washed my hands of it."

Standing now before a marble mantel, Konig stares at the craggy, pitted visage wavering in the smoke-glazed mirror opposite him. The eyes are red and bleary, as if they'd peered too long into a blast furnace.

"Depressing, isn't it, Paul? Being around so many young people?"

"'Specially when you've just had a glimpse at your own EKG's. Ida—who's that fellow with Lolly?"

"I don't know. Some young man she met at achool. I think he's an instructor or something on the faculty."

"Oh?" Konig frowns deeply. "Well, I don't like him."

Stillness hovers about the house with palpable weight,

crouching in shadows and corners, inhabiting rooms and hallways long untenanted. Upstairs now, Konig drifts like a stranger down corridors he has known for a quarter of a century. Past doorways he has walked in and out of, and gloomy spaces still haunted by the aura of occupants long since gone.

In his own bedroom, where he has not slept since the death of his wife, the fine old French furniture—the tall canopy bed, the Louis XVI escritoire, the graceful silken Recamier—is shrouded now in sheets. On a night table on the side of the bed where Ida Konig slept is a yellow, faded photograph—a bridal picture, formal and stiff, depicting a tall, stern-visaged young man awkwardly attired in top hat and tails; beside him, a dark, diminutive woman in long *peau de soie* lace, more handsome than pretty, with a strikingly arresting gaze.

Farther on, a music conservatory. A grand piano sits before a huge bay window with leaded panes and insets of stained glass depicting shepherds and lambs, swains and milkmaids, saltimbanques and saints, funereal crows in laurel branches, all limned in scarlets and cobalts, regal, ecclesiastical purples.

On the music stand on the grand piano, a book stands open to a Chopin nocturne; an air of expectancy about it all, as if the whole setting were simply awaiting animation by the appearance of players soon to come.

Farther on, the lace and tapestried bedroom where his mother died eight years before in ghastly pain. The closets still hung with her clothes, redolent of old persons —camphor and mothballs, the vapory medicants of the sickroom.

Other rooms—guest rooms, sitting rooms. Gracious old baths, generous in size and opulently appointed—sunken tubs, fine old Italian brass fixtures. Certainly not the baths of a civil-servant physician with no visible private means of his own, but very definitely the baths of a young professional man who happened to marry quite well. Even now, the bitter rue of the have-not in a world of haves still rankles in him.

Then, at the far end of a corridor, a sewing room, large and cozy beneath steep-pitched gables, with a stone hearth and a loom. Ida's hideaway. Balls of colored yarn still lie there in wicker baskets, a vase stocked like a quiver full of knitting needles, a beautiful old antique

Singer; and on the loom itself, just as she left it, half completed, a white Bargello needlepoint rug studded with immense blood-red hydrangeas.

Then, finally, another room, smaller than all the others; a silken nook of a room—a small canopied bed, an elegant little vanity flounced with ruffles. Paintings of ballerinas line the flower-papered walls. An exquisitely feminine room, that of a child who had entered womanhood in that room. Once a nursery with a crib where an infant slept, an infant who'd arrived completely unexpected by her parents, long after they'd given up all hope of ever having a child of their own. Ida Konig had for many years appeared to be one of those stubborn and curiously begrudging cases of infertility. Responding to neither drug nor treatment, a mystery to a half-dozen specialists, all of whom were unable to determine the root of her problem. Then one morning, a few days past her fortieth birthday, she woke up and found strange stirrings inside herself. Nausea, flushes, menses long overdue. Even the gynecologist was unwilling to attribute the symptoms to pregnancy, preferring instead to call it some vague hormonal disorder. Then he saw the results of the rabbit test and the urine analysis, and a little later, during the course of an internal examination, felt a tiny fetus clinging to the wall of the uterus. And that night, Paul and Ida Konig lay in each other's arms and laughed themselves to sleep.

Lolly Konig's room was a clutter of pieces and oddments from every stage of her life from infancy to young womanhood. An old moth-eaten hobbyhorse, shelves lined and crowded with every imaginable kind of doll—Dutch dolls, china dolls, Raggedy Anns, cinnamon teddy bears with button eyes, Pinocchios and harlequins, a grenadier with pink cheeks and a shako, ballerinas and toreadors, little Hummel figurines out of Grimm and Andersen. And beneath the shelves of dolls, the shelves of books—*Madeline, Babar, Winnie the Pooh, Alice in Wonderland, Peter Rabbit, The Wind in the Willows, The Secret Garden, Guki the Moon Boy*. Then the somewhat older books—*Heidi, Lorna Doone, Jane Eyre, Vanity Fair, Tess of the D'Urbervilles* and on through Dickens and Twain. Then books about the planets, the life of fish and insects. Later, books on plant histology and art history. Then huge, opulent books crammed with paintings, cave paintings from Lascaux, medieval and Byzantine icon painting, Italian

Quattrocento and Flemish painting, great French and Spanish masters, Impressionists and Russian moderns, and endless books of American painters—Eakins, Ryder, Sargent, Homer, Burchfield, Hopper, and Russell.

In the drawers and the closet, her clothing, piled and hung neatly, awaits her return—Shetland sweaters, tartan skirts, suits of wool and camel, jackets of suede, old patched and faded denim jeans from college days, shoe racks crammed with pumps and sandals, scuffed and beloved old oxfords, girlish saddle shoes and smart, young-ladyish patent leather. And, further on, in the darkest corner of the closet, a silk organza gown, redolent of orange blossoms from a graduation garden party two years prior.

"Lolly, who is this man? Why did you bring him here?"

Konig's finger plays gently over the flaxen head of the Hummel goose girl. From her basket of wicker she strews feed to three plump geese who promenade about her feet.

"Daddy, I'm sorry you don't like Tom's politics, but I can't very well ask him to leave."

Konig flicks out the light, then picks up the small goose-girl figurine and carries it over to the narrow bed. Sitting on the edge of the bed he kicks off his shoes, and still otherwise dressed in the sour, rumpled, death-drenched clothing of his day, he slumps backward into the thick, welcoming darkness, the small goose-girl figurine balanced comfortingly on his chest.

Only now that he is off his feet is he aware that the pain in his leg and back is excruciating. A few grams of Demerol will help, he thinks, but as of late he has been relying too heavily on Demerol, craving it always at night, just before sleep.

Instead of Demerol, he flings an arm across his face and lets the darkness wash over him. It is comforting to hold the little goose girl there on his chest in the dark—in his daughter's bed, on the down mattress and bedding that still bears the imprint of her body, the memory of her weight. He feels somehow closer to her there in that familiar darkness where he has slept night after night for almost five months. He imagines her in some dingy, squalid place, a small, mean cell, a place of self-banishment. And he wonders if at that same moment she is thinking of him.

Suddenly the phone rings. Sitting bolt upright in bed, he hears it ring across the hall in his own bedroom. He sits there, eyes open and staring, nerves trembling with expectation, waiting for it to ring again. But it rings only once and then is silent. A mistake, he surmises, and yet his heart is thumping wildly as he hears the echo of that ring fading through the great, gloomy solitude of the house—a cry of anguish from somewhere far out in the clammy, terror-haunted night, like the bleating of a lost and stricken lamb.

The weekend has commenced now. Spreading out before him, the dreaded hours of idleness and inactivity; hours somehow to be gotten through in order to reach the blessed self-forgetfulness of back-to-work on Monday morning.

≈≈ 16 ≈≈

"Forty-eight separate pieces in all."

"Good—now maybe you can tell me how many separate bodies those forty-eight pieces represent?"

MONDAY, APRIL 15. 9:00 A.M. AUTOPSY ROOM, CHIEF MEDICAL EXAMINER'S OFFICE.

Young Tom McCloskey gazes forlornly down at five large trays of assorted upper limbs, trunk sections, extremities, fragments of bone and muscle, anatomical debris. "Sorry, sir—I'm afraid I don't have the slightest idea how many bodies we've got here."

Konig's eyes swivel around at the half dozen or so of the others gathered about the grisly trays—Pearsall, Bonertz, Delaney, the little Parsi, Hakim, and shifty-eyed Strang.

"Well, then," Konig goes on a little spitefully, "if you can't tell me how many bodies you've got here, maybe you can give me some idea of the age, sex, and approximate stature of whatever the hell it is you've got here."

Konig's eyes, still fastened on McCloskey, glint maliciously. For a moment it appears he's on the verge of laughter. Then suddenly his shoulders slump a bit, as if after great effort, and he sighs. "Well—this is one hell of a goddamned mess, isn't it? We don't even know if we have one body complete. And no heads."

"Flynn rang up early this morning," says Strang. "Said they'd been digging all weekend. Found some more soft parts and sent them over to us yesterday. Thinks he might have more of this stuff for us today."

"Might?" Konig laughs scornfully. "What the hell do they expect us to do with this? Don't they know it's hard to make identifications without heads, without teeth, without fingers to take fingerprints from? What the hell are we supposed to do?" He gazes ruefully down at one of the hands, badly mutilated, the terminal segments of the fingers hacked off to thwart identification, and no doubt lost forever in the tidal muck of the river. "Oh, well," he sighs again, "can you break it down a little further for us, McCloskey?"

"Yes, sir." McCloskey adjusts the glasses on his nose and proceeds to read aloud from a clipboard. "The total number of separate parts is forty-eight, and that includes what came in yesterday. Twenty pieces of bone, twenty-seven pieces of assorted soft tissue varying in size from fourteen inches by eight inches downward. Carefully examined from the point of view of identification, we found no scars or other special marks." The young pathologist glances up from his clipboard. "Shall I take it piece by piece, Chief?"

"Why not?" Konig peers gloomily about at his staff. "We've got the whole morning and no place special to go."

And so the morning begins at the Medical Examiner's Office. Six men huddle about five grisly trays as the young assistant, already sweating beneath high, bright fluorescent lights, begins somewhat falteringly to read.

"Right forearm and hand. Disarticulated at elbow joint. Skin and tissue absent from upper third of forearm. First segment of thumb completely devoid of soft tissue. Terminal segments of all fingers missing.

"Left forearm and hand. Disarticulated at elbow. Terminal segments of all fingers and thumb missing.

"Right thigh. Disarticulated at hip and knee joints. Most of tissue removed from femur except for small triangular flap of skin, five and three-quarter inches by four inches, holding patella in position.

"Left thigh. Disarticulated at hip and knee joints. Small tuft of blackish pubic hair on inner side of thigh.

"Right leg and foot. Disarticulated at knee joint. Toes either mutilated or missing.

"Left leg and foot. Disarticulated at knee joint. Toes also mutilated or missing."

The door of the mortuary swings open and the head of an assistant pokes through. "Dr. Konig?"

"Over here."

"There's a call for you upstairs."

"Who is it?"

"The *Times*. Something about a story they want to do."

Konig glances at Strang, whose eyes drop quickly to one of the trays. "Tell them I'm busy now."

"They say it's important."

"So is this, goddamn it." Konig flings a hand at the trays. "Tell them to call back later. Go ahead, McCloskey."

The door swings closed and McCloskey resumes his grisly inventory.

"Trunk. We've only one trunk. It's malodorous and maggot infested. The soft tissue at the sides of dismemberment shows some putrefactive changes. It's been divided in two parts through the upper abdomen. Spine's been severed in the upper lumbar region. The upper portion contains the whole of the thorax, complete with heart and lungs. Left half's been entirely stripped of covering muscle. Diaphragm severed. We also found five stab wounds in the thoracic wall. Two wounds of the left lung and a wound perforating the left atrium of the heart and transfixing the aorta. Probably inflicted by a small-bladed knife."

"Any hemorrhage?" Konig asks.

"Nothing on the inner surface of the pericardium," Pearsall replies. "No blood or blood clot within the pericardial sac."

"Postmortem wounds," Bonertz remarks.

"Probably." Konig nods. "Inflicted while trying to remove the viscera from the thorax. Made a botch of that diaphragm, too. Get us some tissue sections on the organs for histology, will you, Hakim?" Konig grumbles. "Go ahead, McCloskey."

"Lower trunk portion," the young man continues, scarcely missing a beat, "includes the entire pelvis and its organs with the exception of the genitals, which have been cut out. But we know it's a male pelvis from the bone configuration and the amount of adherent prostatic tissue we found."

"Can't be too sure of that," Strang says archly. "Not at all uncommon to find residual prostatic tissue in female cadavers."

"Yes, sir," McCloskey stammers, "but—"

"Oh, for God's sake," Konig snarls. "You've got the goddamned cock and balls right over there, Carl. I can see they fit. Can't you?"

Strang's eyes flutter from the sting of rebuke. For a moment both men glare at each other. Then Konig turns back to the young assistant. "It's a male pelvis all right. Go on, McCloskey."

The young pathologist takes up quickly where he'd left off.

"Thighs on lower trunk portion disarticulated at hip joints.

"Right upper arm. Humerus disarticulated at shoulder and elbow joints.

"Left upper arm. Humerus disarticulated at shoulder and elbow joints.

"Right forearm and hand. Disarticulated at elbow joint. Hand mutilated by removal of terminal segment of thumb and of each of four fingers. Fine reddish hairs on the back of forearm and hand.

"Left forearm. Disarticulated at elbow joint. No hand present.

"Left hand. Disarticulated at wrist. No mutilation other than extensive abrading of tissue at fingertips, probably done with a file or rasp, and obviously an attempt to obliterate fingerprint pattern. Nails heavily lacquered in purple."

"Ah, the plot thickens," Pearsall sings out, a waggish glint in his eyes. "A tortured love triangle."

"You think so?" Konig grumbles, tilting his glasses back on his head, once again scrutinizing that garish, obscene hand. "Maybe." He shrugs. "Go on, McCloskey."

And so it continues, this grisly inventory through the bright April morning. Sun shining outside. Lilacs blooming. People up above on the pavements scurrying about their business. Lovers, arm in arm, strolling the river promenade.

"Right thigh. Disarticulated at hip and knee joint.

"Left thigh. Disarticulated at hip and knee joint and at joint below the talus. No foot present.

"Left leg. Disarticulated at knee joint and below, through the talus. No foot present.

"Right upper arm. Humerus disarticulated at shoulder and elbow joints.

"Left upper arm. Humerus disarticulated at shoulder and elbow joints.

"Two patellae. One badly damaged, apparently by a hacksaw. Probably slipped." McCloskey glances up. "That covers the hard stuff."

"Any questions, gentlemen?" Konig gazes around at the assembled group.

"All very neat," Delaney remarks, gazing down at the round gleaming head of a femur. "Fellow knew his stuff. Cut neatly."

"Very little damage to these joints at the disarticulation points," Bonertz observes.

"Let's be grateful for that," snaps Konig. "All the easier to reconstruct the stuff. And this fellow hasn't given us too many breaks. Might as well take the soft parts now, McCloskey."

The remainder of the morning is spent listing and tagging soft tissue, cutaneous and subcutaneous—ears, cheeks, buttocks, genitals, gobbets of flesh, torn, severed, hacked out—much of it barely, if even, recognizable.

By noon the tedious business of the inventory is over. The men, still gathered around the trays, gaze ruefully down upon them. With sinking heart, Konig has already gauged the enormity of the task ahead. The task of identification. In the next moment he turns, addressing the small group.

"There are four questions that have to be answered before the police can even begin to move on this. One, how many bodies are represented in all these various parts. Two, the sex of each body. Three, probable age of each. Four, probable stature. I hate to do this and I'd do anything to avoid it, but I see no way out. The obvious first step is reassembly." He glances around at them expectantly, then continues. "This is no simple matter of a single body roughly dismembered by knife or saw. Were it only that, it would be no great feat to put the parts together again. We've got one hell of an anatomical problem here. Number one, there is obviously more than one body. So there's already the complication of which part goes to which body. Number two, there's been gross mutilation of the individual parts by the deliberate removal of skin and soft tissue. Not only have the skeletal parts been separated from each other by disarticulation with a saw and possibly a knife through the joints, but they've also been denuded of much of their covering tissue in a deliberate effort to foil identification.

"Moreover, since the parts of at least two bodies, possibly more, are intermixed, it will be essential that each step in the reassembly of the pieces be proved squarely on anatomical grounds. If by chance there are more than two bodies here—even only a third—the complexity of the task will mount in geometric progression, and the odds that we'll be able to reassemble, let alone even recover, all the pieces are astronomical. Christ," Konig sighs, "what a pain in the ass."

"Offhand," Strang remarks, "I'd say we've got three to four bodies here."

"Would you?" Konig lights his dead cigar. "Well, I couldn't begin to say. I'm not even sure yet which of these limbs can be matched into sets."

"You don't know what else Flynn is going to come up with, either," observes Bonertz.

"Without the heads and the dentition"—Hakim shakes his head woefully—"it's going to be very difficult."

"It'll be difficult with or without the heads," Konig snaps. "Can't worry about that now. We've got to work with what we've got here."

"Well"—McCloskey gazes into the trays—"we know we've got at least a man and a woman."

"Don't let those painted nails fool you." Konig smiles shrewdly. "Anyway, it's the only complete set of fingers we have."

"Doubt we'll be able to lift any prints off them," says Delaney. "Just look at the mutilation of that tissue."

"Leave that to me." Konig starts to pack up his notes. "I'd like a crack at that hand this afternoon. Meanwhile, we'll need some blood types and let's get some tissue samples of the organs up to toxicology. Max"—he turns suddenly to Bonertz—"see if you can't work up a moulage of those two feet. It'll be hard without the toes, but there was a sneaker down at that shack—left sneaker. It's a long shot, but let's see if we can't get a match anyway.

McCloskey, you might as well start cleaning up these pieces before we try any reconstruction. Wash everything down with a weak alkali solution, but save me a couple of the maggots and the larvae. Offhand, I'd say they're *Calliphora*. But let's get a reading from Ferguson anyway. Then dump everything in ten percent formalin and lock it all up in the tanks. I'll be back this afternoon to have a crack at that hand. See if we can't start matching some of this stuff."

The door of the autopsy room swings open again and the same assistant pops his head in. "Flynn's on the phone, Chief."

"Tell him I'll be right up."

Konig gathers his papers and then starts out. "Oh, McCloskey"—he turns at the door—"first-class job."

≈ 17 ≈

"READ ALL ABOUT YA IN THE *Daily News*."

"Swell."

"Right up there. Page four. Picture. Headline. The works. How come they never take my picture?"

"You're unsightly, that's why. What can I do for you, Flynn?"

" 'Chief Medical Examiner scours murder site,' it said," Flynn runs on unfazed. "I was there too, scourin', but not a mention of me. And I betcha don't even know you were on TV last night. Eleven o'clock news, Channel Two. How does it feel to be famous? A celebrity?"

"Marvelous." Konig lights his cigar and flicks through the morning mail on his desk. "What's on your mind, Flynn? I'm very busy."

"That Doblicki business."

"What about it?"

"The Jersey authorities refuse to release the body for reautopsy."

"Don't be ridiculous. They've got to— Tell them—"

"Hold it. Hold it." Flynn's long, disconsolate sigh issues through the receiver. "Will you please lemme finish?"

"Well, then, get to the point, for Chrissake."

"I am—I am—or at least I'm tryin' to. What I was gonna say before you jumped all over me was that while they refuse to release the body to us, they're perfectly willin' to do it themselves."

"Fine. Beautiful. Why didn't you say that in the first place? I don't care if they do it. Just as long as someone does it."

"All you have to do is tell them what the hell you're lookin' for."

"My pleasure." Konig's eyes glance over the details of several of the morning's autopsies. "Who'd you talk to over there? Weinstein?"

"That's the man."

"Fine. He's very good. Studied under me."

"I sort of got that feelin'—from the way he shouted at me all the time."

"Tell him we found no soot or cinders in the trachea."

"The trachy—what?"

"Never mind. Tell him in the lungs. That'll do. And tell him—"

"Hold it. Hold it. You talk too fast."

"You write too slow. Tell him we also found no appreciable CO levels in the blood. Very suspicious finding in a person who supposedly died in a fire. Tell Henry to—"

"Henry?"

"Weinstein. Dr. Weinstein. Tell him to look for a bullet wound around the back of the head or for traces of a slug in the brain. Reason we didn't look for a slug is 'cause we're slipshod around here. The troopers' report described a fatal accident due to drunken driving, and like the goddamned fools we are, we just accepted that. The guy did have a lot of booze in him, but he was dead before he ever set foot in the car. Most of the skull and brain was incinerated in the fire, and the slug itself probably embedded in the debris. But there's a good chance if Weinstein sifts through what's left he'll find some residual lead or a bullet hole."

"—or a bullet hole." Flynn repeats the final words and Konig can hear the sound of his pencil scratching across a pad as he writes. "That all, Chief?"

"That's it. Anything else?"

"Yeah. We gotcha a few more assorted parts from down on the river."

"Heads?"

"Nope. Got a couple of feet though. A few toes. Upper half of a trunk, and some chunks of stuff I can't begin to figure out."

"Where'd you find it? Same place?"

"No—about five hundred yards away. Tide washed it down. What's it all look like so far?"

"A goddamned mess," Konig goes on, his eyes continuing to scan autopsy reports. "Two, maybe three bodies. One definitely male. The others, I don't know. Could be anything. Can't say till I get the stuff assembled. You gotta get me some heads. I need heads."

"And I need prints. Listen—we're liftin' a slew of prints out of that shack. If you could get me some corroborating prints—"

"With what? You've got to have fingertips to do that. I've got no fingertips. All of them were hacked off—"

"You've got the set with the pretty nails though, don'tcha?"

"All the cuticle's been torn off with a rasp," Konig snorts. "The bastard who did this job must be some cool number."

"A pussycat."

"I'm going to try to lift a set off that hand this afternoon. It's tricky stuff. Call me later on. After six. What about that shack?"

"What about it?"

"Said you were checking the Bureau of Records—"

"Oh, yeah—the deed of ownership. Just like we figured. The City owns it. Originally belonged to a widow lady name of Chatsworth. Died intestate about fifty years ago and the place reverted by escheat to the City—who naturally don't do a goddamned thing for it. Past few years it's become a haven for junkies and winos."

"What about that Salvation Army lead?"

"I'm way ahead of you," Flynn snaps. "Been on to the Army this mornin'. They got no record of any of their people assigned to that area."

"Odd."

"Yeah. Still a couple of storekeepers down there insist

they seen some Salvation Army guy goin' in and outta the place from time to time."

"Oh, come on, Flynn. What the hell does that mean? Anyone can walk in off the street to any Army-Navy store and pick up a Salvation Army uniform—"

"That's right, Chief," Flynn smirks into the phone. "Now suppose you let me do my job and you do yours. See if you can't get me some prints off that hand."

"Fine," Konig snorts. "You see if you can't get me some heads."

No sooner does Konig slam down the phone than it rings again. This time it is Carver speaking from just outside the door. "Deputy Mayor been tryin' to reach you all morning."

"Jesus Christ." Konig rumples a wad of paper, crushes it in his fist. "Put him on."

"You know anything about this other man—this Carslin?" snaps the Deputy Mayor.

"Yes. He's very good. Trained under me."

"Haven't they all?" the Deputy Mayor snarls sarcastically. "Harris tells me he's got something of a grudge against you."

"Oh, that old business. Nothing. Just an ego thing."

"Just an ego thing?" A scornful laugh rings through the receiver. "That's precisely why these Robinson people have retained him. Their lawyer is sure this Dr. Carslin will come in with a verdict that will show the boy did not—repeat, *did not*—commit suicide—"

"But was beaten to death by six sadistic prison guards —right?"

"Not so improbable, my friend. It wouldn't be the first time—given all the glories of the City penal system. Goddamn it, it does look funny. As a matter of fact, it stinks out loud. The City Medical Examiner's Office finding no evidence of a beating. Then a hick funeral director up in the boondocks receives the body and finds all kinds of evidence of injuries not mentioned in the Medical Examiner's report."

The Chief Deputy Mayor's voice drones on while Konig's eyes linger on the cartoon grizzly bear of Lolly's birthday card.

"Paul—are you there?"

"Of course I'm here."

"Well, answer the goddamned question."

"What's the question?"

"What sort of injuries would this funeral director be talking about?"

"Maury, we've been through this a dozen times."

"Fine. Let's do it another dozen times. What sort of injuries?"

Konig's eyes roll heavenward, as if seeking mercy. A long, weary sigh expires from somewhere deep within him. "Inverted V-shaped abrasions about the neck—"

"In English, Paul. Plain, simple English for the stupid, unlettered layman."

"Bruises caused by a noose of mattress ticking."

"Okay. Go on."

"Crusted lacerations on the front of the left wrist. Half-inch-long abrasion over the left eyebrow. Fracture of skull. Ecchymosis—"

"Ecce what?"

"Hemorrhage—over the left scalp, overlying the fracture."

"Is that it?"

"That's it."

There's a pause while both men gain time listening to each other's breathing.

"Now tell me this, Paul," the Deputy Mayor continues cagily. "Why isn't any of that down in the Medical Examiner's report?"

"It is down in the medical report. You'd know that if only you'd read it through. But of course you didn't. You had some lackey read it for you and then give you a summary. Am I right?" The silence at the other end provides him his answer. "I didn't expect that you would read it. That isn't the question these people want answered, however."

"Well, what the hell is the question?" the Deputy Mayor asks, a little cowed by Konig's sudden onslaught.

"They want to know if Robinson's death is attributable to any of those injuries."

"Rather than the hanging?"

"Right. What Carslin will try to show is that Robinson died as a result of head injuries inflicted during a beating. That he was then strung up by the panicky guards to make it look like suicide."

"Well, in that case," says the Deputy Mayor, the cagey note coming back into his voice, "what determination did this mystery examiner of yours make with regard to the time the head injuries were inflicted?"

Konig senses the Deputy Mayor inching closer to target. "The determination was that the head injuries occurred after the victim's death. When the body hit the floor of the cell subsequent to being cut down."

"How is that determined?"

"By simply doing a tissue study of the area around the head wounds. If the injuries are inflicted before death, a tissue study will show leukocytic infiltration—thousands of white blood cells flowing to the injured area. That's a vital reaction. It can occur only in a living creature. If Robinson sustained those injuries before he died, Carslin will see those leukocytes under the microscope. On the other hand, if Robinson was dead, as we claim he was, when the injuries were sustained, there'll be no leukocytes. Get it?"

"Perfectly." There is a pause and Konig can hear the Deputy Mayor beginning to zero in now for the kill. "Now tell me this, Paul. Did your mystery man do such a tissue study before submitting his report?"

Konig has been expecting that question. Still, now that it's come, it takes his breath away. He knows he will have to make a plausible response. Any fancy, technical sophistries would be immediately detected and scorned. "No tissue study was done because the pathologist in charge was completely satisfied that the head injuries were superficial and sustained after death." Even as he's saying it, he can hear it falling flat, his own voice sounding hollow with pathetic lack of conviction.

"And you buy that?"

"Yes, I do. I have complete faith in the men of this department. I've trained them all. I'll stand behind their determinations."

"Well—good for you. That's admirable, but I don't buy it." The Deputy Mayor's voice sounds suddenly sympathetic. "And I don't believe you do either. To me the whole thing stinks. It stinks to high heaven. And I tell you something else, my friend, the stink I detect is a very particular stink. It's the stink of Emil Blaylock. I smell Warden Blaylock all over the lot. I feel the oily grip of that fine Byzantine hand behind all this. Covering up the dirty stuff. Sweeping it all under the rug. Prestidigitation —now you see it, now you don't. By the time Blaylock gets finished doing his PR job on the Tombs, the place'll sound like a milk farm in the Catskills. And I'll tell you something else, my esteemed friend, dig a little deeper into that sacrosanct department of yours and you'll find a fink. Blaylock got to your fink, Paul."

"He did not." Konig's voice rises ominously. It is enough to stop the Deputy Mayor dead in his tracks. There is a long pause on the other side, and then, at last, a sigh.

"Suit yourself, Paul. But a word to the wise. If I were sixty-three, with a distinguished record, two years to retirement, and a freightload of enemies, I'd keep a low profile. If the Medical Examiner's report is proved wrong, someone's head down there is going to roll. That's straight from the horse's mouth—repeat, *the horse's mouth*. And when *The New York Times* man shows up here and the Savage Skulls start to build a fire around Gracie Mansion, I'll refer them all to you. See you at the autopsy—Wednesday morning—ten o'clock sharp."

≋ 18 ≋

"The paintings just got sadder and sadder. Got harder and harder to peddle the stuff."

"I see." Francis Haggard nods wearily. "And when did you say was the last time you saw her?"

1:15 P.M. THE FENIMORE GALLERY,
MADISON AVENUE AND 67TH STREET.

"I didn't say," Mr. Anthony Redding replies curtly. "But it must have been about three months ago. She brought in a batch of new things. But we spoke on the phone quite regularly—only last week, as a matter of fact."

"Oh?" Haggard's eyes roam restlessly about the room. It is a room in which he is distinctly uneasy, a room that is aggressively and expensively comtemporary. It seems to cry out, "I am chic. I am modern. I am with it." Actually a suite of rooms, it is a tasteful exercise in eclecticism,

Louis XVI pieces with a lot of stainless steel and leather, Mies chairs and tole, fine old Sirhouks and Khazaks strewn all about. The cork-lined walls are hung with a variety of paintings.

"She called to say she would be sending some new things. Well, I wasn't entirely—"

Mr. Anthony Redding chatters on, a nervous, petulant man who talks incessantly. He too, like his gallery, is very chic. Tall, elegant, patrician, the sort of man who sets Haggard's teeth on edge. A somewhat exotic-looking individual, the great glabrous dome, the compensatory bushy beard flowing out over his throat, the caterpillar eyebrows, the nose, blade-thin and saturnine—all conveying an impression of urbanity and taste. And then the carefully studied attire, the blue denim shirt (not the proletarian blue denim of Navy issue, but rather the blue denim of expensive East Side boutiques) with a red silk foulard tied rakishly around the throat; the exquisitely tailored trousers, tight at the top, flared widely at the bottom, and whispering as he walks. And most grating of all to the detective, born and raised in Coney Island, the obviously affected British accent, carefully cultivated for the titillation of the wealthy uptown matrons who are his stock in trade.

"—thrilled at the prospect of another shipment. As I say, the stuff hadn't been going well. Listen, is she in some kind of trouble?"

"No—no trouble. These hers over here?"

"Right. Those three gouaches—they're all I have left. I did much better with the oils. How'd you know they were hers?"

"Aside from the fact that they're signed Emily Winslow"—Haggard saunters toward a small cluster of paintings—"I recognize the style."

"Oh?" Mr. Redding trails after the detective, looking startled and a bit uneasy.

Redding is right, Haggard muses, standing, arms crossed, before the three pale gouaches. The pictures *are* sadder. Certainly sadder than what he saw in the loft on Varick Street: Even in the state those were in, they conveyed a certain vitality, a kind of serene celebration of the grandeur of simple things—sunlight, ocean, great empty beaches running into sky. They throbbed with a kind of life, flora and fauna abounded. These are rather drab, gray, dispirited things. Terminal subjects. Landlocked. No water about anywhere. One, a shack, squatting like a toad-stool, lists sideways in a vacant field.

Looking at that field, one has the feeling that once it was verdant, full of mint, phlox, pennyroyal, vervain, fringed gentian, scorpion grass. Now, it is dry, sere, a scorched place where only pauper's weed will grow. And the shack has a dismal, unsavory air about it. A door hangs open on a hinge and the punched-out windows have the look of eyeless sockets in a skull. An abandoned, derelict place, you imagine it was once the site of some ghastly act. Then another painting depicting merely shards of broken glass. And then—most disquieting of all—a pair of badly soiled underpants lying in a heap in the dirty corner of some tenement privy.

"When you spoke with her," Haggard continues, his eyes roaming the canvases, "how did she sound?"

"Okay, I s'pose—maybe—"

"Maybe what?" The detective turns and stares at Mr. Redding.

"I don't know. Listen, what's all this about anyway?"

"Nothing—absolutely nothing."

"Oh, come on now." Redding's face grows red and cross. "You come in here flashing badges, asking a lot of questions—"

"She's missing," Haggard growls. "If I knew more, I'd tell you."

"How'd you find me?"

"We found her studio a couple of days ago. We knew she was painting. We knew she was selling her stuff through an uptown gallery on the East Side. After that it was just a matter of the Yellow Pages and about eighty patrolmen making a lot of inquiries. What's your last address for Miss Konig?"

"Miss who?"

"Miss Winslow."

"That isn't what you said before."

"So what?" Something rude and pugnacious leaps from the detective's eyes. "You got that address?"

Mr. Redding appears resentful but cowed. He stalks sullenly across the gallery floor to a small Louis XVI es-critoire with gold fastenings. From a bottom drawer he extracts a small metal file box. He flicks methodically through it, halts at a place, and snaps out a card. "324 Varick Street."

Haggard sighs. "Thanks."

"Anything wrong?"

"Nope—only I already have that address." He starts out.

"There's another one here.'"

Haggard turns. "Oh?"

"She asked me to send her money to some place up in The Bronx."

"The Bronx?"

"About two months ago she called and said she wanted all future checks sent to Fox Street, The Bronx. 1622 Fox Street, care of Eggleston."

"Eggleston." Haggard scribbles quickly into his pad. "Any first name?"

Mr. Anthony Redding glances back at his card. "W."

"W?"

"That's it. Just W. W. Eggleston."

≈≈ 19 ≈≈

"I see a large body of water."

"Yes."

"Not an ocean. Somewhat smaller. A large river—or a bay, perhaps."

1:30 P.M. AN APARTMENT ON WEST 55TH STREET.

Konig sits in a large, shadowy room full of the odors of overstuffed furniture and incontinent cats. He sits at a bare, round, wooden table opposite a woman of Buddhistic proportions with a wen on her nose and a furze of dark hair above her lip.

"I see a small house."

"Yes."

"With a garden outside and a small fence around it."

Madam Lesetzskaya leans forward, rocking gently on immense haunches, eyes glazed, lashes fluttering like butterflies above them. She leans into the shadow, craning her neck, as if trying to hear better, words, or a message, coming to her from far away. Konig sits there in the darkened room, behind the drawn curtains, stiffly, warily, a begrudging tolerance upon his face, waiting for her to speak.

A card pressed on him several weeks before by a friend, and carried in his pocket till only that afternoon, had read: "Madam Paulina Lesetzskaya. Budapest, St. Petersburg, Paris, New York. Spiritualist. Mediumist. Confidante and adviser to—" Then a list of mostly defunct and obscure royalty to whom she had ministered—dukes and princes, shahs and potentates, pages to the royal court. Then the tag line, the kicker: "Contact established with the departed and missing. Results guaranteed," the card promised in the plain, rather unextraordinary verbiage of an exterminator's calling card promising to rid you of roaches.

The two figures lean toward each other in the damp, malodorous shadows, the one rocking slowly back and forth, the other, stiff, recoiling slightly, as if struggling against the impulse to shout.

The tips of Madam Lesetzskaya's fingers tremble across the face of Lolly's birthday card—the shaggy bear in the white copious robes of a doctor, stethoscope dangling absurdly around its neck. Each finger on Madam's hand has a ring, while depending from her neck is a bezoar stone, a scarab amulet, and a fake jade lavaliere.

"I see several people—three, possibly four—"

"Yes."

"One female—early twenties."

"Yes."

"The others, male, somewhat older. Though there is danger about the house, I don't sense any immediate danger to the girl."

Konig sighs, leaning backward, relief flowing over him like a balm. He knows it is all fake, meretricious. That means nothing to him. All he wants now, craves, is the simple analgesic of her words, like the blessed Demerol coursing through his bloodstream.

"I feel her trying to reach you. She wants to talk to you. Make contact."

He cocks an ear toward her, waiting for the next words. "Yes—but where is she? Can you tell me where she is?"

Madam Lesetzskaya's stubby, bejeweled fingers scratching over the birthday card suddenly halt, then rise tremblingly to her temples. Eyes screwed shut, hunched over the table, she concentrates more deeply, rocking back and forth, on her great haunches, huge buttocks spilling over the sides of a small wooden chair creaking rhythmically beneath her. "A cold, remote place. Far north of here." Her eyes suddenly open and she stares fixedly at some distant point on the ceiling. "That's all I see now. The air is beclouded. I have no clear impression. Come back in three days. Bring some article of clothing or jewelry."

"Yes," Konig mumbles and staggers to his feet. "Yes, I will."

Going down the murky stairway, he is full of loathing and self-contempt. Next time, perhaps, it will be an astrologer, or an Oriental guru, or some wizard phrenologist who will read the bumps on his head. He feels like an ass, a fool, a rube who's just been sold the Brooklyn Bridge. And the worst part of it is, he's not at all certain he won't be back there in three days with a piece of clothing or jewelry.

≈≈ 20 ≈≈

2:30 P.M. THE MORTUARY.
CHIEF MEDICAL EXAMINER'S OFFICE.

Konig sits in a small laboratory off the autopsy suites, a jeweler's loop screwed fiercely into his eye, the hand with the lacquered fingernails propped on a desk before him. The hand is rigored now. Hard like stone, frozen into its gesture of beatitude, a curiously penitential expression to it, like a hand broken off a plaster saint.

The hand has soaked all morning in a mild alkali solution, and while the skin has shriveled, the cuticle has softened to the point where Konig's small, jewel-like dissecting knives can begin to work on it.

Through the magnification of the loop Konig can see that the damage to the epidermis around the fingertips has been massive. There's no doubt that a strong abrasive —a rasp, or possibly a file—was used to obliterate the digital and palmar patterns. But by carefully cutting away the totally lacerated outer tissue, he is able to dissect out several small swatches of dermal tissue bearing faint patterns of whirls and ridges.

Konig has been up against this kind of situation before, a situation in which the epidermis has been shed from the fingers through putrefaction or through deliberate mutilation. He knows what the mutilator of the fingers doesn't —that the characteristics of the exposed surface of the dermis are identical with those of the actual fingerprints. Also that the ridges of the papillary layer, just beneath the dermis, are the primary cause of the ridge pattern on the epidermis, which is molded like a glove upon them, thus reproducing their pattern exactly on the surface.

Even under great magnification these dermal impressions are fainter than ordinary fingerprints, but nevertheless, they are there. Extracted painstakingly, several tiny swatches of dermis hang drying now like old laundry on a line of tautly strung black thread. Here a bit of thumb tissue with papillary ridges intact; there a somewhat sharper print found on a bit of dermal tissue taken from the forefinger.

Later, when the swatches have dried, they will go to the police lab, where they will be reversed, photographed and enlarged. Hopefully, the police will be able to establish that the prints from the hand are identical to some of those found in the shack near Coenties Slip. Thus the site of the crime will be firmly fixed.

Like a lapidarist, Konig screws the loop tighter into his eye and bends once more to his work, his tiny blade carefully lifting out the shredded cuticle of the ring finger in order to get at the dermal impression below.

"Chief"—young McCloskey's tousled head pokes through the door—"care to have a look at what we've got so far?"

"Among limb segments, no single region is represented in more than duplicate." Pearsall lounges before the five trays, briefing a handful of staff. "So, we've got four upper arms separated at shoulder and elbow—two right and two left which appear to match in pairs. We've got three forearms and hands—two right and one left, including a pair. We've got four thighs separated at hip and knee— two right and two left which appear to be matchable in pairs. Four legs—two with feet which look like a pair, two without feet which also look like a pair. Attached to each of the thighs forming one pair, we've got a patella; two other patellae, also a pair. In addition there's— Oh, hello, Paul." Pearsall turns to greet the Chief. "Just doing a run-down of what we've inventoried so far."

"Good. Flynn send over the new stuff?"

"Arrived about a half-hour ago," McCloskey says. "Two more feet, badly mutilated—"

"Probably match that set of footless legs," says Strang.

"No doubt," Konig snaps. "Flynn mentioned something about another trunk."

"Right." McCloskey nods. "An upper half with three cervical vertebrae—"

"Looks more and more like two people," Delaney murmurs quietly to himself.

Konig's eyes range avidly over the trays. "I'll buy that, just as long as we're absolutely certain there's not a stitch of evidence that implies more than two—a spare bone, an extra limb that goes to neither. The minute we've got that we've got nothing."

"So far we've found no odd parts. We're in pairs on everything." Bonertz stirs from a far corner. "At least with the bone, and it seems unlikely we'll find it in the soft parts. We've already sent out a dozen samples of bone tissue for age determination."

"Fine." Konig rubs his hands eagerly. "Well, let's see if we can't put Humpty Dumpty together again."

"We've already started with the trunks," McCloskey says. "Looks like we've got an upper and a lower half matched already."

The group now converges on the tray containing the three trunk portions. Hakim now takes over. "Two upper trunks," he begins in his thin, clipped enunciations. "Trunk number one comprising two cervical vertebrae, the full twelve thoracic vertebrae, and two lumbar vertebrae. Trunk number two comprising three cervical, twelve thoracic, and three lumbar. The only lower trunk portion we have contains a pelvis and three lumbar vertebrae—"

"So you matched the lower with your upper trunk number one to get the full five lumbar vertebrae." Konig nods in agreement.

"Yes, sir. When we brought these two sections of trunk together, the lower vertebra of the upper portion articulated perfectly with the upper vertebra of the lower portion."

"So," Konig rattles on, his mind computing, anticipating, "the trunk was divided by cutting through the intervertebral disc between the second and third lumbar vertebrae."

"We even found the knife marks on the bone at that point," Strang says.

Konig cocks a somewhat jaded eye at him. "How many?"

"Three," Strang replies. "The first cut through and broke off the tip of the articular process. The second took off another piece of the same process, which we don't have."

"Probably broke off," says Konig. "Still in the mud down there on the river. Go ahead."

"The third," Strang continues, "cut through the elastic ligament joining the two vertebrae."

"Fine," Konig goes on brusquely, the memory of Strang's treachery still rankling him. "Any X rays?"

"Over here, Paul," Bonertz calls from a far corner where a radiographic scanner, already lit, has the first X-ray print mounted on it.

In the next moment, the assembled group clusters before the ghostly gray-white pattern of a human spinal column showing the lumbar region of a reconstructed trunk.

"Not the most perfect fit, I'm afraid," says Hakim apologetically.

"Still"—Konig scours the screen—"there's little doubt they're from the same body. Reason they're sitting a little lopsided like that is because of that clumsy cut at the tip of the articular process in the second lumbar vertebra. Hand me my dissecting kit, somebody."

The light of the scanner is flicked off and moments later the group is assembled around Konig, bent over the separated upper and lower portions of trunk. Jeweler's loop screwed back in eye, small dissecting knives flashing beneath the harsh white glare of fluorescent overheads, Konig proceeds to carefully extract the small, broken-off slivers of bone. In a setting of absolute silence, he works deftly and swiftly before a rapt audience, a situation he loves.

In a matter of moments he has carved out several minute slivers of bone, then taken the small slivers of extracted bone found on each vertebra and attached them to the articular process of the other vertebra to make a precise fitting—broken-off pieces of bone, one taken from each trunk portion and fitting, respectively, broken surfaces on the other portion.

Removing the loop from his eye, Konig looks up smiling at the assembled group. "I think you'll find now, Hakim, when you X-ray again, that you have here a true anatomical picture."

A small murmur of admiration ripples through the crowd. It is an admiration not only for Konig but for themselves. For it is the rather unique gift of the Chief's to make a group of widely disparate men feel a common sense of pride and self-respect in work well done, the potent combination of skill, knowledge, and a kind of reverence.

Konig's smile beams from one man to the next, until that smile reaches Carl Strang, whereupon it turns into a grin of spiteful malice, and for a moment they regard each other thusly.

"Well," Konig booms cheerily, "now that we've got one whole trunk together, why don't we give it some arms and legs?"

≈≈ 21 ≈≈

"Pigs—goddamn pigs. Whadda hell I s'pose to do now? Dis goddamn mess—I can no rent like dis."

4:15 P.M. 1622 FOX STREET, THE BRONX.

Francis Haggard gazes impassively into the lengthening shadows encroaching on a squalid four-room flat, recently vacated, and from all visible signs, vacated in great haste. He moves slowly around the room followed by Mr. Guzman, the peppery little Puerto Rican superintendent of the building.

"Whadda hell I s'pose to do now wid dis goddamn mess?"

Haggard cannot answer his question. Actually, Mr. Guzman is luckier than he knows. The devastation visited on this squalid little flat with its punctured walls and peeling plaster is nothing compared to what Haggard had seen Friday evening in the loft on Varick Street.

Except for the obvious filth of the place, as evidenced by the battalions of roaches diving for cover the moment they had entered, and the heavy mosaic of graffiti inflicted on every bare inch of wall, the detective sees nothing that plaster, sizing, and several gallons of cheap latex paint won't cure.

His eyes roam searchingly through the spray-can calligraphy—this lingua franca of the slums—for some clue to the whereabouts of the recent occupants. But very little seems to emerge from all the curlicues and numbers other than more street shibboleths of the "Power to the People" variety, cant and sloganeering, bombastic rhetoric, all strident and admonitory. A mixture of agitprop banalities out of the underground press combined with a kind of comic-strip mentality. But suddenly, once again, smeared in bright, gaudy letters near the top of the wall, that opaque and faintly unnerving message he'd read on the Varick Street wall gleams down upon him.

THE DAY OF THE MUFFLED OAR IS COMING

"Alla time here, nine, ten years ago, we got nice people," Mr. Guzman laments. "Family people, hardworking church people, you know? Now jus' a lotta junkies and freaks."

Haggard nods abstractly. His pebble blue eyes watch a wasp dive into an overhead light, collide with a sickening crack, then plummet downward to the floor where it lies on its back buzzing and pedaling its legs fecklessly in the air.

"Now I gotta spend coupla hundred bucks—clean up dis goddamn mess—"

"That's too bad." The detective shakes his head commiseratively. "When did they pull out?"

"I dunno. Two, t'ree days maybe. I come up to collect de rent and dere's no one here, you know? I open up wit' de key and find dis goddamn mess."

"Uh-huh." Haggard nods. "How many of them were there?"

"Here?" Mr. Guzman points to the floor.

"Uh-huh."

"I dunno. A lot. Always different faces. Maybe two,

t'ree regular—maybe five, six. I dunno. Never de same. Come and go all time day and night."

"They bother anyone? Make a lot of noise?"

"No. Dat's one t'ing. Dey very quiet. You never know dey in or out."

"Uh-huh." The detective nods. "Any women?"

"Women?"

"Yeah. Did they ever bring women here?"

Mr. Guzman pauses, baffled by the question, the barrier of language having momentarily stumped him. "Women?"

"Yeah—you know—girls."

"Oh, girls." The clouds part. Guzman smiles deeply, flashing a gold incisor. "Sure. Plenty girls."

"Ever see this one?"

Guzman's eyes roam quickly over the small photo of Lauren Konig on the DD13. "No—I never see." He thrusts it back at Haggard, then jerks it back again and holds it, squinting, at arm's length from his body. "I dunno—maybe. Dere so many. Come here all times of day and night. For the boys. Boff, boff, boff they go—fast. In de bed and out. You know? Den dey go 'way." He looks at the photograph once more and shrugs. "No—I never see dis one. Mostly I see de guys. Longhairs. Freaks. Dirty. Filthy. Never bathe, you know? Stink."

"Yeah, I know. What about this Eggleston?"

"Oh—Mr. Eggleston. He de boss."

"The boss?"

"Sure. He pay de rent. Handle de money. Always telling de others what to do. You go here. You go dere. He very nice. Very polite. Not like de others. Know what I mean?"

"Uh-huh." Haggard nods wearily. "And you got no idea where he's gone?"

"No. How I got an idea where he's gone? If I know where he go, I go get my rent. I make him pay for de goddamn mess here. I go myself. I don't care. He beat me for two months' rent. Now I gotta pay."

The detective listens, making a show of sympathy. But he listens without really hearing, his eyes gliding over the simple-minded wall scribblings without really seeing. But it is the empty carton of TNT sticks that really rivets his attention, the empty canisters of gelignite, the empty boxes of percussion caps and cheap Japanese detonators, the small wisps of wire coil, the unmistakable odor of cordite hanging over the place that scares him sick.

"I ever see dis guy," Mr. Guzman fumes on, "I break his legs. What de hell he do? He sóme kinda crook?"

Haggard turns, evading the question. "I wanna get this guy, too, Mr. Guzman. And you've got my word, I'm gonna get him. Lock this apartment now. Don't touch anything. Don't let anyone in here." He starts out, then turns back. "Listen—these guys ever come back for this stuff" —he waves his arm around the room—"you call me. Hear? Understand?"

"Yeah—sure."

Haggard scratches two telephone numbers on a pad. "You can't reach me at the first, try me at the second. Okay?"

"Yeah—sure. Sure. Okay. Whadda hell you gonna do about my place here?" Mr. Guzman gazes desolately about the wreckage of his rooms.

"First I wanna get some fingerprints outta here. Then I'm gonna send the bomb squad in."

"Bomb squad?" Guzman squeaks. But already the detective has gone out the door without hearing him or seeing the queasy, sickish grin fading in the shadows behind him.

≈≈ 22 ≈≈

"Basically it's a ball-and-socket arrangement. Ball of the humerus to the scapula socket; ball of the femur to the acetabulum socket."

7:15 P.M. AUTOPSY ROOM,
CHIEF MEDICAL EXAMINER'S OFFICE.

Konig and young McCloskey hunch over the trays shuffling long bones around, attempting to match one of the two sets of limbs to the reconstructed trunk. They work on, rapt, intent, unaware that as they have labored through the afternoon, the others, one by one, have gradually departed. They are not now even aware of those departures. It is just them together and the job at hand. Nothing else.

"It's a trial-and-error thing," Konig rattles on. "It's a bitch. Time-consuming. Hardly worth what you get for it at the end. But that's the only way to do it."

For the past several hours they've been trying to match a set of arms and a set of legs to a single trunk—the re-constituted trunk—for that's the only one complete with two shoulder sockets and two hip sockets. The other trunk portion is only half complete, only the upper trunk. To that, hopefully, they will be able to match a pair of arms. But they will have to wait for the men still digging on the river near Coenties Slip to unearth a pelvis and lower torso, to which, hopefully, they will be able to assign a pair of legs.

So they have juggled bones for the past several hours, sorting them on the basis of general appearance, texture, and dimension. Then in turn trying to match each limb segment in pairs of rights and lefts.

"The articulations have to be completely harmonious," Konig muses aloud as he shuffles bones, lifts them, hefts them two at a time, using his own hands like a pair of scales. "You can't force anything in this. The moment you have to force you know you're wrong."

McCloskey watches the skilled, deft motion of the older man's hands, rather like a child watching an old magician at some dazzling feat of prestidigitation. With long cotton swabs he reams out the acetabulum socket of the right hip into which he is about to insert the ball of a right femur. "Every reasonable doubt has to be eliminated."

During the course of that afternoon, while one by one the others had slowly drifted off, McCloskey and Konig have drawn closer to each other, some mutual obsession holding them there long past the hour when common sense has told them to quit and go home, seek warmth and light, respite from the day, a comfortable room, a few genial friends.

But no, they're still there, shuffling bones, both having fallen unconsciously into the attitudes of student and teacher—yet, perhaps, not quite so formal. There's also a touch of intimacy here; two strangers startled and de-lighted to discover they share a common passion.

"See that left acetabulum?" Konig whispers, and the young man stoops to peer into the hip socket on the re-constituted trunk.

"Busted up pretty badly."

"Right. Femur's obviously been yanked out by force."

"It'll be hard to fit it," says McCloskey. "Maybe we oughta start with the right instead."

"Good idea," Konig snaps. "Hand me those two right femora."

Konig holds both femora in his hands thoughtfully, as if he is weighing them. Getting the heft of them. One is clearly shorter than the other, and both femur heads are clearly different in circumference. When Konig in-serts the smaller of the femora into the right hip socket, it slips easily in and can be moved around in all direc-tions. It is just as easily withdrawn.

"A little loose," McCloskey remarks.

"Let's try the longer one."

They do, and with a little manipulation the larger head belonging to the longer set of limbs can also be made to enter the socket and fit snugly there.

"More like it," Konig mutters quietly pleased. "But just to make sure, we'll dissect out all the remaining liga-ments around this hip joint and make a plaster cast of the acetabulum for comparison with the femur head. Then tomorrow morning, when the cast has hardened, we'll measure the vertical diameter of the cast with calipers on a vernier scale. Hopefully the correspondence between the size of the cast and the femur head'll be pretty even — You seem skeptical."

"I just can't get it out of my head that we might be dealing with more than two bodies. What if—"

"—we should find an odd part that can't be matched to either the long or short set?" Konig smiles. "Then we can toss out everything we've done so far. The minute one odd part like that shows up, the mathematical odds of numbers of bodies we're dealing with jumps to ap-proximately seventeen and that means we haven't even begun to salvage a quarter of the parts buried somewhere along the river. Too grim a notion to contemplate. Wipe it from your mind, Thomas, my boy." The Chief cocks an amused eye at the young man. "Anyone waiting for you at home?"

"Waiting for me?"

"A wife? A concubine? A small dog? Anything?"

"No, sir." McCloskey laughs. "I'm not married."

"Well then, how about a break for supper? My treat."

And so they pause for a bright, warm hour in a small Italian restaurant where, under the spell of two martinis and a well-chilled bottle of Verdicchio, Konig waxes more expansive.

Somewhere near 9 P.M. they are back again in the sub-basement level of the mortuary. Returning with a jug of Chianti and some paper cups, they post themselves once more before the trays of bone and tissue, the gobbets of flesh, all waiting to be sorted out.

Alcohol and a bit of companionship have brought a roseate glow to Konig's cheeks. Not only has he grown more expansive, he is, curiously, even more lucid. Alcohol seems to have sharpened his perceptions, honed the dexterity of his fingers to a remarkable pitch. "Now, Thomas"—his voice fairly lilts—"hand me that long left femur."

In the next hour or so they manage to fit the left femur to the badly broken left hip socket, so that the reconstituted trunk now sports a full set of thighbones. Their next job is to match a pair of patellae to each. All of the four kneecaps they have still bear loose portions of flesh and tendon, making the job of identifying a pair more difficult. In the next hour or so Konig and McCloskey go about the business of sorting out these strips of tissue and cleaning the margins of the patellae. Then, finally, Konig fits a kneecap to the right and left femora respectively. *"Voilà,"* he cries out when he sees the ease with which they both articulate. "We're now ready for the lower legs."

And so, before the night is over, somewhere around midnight, two complete sets of lower limbs are reconstructed, and one set attached to the reconstituted trunk. Both sets have been matched by such factors as dimension and texture, as well as by the careful measurement of the bones of individual segments. Once reassembled, the two sets of lower limbs are so manifestly different in length that it is now easy to think of them in terms of the shorter and longer set. Already, each set is able to divulge crucial nuggets of information regarding age and stature; even, but somewhat more vaguely, the sets tell something of the racial history of their former owners and how, possibly, they met their ends.

It is well past midnight when Konig glances up from his work and catches the young pathologist suppressing a yawn. "Call it a day?" The wicked, slightly mocking grin crosses his features. The "I can work you under the table, kid" look that McCloskey knows so well.

Konig stands and stretches. "First thing in the morning we'll X-ray both sets of limbs, make sure the articulations at the hips and patellae are correct. Those acetabulum casts ought to be ready by about ten A.M." He thumps the young man on the back. "Oughta be able to start on the arms tomorrow."

≈≈ **23** ≈≈

TUESDAY, APRIL 16. 2:00 A.M. RIVERDALE.

Sometime around 2 A.M. Konig is back home in Riverdale, padding about upstairs in his bathrobe after a hot shower. He cannot sleep. Even with the heightened dosage of Demerol, the sciatic pain in his leg is once again gnawing remorselessly at his bone.

He tries to read a magazine but his attention wanders, his mind too agitated and full of the day; the budget still due, the list of chiseling morticians from Angelo, the exhumation of the Robinson boy in Yonkers on Wednesday, the Doblicki business in Jersey, Strang's treachery, and the matter of the missing heads. Without heads they will never be able to ascertain precisely the age of the two dismembered corpses. Without the dentition inside the jaws and without the terminal segments of fingers with which to make readable prints, they can never hope to make any real identifications. And despite the strange hand with the lacquered nails that seem to suggest a woman's but feels more like a man's, in the absence of a pelvis and lower trunk, any hope of accurately sexing that skeleton appears remote at best. And then, of course,

Lolly. The thought of her comes creeping back into his head. Voices whisper through the room, all the old oaths, recriminations, guilts, and sorrows.

He rises and goes downstairs, padding through the empty house like a somnambulist. These nocturnal perambulations of his have grown more frequent. Over the past months since wife and daugher have gone, he has grown more restive and irritable. Less able to sleep. What a curse a bed is when you cannot sleep in it.

He goes to the kitchen—spotless, immaculate—where nothing has been cooked in nearly half a year, and nothing eaten, except small snacks nibbled late at night from the nearly empty refrigerator. He pours a glass of milk, hoping it will soothe his stomach, sour now from frayed nerves, too much gin and cheap Chianti. He wanders from there to the library looking for a book, something to get him through the night.

For a physician, Paul Konig is unusually well read. In his youth, fresh out of medical school, with textbook reading comfortably behind him, he developed a voracious appetite for books. Nowadays, his life being the hectic thing it is, he has scarcely time for that. But his library is stacked from floor to ceiling with the passion of those years—history, poetry, biography, novels. His favorite character in all literature is Prince Myshkin, probably because he is nothing like Myshkin. If anything, he's like Coriolanus, proud, angry, incautious, scolding the mob, always confronting them with their stupidity. As a character, Konig loathes Coriolanus.

Now his fingers wander up the shelves and search through the titles, pausing finally at an old, frayed copy of *Lear*. The story of the old, derelict king, bereft of throne, fortune, his daughters, careening over the stormy plain, blind and dotty, wondering what it was he'd lost, or ever thought he wanted, is an old favorite of his. As a senior in medical school he played the part of the mad old king in a laughably inept university production. Lurching and ranting around the stage in an ill-fitting costume—"Blow, winds, and crack your cheeks" and so on—he elicited from his audience a number of embarrassed titters. And the young man who reviewed it in the school paper was able to remark that "Konig's Lear was awesomely voluble if not entirely convincing."

He takes the book down now and pads out into the sun parlor. It is a large, glassed-in hothouse-cum-terrace, moist and verdant, crowded with a tangle of assorted indoor flora, unpruned, unattended, growing wild since Ida's death—the coleus, the schefflera, the huge luxuriant ficus with their great green paddle leaves, the myriad pots of blooming lilies, variegated and of every color, Ida's passion.

He lies back in the sultry, near-tropical greenhouse air, recumbent on a chaise of rattan, aching leg propped high on a cushion, and sips his milk. He starts to read, but after a moment his eyes flutter and close, the glass balanced on his chest, and he nearly drowses. Then suddenly the harsh jangle of the phone, the ring, like a long, cruel needle, drills through the silence of the house. The milk nearly topples and, sitting upright, he waits for a second ring, already believing that, just as the other night, the second ring will never come.

But it does, and suddenly his heart is thumping. He's up, spilling milk, lurching, staggering, hobbling to the phone on a leg with shooting stars in it. Another ring and yet another. His bowels grind with fright. A premonition of danger. Who can it be at such an hour? Possibly the office. Or Flynn. No—they'd never call like this, unless—

"Lolly—Lolly," he murmurs even before the phone is in his hand.

"Hello."

Only silence roaring back at him. Ominous. Anticipatory.

"Hello—hello. Who is this?"

"Dr. Konig?" A voice comes at him.

"Yes—speaking."

"Dr. Konig," the voice proclaims once more, as if he were being officially summoned.

"Yes, this is Paul Konig. Who is this?"

"Listen to this, Dr. Konig."

There's a moment of silence in which Konig can hear the other man breathing. Then suddenly a piercing, wrenching scream, followed by a lewd giggle in the background.

"Dr. Konig," the voice comes again, "did you hear that?"

A cold sweat breaks out on Konig's forehead. His heart

is beating wildly in his chest. The voice continues now more softly. It is a refined, eerily gentle voice.

"Dr. Konig," it resumes, "that was your daughter."

Another loud, wrenching scream. More ghastly. More anguished. Then the phone is slammed down.

≈≈ 24 ≈≈

"If you've got the whole New York City Police Department looking for your daughter and they can't find her, what do you expect me to do?"

"Find her." Konig slams a fist down on the desk.

10:15 A.M. WORLD-WIDE TRACERS ORGANIZATION.
OFFICE OF MR. DANIEL CORY, PRIVATE INVESTIGATOR.

"And you say the FBI is apprised?"

"I told you." Konig wipes a badly crumpled handkerchief across his brow. "Right after they hung up, I called a friend of mine with the Bureau here in New York. Told me they'd known all about it for several months now. Learned about it through a friend of mine. A Lieutenant of Detectives who's been working on the case for almost six months now. They've been following it, they say."

"Well, that's very good. If you've got the police and the Bureau—"

"Not good enough." Konig's fist comes down again. "I want you to find her. Find her. I'll pay. I'll pay you anything."

Mr. Cory is a small, impeccable man with ruddy features and a waxed mustache. The sort of man whose toilet and wardrobe, you gather, are all rather carefully calculated. The disheveled specter seated opposite him, unshaved, in sour, rumpled clothing, a slightly crazed look in his eyes, makes a striking contrast. As Konig's voice grows louder, more demanding, as his fist flails the air more violently, Mr. Cory grows cooler.

"It's not a question of money, Dr. Konig. If it were merely a question of money—"

"Then what is it a question of?"

"That's what I've been trying to tell you." Cory goes on soothingly, a more placatory approach. "Your daughter is not a missing person. If she were, I might be able to do something. From what you've told me, she's right here, somewhere in this city. A captive of some person or persons. That's not a missing person. That's kidnap. Forced confinement. If I'd heard a daughter of mine scream like that— Well, this is simply not a matter for an agency like this. It's a police matter. A Federal matter—"

"The police have done nothing. The Feds are fools."

"That's a strange thing for a man in your position to say."

"Forget about my position, goddamnit." Konig's fist explodes once more on the desk, causing Mr. Cory to recoil and gaze uneasily at the outer door, as if he deplored such a breach of decorum.

"But your position is unique, Dr. Konig. If you weren't the Chief Medical Examiner, if you weren't such an influential man, with such a vast reputation, I'd be more inclined to take you on. But because you are who you are, I'm sure the efforts made by the police and the Bureau to locate your daughter have gone far beyond their normal range of operation. If I were to set out now to find your daughter, I'd only be duplicating what I know they've already done. I don't want to take your money for that kind of duplication, or raise your hopes unjustifiably."

"The police—" Konig blurts out but Mr. Cory cuts him short.

"No, please let me finish, Doctor. The police are really very good at this sort of thing. I repeat, your situation is unique, your daughter does not fall into any of the usual categories. Number one, she's no longer a minor. Number two, she's being forcibly detained somewhere. She's a kidnap victim. Kidnap is not our sphere of operation. That, as I say, is a police matter, or a Federal matter."

Konig slouches wearily in his chair, all the fire suddenly gone from him.

"You've already got the police and the Bureau involved," Mr. Cory goes on. "That's very good. That's a one-two punch."

A look of scorn creeps into Konig's eyes. "One-two punch, ay?"

Mr. Cory is momentarily flustered. "By all means. If the police and the Bureau are coordinating—"

"Coordinating?" Konig's eyes glint more spitefully than ever. "Oh, yes. They're coordinating. And knowing what I do about the reliability of both organizations, I'm reasonably certain that with all their coordination in due time they'll eventually locate my daughter's corpse. Meanwhile, these crazy bastards have my kid. They're hurting her, and no one—nobody—seems able or willing to do a goddamned thing about it."

≈≈ 25 ≈≈

"Well goddamnit—you find him."

"I told you, Chief. I don't know where he is."

"And I told you to find him," Konig bellows at a young assistant detective, sitting in shirt sleeves, gaping goggle-eyed up at him. "Now go on. Go find him."

11:20 A.M. CHIEF MEDICAL EXAMINER'S OFFICE, DIVISION OF MISSING PERSONS.

The young detective's name is Zymansky and all he can manage to do is move his lips but no words come.

"Why the hell isn't he here in his office?" the Chief rants on, flailing the still, musty air of the little office. "What if somebody needed him? What if there was an emergency? Christ—what the hell is he being paid for anyway if not to—"

"But I told you, Chief. He's out on a job—"

"What job?"

"How the hell should I know? He's got about twenty of 'em going at one time. Is there something I can do?"

Konig's face is sickish pale, the color of parchment. Rage has rendered him nearly speechless. The poor assistant detective withers now under the scorching glare of the Chief's eye.

"No." Konig smolders, as if the question asked him was an impertinence. "There's nothing you can do for me. There's nothing Haggard can do for me. I wouldn't give a plugged nickel for the whole goddamned kit and caboodle of you."

The Chief wheels sharply, veers toward the door, knocking over a decanter of water as he goes, not even bothering to glance back as it gurgles over the papers and blotter on Haggard's desk.

"Should he call you when he gets in?" the assistant detective, dabbing furiously at wet mail, cries out after him. "What should I tell him?"

"Tell him to go to hell." Konig slams the door behind him.

"Deputy Mayor on the phone again, Chief."

"I'm not in." Konig barges past Carver, making for the door of his office.

"Already told him that three times. You better speak to him."

"Oh, Christ." Konig flings his palms heavenward. "Okay—put him on."

Inside the cluttered, airless sanctity of his office once again, Konig bites off the tip of a fresh cigar, spits it vehemently over his shoulder, and snatches up the phone.

A buzz. A high ringing. Then suddenly the harsh, crazed nasalities of the Deputy Mayor crackling through the wires. "What the hell do you think you're doing?"

"Beg pardon?"

"Are you trying to fuck me, Paul?"

"What in God's name—"

"Are you trying to screw me? Because if you are, I can assure you—"

"What the hell are you—"

"I've stuck my head out—"

"What is this, Maury? What are you talking about?"

"You know goddamned well what I'm talking about. If you don't you're a bigger fool than even I—"

"Hold it. Slow down," Konig says, half rising off his chair, then falling back. "Will you for Chrissake tell me what the hell's on your mind?"

"This story," the Deputy Mayor splutters, "this goddamned newspaper story."

"Oh, you mean this dismemberment thing on the river?"

There's a pause full of consternation and puzzlement. "What dismemberment thing?" the Deputy Mayor whines piteously. "I don't know anything about any dismemberment thing. It's this goddamned body-snatching thing."

"Body snatching?" Now it is Konig who pauses, bidding for a bit of time.

"It was all over the late editions of the *Post* yesterday. Pages two and three. I've been with the Mayor all morning. He's furious. Fucking furious. Repeat, *furious.*"

"What's it say?"

"What's what say?"

"The story."

Konig can hear the Deputy Mayor panting incredulously. "You really haven't read it?"

"I haven't seen a paper."

Another pause full of bafflement and rage. "You really ought to read the newspapers, my friend. Keep abreast of things. You're a public official. It's always helpful to know what's going on in your own agency."

"All right, Maury, spare me the sarcasm."

"Your own backyard, so to speak."

"Quit the cute stuff, I said. If you mean that someone in this office—"

"That's exactly what I mean."

"—peddled a few names—"

"A few names?"

"—to some sleazy mortician for a few bucks—"

"A few bucks?" A loud, scornful laugh shatters through the receiver. "A million bucks a year the *Post* says. One million bananas. The City's being ripped off to the tune of a million a year. You're very casual, I must say."

"What's a million?" Konig's voice suddenly booms. "Peanuts. Consider the annual rip-off budgets of the Welfare Department, the Highway Department, the Realty Board, and the Bureau of Acquisitions or whatever the hell they call themselves."

"This is no time for frivolity, my friend."

"Who's being frivolous? I'm telling the truth. We're peanuts. Absolute pikers when it comes to municipal rip-offs."

"Paul, I will not sit here and listen to a lot of smart-ass talk. I tell you, the Mayor is—"

"Furious. I know. Repeat, *furious*."

"Okay, my friend." A long sigh and the Deputy Mayor crumbles in defeat. "I have stuck my neck out for you a half-dozen times in the past five years. This is it. You've had it. A cover-up of this proportion—"

"You're right there. I did cover up. I knew about the situation for at least three years and did nothing about it. That was very sloppy of me. I was wrong. I'm sorry—"

"Very noble, very magnanimous," the Deputy Mayor whines gratingly. "None of that, you realize, mitigates one iota the fact that you are now up to your ass in a cover-up scandal that's cost the City—"

"Fine. I plead guilty. What does the Mayor want me to do? Resign? Very well. I resign."

"I didn't say anything about—"

"I'm a doctor. Not a policeman. If the Mayor wants a policeman to supervise the ethics of the personnel in this office, let him goddamned well hire one. I'll serve him gladly. He'll have my complete loyalty and affection."

"Paul, for Chrissake—"

"And my pity, I might add. I've had it with fiscal budgets, requisition forms, bureaucratic Neanderthals, hack politicians, retrograde morons—"

"Paul, listen to me—"

"—petitioning the City in triplicate for pencils and paper clips. I'm a doctor. I'm a—"

"Paul—Carl Strang is in the Mayor's office right now."

There's a pause in which both men listen to each other breathing. Konig can feel a pulse beginning to drum at his temple. "So?"

"They've been closeted for half an hour."

Rue and anger rising in his gorge, Konig suddenly has an image of Strang, unctuous and sycophantic, telling his tale, spilling his guts to the Mayor. He can see the hand-wringing, the breast-beating, hear the woeful litany of such typical Strang adjectives as "regrettable," "deplorable," "unfortunate." And Strang sitting there before the Mayor in the leather-mahogany sanctum sanctorum of City Hall, bowing and scraping, genuflecting like a mandarin, dizzy with adulation, and Uriah Heeping before that exalted personage, His Honor the Mayor.

"Was he summoned?" Konig spits the words out. "Or did he just show up on the doorstep?"

"A little of both, I'm afraid. The Mayor called him

early this morning, after he'd read the story. Suggested offhand that they might chat at some vague, indefinite time in the future. About two hours later, Strang walked through the front door. Paul—this man is no friend of yours."

Another pause in which Konig drops a ball of wadded paper from his fist. "Thank you, Maury. Thank you for telling me that. And if it's any consolation, you may tell His Honor the Mayor that the man responsible for leaking the names of unclaimed bodies has been relieved of his duties. I will also have a complete list of all those morticians and funeral parlors in question on the Mayor's desk tomorrow morning."

No sooner has he slammed the phone down than it rings again.

"Konig here."

"Dr. Konig?"

"Speaking."

"Bill Tracy at the *Times*. You're a tough man to reach."

"Been busy."

"I'll bet you are. I was wondering about your reactions to the *Post* story."

"What story is that?"

"Story in yesterday's *Post*."

"Haven't read it yet so I've got no reactions. Is that all?"

The baffled pause that follows produces in Konig a mild lift of pleasure.

"Well," the reporter plods on, "do you know what it's in regard to?"

"You mean the body-snatching thing?"

"Right."

"What about it?"

"Is it true?"

"Oh, sure—we've been in the body-snatching racket here for years. Been selling the stiffs to fertilizer manufacturers."

"Fertilizer manufacturers?"

"Sure," Konig rants on spitefully. "Good money in stiffs. Too bad some loudmouth had to go blow the whistle and ruin it for all of us. Supported my drug habit for years."

Another baffled pause. Konig lights his cigar with mounting fury.

"I see," says the reporter, a note of chill creeping into his voice as he catches the gist of Konig's quirky humor. "Is it true that you've been aware for several years that people in your office have been selling names of unclaimed bodies to local morticians?"

"Who says so?"

"I'm afraid I'm not at liberty to disclose my sources of—"

"Never mind," Konig snaps, "I know who. Well, if Strang says so, it must be so. Strang's an honorable man."

"Well, I didn't mean, sir—"

"Quite all right," Konig says. "I know exactly what you meant."

Another pause. Konig can almost reach out and touch the puzzled consternation at the other end.

"Well, I was just wondering—" the reporter struggles on. "There's a rumor going around—"

"Rumor? What rumor? I never listen to rumors."

"I don't either—but this one is pretty solid."

"Solid?"

"Impeccable sources. It's about the DA's office."

"DA's office?" Konig's ears perk.

"According to a report we've had here, the DA is planning a full-scale investigation of the Medical Examiner's Office."

"Full-scale investigation?" Konig mumbles, all former levity gone.

"Yes, sir. According to well-placed sources, you've been in collusion—"

"Collusion? What in God's—"

"Yes, sir—with several people in your office. Demanding kickbacks from morticians for the names of unclaimed bodies, knowing full well these bodies were being buried at public expense, and that you plotted to conceal—"

"Plotted to conceal—" Konig mumbles the words without comprehending them.

"Yes, sir—and that you were fully aware that—"

Konig quietly places the receiver on the cradle. For several moments he sits at his desk, numb, spent, musing distantly while the cigar expires in a smog of smoke between his fingers. A variety of emotions churns within him, none of which he is able to define. But fear—fear is not one of the emotions he is feeling. He is not afraid of the

District Attorney, or the Speical Investigator, or the Mayor, or public chastisement from the press. What he is feeling principally is shame.

A sudden vision of old Bahnhoff rises before him, the stern, iron-gray visage glowering at him—he who has brought shame on the Office. Body snatching, faked and shoddy protocols, deliberate concealment of wrongdoing. What would Bahnhoff have done about such shenanigans during his own tenure? The old German would have rooted them out mercilessly. There would have been excoriations, public hangings, all hell to pay, but the Office would have been cleansed.

The phone rings again, jarring his ruminations. A picture of Lolly flashes through his mind as he snatches it up, expecting to hear her voice, or her captors demanding money.

"Konig here."

"Where the hell you been?" Flynn's voice comes pantting and susurrant out of the receiver. "Been tryin' to reach you for hours. Listen—I'm over in Jersey. That Doblicki job. You were right. Gotta hand it to you. The Jersey boys finished with him a couple of hours ago. Pulled a thirty-eight-caliber slug outta the inside of the head. Reason you guys missed it was the goddamn thing was all buried and covered with ash. In the back, just like you said. How the hell didja know it was the back of the head?"

"Never mind, Flynn. Just get on with the story."

"I am—I am," Flynn whines. "For Chrissake, gimme a chance, will ya? What I'm tryin' to say is they got the guy dead drunk, shot him in the back of the head, doused him with gasoline, dumped him into a car along with a lot of gin bottles, and set the whole thing on fire. Then they pushed the car over an embankment to make it look like he drove off drunk. The guy was a big lush anyway. So they figured it would all look pretty plausible."

"They? They?" Konig snaps. "Who's they? Did you get the bastards?"

"Relax—relax," Flynn goes on, barely able to suppress the triumph in his voice. "I'm comin' to that. It was the goddamned brother. Got him dead to rights. Soon as we had the autopsy report from your pal Weinstein, we marched right over to the wife with the remains of the bullet. The brother's right there"—Flynn giggles spitefully—

"just happened to be spendin' the night. Consolin' the newly bereaved widow, don'tcha know? Soon as we laid it on him, he put the whole blame on her. Then she put the blame on him. Ain't love grand? There was a hundred-thousand-dollar straight life policy plus a double-indemnity rider on Doblicki's life. These two bastards were gettin' ready to ride off into the sunset with nearly a quarter of a mil. How d'ya like them apples?"

Konig laughs. It's a harsh, vindictive laugh. Full of a kind of fierce merriment. An unpleasant sound. But it's over in a moment, then once again he's all business. "What about the heads, Flynn? You promised me some heads—"

"I got no heads," Flynn says apologetically. "But I got something almost as good."

"Fingertips?" Konig feels his spirits leap. "Some of those missing tips for prints?"

"No—no missin' fingertips. I got underwear."

"Underwear?"

"Yeah—in the shack. From all that crap we cleaned outta there. Found a dirty pair of boxer shorts, Army issue—"

"So what?"

"So what?" Flynn cries, his voice full of astonishment and hurt. "There's a serial number stamped in the waistband—that's what. RA 12537744—pretty faded, but we got it. Sent down to Washington this morning. Oughta be hearin' somethin' pretty—"

"Jesus Christ," Konig snarls once more. "That's great for you. What about me? I can't verify any identifications without heads—"

"I can't find no heads, goddamnit. We been up and down that shoreline ten times, two miles each way, and still—"

"What about the shack?"

"We been through the shack with a fine-tooth comb."

"Under the shack, I mean. Did you pull up the god-damned floorboards?"

There's a baffled pause in which Konig can hear the detective thinking hard, stalling for time.

"Pull up the floorboards, goddamnit," Konig shouts.

"Listen, you." Flynn's high spirits suddenly snap. "You quit your goddamned shoutin' at me, you hear? I ain't been to bed in forty-eight hours. Runnin' my ass all over the place in Jersey and—"

"I don't care where you're running your ass. I don't care if you never go to bed. You get me those heads, Flynn, or I'll have your head. And you know I'm just the one who can do it. Now pull up those goddamned floor-boards."

For a long time after, he sits there in the gloomy, cluttered shadows of his office. It is twelve-fifteen and everyone has gone to lunch. Thinking he will get a cup of soup somewhere, he starts to rise, then falls back in his chair, riveted to the spot, a cold gnawing in his bowel, as if he had to void himself. "Dr. Konig," a quiet voice whispers in his ear. Suddenly, in his head he hears that loud, wrenching scream, hears it just as he heard it early this morning, as if through a phone receiver, anguished, frightened, like a small stricken animal. Then that lewd, awful giggle. He hears it over and over again, exactly in that order—the quiet voice, the scream, and then the giggle. Over and over again.

His forehead glistens with cold domes of sweat. He feels the knot tighten in his chest, the fist closing over his heart, and his hand fumbles in the lower right-hand drawer for the small phial of amyl nitrite kept there for just such occasions.

He continues to sit there in those shadows heavy with the odor of formalin and cigar smoke, and he waits.

The last time Lolly called the office was four days ago at noon. Somewhere around this hour. If he sits there now, glued to his phone, perhaps she may call again. Or her captors may attempt to make contact. Sitting in sodden, rumpled clothing, he waits, convinced the phone will ring at any moment. He even believes that by bringing the immense power of his concentration to the thing, he can will it to ring. He concentrates on the sound of a ringing phone, but the silence in the room is deafening, and the phone never rings.

Two hours later when he gets up, ready to descend into the mortuary where work awaits him, he is nearly beside himself.

≈≈ 26 ≈≈

"We've got all the lower limb articulations correct."

"Good. What about the casts of the hip joints and femora?"

"Appear to match perfectly."

2:15 P.M. MORTUARY.

McCloskey is glowing as he makes his report to the Chief. The others, assembled about the trays, are all busy at individual tasks.

"You boys really burned the midnight oil last night, didn't you?" Strang smiles expansively.

"Radiographs are beautiful, Paul," says Pearsall. "Beautifully clear articulations."

"Absolutely no doubt," says Delaney, gazing up at the ghostly gray-white bone configurations on the screen. "Those are perfect limb assignments."

"Any serology yet?" Konig mutters, disregarding all the glowing chatter.

"We've got a Type O and a Type AB," Hakim reports.

"Which is which?"

"The long set is O and the short AB," says McCloskey.

"Toxicology?"

"Negative," Bonertz replies. "No drugs. No appreciable alcohol levels. Gas chromatograph picked up reserpine traces in the liver of the short set. Probably hypertensive."

He's about to go on but Konig cuts him short. His manner is rude and abrupt. Konig has a number of unpleasant traits, but rudeness is not one of them. He has never been known to be rude to a colleague. Now, this sudden churlishness has them all puzzled and wary. Uncertain what to expect next.

Konig's bleary eyes are once again scanning the trays and the partially reconstructed corpses. "Any progress?"

"We've made preliminary assignments on both sets of humeri, Paul." For the first time in their relationship, Mc-

141

Closkey is emboldened to use the first name. After all, last night, during dinner and throughout work, they had been more than merely colleagues.

"Oh?" Konig replies and there is something clearly cold and admonitory in the tone of that single syllable.

The young pathologist, however, doesn't detect it. He runs right on, absolutely glowing, full of professional pride and enthusiasm. "We've dissected out the ligament and muscle tendon surrounding the shoulder joints, the sockets on the scapulae, and the ends of the humeri. Then we—"

"What's this pin doing in the scapula?" Konig cuts him short. There's a moment of portentous silence.

"I put it in," McCloskey murmurs, beginning to sense something awry.

"You put it in?"

"Yes, sir. You see, I thought I'd try one of the shorter humeri first—the way we did the other night—and the—"

"So you forced the head in and busted the goddamned acromion—right?"

A hot pink suffuses the young man's face. "Yes, sir, I'm afraid so."

"You're afraid so?" Konig jeers. "You're afraid so? Couldn't you see it was all wrong? Are you a fool? Are you blind? If you've got the longer pair of femora fitting the hip joints of your trunk, you ought to goddamned well know that it's the longer pair of humeri that should fit at the shoulder."

"I did, sir. I was merely trying to eliminate any other possibility—"

"And in doing so, eliminated the acromion. In fact, you busted the goddamned thing."

Young McCloskey appears shattered. His eyes have grown watery; his cheeks are scorched with the shame of public denunciation. "But, Dr. Konig, I do have the longer humeri now fitted in place and the articulations seem perfect."

"Perfect?" Konig shouts. "How can it be perfect? It'll never be perfect. You busted the goddamned acromion. How the hell can you ever expect now to restore the exact fitting in relation to that humerus?"

"But, Paul," Pearsall steps in, trying to draw some of the withering fusillade away from the boy, "the X rays are showing nearly perfect articulations. These arms do go with this trunk."

"Who asked you?" Konig wheels, turns his fire now on Pearsall, whose features blanch under the heat. "Who the hell asked any of you?" He wheels again, his raging, accusatory eyes flashing from one man to the next. Disheveled, bleary-eyed, unshaven, his gray hair tousled wildly, seeming suddenly white, as if it had turned right there before them, Konig has the look of some Old Testament prophet, crazed, half-lunatic, half-divine, a Jeremiah or an Ezekiel, full of lamentation and woe. "Who the hell asked any goddamned one of you?" He flails the air with his fists.

Strang, standing off to the side, arms akimbo, quietly observes this maniacal performance, a slight, enigmatic smile on his thin, taut-cord lips. Konig wheels again, just in time to catch that smile, then turns on him. "What the hell's so funny?"

"Funny?" Strang affects a deeply aggrieved look. "I don't think it's funny, Paul. I think it's very sad. Very goddamned sad." He turns sharply on his heel and strides out.

"Go on," Konig shouts after him. "Go ahead. Run to the Mayor or the District Attorney. Run to *The New York Times*. Maybe they'll take your picture. Put it in the goddamn paper—right on the front page—"

By this time Konig is ranting, his voice bouncing off cold porcelain and stainless steel, shattering the normally sepulchral hush of the mortuary. An elderly Negro attendant inadvertently stumbles on to the scene. His wide, startled eyes blooming open in fright like huge white peonies, he turns and stumbles back out.

"I don't need any of you. I'll do better by myself. Get the hell out." Konig flails the air as the others still stand about, heads lowered out of shame for their leader.

"Go on. Get the hell out. All of you," he bellows like a wounded animal. "Go on. Go on. Get out."

Slowly, one by one, they turn and go—Bonertz, Delaney, Grimsby, Hakim, Pearsall, still white and shaken from the ordeal, until no one is left there but Konig and young McCloskey, facing each other across a table, the two partially reconstructed corpses, stony and recumbent, like figures on Egyptian sarcophagi, between them.

"Well, what the hell are you waiting for?" Konig snarls. "You get the hell out of here too."

McCloskey doesn't stir. For a moment they stare at each

other, the younger man still flushed with shame, his questioning gaze full of puzzlement and hurt. His lips move, attempting speech, but no sound comes. In the next instant he turns and goes.

For a long while after Konig stands there, riveted to the spot, silence rushing in upon him, in a solitude of his own making. Having driven everyone from him, alienated his staff, denounced colleagues, and humiliated a young man whose crimes were nowhere near as great as Konig had magnified them, he is at last profoundly alone.

In the next moment he flings off his jacket and seizes a pair of radii there in the trays awaiting assignment.

≈≈ 27 ≈≈

"I don't give a goddamn if it does stink like a toilet."

"Have a heart, will ya, Flynn?"

"How many holes we gotta dig before ya see it's a bust?"

3:15 P.M. THE SHACK NEAR COENTIES SLIP.

Detective Sergeant Edward Flynn sits in shirt sleeves, tilted backward on a raddled bridge chair, eating an apple, and supervising the excavation of the earth beneath the little shack near Coenties Slip.

In contrast to the night Konig was there, the place is now stark and empty, the sum of its cluttered accretion of refuse and scrap all crated now and carted off to various police laboratories for blood analysis, fingerprints—dust gathered carefully in glass phials, and innumerable little envelopes of nail parings and hair all collected. Dozens of people—specialists—are already at work at various points around the city analyzing, testing, collating. Nothing remains there of the former wilderness of junk and disarray but the large, dirty old Victorian tub with the curiously ornate legs that is attached to no source of water. The solitary nature of the thing just standing there now makes it seem even more grandly ludicrous.

Already most of the floor planking has been torn up

and lies strewn about the place wherever it happens to have been tossed by the two beefy patrolmen laboring there in skivvies and hip waders in yet another fetid, muddy trench.

"Why the hell don't he come down here and stick his own ass in this goddamn toilet?" comes the muffled muttering of one of the diggers from below. "See how he likes standing in all this *bunjara.*"

A spadeful of black tarlike ooze comes hurtling up out of the trench and lands with the plopping sound of cow dung on the floor.

"Quit the goddamn grousing, will ya?" Flynn snarls at the two stooped figures grunting in the hole.

"I tell you, there's nothin' here, Flynn."

"I know there's nothin' there but I'm gonna rip up every square inch of goddamn floor anyway—"

"You're gonna rip up?" A scornful laugh bursts upward from the hole. "Hear that, Del Vecchio? He's gonna rip up."

"Yeah—don't give yourself a hernia, Flynn."

More scornful laughter. More grunting and more plopping. Then after a short while: "If there's nothin' here, how come we gotta break our ass in all this *bunjara?*"

"Because that's your lot in life, dummy"—Flynn pops three Maalox into his mouth all at one time and chews them ruefully—"diggin' sumps. Now if you'd had your asses reamed today like I had— Goddamn him, if he ever pops off at me like that again, I'll haul him up before the Commissioner—I swear it. Goddamn it, next time he pulls that crap on me—"

"Ah, what the hell you care what that old fool says?" Another loud plop of black ooze.

"He's bananas. Like everybody knows, the guy's a nut."

"See the paper? DA's gonna have his ass on this body-snatchin' thing."

"Crazy old fool."

"Quit it." Flynn bolts up, kicking the chair aside behind him. "Quit the goddamn grousing, I told you. All right—I've had it. Let's get the hell outta here."

"Hallelujah."

"Close up that dung hole."

"My pleasure."

Two muddy, befouled figures scramble out of the hole and with a kind of boyish exultation start spading mud

back into it while Flynn prowls uneasily through the shadowy reaches of the shack, his eyes yellow and shifting like
those of a panther stalking prey. He comes to rest at last
before the sorry old Victorian tub. What a curious thing
to be sitting there now in the middle of a bare, malodorous
little shack. It had, no doubt, seen better times. A relic of
a more tranquil age. Probably it had graced the bathroom
of some tawdry old pleasure palace out of the gilded age,
like the Astor or the Ritz, now demolished, its site turned
into a parking lot. It had been witness to the daily ablu-
tions of bankers, brokers, rich matrons traveling with their
hubbies. And it had ended its days ignominiously, as a
butcher's block for a maniac.

It stands there in the corner now, solitary, forlorn, its
pipes all hanging out, plunked down on a six-foot-by-six-
foot strip of old linoleum on which is stamped a pattern
of faded, liverish-colored flowers.

"Okay, Sarge." The two beefy young cops come panting up to him like pups eager to get out to play.

"Finita la commedia," says the more lyrical Italian one.

"Let's blow this shithouse," says the more direct Irish
gentleman. They hustle for the door, leaving Flynn back
in the shadows, still contemplating the tub and the six-by-
six strip of linoleum.

"Wait a minute," he bellows over his shoulder, stopping the two young cops dead in their tracks, just at the
brink of their escape into the sunlight and fresh air at the
door. "Let's just have a wee peek under that linoleum."

"Mannagia diavolo," the Italian moans balefully.

"For Chrissake, Flynn," the Irishman whimpers. "Have
a heart."

"Quit the bellyachin' and pick up that goddamn tub
like I told you."

6:15 P.M. MORTUARY. CHIEF MEDICAL
EXAMINER'S OFFICE.

"There is a better fit of the ends of the supraspinatus
tendon on the right side than on the left. Portions of the
lubricating bursa between the capsule of the shoulder
joint proper on the top of the humerus and the under surface of the acromion are still in position and come together
as the head slips under the acromion. Appear to come
naturally together." Konig scrawls hastily into his pad.
"Thus the two humeri of the longer set of upper limbs
appear to belong to the same body as the reconstructed
trunk."

Working steadily for the past four hours, all by himself
in the solitude of the abandoned autopsy room, no sound
within the place but the dripping of a water tap behind
him, Konig has managed to assign all the remaining limbs
to either one torso or the other. Both now have arms and
legs.

Working that afternoon with both sets of arms, he has
found that the heads of the shorter humeri were too small
to fit the shoulder joints of the reconstructed trunk, just as
the heads of the shorter femora were found to be too
small to fit the hip joints.

But when he attached the longer set of humeri to the
same trunk, not only did the sockets fit neatly, but with
the addition of the longer pair of forearms, the arms appeared in correct proportion to the length of the trunk.
The tips of the fingers, allowing for the removal of the
terminal segments, were suddenly in correct relation to the
thighs. But when the shorter pair of humeri and forearms
were attached to that same pair of shoulder joints, the
fingertips came just below the level of the hip joints, an
impossible proportion for a normal body.

So Konig's hypothetical case based upon only two

bodies is building slowly toward an incontestable fact. He sits silently now before the two broken, battered things, which, albeit headless, nevertheless have begun to bear the unmistakable configuration of mortal man. Though still unidentified, still mysterious, unknown figures, it is now at last possible to see the lineaments of humanity in the reconstituted parts. Both bodies have undergone partial resurrection, and Paul Konig, like an old, demented dollmaker, sits before his half-creations now, still baffled by the numerous unassignable soft parts, odds and ends, human debris scattered all about him. He gazes down upon these half-creatures, pondering their curiously peaceful repose, trying to decipher the riddle contained in a handful of bones.

Number 1 and Number 2—the short and the long—already he knows a great deal about each. Even as he gazes over them, he feels a growing affection, a growing intimacy, a physician's intimacy, as their various parts merge slowly into anthropomorphic form. They're now a bit like old friends. Working on Number 1's badly mutilated feet, which had been viciously slashed across the arches and had had several toes amputated in an attempt obviously to erase some identifiable feature, Konig has found a curious metatarsal deformity, an unnatural curving outward of the big toe, hinting at a painful foot problem. Then, too, Number 2's back in the area of the fourth and fifth lumbar vertebrae reveals definite disc displacement as well as a pelvic asymmetry, as if he'd walked for many years with a compensatory gait in order to alleviate severe sacral pain.

It was curious the way the heads arrived, just as Konig was going to get up and go home. Not that he wanted to go home. He dreaded the prospect, but there seemed nothing left to do, and his leg had started shrieking again. Then they came, in a cheap vinyl suitcase plastered over with a lot of paper college pennants and swabbed with mud. They're carried in by a young cop, looking frightened and a little queasy. He doesn't know exactly what it is he is carrying, only that it's "something" and that he wants to get shut of it as quickly as possible.

Konig, however, knows what it is, knows instinctively the moment he grasps the muddy handle and slings the case onto a table. The heft of the thing and the dull, sickening thud of the stuff inside bumping together tell him all he needs to know.

His fingers tremble as he fumbles with the clasps, and raising the lid of the case, he feels a rising sense of excitement, an inner gush, rather like the confluence of innumerable tiny streams suddenly merging into a single roaring torrent.

All he sees at first is a lot of old crumpled newspaper, as muddy as the case itself and spattered with innumerable tiny spots of red. The paper is evidently there as a kind of cushion for the contents, rather like the way you pack fragile porcelain or glass in excelsior. On top of all that newspaper lies a small white piece of bond, torn from a memo pad, upon which is indited in a large, hectic scrawl:

> Here are your heads.
> I hope you're happy.
> Flynn

> P.S.
> You were right, goddamn you!
> They were under the floorboards.

In the next moment, his hands are pushing through the crumpled newssheet, thrusting aside paper with tiny bits of adherent hair, shards of clotted gore. Then suddenly, there they are.

Konig is not a squeamish man. In nearly forty years of service at the Medical Examiner's Office, he has seen some pretty grisly sights. For the most part, such things have left him unfazed, or at least inured. But the condition of these two heads, or rather what remains of them, has shown him a wholly new, undreamed of dimension of man's capacity for visiting havoc on his fellow man.

Both heads have been drastically mutilated with the deliberate intention of making the possibility of identification extremely remote. Just as the fingers and toes on each corpse had been either mutilated or hacked off, to remove all identification marks, so, too, in the case of the heads, the features of each had been obliterated—eyes, ears, nose, lips, almost all flesh cut away from the face, and nearly all of the hair and scalp removed—violently excised. The skin tissue had been peeled off like a glove so as to reveal the skull beneath; also, many of the teeth in each head had been extracted in order to make identification by means of dental charts very difficult. The less mutilated of the two heads is clearly that of a man. The other—a smaller, somewhat slighter skull—is of equivocal sex. It might well be that of a woman.

The first head, the more mutilated of the two, had been severed from the neck immediately below the level of the chin. Not only have all the visible facial features been removed, but nearly the whole of the skin of the head and face as well. Two small portions of scalp remain, one over the lower quadrant of the right side and the other just behind the left ear opening. The lips have been entirely cut away; the two upper central incisor teeth have been drawn and the tongue, its tip cut off, protrudes slightly in the gap.

The second head had been severed from the neck at a level slightly lower than that of the first. A huge chunk of scalp is missing from the right side of the head and most of the skin and underlying tissue of the forehead and face have been removed. Flaps of skin still adhere to each cheek, trailing down to the chin and below it. Both lips have been almost completely cut off and nearly all teeth have been drawn. Between the jaws protrudes a swollen tongue.

Just before the stump of the left ear there is a tuft of dark hair. The portion of the scalp remaining on the left side of the head bears a curious Y-shaped laceration covered with dark hair. It is clear to Konig that the wound was caused by forcible contact with a blunt instrument. He cannot say for certain whether or not the wound was produced before or after death.

Konig, examining the first skull under a magnifying glass, quickly locates two fractures. The first is a depressed fracture measuring three-quarters of an inch by a half inch, shelving from behind forward. The injury has broken the outer table of bone, causing a slight depression on the inner table. Slightly behind this fracture, and to the left of the midline, Konig pinpoints the second fracture, affecting the outer table only. This measures a quarter inch in diameter. Once again Konig is uncertain whether the fractures have been inflicted before or after death. But he is certain that they resulted from two separate blows with a blunt instrument. Undoubtedly the same instrument that had produced the Y-shaped laceration on

the second head. Had they been inflicted during life, the
blows would probably have been sufficient to produce
unconsciousness, but they do not appear to have been
sufficiently violent to have caused death. He must look
elsewhere now for the cause of death.

In the adherent tissue just under the left eye of the first
skull, Konig's sharp gaze spies a deep-seated bruise,
roughly an inch in diameter. Then a similar but smaller
bruise on the lower border of the jaw on the left side.
These bruises lead his eye down further to the place
where that purple, swollen tongue, with its tip cut off,
protrudes grotesquely just beyond the margin of the jaw.
It is that tongue that really starts to tell the story.

The tip cut from the tongue is about an inch and a half
in length. It seems to Konig that it had been removed to
facilitate the extraction of teeth. If that is so, its removal
is of importance as proof that the tongue protruded just
at or immediately after the time of death.

Studying the tongue further, he notes that the contour
of the palate is imprinted on both the upper and lower
surface with indentations that correspond perfectly with
the remaining dentition in the jaws. These indentations
are shallow in front and become deeper toward the back
of the tongue. Such marks can be made only when great
pressure is exerted on the tongue for an uncommonly
long time, and such a condition is sometimes found after
throttling.

Immediately Konig is looking for the telltale bruising
signs of manual strangulation. None are to be found in
the soft tissue around the neck because this tissue has
been stripped away, as if there had been a need to erase
all evidence of throttling. But in some of the adherent
tissue, Konig discovers several small half-moon impressions, suggestive of those caused by fingernails. He has
only to examine next the hyoid bone in the throat to discover there the clean fracture going through it and to
know finally that the neck had been forcibly compressed
and that the poor, hapless owner of the skull he is now
holding in his hand had died an asphyxial death from
violent throttling.

Gazing at both heads now, Konig is struck again by the
somewhat curious fact that the mutilation inflicted on the
first head is so dramatically greater than that inflicted on
the second. The owner of that first head, he reasons, must

have been the real object of contention here. The rage and hate visited upon that head are simply, even to him, horrifying.

The time now is nearly 8 P.M., though Konig is not aware of that. Indeed, since the awful moment when he drove everyone from the autopsy room, locked the doors, and hurled himself into the task of reassembling the arms, he has been unaware of the passage of time.

The task before him now is purely anatomical. He must assign each of these heads to one or the other torso.

The first part is easy and is solved by simple observation. Attached to head Number 1 are four complete cervical vertebrae, with fragments of the fifth still clinging. Attached to head Number 2 are five cervical vertebrae.

The reconstructed trunk has two cervical vertebrae attached to its upper end; the partially reconstructed upper trunk has three. Since the normal number of cervical vertebrae is seven, it's obvious to Konig that head Number 1 with its four vertebrae belongs to the partially reconstructed trunk with the three vertebrae and that head Number 2 with its five cervical vertebrae belongs to the reconstructed trunk with the two cervical vertebrae.

As with the reconstruction of the trunk, Konig's next job is to bring the two parts together by articulating the lower vertebrae attached to the heads with the uppermost of the vertebrae attached to the trunks. This is delicate work and requires considerable time since he must match badly shattered fragments of these vertebrae, upper to lower, in order to verify that they come from the same source.

This he does with the wholly reconstructed trunk and discovers that these two cervical vertebrae appear to fit together very well in all details. He repeats the operation with head Number 1, matching it to the partially reconstructed upper trunk, and with the same success.

But Konig cannot be content with this kind of facile observation. He must now verify these articulations with X rays, and in order to do this, he spends the next few hours dissecting out the cervical vertebrae from both heads, as well as both trunks, cleaning them by maceration in order to display the margin of the bones. After that, he is ready to connect both sets in complete anatomical series.

The work is laborious and painstaking. He must sit hunched over for a period of several hours under bright lights and wield his knives. But this is not labor for Konig. Time goes swiftly for him. It flies. The anxiety and tension of his day simply fall from him like old sour clothing, and as he works far into the night, he feels not the slightest fatigue, only a kind of strange, heady exhilaration.

Somewhere along about 2 A.M., he's back upstairs in the radiographic room with two completely reconstructed cervical sections, taking X rays of each.

In a matter of minutes, he has taken photographs of both cervical series, front and back views, and while waiting for them to develop, has a cup of stale coffee in his office, smokes one of his dark, noisome cigars, and scribbles more figures into his requisition budget for the Comptroller.

A short time later he is back upstairs padding through the shadowy halls of the large empty building, back to the radiographic room for the developed X-ray pictures of both sections.

Scanning the gray-white ghostly pictures on the illuminated screen, there is a sense of victory. They confirm what he has known all along. Both sets of vertebrae fitted together give the general appearance of anatomical harmony, a harmony that becomes more and more pronounced to his trained eye.

"Marvelous," he whispers to himself almost reverentially, studying the clear, beautiful articulations between these long links of vertebrae and discs. "Goddamn marvelous—what a goddamn marvelous miracle of engineering."

With a small shock of amazement, he realizes that it's nearly 3 A.M. Hastily he starts to scribble notes onto his pad preparatory to writing his longer, more elaborate protocol.

". . . Radiograph 3 shows seven cervical vertebrae present—five in upper part removed from head Number 2—"

"Why can't you be like other men? Come home at night for supper. She's been asking for you all day— hasn't seen you once this week—"

"—and two attached to the trunk—so that the bones of the upper vertebrae match the bones of the lower in anatomical detail, including bone texture, making them appear to be in perfect—"

"*I'm not like other men.*"

"—and proper sequence—that portions of intervertebral disc between 5th and 6th vertebrae exhibit cut and torn surfaces with reciprocal features, making it highly probable that the portions adhering to the two vertebrae—"

"*You know what she said today? She said 'Daddy is dead.' I overheard her telling her friends. She said you'd died and left us all alone.*"

"—were part of the same intervertebral disc."

"*Go upstairs now and say good night to her.*"

"*Good night? For Christ sake, Ida, it's two A.M.*"

"*I don't care what time it is. She's up. She's waiting. Now you go up there and let her see you. For God's sake go up there.*"

"The plane of severance between head Number 2 and reconstructed trunk passes not quite cleanly through the junction of the larynx and trachea—"

"*Paul—I want you to take that job in Rochester.*"

"—between the cricoid cartilage of the larynx and the first cartilaginous ring of the trachea—"

"*And sit on my ass for thirty years in some university teaching a lot of—*"

"—both showing signs of damage, so that not only did cut surfaces fit each other exactly, but on each there was found an attached—"

"*—lumpheads—nothing between their ears but suet?*"

"*Paul—we can't go on this way—*"

"—shaving of cartilage and a cut cartilaginous surface which fit in perfect reciprocal harmony—"

"*What way? What's wrong with this way?*"

"*Don't you see it? Can't you see for yourself? Nothing in common but an address, and a little child—*". .

"—and therefore provide conclusive corroboration of the opinion based on purely anatomical evidence—"

"*Hello, Lolly. Good morning, honey. It's Daddy. How are you, sweetheart?*"

"—that head Number 2 belongs to the same body as the wholly reconstructed trunk and head Number 1 belongs to the same body as the partially reconstructed upper trunk."

"*—and therefore by mutual consent, this Court concurs*

*—for a period of trial separation, not to exceed one year
—at which time such matters as disposition of property—
parental custody—to be remanded to—"*

Konig gazes up into the cavernous quiet of the radiography room, a gray-white picture of a complete vertebral series flickering ghostly patterns on the wall, ghost voices of his imagination ricocheting off the walls, receding now like a dying echo through the room. He rises stiffly, flicks off the scanning screen, and gathering up his developed X-ray plates, he starts back down for the mortuary.

Standing once again before the two reassembled bodies, he is now absolutely certain that he is dealing with only two bodies. What remains for him to determine is the approximate time and manner in which these two hapless creatures met their untimely ends. Already, for purposes of identification, he knows a great deal about the relative stature of both. Based upon even perfunctory examination of the skulls, he can say with fair certainty a number of things about the sex and age of each.

Holding head Number 1 up to the light, rotating it at a variety of angles, he sees a male skull, wonderfully harmonious, with steep forehead, narrow face, delicate lower jaw, and elegant but markedly prominent chin. The rounded eye sockets with thin margins are very large, the cranial sutures not yet occluded, and the third molar not yet erupted.

All that speaks of a very young man, Caucasian, no more than eighteen or nineteen, with fine, rather effeminate features. Konig has been right all along. The lacquered nails had not really fooled him. The mandible, too, of this skull, while small, is somewhat heavier than a female mandible, and the dentition that still remains in the mouth is definitely masculine; the teeth in absolute volume and shape, with the first incisor and canine of about the same height, and the canine of the lower jaw markedly higher, all speak unequivocally of the male of the species.

The state of cloture in the sutures of head Number 2 seems already quite well advanced. From the state of the parietomastoid and the squamous sutures, Konig can read an age of between thirty and thirty-five, leaning more toward the former than the latter figure.

This skull, too, is male—ovoid, cheekbones well defined, forehead high, fairly broad, with heavily developed relief. The eye orbits are large, angular, with strongly sloping margins. From the nasal aperture, Konig can visualize a sharply projecting nose, possibly curved, the bridge of the nose high, the root narrow.

The arch of the lower jaw is narrow and prognathous, that of the upper, massive, suggesting a sharp, projecting chin accentuated by an astonishing degree of alveolar prognathism.

Using the well-known techniques of the Russian anthropologist Gerasimov, Konig can visualize a heavy, coarse, rather brutal face, slightly Slavic in cast.

What in God's name ever brought these two men together? Konig now speculates. What fatal union brought them to those muddy crypts beside the river—the one with the fragile, patrician lineaments of an Egyptian princess, the other with the coarsely brutal aspect of a Tartar horseman.

It is then that his eye is inexplicably drawn to the spattered, crumpled newssheets in which the heads were wrapped. Limping across the room, he removes them from the carrying case and spreads them out on the table. For several moments he sits there in a chair reading them, his head tilted to the side, a little myopically, like an old man reading in a dim light.

When he looks up again after a while, slats of gray dawn are painted like bars against the mortuary windows. A small noise sounds behind him. He turns, and there, stooping in the doorway in a rumpled raincoat, neck stretched, oddly craning, like a large, dirty heron, regarding him silently, is Francis Haggard. Konig watches the detective's gaze wander to the tables where lie the two reconstructed corpses.

"Good morning," Konig growls. "Say hello to Ferde and Rolfe."

≈≈ 29 ≈≈

WEDNESDAY, APRIL 17. 5:00 A.M. MORTUARY.

"Been here all night?" Haggard asks.

"Guess I have," Konig replies, a little astonished. He's had no sense of the fleeting of fifteen hours. "What time is it?"

"Five A.M.," says the detective. "It's five A.M." Once again his gaze drifts past the Chief to the reconstructed corpses, the gobbets of flesh and bone still in trays all about him. "Why do you do it?" he asks, staring at the bleared, red-rimmed eyes, then at the ashtrays full of burned-out cigars, the beaker full of cold, rancid coffee gulped through the long reaches of the night. "Twelve, fifteen hours a day in this rotting, stinking place. You don't need the money." Haggard's face is full of loathing. "Why the hell do you do it?"

But Konig is no longer looking at the detective. Instead he's staring down at Ferde and Rolfe, the two creatures he gave birth to during the night. Already, almost in the moment of having named them, they've become old friends. He feels a curious camaraderie with them. They've exchanged intimacies. Konig knows their little secret. He has the gist of their story. He holds a picture of their faces in his head, and like the inveterate physician that he is, he even knows something of their daily aches and pains. Ferde's foot problem—bunions probably. And Rolfe's osteosacral miseries. What backaches that fellow must have had.

"Why do I do it?" Konig murmurs aloud, more to himself than in response to the detective. "I do it for them," he says, gazing down at his new friends. "For them I do it. Because I hate the goddamn creeps. The zip-gun freaks and the boys in the back alleys with the razors and machetes. If it'd been your wife and kid on those tables"—he flings a thumb backward at Ferde and Rolfe—"wouldn't

157

you want to know that someone was going to get the creepy bastard that put them there? And believe me, I'm going to get the bastard. Why do I do it?" Konig laughs scornfully, working himself up to a tirade. "I do it because no one else will do it. No one else cares. All these here, working with me now—you think they'll do it? They won't. They play at doing it. But they don't really do it. They're all trimmers and fakes. Come here three, four years, put in their time with me, then go scurrying off to some cushy job in the suburbs—a hospital or a university seat. I do it because it has to be done, and no one else will do it. I do what all your fancy-pants Park Avenue sons of bitches with their fancy office hours won't do. I do the shit work. I clean up after the goddamn party."

Konig is red in the face, while the detective stands there impassively, taking the lash of his tongue. "Does that sound arrogant?" Konig rants on. "Very well, it's arrogant. I am arrogant. That's me. And if they don't like it—"

"If who doesn't like it?"

"All of them. The Mayor. The Police Commissioner. *The New York Times.* You. The whole goddamned kit and caboodle of you. If you don't like it, you all know where you can goddamned well shove it. I do this work because I love it. I do it the best way I know how, and I'm going to continue doing it till they carry me out of here kicking and screaming— Where the hell have you been, goddamnit?" Konig snarls, but something like a sob, full of outrage and hurt, issues from his throat. "I've been looking for you high and low. I can't find you. I can't find anyone. All I hear is excuses. Where the hell is everyone when you need them?"

Haggard stares at him quietly. For the first time in the more than twenty-five years he has known the man, Konig appears close to tears. Racked with exhaustion and worry, his body trembles. His voice, full of anger and recrimination, is modified by a deep sense of helplessness—something he is personally unfamiliar with. The effect results in something like whining. "They've got her. They've got my kid. Some kind of freaks have got her. They're hurting her. And they're going to kill her. Where the hell have you been?"

The detective is seething from the lash of that voice. He too has not yet been to bed. He's been out all night crisscrossing the boroughs, chasing down false leads, run-

ning up blind alleys. The two of them gasping at each other
now in the clammy gray of early morning, disheveled,
sleepless, burned-out, have the look of two old derelicts,
both off on an all-night rip, whose paths suddenly cross.

Finally Haggard stirs from some private musing. "I've
been out looking for Wally Meacham."

Konig gapes uncomprehendingly. "Wally who?"

"Wallace Meacham. Alias Walter Eames. Alias Wendell
Barker. Alias Warren Eggleston. Three years Dannemora,
armed robbery. Eighteen months Leavenworth, aggravated
assault with intent to kill. Busted out of Danbury about a
year ago. He was doing six-to-twelve for blowing up a
bank. The Bureau knows him as 86438 912. Their file describes him as 'Educated. Logical. Shrewd. With a tend-
ency to brag, and possibly vicious.' He's a dilly. One of the
beautiful people. Going to make the world a better place
for us all to live in."

"What the hell are you talking about?" Konig booms.
"They've got my kid. They're gonna kill her and you talk
riddles. What the hell has—"

"Paul," snaps the detective, his voice so full of authority that it brings Konig up sharply. He peers, suddenly
mute and petrified, into the detective's face.

"Come upstairs, Paul. I've got some things to tell you,
and you're not going to like them."

≋ 30 ≋

"You might have told me before."

"I didn't know before."

"But you suspected."

"I did suspect. That's true."

"And yet you didn't tell me. Not a word."

"About my suspicions? Why? What the hell for?"

"You could've at least let me know."

"Know what?"

"For God's sake, man, just to let a person know that things are going on."

"Things were always going on—I couldn't tell you more than that until I knew for sure."

"And you know for sure now?"

"Now I know for sure."

5:30 A.M. KONIG'S OFFICE.

Konig and Haggard sit opposite each other across a narrow space of cluttered desk over which they shout back and forth. Their conversation is like an angry tennis match in which two old rivals bang, chop, and slash at each other remorselessly. It has a vengeful quality about it and the room is hot, like a gymnasium, just as if men had been exercising strenuously there.

"What the hell are you doing for me now?" Konig bawls, red in the face.

"Right now?"

"Right now."

"Right now I'm sitting here wasting my time talking to you."

Konig's eyes bulge; the red in his face deepens. "Don't smart-ass me. I warn you. I asked you a question. I want an answer. Now what are you doing for me?"

"For you?" Haggard's expression is a smirk of bitter delight. "For you?"

Konig, catching the significance of that smirk, falters, suddenly aware that he has overstepped the bounds of propriety.

"For her, then," he snarls, suddenly all self-righteousness. "You know what the hell I meant."

For a moment they sit there not speaking, regarding each other warily, getting their second breaths, while the big Regulator wall clock ticks and black, vaporous coffee gurgles in the beaker over the Bunsen burner behind them.

"I'll tell you what I'm doing for *her*," Haggard seethes. "Christ, I'll tell you what I'm doing. I've got you the name of the guy who's got her."

"Meacham," Konig sneers. "What the hell does the name mean to me? What the hell does—"

"Will you let me finish, goddamnit?" Haggard flings the FBI dossier down on the desk where it lands with the sound

of a whip cracking. "I've got his name. I've got his profile. I've got his prints."

"But you don't have him," Konig thunders. "Crap.
Bunkum. That's what you've got."

"I've got verification that the prints in that FBI file are
the same as—"

"—the ones in the loft and in that bomb factory. Crap.
Bunkum, I say. Without him, you've got nothing. Nothing,
I tell you. Nothing. You understand? And meanwhile,
he's got my kid. Meanwhile—" Konig's voice trails off,
his face flushed, twitching with a thousand unspoken questions. Thoughts shuttle wildly through his head like burning cinders. Charges. Recriminations. Suspicions. Deeply
seated fears. At one point his fists, clenched, knuckle-
white, seem about to pummel the desk. But they don't.
Instead they shudder in midair as if contending with an
invisible force, and a question leaps to his lips. That too
hovers there unexpressed, and dies, leaving his great jaws
moving unceasingly, as if he were chewing rubber.

Having answered nearly a full hour of questions, Haggard sits coiled, awaiting the next assault. But it doesn't
come. At least not then. The Chief's line of interrogation,
for the time being, appears to be at an end. And now
the rigidity, that state of alert that has kept Konig sitting
ramrod-stiff for the past sixty minutes, suddenly lapses.
He hunches forward, elbows propped on desk, hands on
either cheek, supporting the immense, teetering dome of
his head. Then slowly, like a pair of curtains being drawn,
his fingers, reeking with the scent of formalin and decayed flesh, slide woefully across his face, covering completely his red, bleared eyes. "Sorry, Frank," he says.
"I'm sorry."

For a while they sit there silently, Konig rubbing his
eyes, Haggard watching him oddly, embarrassed, and
wishing he were not there. "You're right, Paul," he says
finally. "You're absolutely right. I've got crap and
bunkum. But while I don't know where Meacham is, I
might have a lead on a few of his buddies. I got about a
dozen guys picking through that place up in The Bronx.
Going through there with a fine-tooth comb. Sifting, analyzing, lifting prints. They weren't very careful when they
left. Smeared prints all over the place. Apparently had to
get out fast. What I'm hoping for is to pick up a couple
of 'em. Even one. If I can get my hands on just one, I'll

sweat it out of him. I promise you that, Paul. I'll nail this Meacham bastard."

Konig says nothing, merely sits slouched there at his desk, hiding behind his hands, rubbing his eyes with that slow, fierce rhythm, profoundly unconsoled.

"Tell me again," the detective goes on. "What happened when he called?"

"I told you."

"Tell me again."

"She screamed," Konig mutters blankly. "He spoke first and then they made her scream."

"What did he say?"

"I told you," Konig wails. "I told you. Nothing—just 'That was your daughter.' No hello—no goodbye—nothing. It was all just crazy."

"Why didn't you ask them to put her on?"

"Put her on?"

"Sure. Let her speak to you. Verify it. Next time they call—"

"Next time?" Konig gapes.

"Sure. When they call again. You know they're gonna call again."

"Oh, Christ."

"Sure they'll call again. Put her on. Make her scream. Make you squirm."

"Oh, Christ—no." Terror curdles Konig's eyes. He puts his hands up as if to ward off a blow. "I can't. I can't sit through another one of those things."

Haggard slumps back in his chair, pushes his fedora to the back of his head. "You don't think this guy is finished with you?" A short, cruel laugh rips from him. "You don't know the Meachams of the world if you think that one call is the end of it. That's only the beginning, my friend. Now the game really starts."

"Game?" says Konig, stunned, bewildered. "What game?"

"Oh, come on, Paul. Don't give me that wide-eyed crap. Like you never heard this kind of thing before. You know men like Meacham. You've been around station houses long enough to know guys like this. Now comes the shakedown. Money. Moola. Oh, he'll tell you it's for some lofty purpose," the detective jeers. "Wants to feed starving Lithuanians. Milk for the children of

Rumanian gypsies. All very nice, but believe me, pal, it's a crock. It's pure shakedown."

"But why me? Why shake me down? I've got no money."

"You've got enough," Haggard hammers on. "I'm sure he's ascertained the approximate amount from your daughter. He knows there's enough there anyway so he can play Robin Hood for his pals and show a nice profit for himself too. These new idealists are pretty cynical. If Meacham were in paradise he'd be up there running a protection racket. Shaking down the angels. Agitating for reform among the gods while picking their pockets at the same time."

"Reform?" Konig is puzzled. "What the hell does reform have to do with my kid? My kid's no revolutionary."

"No. But that's how she got mixed up with him. She thought *he* was and I guess she thought it was kind of attractive."

"Lolly's not gullible. She's not stupid."

"Right." Haggard nods vigorously. "She's not stupid. Just vulnerable and human. But after a while she saw right through this guy. Saw he wasn't as interested in starving kids and social justice as he was in guns and explosives. Violence and the sense of constant danger. That's Meacham's real kick. The thing that really turns him on. He's the sort of a guy who can only get a hard on when he kills—"

"Quit it." Konig's hands fly to his ears. "For God's sake, quit it."

"I'm giving it to you straight—just like you want it. Do you want it?"

"Yes—yes." Eyes closed, Konig's huge head swings slowly back and forth. "I want it."

"Lolly was a perfect set-up for Meacham," the detective hurtles forward ruthlessly. "An innocent, gullible kid with a few bucks of her own who cared about other people. A perfect set-up for him. He's clever all right. Had a few years of college. Knows when to say Marx, Lenin. 'Power to the People.' There'll aways be some dumb little chick who'll be impressed."

"Like Lolly?"

"Oh, Christ." Haggard reddens. "I didn't mean—"

"Skip it. I know what you meant."

Haggard sighs, much of his momentum gone. "Anyway, make no mistake. He'll call again."

Konig's brows arch ominously. "Then what?"

"Then—then we'll take it from there."

"Come on, come on." Konig drums the table. "You started, now finish it."

"Well"—the detective eyes him warily—"first he'll probably denounce you. Read you the 'Pig Cop' number. Call you an enemy of the people. Accuse you of crimes against fruit-pickers, fags, anything. You're responsible for it. You did it. So you have to pay."

"Okay, okay." Konig waves this aside. "I've heard all that. What's next?"

"Then he'll try and shake you down."

"Okay—how much?"

Haggard leans back uncertainly, his tongue gliding slowly across his lower lip. "Idealism is big business nowadays."

"Come on, Frank. For Chrissake, how much?"

"A quarter of a mil." The detective shrugs. "Maybe a half."

"A half million?" Konig gapes.

"Sure. Why not? That's peanuts compared to what some of these guys ask. Make no mistake, Paul. Meacham's a businessman. He's got something to sell. He'll call again. Maybe four, five times. Maybe a dozen times. He'll put her on the phone again. Make her scream again, this time louder. Loud enough so your tongue is hanging out and you're ready to pay whatever he asks."

"Where the hell would I get a half million?"

"Don't worry about that."

"That's all well and fine for you to say," Konig blusters.

"Don't worry about that, I said." The detective's quiet, forceful manner calms him. "You leave that to me."

Konig sits there trembling, in a sweat. "Sure," he snarls, starting up. "Sure. A sack of marked bills from the City vaults."

Haggard rises, trying to head him off. "Paul—"

"You're not pulling any fancy stuff."

"No fancy stuff—"

"Not with my kid's life, you're not."

"Leave it to me, I said."

"This guy—this Meacham—he can't be that big a fool.

He's not gonna fall for that old sucker game. You guys crouching behind the bushes while I hand him a satchelful of marked bills." Infuriated, Konig starts to pace the floor, Haggard following in his steps.

"Paul, will you—"

"No, sir. No, goddamnit. No. You're not going to play that game. Not with my kid's life. One slip and they'll send her home to me in a box."

"There won't be any slips."

"Goddamned right there won't." At the head of the room, Konig wheels and turns, the detective panting right behind him. "Because, one way or the other, I'll get the money and go out there myself, wherever the hell he is. None of this crouching behind the bushes stuff."

Utterly exhausted, Haggard at last gives up the chase, leaving Konig to barge and flail about the room by himself. The detective slumps back into his chair, lights a cigarette, and puffs deeply. "That'd be a goddamned fool thing to do," he says, spewing smoke through his nostrils, "because, having got your money, he may very well kill her anyway. That's a whole lot less risky than exchanging her for money with the possibility of the law crouching, like you say, behind the bushes?"

Baffled, weary, deeply agitated, Konig regards the detective warily. Sensing a momentary advantage, Haggard continues. "One way or the other, he's gonna call again. And he *will* try and shake you down. Now when he does call, and suggests a deal, you string along. You say yes to everything he wants. You—"

From somewhere far away, outside himself, Konig hears a thin, high voice, the voice of a young girl. Then for a moment he sees a soft, pretty face. Large startled eyes peer up at him, vexed, anxious, reproachful.

"When have you ever—"

"How many times have I come to you and—"

"When have we ever been able to—"

"Did it ever once occur to you—"

Each rebuke is delivered with the rhythm of a lash regularly applied.

"—agree to everything."

Haggard's voice crowds back in upon him, even as Lolly's eddies and recedes until it is no more. Then Konig is gazing blankly down through the broken, dusty slats of the jalousie windows at the cluttered, huddling rooftops across the way. A soft, muted sky glow of yellow decanting downward like a slowly spreading paint stain nuzzles through the dirty gray of early morning; it pushes out the shadows of the night from where they still crouch in alleyways and dark, mean streets.

"I want to see the place," Konig murmurs aloud, abstractly, not to anyone in particular.

"What place?"

"The place where she was. I want you to take me there."

"You mean the loft? Varick Street?"

Konig nods, and once again resumes his seat behind the desk. "And the other place up in The Bronx, too."

"Christ, why?" Haggard is on his feet again, the rumpled tail of his raincoat swaying behind him as he moves up and down the length of the office. "What in hell for? Nothing there for you to see—"

"I want to."

"If at least it would help anything, I'd—"

"It would help me. Make me feel somehow—a little—"

"Just a lotta junk—dirt. Nothing to—"

"—closer. Somehow closer."

"—see. What the hell you gonna do up there anyway?" Haggard nearly shouts, in his mind a vision of the loft, smashed walls, battered canvases, the sour defilement of the mattress, the awful violence visited upon the place.

"I want to see it. I want to see the place where my kid was."

"Nothing to see there, I tell you."

"I don't care, goddamnit. I want to go."

"Aah," the detective fumes, starts for the door. "Go. Who the hell cares? You don't need my permission."

"Goddamned right I don't need your permission." Konig is on his feet bellowing after the fleeing figure. "Don't you forget that, either."

Haggard wheels, starts back, veering toward Konig like a locomotive, all steam and hurtling mass. Then he shudders to a halt before him. "I don't give a goddamn where you go. But if that creepy son of a bitch calls again—"

"Yeah—"

"Before you do a thing, you better damned well let me know. I got a pretty good lead now on one of

Meacham's buddies, see? If I get hold of him, I'm pretty sure I can smoke Meacham out too. I'm convinced Meacham is still right here in this city. Now if you go and fuck this up for me—"

"Don't you talk that way to me. Goddamnit, don't you ever—"

"Shut up," Haggard bawls. "You shut up now. I'm goddamned sick of you, you pigheaded son of a bitch. You think you know it all. You don't know nothing. You hear that? Nothing. You know bones and blood and wounds of the flesh—but you don't know nothing." He lunges swiftly over the desk, a motion so sudden and monitory that Konig rears back, like a man trying to evade a blow. But the motion ends merely with the detective reaching into a pot of pencils and yanking one out, causing the pot to topple, its contents to spill out fanlike across the desk. The next moment he's scribbling an address furiously onto a pad of paper. "I've seen some of her paintings."

Konig's jaw drops and he gapes up at Haggard. "What?"

"I've seen some of your kid's paintings—a gallery over on Madison and Sixty-seventh." He rips the scrap of paper from the pad and with a gesture of infinite scorn flings it across the desk at Konig. "Go see them. They're good."

≈≈ 31 ≈≈

"Nice to see things going so well for you, Charley."

"Can't complain, Paul. Fate's been kind."

9:50 A.M. A CEMETERY IN YONKERS.

Paul Konig and Charles Carslin stand amid rows and aisles of headstones on a grassy knoll situated somewhere above the New York State Thruway. The sun hangs halfway up the eastern sky above the haze-covered hills of lower Westchester. The haze is a mephitic yellow-brown, as much the product of carbon monoxide from the Thruway as it is the earth warming up quickly after a chill night. Blackbirds chug back and forth at each other, foraging between the narrow lanes of stones. Here and there a dirty, scruffy pigeon wambles about, purring disconsolately between the headstones. From below on the Thruway comes the steady muted whoosh of traffic streaming north and south, like the sound of quickly running water. While here, up on the hill, Konig and the brisk, punctilious Carslin chat easily to the thudding sound of dirt being vigorously spaded and the grunting of two Italian workmen laboring knee-deep in an open grave.

"Can't pick up a newspaper without reading something about you," Konig goes on expansively. Even though he has not slept for thirty-six hours, the fresh morning air on the hill and the sweet, green smell of impending spring have revivified him. For a moment he is able to forget his exhaustion, the dull, gnawing pain of his leg, and the awful load of worry he hauls about with him each day like heavy luggage that cannot be put down. He waxes enthusiastic now not because he feels that way, but rather because of some need, call it pride, to look good before a former student who has made his mark in the world.

"One minute you're here testifying in Criminal Court," Konig gushes on, "then I read about a paper you've presented at a symposium in Jakarta or someplace. And I'm delighted about the new professorship, Charley. Much deserved and long overdue. I'm proud of you."

"I had the best teacher in the world, Paul," Carslin remarks coolly. "I don't deny that."

Konig detects the wary, slightly begrudging edge in that response. Something like a smile, crooked and a trifle mischievous, slides fleetingly across his lips, then once again he is all expansive good will. "And I think what you do is goddamned admirable."

Carslin's eyebrow cocks; his back stiffens perceptibly. "Someone has to."

"Absolutely." Konig nods enthusiastically. "Absolutely. Most of these other sons of bitches won't cross the street for you if there isn't a fee in it. But every time I see the DA trying to railroad some poor black or Puerto Rican into the Tombs, I know that Charley Carslin will be there on the side of the oppressed."

Konig is all aglow with earnest admiration, which puzzles Carslin. He has known the Chief long enough and well enough to catch a hint of something slightly mocking in those spiteful, merry eyes,

"You're not really still bitter about that DeGrasso business, are you, Charley?"

"Bitter? I was never bitter." Carslin waves the suggestion aside. "You won that one fair and square, Paul. Made a jackass out of me in court. I learned a very useful lesson from you that trial."

"Oh?" Konig's curiosity is pricked. "What was that?"

Carslin laughs slyly. "If you don't know I won't tell you. Quite frankly, I'm surprised to see you here this morning."

"If there's been a slip-up at my office," Konig flares suddenly, "I want to be the one who sets it right."

"Naturally. I don't doubt that for a minute. Ah—this will be Schroder now."

A dusty Plymouth with a dented fender rattles up the narrow auto path and stops directly before them.

"Who's he?" Konig snaps, instantly wary.

"The Westchester man. Fellow who examined young Robinson at the request of the family. Reported that the bruises around the head looked suspicious."

"Ah." Konig muses thoughtfully as he watches a tall, brisk, fortyish chap shamble up the aisle toward them.

"Morning."

"Morning," Carslin's and Konig's voices collide in quiet response. Carslin, all solemn and professional, makes introductions.

"Dr. Schroder—Dr. Konig."

"Hello."

"How do you do."

"Konig? Not Paul Konig of the New York ME?"

"Yes, sir." Konig straightens. "That's me."

"Oh." Schroder beams. "This is an honor. I cut my forensic teeth on your book. Something of a bible around our office."

"Very kind of you." Konig glows, obviously pleased.

"Not at all. It's simply a fact. It's one of those seminal works. All of our professional lives have been touched by it. Wouldn't you say so, Charles?"

"Absolutely," Carslin replies so acidly that Schroder is momentarily shocked. It's an awkward moment and for a while the three of them turn to the hole where the two Italian workmen, now hip-deep, continue to pitch spadefuls of thudding dirt upward onto a small slope of tumbling earth.

"Well—who are we waiting for now?" Konig inquires, trying to fill the void."

"Deputy Mayor," Carslin mumbles brusquely.

Just then a state troopers' wagon turns into the auto path followed by a large black limousine.

"Ah," Schroder sighs. "This should be him now."

There's a great deal of bustling and small chatter while introductions are made, greetings exchanged. Deputy Mayor Maurice Benjamin has a curt, hasty manner. A no-nonsense, take-charge sort of chap, intolerant of laxity, uneasy during a pause. But as he gets around to Konig, something almost shy and evasive comes over that superbly arrogant manner.

"Morning, Maury."

"Morning, Paul. How are you?"

Konig's glance is so piercing that even the Deputy Mayor cannot confront him squarely. Instead, he veers sharply, moves on to shake other hands.

It's a curious sight, this highest emissary of the Mayor's office, glittering in an expensive hand-tailored suit, all puffing and swelling with self-importance, having just alighted from a shiny black limousine bearing the large, imposing shield of the City of New York on its bumper, having to give quarter to a shabby, rumpled figure with tousled hair and the look of a demented Old Testament prophet.

"Well," the Deputy Mayor blusters, "let's get on with it."

Carslin nods at the mound of fresh earth and the narrow trench with the two men, chest-high, grunting in it. At a loss for further conversation, the four men saunter back to the grave while the two state troopers lounge against the limousine.

"*Ashes to ashes,*" a voice chants softly inside Konig's head as he peers downward into the freshly dug grave. "*Ida Bayles Konig. Beloved wife of Paul. Endeared mother of—*"

The sharp chinking sound of metal impacting on metal. Then suddenly brass and wood coming into view.

"Ah—there we are," says Schroder.

Ropes are quickly produced, and shortly, with more grunting, the coffin, rising, teetering slightly, is hoisted out of the damp rectangle of earth and edged to one side of the grave.

Carslin and Schroder move quickly to the box. Kneeling, Carslin dusts a few crumbs of still-clinging earth from the brass plate and reads:

LINNEL GAINES ROBINSON
May 6, 1954, March 7, 1974

Benjamin moves up quickly beside Dr. Schroder. "You officially acknowledge this to be—"

"I do," Schroder murmurs, peering over Carslin's shoulder.

"We've set up a small lab and a microscope over in the rectory," says Carslin.

"Where's that?" Benjamin asks.

"Just a couple of hundred yards back down the road," one of the troopers calls from the limousine.

"Okay," says the Deputy Mayor with the finality of a judge gaveling a portentous decision. "Let's get on with it."

Konig shuffles forward. "Before you do, I suggest you open the lid slightly."

Benjamin glances queasily at Carslin.

"To release the gases," Konig goes on.

"By all means," Carslin replies, not to Konig but to the Deputy Mayor.

In the next moment the two Italian diggers have released thumbscrews and prized the lid slightly. There is a long, high hiss like the sound of a hermetically sealed jar of coffee being suddenly opened.

Moments later the box is hoisted onto the shoulders of the diggers and the two troopers. Carslin, Schroder, and the Deputy Mayor move out quickly behind the coffin.

"Aren't you coming?" Benjamin turns and calls back to Konig.

"No," says Konig, still hovering above the freshly dug grave. "I think I'll wait here."

Then, in a moment or so, watching the swaying procession wind its way down the auto path, he is alone there amid the chugging blackbirds, the chirruping of spring crickets, the long, neat aisles of placid stones.

"When did you ever—" the fierce, condemnatory voice cries again. *"When have we ever been able to—"*

The figure of a small girl, bangs, laughing eyes, dressed

in kilt and knee socks, wheels toward him on a tricycle
through the cluttered labyrinth of headstones.

"*Lolly.*"

"*You killed her.*"

"*Lolly.*"

"*You killed her.*"

"*I—*"

"*Yes, you did. You killed her—with that stupid, unfeel-
ing arrogance of yours.*"

It is to the figure of the child he talks, but the fierce,
strident voice that answers him is that of a young woman.

"*Lolly—Mother was very sick.*"

"*Never mind. You—*"

"*Incurably sick.*"

"*—rode all over her. You killed her just as surely as
if—*"

He has no words for her grief. He can barely shoulder
his own. "*Lolly—I—*" His voice trails off even as the tiny
kilted figure on the tricycle dematerializes. "*Lolly—*" he
murmurs again but he is staring down into the hollow,
gaping fissure of newly opened earth.

A short time later he sees the two troopers moving back
up toward the limousine. They're followed by Carslin and
the Deputy Mayor, chatting solemnly. Schroder trails a
few paces behind.

Something in the picture, something in the slope of their
shoulders and the way they walk and chat quietly now beside the limousine, the Deputy Mayor's head lowered, Carslin's head tilted slightly toward him, lips moving as if they
whispered words, tells Konig all he needs to know. Besides
which, Maury Benjamin's characteristically restive, ever-
seeking eyes now appear to be assiduously shunning him.

Schroder, hands thrust deep in pockets, shoulders
slightly hunched, comes shambling toward him. Their eyes
meet. Konig feels a sickness in the pit of his stomach, but
he is smiling broadly. "Well?"

"Leukocytic infiltration."

"Ah?" Konig says, feigning surprise, but he'd known it
all along.

"Quite pronounced," Schroder offers sympathetically.
"Want to see the slides?"

"No." Konig shrugs wearily. "No need."

The doors of the limousine and the troopers' wagon
swing open, bang shut, and without so much as a goodbye

nod, the Deputy Mayor, preceded by the trooper escort, rolls imperiously past the place where Konig stands and down the auto path toward the exits.

Shortly after, Schroder too drives off, and Konig is left alone with Carslin, while about the open grave the two workmen, laughing and chattering in Italian, gather up their tools.

"Well, Charley," says Konig with a burst of feeble cheer.

"Well?"

"What next?"

"Well," Carslin sighs, somewhat ruffled, his eyes evading those of his old teacher, "I'll have to file a complete report with the DA. Then I suppose—"

"A hearing," Konig says, completing the sentence for him.

"No doubt." Carslin's eyes scan up and down the cluttered aisles of stones as if they were searching for something there. "Look here, Paul. You have to understand. There's nothing—personal. It's simply a straightforward matter of—"

Konig waves him to silence. "Spare me the lecture on ethics. No recitations of the Hippocratic oath, please."

"I had no intention of—" Miffed, Carslin gazes into Konig's haggard face, transfixed by something strange and awful that he sees there. "Are you all right?"

"Yes. I'm fine. Why?"

"I don't know." Carslin seems embarrassed. "Something about the way you were looking at me just then."

"Oh?"

"I thought for a moment—"

"Yes?"

"I thought for a moment," Carslin murmurs, obviously having a difficult time, "you were going to ask me to do something I couldn't do."

Konig smiles. "I was—but only for a moment. You know, Charley, I'd never ask one of my old students to compromise himself to save my neck. I'd be awfully pissed off with you if you did. Goodbye, Charley." He thumps the younger man on the back, and as he weaves his way through the maze of headstones to his car, conscious of Carslin's eyes still burning on his back, his knees momentarily buckle. He totters, slips, and very nearly goes down. Hearing a rush of movement at his back, coming toward him, he recoveres his balance, thrusts his shoulders back, stiffens his carriage, kicks out smartly with his aching leg, and with a million confluent streams roaring in his head with something like the sound of rushing water, his eyes swimming before him, he lurches blindly to his car.

〰 32 〰

"Hello, Fergie."

"Hello, Paul."

"How's business?"

"Lousy. I trust things are the same with you."

11:30 A.M. OFFICE OF CHIEF MEDICAL EXAMINER.

"I got your buggies here," Ferguson Dell, Chief Curator, Department of Entomology, Museum of Natural History, wheezes into the phone. "Where'd you get these little beauties? No—don't tell me. It's probably something disgusting."

"*Calliphora,* aren't they?" Konig asks, doodling on a pad.

"Unquestionably."

"How old?"

"All depends." With a great gargle of sputum, Dell clears his throat. "Report here says the stuff they were found on had been submerged."

"That's right. I can't tell you how long it had been submerged, but the stuff wasn't down very far. A foot, maybe eighteen inches at the most. Lot of it probably washed up recently."

"Well, you've got to take that into account."

"I already have." Konig doodles furiously. "So what've you got for me?"

"Well, let's see," Dell says. "These little guys generally lay eggs on meat when it's fresh, less commonly when it's decayed."

"Putrefaction on this stuff was not too advanced."

"So you figure this thing took place pretty recently?"

"I didn't say that," Konig snaps. "I said that to my mind the putrefaction on this stuff wasn't too far advanced. He can hear Dell's puzzlement at the other end of the wire. "All I'm saying, Fergie, is that the normal factors that generally control the rate of putrefaction just don't apply here. Very little blood left in the bodies. Only partial viscera recovered, therefore hardly any gastrointestinal microorganisms to feed on and start to break down the tissue. So the whole process of decomposition is delayed. And the thing is further complicated because of the submersion of the stuff—temperature, excessive moisture. I'm trying to put the time picture together, but it's not easy. So I'm falling back on the maggots. What can you tell me?"

"Nothing's ever easy with you, is it, Paul?" Dell sighs wearily. "Well, this variety of maggot deposits its eggs in groups of about one hundred and fifty. Depending on the temperature of the environment, they hatch in—oh, say—from eight to fourteen hours. Cold weather delays the hatching."

"It's been pretty warm all month."

"Right. Unseasonably. Too goddamn warm for me. How I dread the summer."

"Skip the meteorology, will you, Fergie? Just get on with it."

"Okay—okay. All I'm saying is that in all probability that first hatching wasn't delayed by climatic conditions. So we can figure the eggs hatched in, say, eight to fourteen hours after they were deposited on the meat. And they were deposited not during the time of submersion but only after the stuff washed up."

"Okay," Konig grumbles. "Go on. Go on."

"I am, for Chrissake. What the hell's the matter with you, Paul? You all right?"

"Sure—I'm fine."

"You don't sound fine. You sound—"

"I'm fine. Fine. Never mind me. Let's get on with it." Konig scribbles large, intertwining circles on his pad.

A pause of consternation follows, then Dell continues. "Well, as I was saying, that first larval instar persists for eight to fourteen hours. Then the skin of that larva is shed and you get a second instar, similar to the first, but larger. These little guys hang around for two, three days. Do you follow so far?"

"I'm right with you, Fergie." Konig's face trembles and a large throbbing has begun to pound mercilessly at the back of his head.

"Then the third instar is your typical maggot. Typical little bluebottle *Calliphoras*—like those you've got here."

"How long do they feed?"

"They feed like pigs for six days," Dell goes on with mounting zest.

"How old are the ones I sent you?"

"Well, I'm looking right now at one of the largest you sent over, and I can tell you right now that the total life of this little bruiser could not have exceeded twelve days."

"Twelve at the outside," Konig mumbles and scribbles on his pad.

"But was probably less," Dell continues, "since from everything you tell me, it's highly unlikely that these eggs had been laid more than a day or two after the deposit of the remains in the river."

"I'm figuring two days for the tidal wash to have uncovered the remains."

"So," Dell continues, "put the age of the biggest larvae at ten days and that makes a period of twelve days from the time the body was deposited to the time you recovered these maggots. How does that jibe with your thinking?"

"Beautiful." Konig feels the surge of exhilaration that always comes when his own carefully thought out hypotheses have been confirmed. "Just from the state of the remains, I'd already jotted down in my notes a figure of ten to twelve days. That's perfect, Fergie. I'm very grateful to you and your buggies."

"How many bodies you find down there, anyway?"

"Two—I'm reasonably certain of that now."

"When did you find the stuff?"

"April twelfth."

"That means the poor beggars probably got it around April first."

"That's right." Konig's laugh is a snarl. "April Fool's Day."

No sooner had he hung up than the door bursts open and he stares at the short, burly figure of Detective Edward Flynn bulling his way through the door with plucky little Carver, yipping fiercely, like an enraged puppy, at his heels.

"What in God's—" Konig lumbers half out of his seat.

"He just come bustin' through, Doctor." Carver waves her arms wildly through the air. "I told him to wait."

"I ain't waitin' around here all day," Flynn blusters. "I got business too."

"I told him to wait, Doctor. He just come bustin' right on past me."

"That's all right, Carver. You can go now. Sit down, Flynn."

"I don't wanna sit," Flynn snaps. "I wanna stand."

"Stand then." Konig flings up his arms in exasperation. "Stand on your head if you like."

"Who's he to come bustin' in like that?" Carver mutters, deeply aggrieved. "He ain't nobody."

"All right, Marion." Konig, on his feet now, grips her under the elbow and steers her toward the door. "That's all right. You can go now, I said. I'll take care of this myself."

She's still muttering when the door closes behind her, and Konig turns back to the detective. "Now what the hell is all this about?"

"I'll tell you what the hell it's all—"

"First of all, stop your goddamn hollering. This isn't a bowling alley. It's a mortuary. There are mourners here. And the dead. Show some respect."

The argument works. A devout man, Flynn is mortified at his own unseemly behavior.

"Now sit down, Ed," Konig says assuagingly, grasping the fact that the detective's nose is still out of joint from their last phone conversation. In the next moment he thrusts a humidor at him. "Have a cigar."

Red-faced and puffing, a look of puzzlement in his eyes, Flynn reaches for one of the Chief's better cigars. But his hand stops in midair as if invisible forces held it there and something like suspicion creeps into his eyes. "I ain't forgettin' how you talked to me yesterday."

"Sorry about that." Konig's voice melts with a vaguely bogus contrition. "I had to get those heads. They meant everything to me just then. The difference between identifying and not identifying those poor bastards you dug up the other night."

"Don't tell me you got ID's on them already?"

"Not yet, but I'm getting there. Still, I had no business popping off at you like that. I'm sorry. Here—let me light that cigar for you." Konig whisks the Bunsen burner under Flynn's cigar and holds it there while the detective, perplexed and utterly buffaloed, sucks noisily while lighting it. Then, somewhat appeased, he leans back in his chair and puffs contentedly.

"Well, I had no business bustin' in like that either," he says. "Guess I was still just steamin' from that call."

"Okay," the Chief says abruptly. "We're even now. What can I do for you?"

"I just come to tell you that them swatches of skin you sent over to the lab the other day—"

"What about them?"

"We were able to lift a couple of prints off them. Left index, ring, and thumb."

"Fine. So?"

"So?" Flynn rears back. It was hardly the reaction he'd been expecting. Praise was what he'd been hoping for. A slap on the back. A hearty well done. Possibly even some paltry expression of gratitude. Not this jeering, irascible "So?" But, of course, he should have known better. Should not have been fooled by the cigar and the oddly soothing voice. Should have known that the Chief could not stay civil for more than five minutes at a stretch.

"So?" Flynn jeers right back. "So all I wanted to tell you was that I matched those prints to prints we found plastered all over that shack."

"So now you've got the scene of the crime. So what?" Konig shuffles coldly through the papers and the morning mail stacked on his desk. "With that goddamn bloody tub in there, did you ever doubt it?" Flynn starts to reply but Konig rushes right on. "How does any of that help me?" Konig bulls on ruthlessly.

"Well, after all, you've got—"

"What about that goddamn underwear you were blowing your horn about?"

"Well, Jesus Christ"—Flynn's face reddens—"if you'd just let someone else get a word in edgewise."

"Go on. Go on," Konig jeers. "I'm sitting here waiting for the past half-hour—"

"Christ—I ain't been here no half-hour."

Konig checks his watch. "Almost fifteen minutes. Sue me. Will you get to the goddamn point."

"I'm tryin' to—I'm tryin' to, goddamnit." Flynn reddens. "If you'd only let me—I've been tryin' to tell you that I wired Washington about the serial number we found in the waistband."

"You told me that yesterday. So what?"

"So"—the detective appears to be close to apoplexy—"today they wired back." He yanks a yellow sheet of telex paper from his inside pocket and starts to read in a high, shrill voice. "RA 12537744."

"Right."

"The serial number we found in—"

"—in the waistband. Right. Right."

"Belongs to a chap by the name of Browder, Sergeant Raymond Browder. 82nd Airborne, Fort Bragg, North Carolina."

"Fine. So you called Bragg. Where's Browder?"

"They don't know," Flynn says with barely smothered rage in his eyes. "Disappeared around sixteen months ago. Military authorities down there now report him as a deserter."

"So?"

"So—so—so," Flynn booms and a long white ash of cigar crumbles onto his jacket and into his lap. He slaps frantically at it as if he feared going instantly up in flames. "Is that all you can say? So? So? I'm tryin' to tell you somethin' and you just sit there like King Tut. Lordin' it over me like I was dirt. Treatin' me like a turd. Where the hell do you—"

"So," Konig mutters impassively, "tell me more."

"So I'm tellin' you," the detective goes on in a voice ominously low, restraining himself in an act of superhuman will. "This Browder, missin' sixteen months, is a thirty-five-year-old RA type. A paratrooper. Gung-ho career guy, if you get the picture."

"I get the picture."

"Fought in Vietnam. Got all kinds of decorations. DSC, Medal of Honor, Purple Heart. The whole shmeer. Right?"

"Right."

"So about sixteen months ago, the 82nd Airborne is put on alert. Activated and ordered back to Southeast Asia. Vietnam. You follow?"

"I follow."

"So the night before the unit's supposed to pull out, this Browder goes over the hill."

"You said that already."

"I know I did," Flynn smolders. "I know what the hell

I said. But right now, this minute, I'm sayin' this Browder looks like one of them fricasseed chickens you got glued together downstairs."

"So," murmurs Konig, leaning back in his chair, the tips of his fingers forming a bridge above the slight swell of his paunch. "So," he murmurs once again. But this time it is an entirely different so from all the others—the combative and jeering and derisory so's. These are full of rumination, conjecture, inward reflection. "So?"

Flynn leans back in his chair, puffing at his cigar, certain he has at last made his point. "So I sent your set of prints down to Bragg this morning. They'll check 'em against their set. We oughta hear something in forty-eight hours."

"Will they send medical records? Dental charts?"

"I spoke to the CO down there today," Flynn muses. "Funny."

"What's funny?"

"He was very tight-lipped. Evasive. Didn't wanna say too much over the phone." The detective drums the desk with his finger. "Got a feelin' there's somethin' funny about all this."

"But they *will* make medical records available?"

"Oh, sure," Flynn says. "I mean, I guess so."

"You guess so?"

"Well, I mean, they generally do. But this Captain Di-Lorenzo was a little strange."

The great dome of Konig's head nods drowsily. His red, sleepless eyes flutter and momentarily close. Rocking gently back and forth in his seat, he appears for just a moment to be dozing; to be far away, dreaming of some remote and tranquil time, of a place unsullied. "Well," he sighs at last, "I s'pose all we can do for the time being is sit tight and wait."

For a long while after Flynn's departure, Konig just sits there, rummaging dispiritedly through his mail. A letter from a missionary in Zaire querying him on a rare form of schistosomiasis. A physician in Tashkent with a question on blood grouping. An immunologist at Tulane who wants to know—

He sits there reading the same page over and over again, trying to concentrate and failing. He is still smoldering from the outrage of the morning, his humiliation before Carslin, who undoubtedly believed that it was he who performed the shoddy autopsy on the Robinson boy; who saw the moment of weakness in his face when he almost asked his former student to conceal his findings, bury the report, fudge it . . . anything, but save the department. And, of course, Carslin saw all that. Well, thank God he didn't ask. He didn't stoop to that. How much it would have pleased Carslin if he had. An opportunity to rise to new and stunning heights of self-righteous indignation. And that poor Robinson boy. He knew now that Robinson didn't hang himself in his cell, but instead was hanged there by guards who slipped a noose of mattress ticking around his neck and strung him up from an overhead joist after beating him to death. All that would come out now. Good. Some bastard down in the Tombs would pay for it all right. He'd see to that. But what of Strang? What part did he play in it? Was it really an oversight? Omitting to do a tissue study that was almost mandatory in cases such as this? He might be able to forgive mere carelessness. But if Emil Blaylock had gotten to Strang first—made promises, which Blaylock very well could. He was, after all, an extremely influential man in that serpent's nest, the top inner circle of the City bureaucracy. If such promises were made, Konig, who had some friends too—lower-echelon officials within the municipal penal system, people with a strong urge to rise quickly and no great scruples how they did so—would goddamned well find out and there would be hell to pay.

In the next moment Konig flicks a switch on his phone, picks up the receiver and hears Carver's voice on the other end.

"Yes, Doctor."

"Get me Bill Ratchett's office down at the Tombs," he snaps, then bangs the receiver back down. Once again he is sitting there fuming. Expecting at any moment the Deputy Mayor's phone call. The stern rebuke. The chilling admonitions. Hints of dire things to come, all uttered in the lofty verbiage of municipal officialdom, expressing His Eminence the Mayor's high moral dudgeon—"peeved—vexed—outraged—furious—repeat, *furious*—"

The buzzer on his phone sounds and it is Carver again. "Ratchett's not in, Doctor." Konig grumbles something about leaving a message to call back, slams the phone back down and rises. He has a need now to get away from his desk, away from his office, away from himself. In the next moment he is out his door, storming down corridors emptied by the noon lunch hour, clattering down the green descending spiral of Stairway D.

He has not been down to the mortuary since Haggard found him there in the early hours of the morning, but even at this late hour, four or five gurney carts are still lined up in the receiving area, their grisly cargoes still sacked in canvas, waiting to be unloaded into the huge purring refrigerators.

For a while, cut off from all the world above, he stands there waiting for the silence and the curious isolation of the place to soothe him. But standing there in noonday silence, he feels only estrangement, an alienation, a curious revulsion from things he had formerly loved. For the first time in his life he feels like a stranger here. Like a man who had inadvertently wandered into someone else's nightmare. Suddenly, the place to him is a horror, a freak show, and he must flee it. Get the stench of it out of his nostrils. Get back up to the sunlight and the fresh air above.

He turns, but in that moment he is suddenly aware of faint scratching noises coming from the autopsy suites behind him. At once, in his feverish, overwrought mind, he imagines more foul play. Who's in there now—at this hour when everyone is supposed to be out to lunch?

He crosses quickly to the doors leading to the autopsy rooms. Reaching there, he peers through the glass window panes set in the doors and sees there the tall, white-robed figure of Tom McCloskey hovering above the reconstructed Tinkertoy figures of Ferde and Rolfe. With a long steel tape, like a tailor measuring a man for a suit, the young man is very carefully taking limb and torso measurements, then tabulating them in a notebook.

Konig watches, with an odd pleasure, the quiet, purposeful motions of the young pathologist—all smooth, thorough, methodical. Then suddenly, for the flicker of an instant, Konig is forty years younger, a boy of twenty-three or so, just out of medical school. He is standing in that same suite of rooms, just where McCloskey is standing now, wearing just such a long, white, foolish surgical robe. Beside him stands old Bahnhoff, that black noisome cigar screwed into the center of his mouth, puffing furiously, and observing with a finicky vigilant eye the young man hovering there, above a flayed body, scalpel in hand, carrying out an extremely delicate arterial survey.

Such an ache comes suddenly upon him. Such a longing. Such a need to reach out and touch that moment again, drag it forcibly back across the spate of years, hug it to his chest as you would a lost child—those two figures lost irretrievably somewhere in the vanished years. As if he might simply walk through those doors and be that boy again. Stand there trembling beside old Bahnhoff, trying desperately to please him.

A rush of curious affection suddenly overtakes him. Not for the ghost of his vanished youth. That he knows was too mawkish and painful to feel anything other than contempt for. But it is rather an affection for young McCloskey with his tape measure and pad—and that ridiculous, ill-fitting surgical robe. Such affection. Such grief. If he could only warn the boy.

In the next moment, he turns and goes.

≈≈ 33 ≈≈

"Who did you say is the artist?"

"Emily Winslow. Name's right there in the corner."

"Oh, yes, of course . . . Winslow."

"Not terribly well known yet. But she will be."

1:00 P.M. THE FENIMORE GALLERY, MADISON AVENUE AND 67TH STREET.

"Greatly talented," says Konig.

"Yes, she is."

"Greatly talented," he murmurs again a little foolishly. "Greatly talented."

And for a while the two men stand there, Konig and Mr. Anthony Redding, gazing at the three little gouaches.

"And you just have the three?" Konig asks finally.

" 'Fraid so." Redding glances somewhat disapprovingly at the rumpled figure with tie askew and slightly demented eyes. "We've sold quite a bit of her painting though. This is all we have left. Unfortunately," he goes on apologetically, "these are not the most appealing of her works."

"Not appealing?" Konig's brow arches. "On the contrary, I find them very appealing. Oh, I s'pose there is a certain air of morbidity about them. I quite agree. But still I find they say something to me."

"You do?"

"Yes, I do," Konig goes on, fiercely protective, warming to his subject. "Something universal. I'm profoundly touched by them."

"You are?" An expression of puzzlement and suspicion mingles on Mr. Redding's sallow features. "Well," he goes on agreeably, "she is a superb draftsman. Unusual to see that kind of discipline in one so young."

"Is she young?" Konig asks slyly, enjoying in some odd way this utterly bogus role he plays.

"Yes, quite young. Early twenties, I should judge. I'm not sure. And utterly different from the other young painters of her generation, opportunists all trying to look chic and trendy. Winslow's not trendy at all. Not voguish. Not afraid to be conventional. A little old-fashioned. Not hung up on style for style's sake, and absolutely determined to master the tools of her craft. Yes, she has something to say. She is very good."

"Yes." Konig swells a bit with pride. Oddly enough, he's moved. At a loss for words. Once again his eyes pore hungrily over the three little canvases. Displayed rather prominently as they are in this sleekly elegant gallery, exuding opulence and taste, they seem to take on a curious air of importance. Oddly enough, he's impressed. But still, the paintings are profoundly sad. That woeful little shack in the burned-out field—so desolate, so forlorn. And even more disturbing, the study of broken glass, lethal little shards. And then the soiled underpants moldering in the fetid shadows of some tenement gloom. Something like a shiver courses through him.

"I'll take the three," says Konig suddenly.

"You will?"

"Yes, of course." Konig is a little shocked at the sound of his own voice. As if someone else had spoken those rash words. "I said so, didn't I?"

A look of something like wariness comes into Redding's eyes. This man in his tatty suit—hardly the sort of person he's accustomed to selling paintings to.

"They're not inexpensive," Redding says rather grandly.

"I hardly imagined they would be," Konig snaps, matching the grandeur.

The gallery owner is baffled. Somewhat at a loss. Not certain whether the man is a wealthy eccentric or merely a crackpot in off the street. "I can let you have the three for fifteen hundred," he offers cautiously, half expecting the man to bolt out the door.

"Fine," says Konig, whipping out his checkbook. "You will take a check?"

"Certainly," says Redding, suddenly in a tizzy. Even his British accent lapses. "Come right this way to my desk, Mr.—"

"Konig."

"Yes. Of course. Mr. Konig. Come right this way. We'll make out the papers."

Redding, on little maroon velvet pumps, scurries up to the front of the gallery, with Konig trailing a short distance behind.

Redding slips easily into the Mies chair behind the elegant little escritoire. "You have some identification, Mr. Konig?"

"Certainly."

The gallery owner glances through driver's license, registration, AMA card, jotting down details. "Ah, I see it's not Mr. but Dr. Konig," he says, by this time glowing with that kind of benevolence that only hard cash can engender in a merchant's heart. "Very good, Doctor," he says, handing back the identification. "I think you've chosen quite shrewdly. This girl's work is going to be quite valuable some day. Funny, you know, only the other day, another gentleman was in here inquiring about her."

"Another gentleman?" Konig's eyes narrow to slits. "Who?"

"A very big collector from the Middle West. I'm not at liberty to divulge his name, you understand."

"Yes, of course," says Konig, his curiosity raging. "I don't suppose you could tell me what he looked like?"

Redding seems startled by the request, yet for Dr. Konig and his checkbook, he seems eager to comply. He laughs a little uneasily. "Well—he was a big man. Quite tall; white curly hair—"

As Redding drones on animatedly, it suddenly dawns

on Konig that the big collector from the Middle West was obviously Frank Haggard, and that Mr. Anthony Redding is lying in his teeth.

"—and that's why I say, Doctor," he effuses, "you made a very sound investment today. Within the next few years Winslow's work is going to be very much in demand. Big people are beginning to take notice. If you'd like, I can have those three gouaches sent up to you in Riverdale today."

"No—I'll take them with me."

"But—"

"That's all right," Konig says emphatically. "They're small."

"Well"—Redding shrugs—"you're the boss, Doctor." He giggles a little foolishly. "If you can wait just a minute, I'll have my boy pack them for you."

Redding scurries to the back of the gallery where Konig can hear him calling down to someone on the floor beneath. In a few minutes he returns, face glowing unnaturally, and carrying a three-foot-by-four-foot package wrapped in brown paper.

"A fantastic coincidence, Doctor," Redding bubbles excitedly. "I was just down in our storeroom. We had a shipment come in around two weeks ago. Most of the stuff is not even unwrapped yet, just sitting around down there waiting to be catalogued and inventoried. Anyway, look what I found right on the top of the heap."

He thrusts the package at Konig. Large, black Crayola letters in the upper left-hand corner read: "Emily Winslow. 324 Varick Street. New York City."

Suddenly Konig's legs are trembling beneath him.

"Shall we open it, Doctor?"

"Yes," says Konig, his mouth suddenly dry. "By all means."

"I'm dying to see it myself." Redding slashes the cords rather gleefully with an Exacto razor. Then the two of them are tussling with the wrappings. Beneath the coarse brown outer wrapping is a layer of newssheet lying directly over the canvas. They lift that in turn and then step back.

For a long moment Konig stands there gazing down at the canvas, not speaking, seeing only a flood of color and light—grays, greens, blues, dazzling ocher, and yellows. Then gradually a configuration of line and motion come together on the canvas, and suddenly Konig is aware of cold sweat erupting on his forehead. His legs buckle and he nearly sags.

"Marvelous," Redding enthuses, unaware of Konig's reaction beside him. "Isn't it marvelous? Look at the gorgeous way she's handled—"

Konig's feverish eyes range avidly over the familiar lines of his house in Montauk. There it is, lovingly recreated. Every last detail of it—windows, balconies, decks, shrubbery, the dunes running out from the back of it. And there's the high sand bluff on which it sits, the long sweep of empty beach below, and beyond that a gray-green slab of gently undulant surf, glinting with sunlight, unfolding like a scroll onto the beach below.

But it is not that, not simply that, that has caused his wrenched heart to slug so in his chest, beneath his shirt, like a huge mallet. It is the face in the center of the canvas, the dear, beloved face of Ida Konig smiling out at him from beneath the huge brim of an old, floppy sunbonnet. How well he knew that bonnet. It is still out there in Montauk, stored away somewhere in the attic in a stack of cartons that contain the rest of her things, hastily packed and stored away when she died. Her eyes smile warmly out at him. She is kneeling in the garden, her garden, with huge blood-red poppies nodding all about her. The poppies seem like living creatures, tall, slender, graceful things with fiery heads. They delight in her presence.

The painting is literally awash with sunlight. Suffused with love. And in all that dazzling incandescence of feeling, there is only one shadow—rather large and portentous —a gray eminence framed in an upstairs window. It is a faceless figure staring down on the scene below, and though it is small in relation to the size of the painting, it nevertheless succeeds in casting a pall over everything else in the canvas. It is as if the artist, having succeeded out of love (for the painting was pure love) in recapturing some precious moment of her past, then had, for inscrutable reasons, known only to herself, to ruin it, deface it, sully it, with this rather dirty thumbprint stain of gray.

"Simply smashing," Mr. Anthony Redding enthuses, manufacturing fresh banalities in his quickly regained fraudulent British accent.

"I'll take it," Konig says. He can barely speak. His voice is choked.

"Oh, but Doctor—I'm afraid—"

"I'll take it." Konig turns fiercely on him.

Redding gapes into that wild, demented face. "But I don't even know what to ask. I have to at least consult the artist."

"Then consult her. Speak with her," Konig shouts, scarcely fathoming his own words.

"But I can't." Redding pleads, now genuinely terrified of the madman standing there before him. "I can't. I haven't been able to reach her in weeks. I've got money here for her. A few thousand in addition to what you've just given me. She must be out of town. She'll be back. Listen—the minute I get in touch with her, I'll—"

"I have to have it now." Konig snatches the painting. Redding tries in turn to snatch it back. Then for a moment or two they do an idiotic little dance, a tug of war with the canvas jerking back and forth between them.

"Doctor—please, please, Doctor."

"I'll pay you whatever you want."

"I can't," Redding pleads, "at least not until—"

"I must have it now." Konig's voice brings Redding up sharply. Something he's heard in that strangled sob alerts him, tells him something is profoundly wrong here. At the same time his shrewd merchant's mind is quickly computing a hefty price to attach to the painting, as well as exacting a neat profit for himself in the transaction.

At last Redding sighs, letting go his end of the canvas, capitulating nobly, as if he'd fought the good fight. "I don't think I can let it go for a penny less than three thousand." As he utters the figure, even he is a little awed at his own audacity. But there is in this man, this wild, rumpled apparition, with the mad eyes and the awful odor of hospital antiseptic all about him, clutching the painting in one hand and waving a checkbook at him with the other, something that tells Redding to try to get shut of the man. Get his money and get him out of there as quickly as possible.

Together they stagger back up to the front of the gallery, Konig still clutching the painting, refusing to relinquish it for even a minute. Even as he scribbles another check, he holds tight to the canvas with his free hand.

Redding dabs petulantly at his brow with a silk foulard, muttering, "Highly irregular. Highly irregular."

"Here's your check."

"Are you taking the big one with you, too?" Redding leans back, exhausted.

"Yes."

"Then at least let me wrap it so that you don't damage—"

"No time now."

"It'll take just a minute."

"No time—no time." Konig backs toward the street door, bowing and smiling foolishly, canvases jammed under both arms.

"Are you sure you're all right?" Redding, terrified, trails him out.

"I'm fine. Fine."

"Dr. Konig." Redding cries after him.

Startled, Konig turns. "Yes?"

"You're her father, aren't you?"

For a moment they stand there gawking at each other across a troubled space. Then in the next moment, Konig is out on the street, in the warm April sunlight of Madison Avenue. Running. Jostling through startled lunchtime crowds. Flying like a wild man, not even aware that he is crying.

≈≈ 34 ≈≈

"Digital imprint on wine bottle in kitchen."

"Sixteen ridge characteristics in agreement with left forefinger."

"Digital imprints on plate in kitchen sink."

"Fourteen and ten ridge characteristics in agreement with left middle and ring fingers respectively."

2:20 P.M. PRINT LAB, 17TH PRECINCT, NYPD.

"Digital imprint on canister of gelignite Type C in front foyer."

"You got there sixteen ridge characteristics in agreement with right middle finger. Imprints of finger and thumb also identical."

Haggard scribbles hastily on his pad. "What's that left palmar imprint on the dining-room table look like?"

Sergeant Leo Wershba holds a set of print cards up to the light, scanning them quickly with his bright, shrewd eyes. "Pretty messy," he says after a while. "It was a glass tabletop and it looks like somebody wiped it. But we got thirteen ridge characteristics in agreement."

Haggard sighs, snaps his pad shut, and leans back in his chair. "Looks pretty good, doesn't it?"

"Couldn't look better, Frank. This is your boy."

For a while the two men regard each other silently.

"Lemme see that ugly puss again," the detective growls.

Wershba tosses a standard police mug shot across the desk at Haggard, who lights a cigarette while studying it intently. "Janos Klejew— How the hell you pronounce that?"

"Klejewski—the w is silent."

"Klejewski." Haggard says it over and over again, forming the word slowly with his lips. "Lovely-looking boy, isn't he?"

"I'm sure his mother thinks so." Wershba, a short, moon-faced man with a bald head and enormous compensatory mustache, smiles brightly. "I got a book on this guy as thick as the Manhattan Yellow Pages."

"Klejewski." Haggard resumes his quick, barely audible lipreading. "Known to associates as Kunj or Kunje. Has repeatedly been identified with persons who advocate the use of explosives and may have acquired firearms. Considered extremely dangerous."

The detective's eyes range over the broad, flat, slightly acromegalic features. They are thick and not at all sharply defined. There is, too, something profoundly disquieting about the eyes, a blank, drowsy quality beyond which lurks an air of easily eruptible violence.

"Big mother, ain't he?" says Wershba, reading the detective's thoughts.

"Got any leads?"

"Maybe. Who knows? Nothing that amounts to very much anyway. Got an all-points out for him now, but the guy's been at large two years. Busted out of stir twenty-three months ago. And this bombworks up on Fox Street is the first pickup we got on him in all that time."

"What was he in for?"

"Arson—Kunje has a fondness for matches and big firecrackers."

Haggard nods slowly. "Where'd you say he busted from?"

"I didn't. But it was Danbury."

"Danbury?" The detective ponders the word aloud, his fingers drumming on the arm of his chair. "Wasn't that where—"

"—Meacham was," Wershba says, glowing like a Christmas light. "Right you are, pal. That's where the two lovelies met."

"Jesus." Haggard's fist cracks loudly in the palm of his hand. "If I can only get my hands on the son of a bitch he'll lead me right to Meacham."

"What makes you so sure they're not together right now?"

"No way." Haggard shakes his head. "All you hadda do was see this place up in The Bronx. Clothes in the drawers, food still on the plates in the kitchen. They left prints all over the place. They got out fast. Then all of 'em split. Went separate ways."

"What makes you so sure?"

"A mob that size? Eight or nine freaks traveling together? Stand out like a sore thumb. Nope—they split, probably with plans to meet at some future time. Meacham and maybe two, three of the other freaks took the girl with them. The rest of 'em all went their own ways." Haggard hops to his feet and starts pacing. "Identify any of the other prints up there?"

"Not yet. Still working on it. But Meacham and Klejewski we got nailed. Both on the Fox Street place and the loft on Varick. We'll get you the others too. All we need is a little time."

"That's all you got, Wershba. Just a little. If I read this Meacham right, he isn't giving us much more than that."

"Humerus—32.3 centimeters."

"Is that left or right?"

"Right. But the left is the same."

2:30 P.M. MORTUARY. MEDICAL EXAMINER'S OFFICE.

"Radius—23.3 right, 23.2 left." Tom McCloskey deftly completes tape measurements of a set of upper limbs and proceeds without pause to the legs. "Femur—43.1 centimeters right, 43.1 centimeters left. Tibia is 34 on both right and left."

"Thirty-four both right and left tibia." Pearsall jots figures quickly on a pad. "So directly measured with trunk length, neck, head, lower limbs, and deducting the two centimeters for postmortem lengthening, that puts our friend Rolfe at 188 centimeters. Right?"

"Right." McCloskey nods. "Say about six feet two inches."

"About six feet two inches." Pearsall scribbles on his pad. "Okay. What do we have on Ferde?"

"Nothing as good as we have on Rolfe."

They have both fallen quickly into the use of the adoptive names with which Konig has christened the dismembered corpses and taped to each of their wrists the night before.

"Since the torso's incomplete, I had to rely entirely on the Pearson formulae."

"No choice, really." Pearsall sighs and peers through bottle-thick lenses at McCloskey's carefully elaborated tables of computation. "At best, all we can say we have then on Ferde is a projection of stature based on average proportion of limbs in relation to total stature."

" 'Fraid so." McCloskey shrugs. "With a built-in probability of error of two to eight centimeters."

"Which I see you've already figured in," Pearsall says,

studying the chart. "So with all things considered, you put Ferde at—"

"One hundred and sixty-four centimeters."

"Small—five feet four, five feet five."

"Roughly speaking. And I still find the sex ambiguous."

Pearsall glances up, a little surprised. "You do?"

"Sure. No lower torso. No pelvis. No genitalia. That's pretty ambiguous right there."

"You used Pearson's tables for sexing the limbs?"

"I did. And it's still ambiguous. Could be either a female or a very small male."

"What about secondary sex characteristics?"

"Nothing conclusive. There are just too many variables and overlappings in the secondary system. And all that hair and musculature stripped from the body." McCloskey shrugs again. "I just don't know."

Pearsall, followed by the younger man, walks back to the long steel tables where the two reassembled corpses lie supine and oblivious, like sarcophagi figures—ancient kings, newly excavated.

Pearsall begins a casual examination of the corpse called Ferde. First he studies the head and face, or what remains of them. Because the skin has been completely peeled from the skull and face, except for two tiny patches, the hair of neither head nor face remains to give any hint of sex.

"What about the larynx?"

McCloskey smiles wearily. "See for yourself."

In the next moment, Pearsall, armed with tape and calipers, is measuring the cadaver's larynx.

When Ferde's head was severed from the trunk, the larynx had remained attached to the head. The level of decapitation was between the fourth and fifth cervical vertebrae. And, although the larynx normally extends down to the sixth cervical vertebra, Ferde's was so small that it was found almost *in situ* above the plane of severance, which extended backward from the level of the lower border of the chin.

Pearsall is well aware that the larynx of a man is, on the whole, about one-third larger than that of a woman. The average length of the adult male larynx is nearly two inches. That of the female, about an inch and a half. Ferde's larynx on Pearsall's calipers measures 3 centimeters, or less than an inch and a quarter.

"That *is* a small larynx for a male." Pearsall shakes his head perplexedly. "Even a very young male. How old did you figure this one?"

"Just based on limbs and skull sutures," McCloskey stares ceilingward and computes aloud, "oh, I'd say between eighteen and twenty."

"Odd," Pearsall ponders aloud. "A larynx of that size in a male of that age."

"Couldn't agree with you more." McCloskey nods. "That's why I say it's ambiguous."

"I wonder where Paul gets the idea this is a male?"

"Beats me. If it is, it's a very small one."

" 'Lo chaps," a voice booms cheerily behind the two men. They turn in time to see Carl Strang breeze through the swinging doors and bound energetically up to them. He stops dead in his tracks, seeing the consternation on their faces. "My, my, pitched in gloom, you two. So sober. So earnest."

Pearsall's brow furrows. "We're stuck on the sex of this damned thing."

"The Chief seems pretty sure it's a male," McCloskey says.

"Oh?" Strang's eyes sweep quickly over the corpse and settle on the paper wrist tag. He tilts his head to read it. "Ferde, ay? Doesn't look like any Ferde to me."

Pronounced at once and with such finality as to give it the ring of Holy Writ, both Pearsall and McCloskey are momentarily stunned. Strang continues. "It's perfectly clear to me this little beauty is a female, and it's not simply the fancy fingernail polish either. Just look at the stature of the thing—the limbs, the larynx."

"We've just been all through the limbs and larynx," Pearsall mutters impatiently.

But Strang barges ahead cheerily. "I don't have to measure the damned thing to see it's the larynx of a small female—say about nineteen or twenty. And for Chrissake, look at the skull. That's no male skull. See how delicate it is. How effeminate. Feeble superciliary arches. Thin orbital margins. Vertical slope. Distinct frontal eminences. And just look at those occipital and mastoid regions. Small mastoid process. No muscular markings. My God—you can read it like a book. That's no male, chaps. That's a lady. A poor, sweet young thing come to a sticky finish." Strang's lecture concludes with a triumphal flourish, a burst of laughter, and patronizing good will for his baffled colleagues. "Now cheer up, the both of you."

But Strang's breeziness, his absolutely unhesitating certainty, rather than relieving their doubts, have only pitched them into deeper gloom.

"You make it sound very convincing, Carl." Pearsall frowns.

"It *is* convincing because it's true. You know it's true. Both of you." Strang's manner has gone from good will to that of faintly amused scorn. "Know what's wrong with you chaps? Not only you two but all of this damned staff around here. You're all afraid to think for yourselves. To make an independent judgment. And do you know why? I'll tell you why." Strang smiles and there's a spiteful glint in his eyes. "It's because you've all had your balls cut off by the man upstairs. Dr. Big. Lord God Almighty, for whom we labor daily to his greater glory. He sticks a male name tag on the wrist of a stiff and even though all your training, all your experience, tell you that stiff is a female, you can't get yourself to believe that you're right and Dr. Big is wrong. What a funk. What a goddamned pitiful funk you're all in."

McCloskey stands there frozen speechless. Pearsall's frown has turned to a glower. A broad swatch of crimson has leaped to his throat and is now beginning to flame up his cheeks. "That's true, Carl," his voice chokes. "What you say is perfectly true. We do listen to Paul Konig. Wait for his final reading on a case. What Paul Konig has already forgotten, most of us have yet to learn. He knows more in his little finger than the whole goddamned total of us combined." He struggles to suppress the tremor in his voice. "Now if Paul Konig has come in here and tagged this cadaver Ferde, it's because it damned well is a Ferdinand and not a Sally or a Joan. If Paul Konig says this poor battered, chopped-up heap of flesh and bone is a male cadaver, then it damned well is a male cadaver. Konig is the Chief, and when Konig speaks, he knows. He's proved that time and time again in more cases and throughout more years than I care to remember. He's got a track record no one else in this business has ever come close to. That's why, Carl, when Konig speaks, we listen. He's the Chief and he's still the best. When you're the Chief, hopefully we'll be able to listen to you too."

≋ 36 ≋

"Sarcoma . . . myeloid . . . bone-marrow tumor . . . metastases . . . widespread massive invasion . . . three, four months at best."

"Lie."

"No lie . . . true . . . sorry . . . sorry . . . sorry."

Words, echoes in a locked room. A shuttered house. Dust of old lost summers. Sand blown beneath a door. Shuttered windows. Furniture shrouded in sheets. Cold floors covered with strips of yellowing newspaper. Small black pellets of mouse droppings and the tracks of innumerable small wild things everywhere in evidence. The creatures of dune and moor who have huddled there for winter.

"How can they be so sure?"

"Biopsy. X rays. Three of the biggest radiologists in the country . . . No mistake."

"What did Brainford say?"

"Hopeless."

"And Keefer."

"He said 'cut.' "

"Then in God's name why not?"

Sun flooding through an upstairs window beyond which can be seen a flat gray disk of ocean, timeless and immense, spreading to the sky. So still it seems almost to have been painted there. And from just below the window sounds the quick, purposeful click of garden shears.

"Because it would be futile. They have to take off a leg. Why put her through the torture?"

"But if there's a chance—any chance—one in a million. Why not?"

"Because there is no chance."

"Then why did Keefer say cut?"

"Because he didn't know what else to say. Because he's a surgeon and 'cut' is almost axiomatic with surgeons. They say it the way you and I say 'eat' and 'sleep.' "

"And you're willing to take the responsibility of saying 'Don't cut'?"

"I saw the X rays myself, Lolly. I saw the biopsy reports. Completely invaded. Massive involvement. Why torture and mutilate? For a few additional months of agony? And that's a fallacy too. Soon as you touch these damned things they spread like wildfire."

Click . . . Click . . . Click. The garden shears, like the tick of time, click inexorably in the garden below. And the tall, striking lady in the wide-brimmed floppy sunbonnet moves placidly on all fours through a profusion of blood-red poppies, causing the great fiery heads to nod gently on their tall stalks as she passes by. The plucking of each, taken in the moment of their fullest glory, is like an augury of her doom.

"What will it be like?"

"At first, nothing much. Anemia. Neuralgic pain. Then swellings on ribs and skull. Then spontaneous fractures. Very painful."

"And she agreed?"

"Agreed to what?"

"To do nothing? Not even try?"

"Lolly, your mother and I have decided . . ."

"You decided? What the hell does it have to do with you?"

". . . to live these last few months together calmly."

"I repeat: What the hell does that decision have to do with you?"

"Calmly, I said, Lolly. Without tirades and histrionics, which we can all do without. She says she would like to stay out here. I've already arranged for a leave of—"

"So it's all agreed. All decided. What gall. What arrogance."

"Lolly—please stop shouting. She can hear you down there."

"Just let her die—without even trying."

"That is your mother's wish. I respect it. It's very

wise. If you'd seen as many of these sarcomas as I have
—and the aftermath of surgery—"

"That's just your own personal prejudice. You hate
surgeons. You hate all other doctors. Because you're jealous. They have all the glory and prestige of saving lives
while you do nothing but poke around with dead flesh in
a hell-house, a ghoul show that's little better than an
abattoir."

"It's true," he says, aching, full of hurt because she
could never respect his work. It hurt him that his job was
a source of embarrassment to his daughter. It always had
been. Once, when she was still a child, no more than eight
or nine, he overheard her chatting with another little girl,
describing her father as a "great healer." She carried that
embarrassment into adolescence and young maturity. It
hurt him. Not so much that she had to lie about his work,
but that he wasn't a great healer in her eyes. His work
had nothing whatever to do with healing. He was not the
least bit interested in healing.

"Yes, it's true—I do distrust most doctors. I am sus-
picious of surgeons with a lot of fancy, self-serving initials
after their names. Most are numbskulls who don't know a
tumor from a wart, and I will not permit your mother to
be the guinea pig for some prima donna's megalomania.
But the men I took your mother to I trust. I took her to
these men because I have the highest regard for their
work."

"And one of them told you to operate. To cut."

"Because, as I said, there was nothing else he could tell
me. I could look in his eyes and see that. But I don't need
Keefer to tell me what the prognosis is for your mother.
With or without surgery. And if you want to talk about
abattoirs, I'll tell you a few things about the surgical
ward. I'd be glad to take you to one and let you see for
yourself. In the absence of any real hope, that's an ab-
attoir I will not subject your mother to."

"Goddamn you."

"Lolly, for God's sake—"

"You've written her off. Goddamn you. You killed her."

"Lolly."

"You killed her. You killed her. You killed her."

3:00 P.M. KONIG'S OFFICE.

Voices reverberating. Receding through the shadows
of the dying afternoon. Paul Konig's wet, red eyes stare

fixedly at the sun-flooded canvas propped on the arms of the chair opposite his desk. And even as the colors of it waver and fade, the foreground of the painting with the bright, smiling face of the doomed lady moving serenely through the poppies, a nimbus of light glowing all about her, still shimmers brightly before him. But up above, in the right-hand corner of the painting, where a breeze-blown curtain billows gently outward from an upper casement, there is still the large gray spot, the gray eminence . . . shapeless, oddly foreboding. It is, he knows, the single bitter note in a canvas otherwise flooded with love. And looking at it, ever more closely, he also knows quite well, quite beyond any reasonable doubt, that the spot, that dirty gray stain, like some obscene unspeakable filth, is without question himself.

Somewhere far away a phone rings. Three . . . four . . . five times. Eyes still riveted on the smiling visage in the sun-drenched painting, Konig reaches for the phone on his desk.

"Hello."

"Deputy Mayor for you, Doctor." The warm, husky tones of Carver's voice summon Konig back once more into the real world. He sighs and feels a throb of tension commencing at the back of his head.

"Put him on," he growls.

So here it is at last. Sooner, actually, than he'd expected. He'd thought they'd at least spend a few days whispering amongst themselves behind closed doors. Planning a campaign of retribution and self-righteous face-saving. The Mayor and the forces of justice combining to ferret out mischief and incompetence within City agencies. What the editorial writers are wont to call "housecleaning." Castigation and disgrace. But very gentle, of course. Civilized. Full pension. Early retirement for reasons of health. The mushy cudgel of justice in high places.

"Hello, Paul." Maury Benjamin's voice is gruff with fatigue. "Long day?"

"They get longer as you get older, Maury."

"Nasty up there today. Don't like cemeteries. Opening that box. Watching Carslin go through that grisly charade—"

Konig chuckles wearily. "Bet you could hardly get your lunch down at Caravelle."

"Don't be funny, Paul. You've got yourself a peck of trouble here."

"How much is a peck?"

"What?"

"Never mind. How much does the Mayor know?"

"How should I know? He reads the papers. He's got a mob of people on payroll around here with fancy salaries and nothing better to do all day than whisper in his ear. This body-snatching thing infuriated him. And now the Robinson business. You know your friend Carslin has been down here all afternoon beating war drums about that. He tends to beat louder when he sees a reporter around. I don't like your friend Carslin."

"Charley? I don't see why." Konig's fingers pry loose the cap from the phial of amyl nitrite in his lower drawer. "Very talented boy."

"He's a goddamned fink. Self-righteous, self-serving, stuffed-ass, son-of-a-bitch prig."

"All of that?" Konig chuckles and pops the small span-sule into his mouth.

"Like all the rest of them," the Deputy Mayor fumes into the receiver. "Whoring after a bit of glory."

"Which you've never done. Right, Maury?" Konig taunts wickedly. "You've never been interested in ripping off a bit of glory here and there."

"I've never been so goddamned brazen about it, like these guys."

"Nothing wrong with a bit of glory," Konig goes on, chuckling. "Good for the soul. And more important, the blood pressure. Glory has a salubrious effect on the blood pressure."

"Your blood pressure won't be too salubrious, my friend, now that Carslin's report has hit the DA's desk." The high, shrill, accusatory thing is back in Benjamin's voice. "Don't expect any favors here."

"I'm too old to expect favors, Maury." Konig smiles wearily into the receiver. "When the DA is ready to see me, I'll be there."

There is a pause in which the two men listen to each other breathing through the receiver.

"Maury?"

"Paul?"

Their voices collide and halt but it is Benjamin who

quickly takes up the slack. "Paul—don't you want to tell me something?"

"No."

"I don't see why you should take the heat for some son of a bitch who did a sloppy job down there."

"My sloppiness too. I never questioned the report."

"You've got thousands of reports to process. How can you possibly question every one of them?"

Konig can now sense in the Deputy Mayor's beseeching voice, in his thread of reasoning, an old friend already building a line of retreat for him. A way out. "Forget it, Maury. Who conducted what autopsy around here is strictly the Chief's business and the Chief's business only. That was one of Bahnhoff's cardinal principles and it's a good one. The man who did the PM on the Robinson boy is one of my deputies. I know what he did and I'll deal with him in my own way—privately, in this office. But don't expect to ever learn his name."

There's another pause in which Konig can hear the agitated breathing of the Deputy Mayor's mounting fury.

"Okay, my friend," Benjamin finally snarls. "That's fine with me. Remember, I told you that Calvary was coming. Well, get that old crown of thorns out. It's just about here. And when it comes I'm sure you'll love every minute of it. God—you are a fool."

Konig hunches wearily over the phone and nods his head. "You run your office, Maury. Let me run mine."

"Well, quite frankly, my friend," Benjamin snarls, "I don't think you'll be running yours too much longer. If you think your press was bad the other day, wait'll you see tomorrow morning's. I tried to keep Carslin quiet but the minute he saw those reporters he swung right into his Lincoln Steffens number—that ol' muckrackers' shuffle. That's all I have to say. PS—the DA wants you down here Friday."

"What for?"

"What for?" Benjamin starts to giggle a little insanely. "What for? Listen to the man. Oh, I can't believe it. What for? Why, to have a cup of tea. Talk about the funnies. Swap dirty jokes. What would you think for?"

"What time does he want me there?" says Konig, wanting very much to get off the phone.

"Ten A.M.," Benjamin shouts. "Repeat, ten A.M.—
Friday. You be there, goddamn it," Benjamin howls
through the speaker. "What in God's name was wrong
with you up there today? My God—you looked awful."

⚡ 37 ⚡

"Twenty-nine out of the full complement of thirty-two
teeth gone. Fifteen of those old extractions, fourteen recent."

"Postmortem?"

"No doubt. See how the bones healed in the old extractions and the sockets closed completely? Now look
at the recent."

"No clotting."

"Right. And the sockets are still open. Those were
yanked to make identification by charts impossible."

3:20 P.M. DENTAL LAB, MEDICAL EXAMINER'S OFFICE.

Dr. Barnett Rossman, forensic odontologist, squints up
at a series of freshly developed X rays illuminated on a
scanner. The room in which the two men stand is full of
skulls, jawbones, grinning dentures mounted on stands,
plaster casts of jaws and mandibles with teeth set in them.
And all around them teeth—thousands of teeth—and gold
crowns, and the air reeking with the thick, smarting
fumes of the hypo in the developing tanks.

"And something else," Rossman goes on. "Those extractions were made with dental forceps, and by someone
who knew how to use them."

"Oh?" Konig's brow cocks upward. "Anything else?"
He scribbles something onto a pad under a list of general
data headed "ROLFE."

Rossman shrugs. "With only three teeth left in the jaws,
there's not a helluva lot to go on. And two of those three
are just stumps—the upper left second premolar and the
third molar. The other one—the lower right third molar—

has a crown, but the tooth's nearly completely destroyed by that large cavity you see there."

Together the two men ponder the ghostly gray-white illuminations on the screen.

"But here's something that might be of interest." Rossman jabs a pencil up toward one of the illuminated negatives. "Look at this area right here. See the gap? Upper left lateral incisor, canine, and first premolar?"

"It's continuous," says Konig, catching instantly the seed of an idea.

"Right. Would have been very obvious and very unsightly during life, unless—"

"—he wore a denture," Konig says, completing the thought.

"A possibility. Probably a Nesbitt type. Lousy dentistry. Anyway, I took a few X rays of the upper left second premolar."

"And?"

"Well, see for yourself." Once more Rossman's pencil jabs upward at something that looms on the screen like an immense Arctic ice floe seen through curling mists. "See how the convex surface of the stump is nearly level with the gum? There's a complete root canal there. Has the appearance of having been recently ground with a dental drill."

Konig glances away from the screen. "Meaning that at one time the stump might have carried a supporting clasp for a denture."

"I'd say so." Rossman beams. "I'd say very probably."

Konig scribbles hastily onto his pad. "Anything you can tell me about the age, Barney?"

Rossman sighs, removes his bifocals and set them carefully on the desk, then proceeds to slowly rub his eyes. "Well, all the wisdom teeth were erupted. Two of them shed for some considerable time. So he had to be over twenty-five years of age. Afraid that's all I can offer you there."

"Over twenty-five," Konig murmurs aloud as he scribbles more notes. "Well, at least that gives me the lower range. I've got an upper range in my figures here of about forty to forty-five. Truth probably lies somewhere in between those limits, but I'd say more toward the upper."

"What'd you get from the skull?"

Konig licks his thumb and flicks back several pages

through the pad, his eyes skimming up and down the dirty, hectic scrawl there. Slowly, he starts to read aloud. " 'Cloture of sagittal, coronal, lambdoidal sutures nearly complete.' That starts somewhere around age thirty. Then I found incipient cloture of the parietomastoid and squamous sutures on the inner surface. You don't get that till somewhere between thirty-five and forty."

"What about the limb bones?" asks Rossman.

Konig starts to mumble over his pad again. " 'Epiphyseal ends of all limb bones completely united.' That takes place between twenty-two and twenty-five years. Which jibes with your minimum figure of twenty-five."

"So you're between twenty-five and forty-five, but leaning toward the upper limit?"

"Only because of the skull sutures and the amount of calcification at the epipyhses. There was also a great deal of ossification in the thyroid and cricoid cartilages, and osteoarthritic changes in the right hipbone—sacroiliac joint. Lipping changes in the cervical vertebrae. You don't see that sort of thing until middle age. Poor bastard must have had some God-awful backaches. Also the entire thymus had turned to adipose tissue."

"So the total picture sounds pretty much like"—Rossman's eyes narrow as he calculates aloud—"oh, I'd say —about age thirty-seven."

"Right." Konig nods. "And that's just where I'm placing poor Rolfe. Thirty-seven years—maybe forty. Now what d'ya have for me on Ferde?"

Rossman moves quickly around his desk and back to the scanner. "Ferde's more interesting. Wait a sec while I stick up his pictures."

In the next moment both men are back at the scanner, staring up at a row of seven X-ray negatives depicting skull, jaw, mandible, and dentition from various angles. "Now Ferde," Rossman begins, "was left with twenty-five teeth. All seven of the missing teeth are postmortem extractions."

"Postmortem." Konig scribbles into his pad.

"There's extensive abrasion due to bruxism. He was a tooth-grinder. Probably high-strung. Nervous type."

"Fine." Konig scribbles rapidly. "Keep going."

"I found innumerable carious lesions. Ferde was undoubtedly a big candy eater. And absolutely no fillings at all."

"None?" Konig glances up questioningly.

"None. Not a filling in his head."

"Curious."

"Not really. Not in lower-income classes. Fairly common. They're generally big sugar eaters, and they don't get their teeth cared for. Just chew with them till they fall out, then chew with their gums. But I did find something curious. Look over here on the lower left central incisor. See that milky white patch?"

"Where?" Konig squints upward at the scanner.

"Right there. Incisal third of the outer surface."

"Oh, yes." Konig nods. "Small stain in the center of it. What is it?"

"Don't know." Rossman shakes his head. "Can't figure out what the hell it is."

"Nicotine?"

"Wouldn't think so. Those are not smokers' teeth. No signs of tar anywhere else."

"Looks like a fairly young mouth," says Konig.

"It is. All four of the wisdom teeth are unerupted. But the left upper is showing signs of impaction. See there? Just look at the jaws."

Squinting up at the negatives, Konig can see clearly all four of the wisdom teeth still embedded in the jaws, completely unerupted. He knows quite well that wisdom teeth rarely appear before the seventeenth year, and that they are most commonly all erupted by the twenty-first to twenty-fourth years.

"And look at those roots, Paul," Rossman chatters on eagerly. "Note how they don't appear completely in the radiographs."

"Meaning they're not fully calcified?"

"That's right. That suggests a person not fully mature."

Konig's steely eyes quickly run down a list of notes on the condition of Ferde's remains . . . " 'No sign of cloture in any of the skull sutures. All epiphyseal seals of limb bones united but some not completely fused.' " He looks up from his notes. "I'd say between eighteen and twenty-five, but based on the unerupted wisdom teeth, I'd say closer to eighteen. Ferde eighteen. Rolfe thirty-seven." Konig scribbles into his pad then claps it shut. When he looks up again, Rossman is beaming down upon him with pleasure.

"Thank you, Barney. That was very helpful."

"Always a pleasure, Paul. Oh—just one other thing. Just as a matter of passing interest, the job done on Ferde was not as clean as the one done on Rolfe."

"Nor as thorough," Konig agrees. "Only seven extractions as compared to the fourteen done on Rolfe."

"Right." Rossman nods. "It's as if the maniac who did this—"

"—ran out of time," Konig says, completing the thought for him. "The dismemberment obviously started with Rolfe, took more time than was anticipated. The cutting is much cleaner, the mutilation much more extensive on the older cadaver. By the time our man got to Ferde he was getting sloppy. Either he was tired or he was running out of time. Yes, Barney, I thought of that too."

For a moment the two men gaze at each other. Suddenly Rossman's phone rings. As he picks it up Konig waves at him and starts out.

"Yes, he's here," Rossman murmurs into the phone. "Just a moment, please. For you, Paul."

Moving back across the room Konig feels an icy sense of mounting fright. Almost afraid to take the call, his hand trembles as he reaches for the receiver. But it's only Carver. The moment he hears that warm, husky voice the fear melts. Once again he's in command, brusque and as imperious as ever.

"Ratchett calling, Chief. You want me to switch it up there?"

"No"—Konig chews furiously on the end of a cold cigar—"I'll take it in my office."

≈ 38 ≈

"I can't do that, Paul."

"Why can't you?"

"Are you kidding? They'd fry me alive if they ever found—"

"Oh, cut the crap, Bill. Listen, you owe me a couple, don't you?"

"Sure. I'm not saying I—"

"Don't forget that Mendoza business."

"I'm not, but—"

"I've got a whole file on that. Then there's the Bartholomew job. To a lot of people I know downtown that still stinks out loud. And I'm not forgetting—"

"Okay. Okay, Paul. What the hell do you want exactly? Just spell it out."

4:00 P.M. KONIG'S OFFICE.

Konig leans back in his chair, puffs deeply on his cigar, then withdraws it and for a moment regards its glowing tip. "Blaylock's appointment book," he says very quietly, "for the month of March."

There's a pause in which Konig can hear the agitated breathing, the palpable desperation on the other end. Finally it erupts in hissing torrents. "Are you mad? Crazy? He keeps that right on his desk. He'd know in a minute if—"

"You're an appointments secretary, aren't you, Bill?"

"Yes. What the hell's that got to—"

"You keep a log of his appointments, don't you?"

"A log?"

"Don't play dumb, Bill. I'm in a rush. I've got no time for games. You're an administrative assistant. No one sees Blaylock without going through you first. Right?"

"Right, but—"

"No buts. So you have a log. Right?"

"Yes, but—"

"Where is it?"

"In my desk drawer." Ratchett's voice is now grim, resigned, all the protest leaking out of it.

"Very good. Now, take it out of your drawer."

"Now?"

"Now."

"Paul—I can't do it now. Let me have twenty-four hours on this. First I've got to—"

"Now," Konig growls into the phone. "If I don't get the information I want from you this minute, the Mendoza file and the Bartholomew file are going to be tied up in pink ribbon and hand-carried to the District Attorney's office."

There is complete silence from the other end of the phone. For a moment Konig believes they've been disconnected or that Ratchett has hung up. But in the next moment he can hear quite distinctly the slow, rasping sound of a drawer sliding open a few miles south of where he himself is sitting at that moment. Then comes the sound of papers rustling. Then William Ratchett's agitated breathing back on the horn.

"Okay," says Konig. "You got it?"

"I got it."

"Fine. Now open it to the month of March."

Konig can hear papers flipping quickly.

"Okay," says Ratchett. "I'm at March. What part of March are you interested in?"

"Linnel Robinson was found dead in his cell on March seventh. He was autopsied here March ninth. I want you to tell me if between the seventh and the ninth Blaylock had a visit from Carl Strang."

Konig carefully lays the receiver down on his desk and rummages through a protocol while all the choking and gagging come sputtering through the receiver. When the voice seems to have quieted, he slowly lifts the phone again. "Finished now?"

"I can't, Paul."

"But you will."

"I can't. I'm sorry. I just can't."

"Fine," says Konig, a strange, resolute calm in his voice. "At least you can't say I didn't warn you of my intentions." He starts to put down the phone.

"Paul—wait."

"Yes?"

"Paul, if I divulge that information they'll know. They'll know—that kind of thing could only have come from me."

"Probably." Konig nods sympathetically. "But you're a resourceful fellow, Bill. Well versed in the manly art of survival at City Hall. I'm sure you'll be able to find someone else, some poor duffer, to hang it on."

"Paul—"

"Goodbye, Bill."

"Paul, wait."

"I'm still here, Bill."

The pages flip again—a rapid, susurrant sound. Then Ratchett's weary, beaten voice croaks through the receiver. "Strang was here to see Blaylock on the seventh and the eighth of March."

"Thank you, Bill. That was very helpful."

"And you say the man wore a uniform?"

"Yes, sir. A Salvation Army uniform."

"People saw him?"

"At least four people claim to have seen him."

"Going in and out of this awful place you describe?"

"Yes, sir. Just a shack, really."

"Sort of a crash pad for derelicts and outcasts?"

"Yes, sir."

"Poor devils. What a ghastly business."

"Business?"

"What they do to each other."

"Yes, sir."

4:20 P.M. GENERAL HEADQUARTERS, SALAVATION ARMY.

"And the chap in our uniform," says Major General Henry Pierce, Division Leader, Salvation Army, Eastern District, "he's a suspect in this grisly business?"

"Yes, sir," Flynn says in quiet awe of the tall, elderly gentleman sitting in uniform across the desk from him. "I'm afraid so."

"You know, of course, Sergeant, it's not at all difficult to come by one of our uniforms."

"Yes, sir. I know most Army-Navy stores carry them."

"And will sell them to just about anyone. They're not supposed to without written authorization, but they do."

"Yes, sir, I know that."

"It wouldn't be the first time we've had people posing as officers in our Army, supposedly doing the Lord's work but actually out hustling money for themselves."

"Yes, sir. I can appreciate that. All the same—"

"—the possibility still exists," General Pierce muses quietly, "that the chap seen going in and out of that shack was actually one of our people. I quite agree, Sergeant."

"Yes, sir," Flynn murmurs awkwardly, his eyes stray-

ing out the window, where the head of a pigeon has suddenly appeared, bobbing along the length of the ledge.

General Pierce catches Flynn's preoccupation and
smiles. "Pretty soon you'll see his friends come along and
join him out there. We put crumbs out along about this
time."

The General rises, hobbles stiffly to a closet at the back
of the room, then disappears within it. In the next moment
he's back out carrying a plastic bag of stale rolls and
bread. "You can almost set your clock by them. Four-
twenty, four-thirty, they're here, cooing, making an awful
racket, looking for their crumbs."

In the next moment the General flings open the window.
Suddenly, Flynn sees an explosion of feathers just outside on the ledge. The noise of the cooing mounts till it
sounds like the hum of a single huge generator, and the
upper half of the General's body at the open window
merges joyously with his feathered flock.

Shortly after the disbursement of crumbs, he closes the
window, hobbles back to his desk and sits. "Still"—he
resumes his thread of thought now, as if he'd never paused
for a moment—"it's extremely improbable that this person is one of our people."

"How so, sir?" Flynn asks, leaning forward.

"Well, for one thing, we no longer run a shelter in that
area. Used to have one on the old South Street pier until about ten years ago, before the area underwent this
big urban-renewal transformation. In those days you'd see
a lot of lost souls down that way—derelicts, drunks, run-
aways, aliens avoiding the immigration people, sailors
who'd jumped ship. Old neighborhood then, full of elderly
people and artists who could rent cheap space down there.
Quite charming in its way. Colorful. Now the place is
full of glass skyscrapers. Bankers. Brokers. Wealthy
merchants. And now, of course, the old seaport's a tourist
attraction. Can't have a lot of these poor souls lurching
all about the place bumping into people. The police have
understandably chased them all out. So there was no further need for us to run a shelter down there. No flock to
minister to. Those people have all crept into different
areas of the city now and we've followed them."

"I see," Flynn says quietly. Part of him is still out there
on the ledge, wondering where all the pigeons have gone.

"What happened to the people who used to run that shelter for you?"

"The old South Street shelter? Oh, they've all been re-assigned. Some of them, I imagine, are dead."

"Yes, sir," Flynn muses on. "Still, I wonder if you keep a record of the names of people who did staff that shelter."

"We keep a duty roster for every shelter in the city. Still, it's been ten years. That's a long time."

"Is it still down there?"

"The shelter?"

"Yes, sir."

"Oh, yes. We still own the property and the building. Probably sell it soon. Real-estate market is booming down that way. We've already had a number of inquiries on it."

"I don't suppose I could go down and have a look around the place."

Mildly astonished, the General looks up. "Can't imagine what you'd find. Place's been locked up for years."

"Probably just a lot of roaches and rats." Flynn shrugs. "But I'd like to have a look anyway."

The General's long, finely tapered fingers roll a pencil mindlessly across the blotter of his desk. Then he smiles. "Why not? I'll arrange to get you a key."

"That would be fine, sir."

General Pierce rises suddenly as if to signal the termination of their meeting. "Now you wanted the duty roster for the old South Street shelter too?"

"Yes, sir." Flynn bounces up, falling into step behind him. "If you've got one."

"We'll never know till we look." The General turns and beams back at him. "Right, Sergeant?"

≋ 40 ≋

"This is far too big, Max. It'll never fit."

"Push a bit harder."

"I am. It won't go, I tell you. It's no fit. The damned sneaker's about ready to burst."

"All right. Hand me the other mold."

4:45 P.M. MEDICAL EXAMINER'S OFFICE. MORTUARY.

"Want me to powder this one too?" Arthur Delaney asks.

"Sure," says Bonertz. "But slip the sock on first."

It's near the end of the day now. All the autopsy tables are cleared and the dieners are scrubbing and scouring them in preparation for the daily morning onslaught.

A number of the others, finished for the day, stand about—Grimsby, Hakim, Strang, McCloskey, Pearsall—taunting and teasing their colleagues. There's a great deal of jesting, the objects of which are two casts of the human left foot. One of these is the foot of Ferde, the other that of Rolfe.

For each foot, a skilled specialist has produced a master cast taken directly from the badly mutilated left foot of each corpse. From that a piece mold was produced in plaster, and from that a further refinement—a perfect copy of each left foot reproduced in a flexible material made from gelatin, glycerin, and zinc oxide, a compound used because of its great plasticity and because it can be made to imitate very well the consistency of the living foot. Also, there is virtually no risk of breakage.

With great comic flourish, Carl Strang applies huge puffs of talcum powder to the inside of the ragged sneaker, filthy to the point of a green moldy patina—the same sneaker found in the shack near Coenties Slip. At the same time Delaney slips a navy-blue sock onto the moulage of Ferde's left foot.

"All right, Carl." Bonertz scowls. "Enough with the powder already. I'm choking on the stuff."

"Sorry, old man," Strang clucks sympathetically, "but the foot odor from this thing is atrocious."

More jesting and bawdy hilarity as Bonertz snatches the powdered sneaker from Strang and prepares to fit it onto the mold. "Now, gentlemen," he proclaims, "the big test."

For a moment there's breathless silence as the sneaker slides smoothly onto the stockinged mold.

"*Voilà*," squeals Hakim and ties a huge bow with the laces.

"Perfect," says Delaney.

"Looks pretty good," Bonertz agrees dourly. He removes the sneaker from the mold and studies the inside of it. "The widest part of the foot corresponds perfectly with the widest part of the sneaker," he murmurs. "And the projecting base of the big toe fits reasonably well into the concavity of the sneaker."

The others gathered around him nod their assent.

Suddenly Strang snatches both molds and proceeds to march them around the room and up the walls. There is something wildly funny about the way these two disembodied left feet stride up and down the walls, and soon several of the others are marching after the feet with a great deal of hooting and raucous laughter. Shortly the place resembles a locker room full of boisterous, hell-bent undergraduates.

"What the hell's all this?" Konig booms, appearing suddenly, like a specter, through the swinging doors. The laughter dies on a stifled guffaw and for a moment Strang, standing on a chair, teeters foolishly off balance, still holding the two molds wearing their oddly incongruous cotton navy socks.

"Anything wrong?" Konig stares up at Strang.

Strang grins sheepishly and steps down from the chair. "Nothing, Paul. Just cutting up a bit."

The two men regard each other silently while the others shuffle awkwardly and study the floor.

"Had a bit of luck, Paul." Bonertz bustles forward with the sneaker.

"Oh?"

"We've matched the sneaker to the mold of Ferde's left foot."

Konig limps stiffly to the table. "May I have a look?"

Strang hands the mold to Konig, who silently examines it, along with the sneaker. "What size did the chiropodist say the mold is?" he asks.

"Eight and a half, triple E," says Bonertz. "Same as the sneaker."

"Luck." Konig smiles. "The other mold must've been far too big."

"Couldn't even begin to get it on," says Delaney.

Konig whips out a pad and jots a few notations in the Ferde section. "Chiropodist find anything else unusual on the foot?"

"Well, of course," says Bonertz, "there was a great deal of mutilation. Some toes missing. Skin stripped from the foot. A deep slash right through the sole of the foot."

"Right," Konig snaps, the line of his jaw tautening as he waits for information. "So?"

"The chiropodist's report says that from what was left of the foot, toe bones specifically, he could determine that several of the toes were bent up and humped. Evidence of bunions."

"Right." Konig nods emphatically. "I know that already. Anything else?"

"X-ray examination of the foot showed that the first phalanx of the left big toe was deviated outward."

"Ah, exostosis of the first metatarsal bone." Konig scribbles hastily into his pad. "Hallux valgus."

"Right," says Bonertz. "And that's about it."

"Good. Every little bit helps, gentlemen." Konig glares around, snaps his pad shut and starts to turn.

"Paul," a voice calls after him.

Konig turns and stares into the faintly mocking eyes of Carl Strang.

"Will you clear up a problem for us?"

"Problem?"

"Yes." Strang saunters forward now, jaunty, self-assured. "A few of us are still a bit confused as to the sexing of Ferde."

"Why?" says Konig, seemingly perplexed. "It's a male cadaver."

"Yes." Strang nods. "We know you've said that, but it has the classic dimensions, musculature, bone formation of a female. What made you tag it male?"

Konig gazes quietly at Strang. He can hear the taunt

and challenge in the voice, read the smirk of cocky self-assurance on the face. His gaze now swings around at the others, who all appear to be watching him rather closely. Alert, vigilant, looking for a falter, a fatal hesitation, that first sign of weakness in the Chief.

"In all honesty, Paul," Pearsall says almost apologetically, "it is ambiguous."

"Ambiguous? How so?"

"Well, as Carl said, all evidence of sex in this cadaver seems to come down more heavily in favor of a female than a male."

"Oh?" says Konig. A small pulse begins to throb just beneath his eye. "Such as?"

"Well," says Pearsall, "since we don't have any primary sexual organs with this trunk, the skull, the larynx, the limb bones—"

"You used Pearson's tables for sexing the limb bones?" Konig asks.

"Yes, sir," McCloskey blurts out. "I did all that."

"And?"

"I found that the lengths of both upper and lower limbs were much closer to the female average than the male."

"They are." Konig smiles. "But what about the heads of those limb bones?"

"The heads, sir?"

"Right. The heads of the humeri and femora. Did you also measure those?"

"No, sir. I'm afraid I—"

"Perfectly natural oversight." Konig's voice is suddenly soft, unnaturally gentle. As if he had a need now to make amends for the inexcusable attack on McCloskey the day before. "That's a mistake a lot of older, more experienced pathologists than you still make. That's because length of limbs is so frequently enough to make a fairly accurate sexing of skeletal remains. But in this case, it isn't. You're absolutely right, Tom. The sex of this cadaver is ambiguous. Highly ambiguous. I went through all the same measurements you did—skull, larynx, limb bones. But because it was so ambiguous, I also did the heads of the humeri and femora."

As Konig speaks the men have drawn almost unconsciously around him, until they encircle him. A hush has fallen over the place, the levity of a few moments before all gone, and once again he, Konig, is the teacher and they the students.

"I found a vertical diameter in the humeral head of 48.7 millimeters and a transverse diameter of 44.6 millimeters. For the femoral head I found a vertical diameter of over 48 millimeters. Those are distinctly male scores."

There is a stir in the room. Murmurs of approval. Only Strang is scowling.

"Still, Paul," he persists, "you're not suggesting that those measurements by themselves are sufficient to impute male sex?"

"Cetainly not, Carl." Konig smiles, more expansive than ever. "And I appreciate your passion for thoroughness and accuracy."

Now it is Strang who can hear the ring of mocking irony in the Chief's voice.

"So, in the absence of more conclusive proof," Konig goes on, warming wonderfully to the subject, "I also measured the sternum of this cadaver. As you very well know, Carl, the proportion of the two main sections of the sternum is also influenced by sex. The upper part—the manubrium—is larger in proportion to the middle part in the female than it is in the male. The average proportion in the male varies from 1 : 2.0 millimeters to 1 : 2.6 and in the female from 1 : 1.4 to 1 : 1.9. You know that, of course, Carl." Konig's eyes have narrowed and they are glowing like ingots. He is using his voice like a whip. "I measured the sternum of this cadaver and found a proportion of manubrium to middle section of 1 : 2.3. And as you, above all, Carl, know very well, that is the score for a male, not a female, sternum."

By this time Strang's features have turned a pasty white. And the cocky smirk he wore so self-assuredly only moments before has turned into a look of positive queasiness.

"But let's skip all the fancy stuff, boys," Konig goes on, more expansive than ever, for he's flying high right now, zeroing in for the kill. "Just go over and look at the hand on that cadaver. Look at the fingernails with the pretty polish that makes you all think it's a female; then look at the way that polish has been applied. Then tell me what woman you know has ever applied her nail polish widthwise on the nail rather than lengthwise. In forty years of practicing medicine, and nearly sixty-five years of life, I have never seen nail polish applied to a woman's nail in that fashion. Women simply don't do that. It would be like buttoning your fly from the top button down."

There's a burst of laughter and a bit of scattered applause.

"No, gentlemen," Konig continues, "that badly battered, pitifully mutilated cadaver over there, the one I call Ferde, is male—a young boy, eighteen or so, slight, frail, with a fairly common sexual hang-up. He liked to wear fingernail polish, and I'd be willing to bet he also enjoyed dressing up like one of the girls." The Chief beams about at his staff, then suddenly, his mood shifting, his stern gaze falls on Strang. "Now, Carl, if you don't mind, I'd like a word with you. Upstairs in my office, please."

≈≈≈ 41 ≈≈≈

"Leukocytic infiltration."

"Where?"

"Precisely where you'd expect to find it—the wounds about the head."

"I see. . . . What do we do now?"

"We?"

"Me. You. Whoever. What do we do?"

"We do nothing. The ball's out of our court, Carl. It's now in the DA's hands. I gather the story will hit the papers tomorrow. Then all hell breaks loose. I'm afraid all we can do now is sit and wait."

5:30 P.M. KONIG'S OFFICE.

"I take it I'm to be the sacrificial goat, the chief villain of the piece." Carl Strang sits stony and bitter opposite Konig, a broad slab of late-afternoon shadow slanting across his face.

"The press wouldn't be too far from wrong if it did draw that conclusion, would it, Carl?"

Konig awaits his reply, but it doesn't come. So he continues. "Be that as it may, the press doesn't have the fog-

giest notion who handled the Robinson autopsy. Nor does
the Mayor, nor the Deputy Mayor, nor the District Attorney. As far as I know, no one who really matters
knows either. And I for one do not propose to tell them."

For a moment hope, relief, even gratitude, flare in
Strang's eyes. Still, his gaze, narrow and darting, is as wary
as ever.

"I've made that perfectly clear to the Deputy Mayor,"
Konig continues.

"Thank you, Paul. That's really extremely decent—"

"No—please—" Konig's hands rise before him, almost
a defensive gesture. "Don't thank me. I'm not doing this
for you. That has always been the policy of this department ever since the days when Bahnhoff ran it. Except in
cases of gross incompetence, such confidences are to be
protected."

"I agree."

"I have always seen the value of that policy and see
no reason to change it now."

"No." Strang nods compliantly. "Certainly not."

"However," Konig goes on coolly, "I will have to go
now to the DA's office, and in the face of Carslin's extremely damaging report, I will have to lie. Oh, I won't
actually lie. But I'll have to do something even more
despicable to me—I'll have to weasel."

"But, Paul—"

"No—please—" Konig's hands fly up again. "Let me
finish. I will have to weasel and fudge this thing—not
to save you, which is totally unimportant to me, but to
save the reputation of this office, which is everything to
me."

Strang's eyes drop to the floor. "I'm very sorry, Paul."
He has the look of a chastened boy. But if he is chastened, truly redeemed, it is to Konig a sham redemption,
too fast, and too easily won.

"However, Carl," Konig says in the next breath, "I
think it only fair to tell you that as far as this department
is concerned, you're finished."

"Finished?" Strang leaps to his feet, yelping the word
like a small dog violently struck. The hurt, chastened
eyes of a moment before are raging now with indignation.

"Sit down, Carl." Konig's tone is ominously quiet.
"I'm not through yet."

Mute, baffled, Strang sits, or rather tumbles backward into his chair, his jaws working restively.

"I know that you think of yourself as my successor," Konig goes on softly. "So do a number of people in very high places. I confess, at one time, I also thought of you in those terms. I must now tell you I no longer do."

"Now see here, Paul."

"Will you please let me finish? Then you can have your say. Understand—I don't ask for your resignation. You can stay on here as long as you please. Do autopsies, research, whatever you want. The facilities here are at your disposal. Or, if you wish to go elsewhere, I'll give you decent recommendations. That's all up to you. But I must make it perfectly clear to you now, lest there be any misunderstanding later on, if you do stay here, you will never be any more than what you are today."

Strang, arms crossed, sits there rigid, fuming. His eyes blink rapidly and his dry tongue darts out lizardlike along his lower lip.

Konig watches him coolly, evenly. A magnificent calm has overtaken him. "All right, Carl, I'm finished. Your turn now."

"You bet it is." Strang's voice is a dry rattle. "And I have plenty to say. But not to you. I'll say it to the people who matter."

"Like the Mayor or the Deputy Mayor, whom you went to see yesterday about this body-snatching business that's cost the City a million dollars a year and which you tried to blame on me."

"Right, right," Strang shrieks. "I did go there. I don't give a goddamn how many of your spies told you."

"My spies?"

"Spies. Informers. Whatever the hell you call them. I went to the Mayor because I found the situation here intolerable. And I did blame it on you. You were perfectly willing to let this shabby bilking of the City go right on, just to protect an old man—"

"That's correct," says Konig, a bit startled and unnerved to find that Strang knows about Angelo. "That old man has given more than twenty years of devoted service to this office. In the last few years his luck has gone against him. He had big expenses and he made a few mistakes. I preferred to overlook them."

"You preferred to overlook them?" Strang twitches in

his chair. "Well, I've given fifteen years of devoted service to this department. Thankless, bitter, poorly paid
years. And I made one mistake too. I admit it. I made a
mistake. Why don't you prefer to overlook mine?"

A small smile crosses Konig's lips. As if Strang has
asked him precisely the question he's been waiting to
hear. He leans back in his chair now and sighs. "Had
yours been merely the simple mistake of omitting to do
those tissue studies, Carl, we would never be having this
conversation now. I would have had a few cross words
with you, then tucked the matter away somewhere forever. But you really fouled your nest when you went to
Emil Blaylock's office on the seventh and eighth of
March, then came in and performed the Robinson autopsy
on the ninth, neglecting to do those studies. That—for
whatever promises Blaylock made you—I find unforgiv-
able."

Konig leans back in his chair now, rocking slightly and
awaiting the explosion. But it doesn't come. The initial
shock of the Blaylock bomb, which he felt certain would
strike like a thunderbolt, seems scarcely to have fazed
Strang. In fact, he's even smiling. Then, incredibly, much
to Konig's dismay, laughing openly. Sitting back in his
chair rocking with laughter. And all the while he laughs
he is looking at Konig. It is a look of solid admiration,
the way one looks at a wily and absolutely brilliant
adversary.

"Very good, Paul. Excellent. Hats off to you. You're
a man after my own heart. Only a man like me could
appreciate a man like you."

Konig smiles in spite of himself. "True—it takes one
son of a bitch to know another." He starts to laugh and
for a while they're chuckling together like old friends.

"But, Paul," Strang says, suddenly serious and wiping
his teary eyes, "I must tell you that I don't share your
gloomy views on my prospects for the future. There are
several people in very high places in this Administration
who are determined to see you out as soon as possible
and me in as the new Chief ME."

"I don't doubt that, Carl." Konig smiles wearily. "There
have been for the past twenty-five years. Blaylock for
one."

"Blaylock among others." Strang smiles back maliciously. "So I'm afraid, Paul, you're not the last word on this question." He starts to chuckle again softly.

"No, not the last, Carl." Konig chuckles lightly. "The first. And I can assure you, with what I have in my files now on Blaylock and you, the question of your advancement will never get any further than that."

For a long while after Strang's departure, Konig sits in the close gathering shadows of his office, gazing with an oddly rapt expression at Lolly's painting of Ida and the beach house in Montauk. It is comforting to sit there quietly in the partial dark, letting the throbbing at his temples gradually subside. It is comforting to sit there looking at the painting of Ida and Montauk and think of nothing else.

"Good night, Doctor."

Konig's reverie is jolted by Carver's husky, lilting voice. Poking her head through the half-opened door, she waves at him.

"Good night, Carver."

"You go on home now, Doctor," she exhorts him. "Don't you hang around here all hours. Get some rest."

"I will. I will."

She starts to turn, then turns back. "Oh—you had a call while you were downstairs this afternoon."

"Who?"

"He wouldn't say."

"Oh?" Konig's ears cock. For some reason he can feel his bowels turn. "Any message?"

"No. Only that he'd call you at home tonight. Very nice, soft-spoken gentleman. Lovely voice."

≋ 42 ≋

"Hah?"

"Janos."

"Hah?"

"Janos Klejewski."

7:00 P.M. AN APARTMENT BUILDING IN ASTORIA, QUEENS.

"Your son—Janos," Frank Haggard barks at an ancient, doll-like figure stooping on the other side of a chained door. He is standing in a dimly lit hallway redolent of boiled cabbage and cauliflower.

"Oooh?" she asks, craning her hag's neck up at him, blinking through the narrow open space.

"Janos," Haggard nearly bellows. "Janos."

"Oh—Janos." She blinks into the shadows, peering at the badge he holds in his hand.

"Your son," Haggard barks again, leaning toward her cocked ear, extending the badge through the opening. "May I have a word with you?"

"Hah?"

"I said may I have a word with—"

The door starts to squeal closed and he just barely snatches his hand out of the narrow space before the door slams. "It'll only be a minute, Mrs. Klejewski," he shouts through the closed door, thinking she's locked it on him. But in the next moment he can hear the chain scraping through the brass slide and several locks being turned. He can see the knob rotate and in the next moment the door creaks open. Standing there before him in the half-light is a stooped, wizened creature with bright little gimlet eyes and white frizzed hair, some of which has fallen out in great unseemly clots, revealing the pale, blotchy scalp beneath.

This then is what has brought the detective here on a tip from Wershba. This sticklike little crone in black

222

bombazine, with a voice like a scraping violin. She is the mother of Janos Klejewski, confidant and first lieutenant to Wally Meacham. The detective has come to this shabby block of huddled, crumbling structures across the river in Astoria, Queens, another one of those old-world neighborhoods forged out of the 1900's when countless immigrants, fleeing hardship and persecution, flocked to these shores as a haven of hope.

Then it was a neighborhood made up of working-class people—Irish, Germans, Poles, Jews—hardworking, brawling, pious, stolid people who managed somehow to reconcile differences and live in peace. They had no time to prey upon one another. Hardship and struggle were their common enemies, occupied all of their waking moments. Now suddenly that same neighborhood, like so many others throughout the city, has had to undergo the upheaval of a whole new wave of integration, that of the blacks and the Hispanics, as well as a flood of addictive drugs. And now change has come swiftly to this neighborhood, change often attended by violence.

Where once there was O'Malley's corner saloon, now one finds the fried chicken kiosk and the *bodega* with the odors of burned gizzards and *cuchifritos* drying in the window. The German pork butcher's is now an all-night check-cashing establishment. And the kosher delicatessen has become a storefront Pentecostal *iglesia* with a crude, almost childlike, crucifix limned on its windows.

The building that Janos Klejewski had grown up in is of a fairly common 1910 vintage. Six stories, red brick, fire escapes running up and down its rear face above an alleyway where wash flutters disconsolately in the balmy evening breeze. Its residents used to pride themselves on its solidity and safety. Also its eminent respectability. Now, entering the murky, dimly lit shadows of the hallway, with its peeling plaster and its single naked light bulb glowing eerily up ahead, one must be wary. Very wary indeed.

The elevator that Haggard rode up in, after having to strike a match and search out the apartment number on the mailboxes, once a handsome thing of brass and mahogany, was now in ruins. A shambles. Into every square inch of its wood, kids have gouged their initials, along with a rich intaglio of obscenities and pictoglyphs of sexual organs. Most of its brass has been stripped for resale at local junk shops, and the small space reeks of urine.

"I'm looking for your boy," Haggard says, stooping as he enters and removing his hat.

"Hah?"

"Your boy—Janos. Janos—do you know where he is?"

"Hah?"

"Janos," he cries at her over the noise of a small television, volume turned up to maximum, where a game-show master of ceremonies bounces and careens about like a buffoon.

The tiny, wizened figure hobbles on a cane to a rocking chair and with a great effort sits. While Haggard's eyes tunnel through the shadows of the place a fat old calico cat rubs up against the detective's leg and purrs.

"Police?"

"That's right." Haggard nods.

"I no see Janos for long time," the little widow lady says, her head shaking with a mild palsy.

"For how long?"

"Hah?"

"Would you mind turning that TV down a bit?"

"Hah?"

"I say, how long since you've seen him?" the detective bawls at her ear.

"Oh, mebbe two year. He run from the prison. You find him?"

"No—I'm trying to."

"Hah?"

"I say, I'm trying to find him. He never calls you? Writes? Nothing?"

"Writes?"

"Yes. Letter? Postcard? Anything?"

"No, no." The old lady shakes her head, smiling sorrowfully. "He no write. Call. Nothing. He no good, Janos. Other brothers, sisters. All good. Work hard. Janos stupid. No good. Always trouble. School. Girls. Police. Always trouble. He in trouble now?"

As the old lady cranes her neck and squints at him, there is something strangely reptilian about her, something prehistoric, elemental; a lizard slowly switching its tail in a Pre-Cambrian twilight. Her toothless jaws move endlessly, gumming nothing.

"I don't know," Haggard says, his eyes swiveling all about the room. "He may be in a lot of trouble."

"Hah?"

"Lot of trouble," the detective bawls. "Lot of trouble."

"Yah, yah." The old lady nods. "Lot of trouble."

"You haven't seen him?"

"No—I no see him mebbe two, three year."

"Now it's three years?"

"Hah?"

"Nothing." Haggard smiles. "Never mind. Okay if I look around?"

"Look around?" The old lady, head shaking unceasingly, gapes up at him.

"Yeah—look. Look around the place."

"Look?"

"Yeah. Look." Haggard gestures toward the shadowy rear of the apartment.

"Sure. Sure. Look. Look." She waves abruptly, as if dismissing him.

The detective turns, leaving the gnomish little creature to the game show with its oafish noises and its gray flickering images of idiocy.

Toward the back of the apartment there is a little bathroom, vile and pestilential, with a lot of sodden pinkish-gray old lady's underthings hanging on a dryer in the tub. Then a kitchen, the floor of which is strewn with saucers of milk and pet food, and liberally scored with cat stools in varying degrees of desiccation.

Farther back is the bedroom. This is a large, shadowy place furnished with heavy, garishly carved oak pieces. There is a big unmade bed with an immense headboard of carved scrollwork. Above that hangs a crucifix. In the corner stands a huge, clumsy chifforobe propped up with books where one of its legs is missing. Beside that is a cheval glass, its mirror cracked. There is one window in the room, curtainless and with a shade hanging askew.

Above all this hovers the smell of old age, that mixture of camphor and medicaments that Haggard associates somehow with approaching death. From somewhere far below in the street comes the squeal and shriek of children playing, then a burst of rapid-fire Spanish hailing down upon them from a window above.

The detective's eyes sweep quickly through the place.

Then in the next moment he crosses to the closet and yanks open the door.

Nothing there but old-lady clothes—black dresses, a couple of hatboxes, a flannel robe, a tatty fur-collared coat with the little, beady fox heads still intact. Nothing there. Nothing out of the ordinary, he feels, starting to turn. But then, there on the floor, along with several pairs of old lady's black shoes, each pair indistinguishable from all the rest, is a pair of men's shoes. They too are black, rather formal, and not old. Not the shoes, for instance, of a dead husband, or a married son long gone from the house. No, these are quite new, and with the stubbed toe and greatly elevated heel so modish among the young.

Haggard stoops slowly and lifts the shoes out of the closet, standing there a while and studying them in the shadows. Then, in the next moment, taking the shoes, he strides back out into the living room where the old lady, seated in her rocker and hunched over her cane, watches the game show. The master of ceremonies is now embracing some screaming, mildly hysterical housewife who's apparently just won a garbage-disposal unit.

"Whose shoes?" He holds them out before her.

"Hah?"

"Whose shoes?" He gestures elaborately at them.

"Hah?" The old lady gapes up at him blankly, her jaws moving unceasingly. But for a fraction of a second he is certain he has seen cognition register in the sharp little gimlet eyes, and something like fear as well.

In the next moment, smiling, he leans down as if about to speak directly into her ear. But he doesn't. Instead, with the shoes tucked under his arm, he claps his hands briskly beside her ear. One sharp resounding crack. Instantly, her eyes widen, flutter, and she winces.

Still smiling, Haggard places the shoes gently on her lap, straightens up and waves at her. "Okay, Mama—you win."

≈ 43 ≈

Old dresses. Old blouses. Old jeans, patched and faded. Tartan kilts. Slacks. Skirts. Suits—a navy, a plaid. The gown of silk organza with the faint fragrance of orange blossoms still clinging to it. An old terry bathrobe, buttons missing. On the door a shoe bag. Pumps and sandals. Loafers. Saddle shoes. A pair of clumsy cork-soled brogans purchased on a trip to Scotland. She used to rake leaves in them in the fall. Sneakers on the floor. Moccasins. A pair of absurd, floppy purple powder-puff slippers.

9:20 P.M. KONIG'S HOME.

Paul Konig stands inside the closet in his daughter's bedroom, sorting through her things. It is a large walk-in closet, full of good, familiar odors. The orange blossoms, of course, but also that unmistakable mixture of soap and cologne that used to permeate her hair, the slightly animal smell of youthful exuberance; these are still in the closet, clinging to the dusty, mote-filled shadows that hover there above the racks of garments.

Konig removes the terry robe with the patches and the missing buttons, folds it carefully and packs it into a large cardboard carton, along with a lot of Lolly's other old things. He'll buy her a new robe this weekend, he tells himself. Take a trip down to Saks or Lord & Taylor's. She's had that old robe since high school. She'll need a new one. And all those shoes in the bag are shot now. All badly scuffed and some are out of style. Hardly worth repairing. She'll need new ones. What about some of these new things the girls are wearing now? Damned pretty, he laughs. Much more stylish than in my time.

He takes the shoe bag down from the door and starts to carefully pack all of Lolly's old shoes in a separate carton. He whistles softly to himself as he works, feeling a curious exhilaration, totally inexplicable in the light of the

227

events of that day. Still, he feels good. Relieved about the Strang business, and, oddly enough, optimistic about Lolly. Yes, Lolly was going to be all right. He had no reason to make such an assumption but he knew that, down deep inside. He knew it with as great a certainty as it was possible to know anything.

These people would not harm his daughter. They wouldn't be that stupid. Oh, they would threaten to all right. Taunt him and demand a large sum of money, which he would give them if he had to. But they wouldn't hurt Lolly. She was, after all, the daughter of a fairly influential man. The Chief Medical Examiner of New York City, with powerful connections and very close links to the NYPD. It would be a little foolhardy to invoke the wrath of that kind of man. They might rip him off for a goodly sum, but they wouldn't be stupid enough to hurt his child. The police would never close the books on a case like that. Yes, he would pay them the money and they would give him back his daughter. Fairly straightforward business. Almost routine in this lunatic day and age. The police might even recover some of the money, but he didn't care particularly about that. Yes, he was certain—very soon now his little girl would be coming home to him.

He whistles as he pulls out three or four pairs of old jeans in execrable condition. What in God's name do kids see in these old rags? Christ. Make a religion out of them, they do. Buy 'em already torn and filthy. He laughs and chucks them onto a pile of other old things in a corner, destined to be tossed out with the morning trash.

Still, as he works, whistling, spirits lifted as they had not been for weeks, months, something gnaws at him. Some queasy unease; a faint sense of constriction in the chest. He is waiting for the phone to ring. He has been waiting for it to ring ever since he got home that evening. Not consciously waiting, for he doesn't even know that his ears are cocked, and every nerve of his body coiled, waiting to spring at the sound of a bell. For several hours, in fact, he has been waiting to hear that voice—what did Carver call it, "Lovely—soft-spoken—said he'd call you at home tonight."

Still, that is not what he's been thinking about. He's been thinking only of her. What it will be like having her home. How he will try to make things up to her. They might take a trip. Now that it was spring and the weather beautiful, they might go off somewhere together. Ideal time for Europe or why not even the Orient? Both Lolly and Ida had always wanted to see the Orient. But he'd always pooh-poohed it. There was always a conference he had to go to in England, France, or Germany. So they'd always wind up going there. More civilized anyway, he'd tell them. Less chance of disease. Orient's a filthy place. Can't stand the food, and besides, the weather's beastly. So, in the end, they'd do it his way. Always his way. God—what a selfish, insufferable bastard. Well, things would be different now.

Suddenly he wheels, staring down hard at the floor. "What was that?" he murmurs half aloud to himself, thinking he's heard a phone ringing. But it isn't. At least not in his house. Possibly across the way at the Cruikshanks'.

He goes back to the cartons once again and the old clothing, working in a desultory way now. Soon, he feels a little tired. That Strang thing—nasty business. Ugly, unpleasant. But glad it's done with. Should've been done years ago. Cleared the air. Never liked Strang. Competent enough pathologist. But sloppy. No passion. Really doesn't care. Just intent on rising. Next-step-up sort of thing. That's the whole game with him. All this young breed—just winning—no real passion. Relieved now it's over. Although he knows that as far as Strang's concerned, it's only just begun. Won't take it lying down. Probably on the phone right now with his bigshot City Hall pals. But even that won't help. Mayor might very well have my head Friday, but Strang will never be my replacement. Strang will not be ME of New York City. Not over my dead body, he won't. "Now what in hell do you s'pose she wants with these?" he mutters, pulling out a pair of bright, filmy culottes, shaking his head and holding them up to the light. "Good Christ." He laughs. "There's a side of her I never knew." And suddenly the phone is ringing. Not in his head this time, but somewhere in the house. So intently has he been awaiting that sound that hearing it now, at last, he doubts its actuality. Or at least he doesn't understand it. Instead, he stands there stunned and baffled, listening to it ringing in his bedroom down the hall.

Then, finally, the significance of the sound dawns on

him. He stirs, and in the next moment he is moving, first walking, then running, actually running. He turns the corner to his room, stumbles, barks his knee, trips, then bangs his jaw down hard on the edge of the night table. His teeth crack together and for a moment, sprawled there on the floor, hugging his knee, a cold, numb spot in the center of his forehead, he sees stars. The ringing, like a pulse, stabs relentlessly through the shadows of the room. Terrified it will stop, he staggers to his feet and lurches at the phone. Mustn't stop. Mustn't.

"Hello. Hello."

"Dr. Konig?"

"Speaking."

A pause, then suddenly the awful shriek. One, then another. A high, stricken sound, like a small animal being slaughtered.

"Hello," Konig shouts. "Hello."

Someone is breathing back at him from the other end but doesn't speak. Then another shriek. A long, sustained wail of unutterable horror that stands Konig's hair on end. "Leave her alone," he shouts, but there's a note of pleading to it. "Goddamn you. Leave her alone."

Another pause in which he can still hear the breathing on the other end. Then another ghastly scream. A sound so awful, so horrifying, he must make it stop. Must get it out of his head.

He flings the receiver down with a crash onto the cradle and crouches there shivering on his bed with the sound still shrieking in his ears, and, curiously, the taste of salt in his mouth. He's unaware of the blood seeping from a broken tooth in his jaw.

In the next moment the phone rings again. Just as violently as he slammed it down before, he now snatches it up; and there again is that awful, hideous sound.

"Leave her alone. Please. I beg you, whoever you are. Leave her alone. I'll pay. I'll pay you anything. *Anything.* Just don't hurt her anymore."

Suddenly the screaming ceases as abruptly as it had started. And he's left there, beads of sweat glistening on his forehead, blood streaming from his mouth onto the bedspread.

"Good night, Dr. Konig," says a refined voice whispering at him from the other end.

≈≈ 44 ≈≈

INTERMINABLE NIGHT. NIGHT OF CALLS. NIGHT OF RING-
ing phones. Dialing and waiting for call-backs. Konig's old
friend the Police Commissioner. Very calm, very wise.
Sympathetic. Counseling patience. "Yes, the entire force
is on it. . . . Key people detailed . . . Investigation going
speedily forward . . . Very quiet . . . very discreet. Hang in
there, Paul." Then down to Washington. To the Bureau,
and by midnight, back to New York, his friend the Bureau's district head in New York, whom he'd gotten out
of bed. He'd talked to him only a week ago, and now he
could sense the edge of impatience in the man's voice.
More than faintly piqued. "Yes, we've got some leads.
Nothing definite, mind you, but everything is being
checked out. Followed up. These people are obviously
well financed. Techniques fairly sophisticated. Sufficient
evidence to indicate that Meacham had been the brains
behind several other kidnappings—identical patterns—in
recent years. All under different names. Mountain of information. Files. Dossiers. Police reports. All being col-
lated, analyzed. Very definite picture starting to emerge.
If he's made contact with you, certain we'll have something tangible in the next week or so."

"Next week or so?" Konig murmurs, letting the phone
drop back onto the cradle, cold pockets of sweat at the
small of the back, in the armpits. And Lolly—that awful
sound still resonating in his head.

Hands trembling, he flips through an address book on
his night table. Finding Haggard's home number, he dials.
Gets a wrong number. An irascible voice at the other end.
Jarred from sleep and hissing oaths, obscenities; even as
Konig apologizes and hangs up. Dials again. This time
the quiet, mildly apprehensive voice of a woman unac-
customed to late night calls.

"Oh, yes, Dr. Konig. Frank's right here."

231

Then Konig, breathless, panting, spewing over into the phone. Frantic. Incoherent. Aware he's making no sense whatever.

"Hold everything," the detective says. "I'll be right there."

"Thank you, Frank. Thank you." Still saying "thank you" even after he's hung up.

Then suddenly alone there, the silence of the house closing in upon him. Sitting there, terrified of the silence, not knowing what to do next. Bathed in sweat, body coiled taut as a spring, he sits there, rigid, erect, waiting he cannot say for what. Possibly the phone. Afraid it will ring again. Afraid it won't.

He goes to the bathroom and takes a pair of Librium, then for the first time that night sees his face in the bathroom mirror and he's alarmed. Truly alarmed. Gray, haggard, vaguely demented, he looks, with a gash of blood now dried at the corner of his mouth and at the crease of his chin, a line moving downward, coagulated russet on the collar of his shirt. Tentatively now, like a man avoiding pain, he glides his tongue over the jagged edge of broken tooth at the back of his mouth. There is, too, inside his mouth, badly abraded tissue where on impact the tooth bit deep into the soft flesh of the inner cheek. But it is that bluish cast to his lips that really alarms him. That ghastly cyanotic blue.

Konig pads back to the bedroom, still in his clothes, and stretches out full length on the bed, lying there, still panting like a winded, harried animal.

He's dead tired but lying there is more of an effort than being up. He must be up now, doing things. Out looking for her. She's somewhere. Somewhere out there. But he can't go. Haggard is coming. What for, though? To what end? Useless. Utterly useless.

Then suddenly a name, like a melody inexplicably recalled, goes through his head. Ginny—Virginia. Can't recall the last name. Lived in Riverdale though. Lolly's best friend. High-school chums; later, college. Thick as flies the past ten years or so. Maybe she knows. Maybe Lolly's called her from someplace. Looking for help. Contacted her, trying to borrow money. Might know something. Some small thing. A clue of her whereabouts. Anything. Oh, God, what was her last name?

Then back to Lolly's room. The Fieldston High School

yearbook. Flipping hectically through the pages. Girls all listed together with photographs in one section. "Where is she? What the hell was her name?"

Back and forth he goes, several times. Then suddenly, at last, a bright, round, rather cherubic face. Blond hair, laughing eyes.

ALCOTT, VIRGINIA
NICKNAME: Beanie
MOTTO: Might've been a headache but I never was a bore.
AMBITION: Law
SCHOOL: Barnard

Konig dashes back to his bedroom, snatches the phone book, flies through the A's. Alcott, Nathaniel. Oxford Avenue, Riverdale. Only Alcott in Riverdale. Breathless, in a sweat, he dials. Three rings, then the voice of an operator asking him what number he dialed, then informing him the phone's been changed to the following number in Hartford, Connecticut. Scribbling the number down he breaks the point of his pencil, and in his fury literally carves the number into the pad with the broken stump.

Then dialing again, that same mad, furious haste, making his fingers fly across the dial, jamming them into the holes.

A man answers. A gruff, coarse, but not uneducated voice. At that hour he, too, like Mrs. Haggard before him, is wary.

"Ginny? Christ. Do you know what time it is?"

Konig, frantic, thinks to himself, Good God, he thinks I'm a suitor. Apologizes. Tries to explain, realizing he's made a botch of it. Sounds demented. "Dr. Konig," he says once more. "Lauren Konig's father."

"Lauren's father?" A significant pause.

"Yes—must talk to your daughter."

Another pause, this one in which Konig can almost hear the consternation and puzzlement in the man. Then the sound of a woman's voice in the background and the muffled whispers of them both. The man has evidently covered the receiver with his hand.

"One moment, Doctor. My wife will be right with you."

Another pause while Konig's heart slugs unevenly in his chest. Then the woman.

"Yes, Dr. Konig. Remember you very well. Anything wrong?"

"Lauren—missing— Yes, almost six months. Yes—I'm afraid so. Yes. Mrs. Konig passed away. Oh, you heard? Yes—over a year ago. Yes."

He tries frantically to explain about Lolly. Once again it's all garbled. Incoherent. "Thought possibly Virginia might know something. Might've heard something. Closest friend, you know."

"Yes, of course. But I don't think they've seen each other in a few years. Not since graduation anyway. Ginny's in St. Louis now. Married. Baby coming."

Konig tries to say something apposite. All he wants, needs though, is her number.

"Do you think I might call her?"

"Now?"

"Yes. Please."

"It's very late, Doctor. I hate to alarm her."

"It's sort of—an emergency."

She can almost hear him pleading.

"Yes, of course," she says finally, reluctance overcome and a little frightened herself. "Just one moment. I'll get you the number."

Then, once again, in a feverish sweat, dialing. The wires singing a third of the way across the continent. The voices of operators and the intermittent chatter of distant strangers caught momentarily in crossed wires. Then a rather flat, curious buzzing sound denoting a phone ringing almost one thousand miles away. At last, the startled, rather anxious voice of a young lady he knew as a child, a little girl in his kitchen, in his backyard, hanging upside down on a Jungle-gym. Watched her, along with his own child, graduate high school, college, now mother-to-be.

"Virginia? Hello, Virginia." Struggling to contain the tremor in his voice, he sounds almost cheerful. "Virginia Alcott?"

"Yes, this is she."

"This is Paul Konig."

"Who?"

"Lauren's father."

"Oh, yes, of course." Laughter. Relief. But apprehension is still there. "Dr. Konig. How are you?"

"I'm fine. . . . Virginia, don't be alarmed," he says gently, recalling the hour and the girl's condition, then

realizing his very efforts to calm her have evidently
alarmed her even more.

"Is anything wrong?"

"That's why I'm calling. You see, Lauren—"

"Lauren?"

"Yes—I'm afraid she's missing."

"Missing? Oh, my God."

He struggles to tell it sanely this time, present the details in meaningful sequence, and he can hear it register-
ing clearly with the girl.

"She hasn't tried to contact you? You haven't had a call
or a letter? Anything at all?"

"No. I haven't spoken with her in about two years.
And she was still living at home then."

"Yes, of course," he murmurs, crushed, the disappoint-
ment so heavy in him, although he never really believed
for a moment that he would get anything at all out of the
girl in the way of useful information. For a moment he
considers telling her about the other thing . . . the
Meacham business . . . the screams on the phone. Spilling
it all. Sharing the load with someone else. But he cannot
inflict that on this girl now. Especially since he can hear
distress in her voice already.

"I just can't believe she's run off like that," the girl goes
on agitatedly. "Without a letter. An explanation. So unlike
her. Have you notified the police?"

"Yes, of course. Well . . ." His voice trails off. "Thank
you, Virginia."

"Nothing I can do?"

"No. Afraid not. Just pray," he says, and is surprised at
himself for saying it.

"She was always so good, so kind," the girl says, unconsciously slipping into the past tense. "Could always talk
to Lauren. Like a sister to me. Are you sure I can't help?"

He is touched by the sudden unashamed swamp of her
emotion.

"No—nothing," Konig says, struggling with his own
voice. "Nothing to do. Nothing to do."

"She'll come back. I know she will."

"Yes—I think so too," he says.

The girl is now crying openly. And suddenly, so is he.
The two of them together on the phone. The removal of
great distance making it easier for them both. Sharing their
grief.

"So good. So kind. Like a sister to me."

"Didn't mean to upset you like this."

"Nothing It's nothing. Just sorry I can't—"

"Heard about the baby. Congratulations." He laughs idiotically "Go back to bed now. Need your rest."

"Yes—sorry. Sorry."

"Go to bed."

He can still hear her crying when he hangs up the phone.

At 2 A.M. Haggard arrives. Dirty raincoat over his pajama tops. Trousers pulled on hastily. Fedora sitting absurdly on the back of his head. He swings past Konig into the library.

"Good Christ. What an hour. You got a drink?"

Not speaking a word, they sit there for the first few minutes drinking large shots of undiluted Scotch. Konig has three in rapid-fire succession, trying to deaden pain as one does for a massive toothache.

"Tell me what he said," Haggard finally says, seeing the Scotch take hold in the slackening of tension around Konig's jaws.

"Didn't say anything."

"Nothing? No money? No ransom?"

"Nothing Just the screaming."

Emanating from partial shadows, Konig's voice sounds distant.

"Have another drink." The detective tilts the bottle and splashes another massive shot into Konig's glass. "Didn't stay on long enough for that tracing device to work, did he?"

"No more than a minute or so." Konig gulps down his Scotch with a shudder. "Called twice."

"Twice?"

"I hung up once."

"You hung up?"

"Couldn't take that screaming. That goddamned screaming. Couldn't take that." Konig gulps deeply and reaches for the bottle this time pouring his own drink. Haggard, sitting there looking ludicrous in fedora and pajama tops, studies him closely.

"That screaming—"

"What about it?" Konig grumbles, his voice and manner growing more vague, diffuse.

"Could be a phony, too, you know."

"A phony?" The word jolts Konig out of his daze.

"Sure. One of the girl friends screaming into the phone on cue. Just an act. Make you think it's her. Just to soften you up."

"Oh, yeah?" Konig laughs harshly, a bit of the old truculence coming back in him. "Well, I'm softened. I'll pay. Just let 'em tell me what they want and where. I'll pay. Christ— I'll pay anything. I'll be there with bells on."

"Okay." Haggard stands. "Whyn't you go up to bed now?"

"Bed? What the hell do I want with a bed? My kid's out there and— " Konig's voice cracks and he turns sideways, back into the shadows. "Hurting her like that. Sons of bitches No need- no need—"

Embarrassed, the detective turns away and saunters up the length of the library, eyes riveted upward at the shelves of books, pausing every now and then, pretending to study titles pretending not to hear the sad noises coming out of the shadows.

"Come on," he says after a moment. "Go on up to bed. You look awful What the hell did you do to your mouth? Looks like somebody smacked you in the chops Go on now. I'm gonna sit right down here and drink Scotch. I don't get such good Scotch at home." He starts around the desk where Konig sits and reaches for the slumped, slightly stuporous figure "Come on. I'll take you up."

"Take your goddamned hands off me. I'm not going to bed."

"Come on. Come on." Haggard laughs and hauls the hefty, lumpen figure to its feet.

"Lay offa me. Lay offa me. I'm not going to bed, I tell you."

The detective laughs louder, taking the great, stumbling hulk of the man hard against his hip.

"You son of a bitch," Konig bawls as he's dragged gently to the stairway then up "Take your hands offa me. Take your goddamned hands offa me, I tell you."

" 'Atta boy, Tiger." Haggard's hearty Irish laughter roars upward through the gloomy silence of the house. "That's my boy talking now."

MEDICAL EXAMINER LINKED TO COVER-UP IN TOMBS
DEATH; MAYOR TO SEEK MAJOR CLEAN-UP
The New York Times

BODY SNATCHING: THREE MIL $ RIP-OFF AT THE NYME
Daily News

THURSDAY, APRIL 18. 9:15 A.M.
MEDICAL EXAMINER'S OFFICE.

Paul Konig sits numb and listless, gazing down at the
morning papers. They're strewn across his desk exactly
where he'd tossed them at 7:15, when he'd first arrived
there, driven by Haggard, who had spent the night with
him in Riverdale.

"Medical Examiner Linked to—" Once again his eyes
glance over the front-page story in the *Times*. His picture
is there and he scans it perfunctorily, with a kind of dull,
limp indifference, as if the face were that of someone else,
a perfect stranger, a silly ass who'd gotten himself in a
God-awful mess. Even the frequent recurrence of his own
name on the page has a curiously alien look. He cannot
associate it with himself.

He had not slept the night before. Haggard had put
him forcibly to bed, turned out the light and shut the
door. But even with nearly a half a fifth of Scotch in him,
he didn't sleep. Dozed fitfully, for a few minutes at best,
but didn't sleep. Early in the morning there was a drenching downpour. He lay there for some time in the predawn
hours listening to it drilling on the ground outside; then
later, after it stopped, to the doleful dripping of the trees
around the big old Tudor house. But nothing, no sound,
could stop, or even muffle, the screaming that persisted in
his head. All he could do was lie there, constricted in his
sheets, laved in a cold sweat, a great pulse thudding at his

temples, trying not to hear the screams, and waiting for the first gray streaks of dawn to poke through the chinks of the window blinds.

At 5 A.M. he rose, unrested, unrefreshed, stripped off the clothes he hadn't changed since Tuesday, then showered and dressed. Downstairs, he found Haggard asleep in a chair, his raincoat spread over him, the gray felt fedora tipped forward over his eyes and nose, his mouth slung open just beneath it.

They made some coffee and at 6 A.M. they were on the road, motoring downtown in Haggard's car. The detective had dropped him off at the office and then had gone home for a fresh shirt and tie.

"You get another of those calls, you lemme know," he urged just before driving off. "Don't try anything on your own."

Konig mumbled something and went inside.

When he got to his office, there amid the copious mail were messages taken by the night man to call *Newsweek* and *New York Magazine*, the latter wanting to do a two-part story on the "body-snatching racket at the morgue."

Channels 2 and 5 wanted to come down there and take his picture, presumably to lambaste him on the evening news for the "cover-up at the Tombs."

"Medical Examiner Linked to—" Once again his eyes glide ruefully over the banner head of the *Times*, but he is long past caring.

Limp, groggy, the way one is after a bout of drinking and massive doses of Librium, he has been dimly aware of the increasing tempo of the workday outside his door, the building coming to life. He decides now to take a stab at the mail, but his hands tremble so that he cannot get the envelopes open. Still, he riffles through all the envelopes, each and every one, thinking something will be there. A message with instructions. Something about Lolly.

But there's nothing there. Only the bills, notices of medical conferences going on halfway around the world, the interminable flow of letters from colleagues seeking his advice, universities and foundations petitioning his services. Then, a long, white envelope, expensive bond with a richly embossed letterhead: Graham, Dugan, Lamont, Peabody. A Madison Avenue law firm representing the family of Linnel Robinson, serving the Medical Examiner's Office and the City of New York with a $3 million lawsuit for damages. "Modest, aren't they?" Konig mutters. "Christ, these lice move in fast." He jams the first cigar of the day into his mouth.

Carver bustles in now with his coffee, an anxious, wary look on her face. She knows something's wrong. She knows nothing about Lolly, but she too has seen the papers this morning. "You want to talk to them people?"

"What people?"

"The TV people. They called again."

"Tell 'em to shove it."

"What?"

"Nothing. Tell 'em I'm not in. Tell 'em I'm at the dentist."

"Dentist?"

"That's right. Broke my tooth. Got an appointment for this morning."

"You not gonna be here this mornin'?"

"That's what I just said, didn't I?" he growls at her, but in twelve years of serving him, she's learned not to take his growling seriously.

"What about the others?"

"What others?"

"Those newspaper people."

"Tell 'em all to shove it."

"What about Flynn?"

"What about him?"

"He called too."

"Why didn't you say so?"

"I did." Muttering, fuming, she marches around the desk, plucks out of the chaos scattered there a small piece of memo paper and pokes it at him.

"Oh," he blusters, "—well, you could've told me."

"Well, goodness—I just did, didn't I?" She groans wearily. "Been sittin' right there under your nose all this time."

"What's he want?"

"What's he want?" She gasps at him incredulously. "Now how would I know what that man got in his head this hour of the day?" she asks and suddenly she can see how tired he is. "Whyn't you go on home. I'll take care of all this—" She waves disparagingly at the mess on his desk.

"He say he'd call back?"

"In a half-hour, he said." The phone on her desk rings.

"That's probably him right now." She starts out toward the ringing.

He jams the cold, unlit cigar back into the center of his mouth and lifts the phone. "Konig here."

"Mornin', Chief. Just been readin' all about you in the funnies.."

"What's on your mind, Flynn?"

"That's a pretty picture the *News* ran of you."

"Skip the gags, will you? Just get on with it. I've got no time this morning."

"Tut, tut, no time?" Flynn clucks into the phone. "Soon as these people get famous, with their faces plastered all over the papers, they're suddenly too busy for old friends, got no time. Listen, I spoke to Bragg this mornin'."

"Oh?"

"Them prints I sent down there that were s'posed to be Browder's?"

"Yeah?"

"They weren't."

"Weren't?"

"That's what I said. People at Bragg checked them against Browder's file and they're not his prints."

"Swell," Konig mutters wearily. "So we're right back where we started."

"I didn't say that, did I?" Flynn laughs, suddenly coy and playful. "Those prints you took off them sexy, pretty painted lady fingers?"

"Yeah? What about 'em?"

"Are you sittin' down?" Flynn taunts merrily.

"Come on, Flynn. Will you cut the crap? Get on with it."

Again Flynn laughs. There is a hard edge to his laughter. More like a triumphant jeer. "Those prints you lifted belonged to a chap by the name of Ussery."

"Ussery?"

"Private Billy Roy Ussery from Seven Parishes, Louisiana. Also, like Browder, late of Company G, 82nd Airborne, Fort Bragg, North Carolina."

For a while the two men are silent, listening to each other's breathing.

"Good God." Konig stirs finally out of his stupor, a man waking from sleep. "How'd they catch that?"

"Like I said. They checked the prints we sent down

against those in this Sergeant Browder's file and they didn't jibe."

"So?"

"So then they checked them against this Ussery's and they were the same. Right on the button."

"But what made them check this Ussery's prints?"

Flynn chuckles again. "Therein lies the tale."

Konig puts the guttering flame of the Bunsen burner to his cigar and draws deeply. "Yeah? Tell me."

"Well, 'member I told you this Browder guy went over the hill about sixteen months ago?"

"Right." Konig puffs deeply at his cigar. "Night before the unit was supposed to ship out to Vietnam."

"Right. Well, anyway, the night Browder disappeared so did this Ussery."

"Ah." Konig tilts far back in his chair, his eyes rolling ceilingward through a mist of curling blue smoke. "I see."

"Seems Browder and Ussery were close friends."

"I see. How close?"

"Very close, if you get my meanin'." Flynn snickers.

"I get it. Just get on with it, please?"

"I am, I am—hold your water. Anyway, this Browder and Ussery got to be so buddy-buddy, so goddamned palsy-walsy, it got to be a helluva embarrassment for the other guys. I mean the Airborne don't like that kind of thing. Not good for their image, if you get my meanin'."

"I get it. I get it."

"So they decided to separate them. Browder was to be shipped out to 'Nam. Ussery was to stay on at Bragg."

"I see," Konig muses through a loop of curling smoke. "So they decided to bust out together."

"Right. Night before the unit shipped, they split. That was sixteen months ago. Right around Christmas of '72. Haven't been heard from since."

"Who told you all this?"

"CO down there. A Captain DiLorenzo. 'Member I said this guy was very tight-lipped, cagey—first time I talked to him?"

"Yeah?"

"Well, he was this time too. Just gave me the general details. But I could read between the lines."

"You could?"

"Well, I don't have to be no Sherlock Holmes to know I'm dealin' with a pair of queens."

"You're brilliant," says Konig acidly.

"Beg pardon?"

"Never mind. They give you any details on this Ussery chap?"

"Just general stuff. Enlisted in the Army on his eighteenth birthday. Was in less than a year. Make him about twenty years old now. Height, five feet six. Weight, about a hundred and thirty. Little guy."

"Sounds about right for Ferde," Konig mutters half aloud.

"Ferde? Who's Ferde?"

"Never mind. What about Browder? Anything on him?"

"Same kind of thing. Age, thirty-six. Height, six feet three. Weight, about a hundred and eighty."

"Looks like we got him, too."

"No kiddin'." Flynn whistles. "You boys work fast, don't cha? Well, we won't know for sure till I get a set of his prints. They're sendin' them up from Bragg today."

"What about dental records? Medical records? They sending them too?"

"I don't know."

"You don't know?" Konig snarls. "What the hell am I supposed to do without records?"

"I told you this DiLorenzo guy was very cagey. Ordinarily they'd send these records right out. They're as anxious to clear their books on these things as we are. But this—like I said—is pretty sticky stuff."

"Sticky?" Konig nearly shouts. "What the hell's so sticky about a couple of queens? Grow up, will you."

"Well, for Chrissake, if it was your kid mixed up in a stink like that—"

Lolly's laughing face flashes before his eyes, and suddenly the old ache, the old grief, are back upon him.

"—would you want all the goddamned private records made available to a public agency? First they gotta notify the next of kin. Then see if the records can be released."

"I see," Konig murmurs, the great ache, the great tiredness taking hold.

"Hey," Flynn snaps into the phone, "you still there?"

"I'm here."

"Oh. Thought you'd hung up."

"No—I'm here," Konig says again.

Knowing nothing about Lauren Konig and the raw nerve he'd just struck, Flynn pauses, perplexed by the abrupt shift in the Chief's tone. "You okay?"

"I'm fine."

"You sure?"

"I'm fine, I said. Just a toothache."

"Oh," Flynn says, still perplexed. "Anyway, this CO, this DiLorenzo guy, knows we need dental and medical records to establish identities. So he said if you call a Colonel McCormick down there—he's the chief medic— they'll try and furnish you with most of the pertinent stuff right over the phone. This way they get around havin' to release the records."

"Colonel McCormick," Konig mutters aloud and scribbles on a desk pad, "Med Corps, Fort Bragg, North Carolina. When's he want me to call?"

"Today if you can."

"Okay."

"Soon as I've got Browder's prints checked, I'll call you."

"Fine. Got any more leads?"

"On what?"

"On what?" Konig gnashes on his cigar. "What the hell have we been talking about the past quarter-hour?"

"Oh, that?" Flynn laughs. "Nothin' really."

"What about the Salvation Army guy?"

"Nothin'. Not a thing on him. Just a couple of dead ends. Listen—gotta run now. Goin' down to look at some real estate."

"Real estate?"

"An old warehouse. Downtown."

"Warehouse? What the hell you want with a warehouse?"

"Oh, just business speculation." Flynn chuckles slyly. "You don't think I'm gonna be a dumb cop all my life, do you?"

"You're gonna be walking a beat out in Staten Island if you don't get on the stick pretty fast," Konig snarls into the phone. "Now you've got the identity of these two fellows. Forget about the goddamned real estate. Find that Salvation Army guy. He's out there somewhere. You get that bastard for me, Flynn."

≋ 46 ≋

11:45 A.M. VICINITY OF WASHINGTON SQUARE PARK.

Mouth slung open, lips slack, still numb from Novocaine, Konig plods eastward from the dentist's office. Already a dull pain has begun to creep back into his jaw where he'd been drilled and chiseled and gouged for the past hour and a half, a temporary cap now fitted to a badly shattered molar. His heavy, slightly lurching footsteps take him eastward now, back to the office, through Washington Square Park.

Though the torch of sciatica rages up and down his leg, nevertheless he's chosen to walk rather than take a bus or cab. It is a warm, bright morning, people gliding lazily through the prenoon hour in the park. Already the quotidian lunch-hour spectacle is being staged there. That curious amalgam of park people are slowly taking up their chosen positions—the unconscious players in this daily Village pageant.

The chess players are already out at the tables. The folk singers and the bongo players. Governesses from cushy town houses out pushing carriages. Septuagenarians drowsing on benches. Miscegenate lovers doing their thing in the grass. The resident winos stumbling and lurching. The young panhandlers, sullen, vaguely menacing. Secretaries with bag lunches, cartons of milk. The bearded young students around the fountain, posed in carefully studies disarray, copies of Sartre, Kierkegaard, Marcus Garvey conspicuously displayed.

Konig wanders through this bazaar trying to forget himself in it, lose himself in the spectacle there. Anything rather than return to the office with all its attendant grief. There wait the daily complement of battered and slaughtered, the endless protocols to be written, phone calls to be answered, intriguing colleagues, clamoring reporters buzzing all about the place, the Mayor's mount-

245

ing wrath fanned by a press bent on conjuring up the requisite media event. And then, of course, Lolly. Perhaps a phone call awaits him, a message from Haggard. He must get back.

He moves out through the park, going east on 4th Street toward the river, his lagging steps leading him inexorably through those very ghettos he somehow associates with his lost child.

The street is a feast of sights and smells, an intaglio of ethnic mix, layers of diverse, antipathetic cultures. It throbs with a kind of vitality, and amid it all a distinct air of imminent violence. Always, he walks these streets with a sense that suddenly she will be there.

"Daddy, can we—"

"Not now, honey. I'm busy."

He turns. A small girl on skates rolls past him on the pavement, chasing after the sauntering figure of her father up ahead. On a street corner he passes a man in black tights, black cutaway coat, a top hat, *commedia dell'arte* face of white grease paint, red swirling Cupid lips, black pencil-line eyebrows and lashes limned sharply against the white. A small rhesus monkey in a red velvet jacket clings wretchedly to his shoulder, and the man wears a placard on his chest that reads: "HELP ME TO HELP THE TINY CHILDREN." He does not move. He does not speak. His expression is disquietingly blank. He holds a tambourine out straight-armed before him, and when someone passes he jingles it with a rather quick, peremptory motion. The physique under the black tights ripples with a sleek, powerful musculature. There is something profoundly unnerving in the clown figure—its white expressionless mask; its blank, curiously unseeing eyes; its sudden, monitory movements. Konig passes quickly on, with the sound of the tambourine jingling faintly behind him.

Somewhere around Tompkins Square, he pauses to rest momentarily on a bench. Sitting there are more people, jackets off, shirt-sleeved, pale, winter-worn faces thrust upward at the bright, benevolent April sun. The young are lolling on the grass. Hero sandwiches, guitars, Orange Juliuses. On the ground beside his bench a young girl with dazed eyes plays a reed pipe—no more than a toy, really. She plays for no one. Not even for herself. Indeed, she seems scarcely aware of where she is or what she is doing. The tune she plays is aimless and a little mournful.

For a moment Konig thinks of Heather Harwell, nee Molly Sully, the small pretty face with the avid eyes, the pathetic little packet of picture postcards concealing pornographic views of herself.

The ache in his jaw grows sharper as the Novocaine wears off. He rises stiffly, and in that moment a young girl passes. He sees her fleetingly in profile, a woozy specter, not so much a person as a presence, an aura of something sharply, achingly familiar. Suddenly his heart bounds in his chest and he lurches out after her, following the back of her head, some fifty feet ahead.

She is a young girl, late teens to early twenties. The configuration of back and head acutely familiar. That stride, hurried but aimless, he has seen before. That certain slouch, not slovenly, but dispirited—the sad slump of shoulders. Even from the back, he can intuit a certain prettiness.

She's no more than a few paces ahead now, easily overtaken. Still, he hangs back, without any intention of ever closing the gap. Knowing this illusion, having experienced it many times before, he wants only to linger in its wake, savoring it a while. For the time being, it is Lolly up there walking in the jacket and paint-spattered jeans. Must be a painter, he reasons, the illusion growing sharper in his drugged, slightly disoriented mind. "Oh, Lolly— Lolly."

He follows the figure through a narrow street to a luncheonette, loitering outside while she has a cup of coffee and scans a magazine. Then she's outside and once again he's following her, north, up Avenue B.

Quite a picture he makes, this untidy, fitful-looking man with the tousled hair, the tie askew, the soiled raincoat open, flying behind him. The girl goes into a small grocery store on 12th Street while once again he hovers outside in the doorway of a shoe repair shop with its door open to the balmy spring day. Inside, two diminutive Italian cobblers bark back and forth at each other over the repetitive banging of a compressor.

Out she comes again, this time with a small bag of groceries. He waits for her to move up the street, then moves out directly behind her. After twenty or so paces, she stops short, glances into the window of a small Japanese gift shop featuring incense and cheap bric-a-brac. He stops short too, botches his attempt to make it appear casual, and in that moment she darts a backward glance at him, then starts quickly north again.

In the instant of that backward glance, she'd turned her face to him. But so ephemeral was the impression that the features remain only a blur in his mind. Still, he fancies now that in that fleeting second when their eyes met, he detected a familiar frown—Lolly's frown—and that was Lolly's look of mild displeasure.

On she goes, north to 14th Street, west for a few blocks along 14th, then north again on First Avenue, he trailing behind, trying not to appear conspicuous. He feels a vague sense of loathing in himself for this furtive lunatic indulgence. It's not Lolly. He knows that. That's perfectly clear. Turn off, he tells himself. Go back. Go back. Back to the office. Needed there. Things to do. Questions to answer. Why this madness? Still, that is the back of Lolly's head up there. He holds his breath lest the vision pass.

Somewhere near 16th Street the girls halts and waves at someone across the street. He halts too, turning frantically to gaze into the window of a hardware store. In the next moment a young man in jeans and navy turtleneck crosses the street and joins her. He's a big, burly youth; like the girl, in his early twenties.

Konig fumbles about, stalling there in front of the window, his eyes riveted madly to power saws, claw hammers, gallon cans of Dutch Boy and Sapolin. They are only about fifty feet up ahead of him now, and without having to look, he knows they're both staring back at him and laughing.

He flushes, hot and mortified at the idiocy of his situation. He wants desperately to bolt, to get away from there fast. But he can't move now without incriminating himself. Suddenly the girl is laughing louder. It's a rather high, shrill laugh, with a spiteful edge to it. The sound of it compels him to turn and gaze at her. Instead of Lolly's quiet, contemplative prettiness, he is staring now at a rather gaudy, pinched face twisted into harpy indignation.

"What the hell you want?" she screams. "What the hell you looking at?"

He gapes, paralyzed, unable to reply. But she's still screaming. "Beat it, creep. Fucking old creep." Suddenly she whips open her jacket and thrusts jutting breasts out toward him. Howls of laughter from the boy. People passing by stop to stare.

Flushed with shame, he wheels quickly and bolts, limping, out into the heavily trafficked avenue. Horns blow. Tires squeal. Cabdrivers shout oaths from quickly rolled down windows. But behind him the shrill cries, the gales of laughter, still ring in his ears. "Creep. Fucking creep."

Feeling soiled, like a molester caught red-handed at his vile work, he reaches the other side of the avenue, mortified at the sight of gaping faces staring at him—nasty smirks, frowns of disgust, glares of loathing, outraged self-righteousness, and he fleeing the awful place, the girl's cries still ringing on the air.

"Creep . . . creep . . . creep."

≈≈≈ 47 ≈≈≈

A shaft of sunlight streaming through a barred window. The floor beneath it strewn with rubble. The sound of water dripping somewhere, and, all about, the damp, rather moldy odor of a building long shut up.

12:00 Noon. The Old Salvation Army Shelter, South Street.

Sergeant Edward Flynn wanders through a labyrinth of empty rooms, the slow but regular clicking of his footsteps ringing upward through the four stories of dusty halls and furniture-crammed corridors above him. The building is an old one, built sometime in the final decades of the last century. Four stories. Red brick. Old pipes, festooned with cobwebs, traveling the length of the ceilings. Joists exposed. Paint peeling down the walls.

Beyond the dust-blown iron grating of a window, Flynn can see a jagged sprawl of skyline, a broad brown swatch of river, people rushing headlong about their business. Here, on the first floor, it is quite easy to hear the din of traffic, gulls shrieking and wheeling above the water, the great clanking sound of steamships, tied up in berths, being off-loaded onto the barnacle-encrusted piers all along the Lower East Side waterfront.

Flynn is standing now in what was once a recreation room. Broken furniture, one piece atop another, is stacked all along the walls. Here is a large, ancient console-model television, its wires disconnected, innards eviscerated and pillaged. There, in the center of the floor, is a Ping-Pong table, net sprung, listing precariously on three legs. Stacks of old magazines are tied up in cords and stashed all along the walls—*Life, Look, Collier's, Saturday Evening Post*—publications long-extinct, out of whose faded covers peer glossy portraits of celebrated people, long since dead.

Flynn's lagging footsteps take him out into another long corridor. More furniture stacked in the cool, dusty, mote-filled shadows. Steel desks, file cabinets, swivel chairs, water coolers, wastebaskets stored one inside the other.

Another turn, a twist, and then a long, greenish dining hall veers suddenly into view, rows and aisles of refectory tables, wood benches piled upside down upon them. At the head of the room, serving tables, steam tables, glass display cases, huge aluminum coffee urns, the scene, Flynn imagines, of many a Christmas past. The long lines of derelict and outcast, shaggy and unwashed, shuffling quietly past the steam tables, cup and plate outstretched. A bit of turkey and cider, a slice of mince pie, some warmth and companionship, a brief furlough from the cold, mean streets.

Flynn moves on slowly, almost dreamily, through the room. It is full of that musty forlorn air of places long deserted and fallen into desuetude. But the hushed gloom of it all is strangely comforting. His footsteps lead him nowhere in particular. What he's looking for he cannot say.

On past the steam tables, through the swinging door, and into a huge kitchen in the back. More barred windows, these so high you cannot see out them. Scullery and cupboards, big, old gas ranges, zinc-lined walk-in refrigerated lockers, their doors hanging open. Then aisles of cabinets full of cheap white crockery, much of it cracked; shelves from floor to ceiling, with still an occasional pan, skillet, poacher—all battered, punctured, deemed even unworthy of common pilferage.

A sudden bang. Flynn wheels in time to see a board clatter to the floor and a huge gray rat wamble off into the shadows.

Now a dormitory, that saddest of rooms. Here numberless people, strangers all, lay down together for a night or two of rest. Aisles of rusty steel cots. Rusty springs. Mattresses thin as pancakes, with urine-stained ticking, rolled up neatly at the foot of each cot. An old shoe on the floor beneath a cot; a moldering suit jacket hanging limp and disembodied on a wire hanger. Naked light bulbs depending from long, frayed wires. At the head of the room a large plaster crucifix; an infinitely sorrowing Christ, His nose broken off, His toes nibbled by rodents, gazes down upon the scene.

The place still has the sour, fetid smell of the flophouse. Strong disinfectant, human perspiration, and filth. Flynn fancies he can even hear the endless hacking coughs through the night, the stifled cry of bad dreams or delirium tremens. He moves on, drawn ever upward into the thickening shadows.

Why am I here? he asks himself. What do I expect to find? This alleged Salvation Army figure seen by several shopkeepers as well as a resident of the neighborhood? They'd all said the same thing. They'd seen such a person going in and out of the shack near Coenties Slip. How in God's name was he to find this person? And even given the miracle of turning up such a person, it was highly improbable that this would be his man. If such an individual did actually exist, then most probably he was a legitimate Salvation Army officer who'd stumbled inadvertently into that desperate little warren of outcast men and tried in some small way to help them.

No, the man he was looking for was undoubtedly one of the residents of that shack. One of the desperate, harried men who cowered there through the long, dismal winter months, feeding on scraps, panhandling an occasional pint of muscatel, and waiting for a break.

There must have been at least a half dozen of them living there at one time, Flynn speculates. They'd found at least that many sets of separate and distinct fingerprints. Starving, freezing to death in that unheated little shack, without sanitary facilities, no doubt they became increasingly desperate, quarrelsome, ultimately preying upon one another for small treasures—a crust of bread, a few coins. At a certain point they fought. Two of them were unlucky. Those were the two poor bastards they'd exhumed from the mud along the river. After the awful thing was done, the others must have then fled. Each going his own separate way.

So the man he was looking for, he was reasonably certain, would be an itinerant, a drifter. A man with no address, no next of kin, and a record of arrests ranging from common vagrancy right on up to assault and manslaughter. He'd seen enough of such men in his time to know the type.

Upstairs, on the fourth floor, he stumbles into an old music room and startles a fat, sleek grackle that had, no doubt, entered through one of the numerous broken windows. The frightened bird rises, the awful drumming of its wings whirring past the detective's shoulder, and soars upward to the high pitched ceiling where it bats about, making its awful chugging sound and skirling beneath the eaves. Finally it comes to rest on an overhead pipe and, perching there turns its yellow beady eyes down upon the detective. They stare at each other for a while, as if carefully taking the measure of each other. "Sorry, pal." Flynn chuckles softly and waves at the bird. "Didn't mean to disturb you." He shrugs and turns. He really hadn't expected to find anything there. But after days of checking fingerprints, studying mug shots, checking out leads that invariably terminated in dead ends, he was ready to try anything.

Out in the corridor once again, he starts down through the gloom, his slow, descending steps reverberating on the floors below.

Curious, how ghastly noise sounds in a deserted place where none should be. Especially one's own noise, as if the mere sound of it made one suddenly vulnerable Flynn tries to step more lightly, to go down more slowly, to reduce his own noises.

Down he goes, and still there is that sound of dripping water, loud, regular, and echoing through the cavernous structure. But here, on the third floor, it seems loudest of all.

Inexplicably he veers toward the sound, never having intended to, drawn toward it as if tugged forward on some invisible leash. For Edward Flynn is a finicky man. Parsimonious and rather compulsive. The sort of man who straightens wall pictures and turns out electric lights in unoccupied rooms. The dripping, profligate water tap needs his immediate attention.

His steps lead him past a succession of small, cell-like rooms, austerely furnished but better appointed than the dormitories. Better beds, thicker mattresses, a small bureau, a night table, a standard mail-order lounging chair, and a floor lamp in each. Identically furnished; one indistinguishable from the next. And each with its own private lavatory.

Undoubtedly staff quarters, Flynn reasons, and enters one of the lavatories. A sink, a wall mirror, a toilet, a stall shower. All very correct, utilitarian. All as uniform and unimaginative as the bedroom. Smiling, he gazes at the dripping faucet, as if he, the detective, had tracked the criminal to his lair. He walks slowly toward it. The spigot is cold and clammy to the touch, beaded with sweat. "Washer's shot," he murmurs to himself, twisting back hard on the faucet handle as far as it will go. Still he cannot get the drip to stop.

Although he's late now, due to report back to the precinct within the hour, the drip has nevertheless become something of a *cause* for him. He stands there, scratching his head, pondering a solution. If only he had a wrench—

In the next moment he twists the faucet full on and a rush of clear cold water gushes noisily into the sink.

"Now that is odd," he muses, turning the spigot off so that it settles once more into its steady drip. Not the gush, of course, but the fact that the water in a building shut up for ten years has never been turned off. And something more—that clear cold gush of water. Taps that have gone unused for a decade are invariably rusty. When first turned on, they tend to cough and spit. And the first water to flow out of them is usually rusty, full of sediment, and putrid.

"Odd," he murmurs once more, suddenly seeing his own gray, puzzled face peering back at him from a mirror above the sink. The mirror is the door of a medicine cabinet. Jerking it open, he sees a half-dozen roaches disporting themselves on the back wall of the cabinet. The sudden intrusion of light sends them all off in different directions, scurrying for cracks.

Left there now are three dusty glass shelves with a meager scattering of abandoned toiletries—old bottles of prescription medicines, an eyecup, a mug of shaving cream, an injector razor, a beaver-brush applicator, and a toothbrush.

It is the injector razor that first attracts Flynn's eye. Not that it is in any way an unusual injector razor. The model is a fairly common well-known brand name—a Gillette Trac II. Ordinary enough, but not the kind of razor one associates with a decade ago. This, to Detective Sergeant Edward Flynn, has a fairly current ring to it. Also, the blade is by no means rusty. On the contrary, it looks rather fresh.

And then, the beaver-brush applicator. Damp, rather wettish to the touch. Now that is odd, he thinks.

Shortly after he leaves the old South Street shelter, clapping shut the big brass padlock on the front gate, Flynn ducks into a coffee-shop phone booth. In the next moment or so he is talking once more with General Pierce at the Army's division headquarters. Had the Army made any provision for keeping a watchman on the premises of the old shelter at night, he inquires of the General, and is promptly informed that no such provision is now or, indeed, was ever in force.

≋ 48 ≋

"You Haggard?"

"Right."

"Sid Fox. Wershba told me you were coming."

"Oh? Did he say what for?"

"Just a little. Come on in. We're holding three of 'em over in the mail room of the First National."

2:00 P.M. PAN AM BUILDING, 45TH STREET ENTRANCE.

Patrol cars. Fire engines. Mobile TV vans. Throngs of people milling about the entrance of the building. Police cordons. The sound of sirens converging on the spot. Thrown about the 45th Street entrance, a large semicircle of patrol cars, doors open, dome lights rotating. More patrol cars nosing their way slowly up through the cordoned-off street between Vanderbilt and Lexington Avenues.

The door of the patrol car slams behind Haggard as he and Sergeant Fox push through the crowds, preceded by a flying wedge made up of a half-dozen patrolmen running interference.

"How come you got 'em in the bank?" Haggard asks over his shoulder. "They try to bust the place?"

"Nope—just happened to be convenient. Right up ahead there through the lobby, Lieutenant. Ground floor on your right."

They spin through revolving doors. Several firemen speed past—men in helmets, bright-red riot jackets— hauling buckets of sand, lines of fire hose.

"How many of 'em you say you got?" asks Haggard.

"Three. There are two more up there. Got 'em pretty well sealed off between the thirty-fifth floor and the roof-top. Pulled around a half-dozen bombs out of the place already."

"Where'd you find 'em?"

"Trash cans. Mail chutes. Stairwells mostly. They were seeding the joint."

"Think you got 'em all?"

"Don't know. It's a big building. We're scouring the place from boiler room to rooftop. Got a restaurant up there. Caught a lot of people eating lunch."

"Get 'em all out?"

Up ahead a patrolman swings a pair of heavy glass doors open before them.

"That was easy," says Fox. "Manager wasn't all that happy about it. Wanted us to wait and let 'em have their dessert so he could charge 'em full price."

They swing on through the glass doors of the First National City Bank, located just below the mezzanine. Inside the bank the hum and buzz of disrupted enterprise going on amidst a semblance of order. Bombs or no bombs, it is business as usual at the bank. Unsuspecting clients bustle in, wanting to cash checks, make deposits, negotiate loans. They're suddenly caught up in the sub-dued chaos of the place. Hordes of police, frightened tellers, harried bank officials scurrying about, red in the face, talking in whispers, calming, soothing, reassuring both clients and personnel.

"Right up this way, Sarge." A patrolman waves them on through a small corridor leading to the back.

"Get anything out of them yet?" Haggard asks.

"Nope. Shut tight as clams."

Haggard sighs, pushes on through a heavy walnut door and then another door with a pane of frosted glass, the words MAIL ROOM stenciled in gold letters upon it. "All right—let's take 'em one at a time."

Beyond the glass door a large mail room. Boxes, cartons, U.S. Post Office canvas wagons, Pitney-Bowes franking machines, an immense wall of pigeonholes, each crammed with envelopes, more bundles of letters waiting to be sorted. And the place crawling with patrolmen and detectives.

Off to one corner, three white youths sit. Somewhere between the ages of eighteen and twenty. They wear identical outfits consisting of fatigue jackets, combat boots, berets. They sit dazed and sullen, slumped in chairs against the wall, while a beefy Irish patrolman named O'Doyle hovers above them, pad and pencil in hand, apparently questioning each.

"Okay, O'Doyle," says Fox, marching up, "I'll take it from here."

"Right, Sarge." The cop shoots a disapproving scowl at his charges.

"Get anything out of 'em?" Haggard asks.

"Not a thing, Lieutenant. They're nasty little beggars." O'Doyle shoots another scowl toward the three youths, speaking suddenly quite loud. "If they give you any smart-ass, Lieutenant, just let me know. Particularly that little mouse-eared bastard over there. Thinks he's a tough one."

O'Doyle juts a stubby finger in the direction of a small, pallid, intense youth, more sullen, obviously more defiant, than the other two. "Just lemme know if he gets funny with you, Lieutenant."

"Righto," Haggard murmurs softly, his restless, searching blue eyes already recording, assessing, evaluating. "Leave that one here for me. You can take the other two out with you."

The big patrolman lumbers swiftly toward the youths. "On your feet, you two." He turns then to the small, sullen youth left behind. "Hear that, sonny?" O'Doyle snaps.

"You smart-ass the lieutenant here, I'll tear your nose off."

A few of the other patrolmen chuckle, then move out behind O'Doyle and the two boys.

For a long while after they've gone Haggard ignores the boy. He studies some notes, gazes thoughtfully around the room, chats quietly off to one side with Fox, letting the youth stew a bit.

Then suddenly he turns, marches back, coming abruptly at the boy, taking him by surprise. "Stand up."

"What?" Startled, the boy gazes up only to see those two small pebbly blue eyes boring down upon him.

"Stand up, I said."

The boy continues to sit, an impudent little smirk creeping slowly across his face. In the next moment he is jacked straight to his feet, hauled up unceremoniously by the collar, and rammed up hard against the wall.

"When I say stand," Haggard snarls between gritted teeth, "I mean stand."

"Hey, now look, man—"

"Man?" Haggard's eyes bulge from his head. His voice booms like a clap of thunder. "Man? Who the hell are you calling man? My name isn't man. When you address me, it's Lieutenant, or sir, or your Lordship. None of this man crap. Get it?" He crowds the boy up harder against the wall, twisting the collar tighter around his throat, so that he makes a gagging sound. "Get it, sonny?"

Red-faced and gasping, the boy nods with some difficulty, while Haggard's huge paw tightens its grip on his collar.

"Now, what's your name?"

This time the youth, cheeks flared red, eyes tearing not from hurt but inner rage, swallows hard.

"Name?" Haggard says once more.

"I refuse to answer any questions until I've had benefit of counsel," the boy says, bristling with defiance. He's obviously educated. Middle class. And with that snotty, well-fed, never-deprived manner, that you-can't-do-anything-to-me attitude of a youth brought up in a comfortable suburb who's never had to contend with anything more than his own boredom.

"Benefit of counsel." Haggard whistles, and calls over his shoulder at Fox. "I take it he's been apprised of his rights."

"He has, Lieutenant. Name is Douglas Mears. Seventeen years old. Comes from Greenwich, Connecticut, according to identification in his wallet."

Haggard's beady eyes pin the youth back hard against the wall. "Don't you have anything better to do with your time, Douglas, than making a goddamn pain in the ass of yourself?"

"I refuse to say another word until I've had the benefit of legal counsel."

"Endangering the lives of a lot of innocent people? Dressed up in that silly costume—a beret and a fatigue jacket? Like a road-company Fidel Castro."

"I refuse to—"

A sharp crack across the jaw from Haggard's open palm stifles the rest of the reply.

"He call his lawyer?" the detective asks.

"His father's his lawyer."

A slow, mean grin widens Haggard's features. "That so, Douglas?"

"It damned well is," the boy hisses. "And you're gonna be sorry you used your hands on me."

"Me? Sorry?" Haggard laughs out loud. "That little shot's given me more pleasure than I've had all week."

Fox lifts a heavy section of lead pipe and walks it slowly across the room to Haggard. "Caught him with this little beauty in a stairwell on the thirty-second floor."

Haggard takes the device, now safely deactivated, and studies it. It's a pipe bomb of a fairly typical sort—center filled with about a pound of gelignite, simple wire fuse. A fairly crude thing. A child might have easily assembled it.

"Pretty stupid for a smart boy like you, Douglas." Haggard slowly shakes his head from side to side. "Getting caught like that, holding all the goods. Hope Papa's a good lawyer."

Haggard and Fox both laugh spitefully. In the next moment, the boy's cockiness appears to melt a bit. Suddenly his eyes seem puzzled and not a little frightened. "Like I told the other pig—"

"Pig?" Haggard wheels and peers hard at him.

"That's right." The boy sneers. "That pig cop." He thrusts a finger at Sergeant Fox.

"Hear that, Fox," Haggard calls over his shoulder. "Douglas here calls you a pig."

"That's a lie," Fox says, deeply aggrieved. "I'm a Democrat."

' "That was very unkind of you, Douglas," says Haggard sorrowfully. "The sergeant here is a very fair man. A Democrat. A husband. A father. Would you call his children sucklings?"

"I'm sorry," young Mears stammers, obviously baffled. "I didn't mean—I meant only him. That guy."

"What guy?" says Haggard, staring around as if he saw no one.

"That guy." Once again the boy thrusts his finger at Fox.

"Oh, you mean the sergeant?"

"That's right."

"Well then, Douglas, say that. Say 'the sergeant.' "

"Yeah—like I told him."

"Not *him*, Douglas—the sergeant. Say *'the sergeant.'* "

"The sergeant—like I told the sergeant."

"That's better," Haggard says gently.

The boy's face is flooded with exasperation. "I was just standing around—"

"In the stairwell?"

"Yeah—in the stairwell."

"Do you always stand around in stairwells, Douglas?"

"Like I told the sergeant here, I was delivering a package to one of the offices up there—"

"Good. We can check the package and the return address on it later. Please continue."

"And this guy comes up to me."

"In the stairwell?"

"Yeah—in the stairwell. And he hands me that."

"The pipe?"

"Yeah. And he says, 'Hold this for me, please. I'll be back in a few minutes.' "

"Oh, I see," says Haggard with his most effusive magnanimity. "This guy, the one who comes up to you in the stairwell. Ever see him before?"

"No. Never." .

"And so you just stood there holding the pipe for him?"

"Yeah," the boy says, full of fake bravado. "That's right."

"Sounds perfectly plausible to me." Haggard nods sympathetically. "What about you, Sergeant?"

"Sounds beautiful to me, Lieutenant."

"Well, Douglas"—Haggard's eyes twinkle merrily—"I hope Papa's a real good lawyer. If he's not, you're going away for a long, long time."

Haggard watches the defiance ooze from the boy's eyes. Soon, he is certain, in just a few more minutes of questioning, those snotty, self-assured postures, all learned and imitated from trashy TV crime serials, will start to run all leaky and soft, like an overripe cheese.

"As it turns out, Douglas," the detective goes on now, almost liltingly, "I'm not very interested in you. You're too dumb to hold my attention very long. You're small stuff. A fart in the blizzard, as they say. But I do have a few questions I want answered. If you can answer them, who knows—it may win you some points from the judge. Personally, I hope it doesn't. Personally, I hope they toss you into a hole for about thirty years and bury you there. Thirty years. That's what the bombing of public buildings is going for on the open market these days. Am I right, Fox?"

"That's right, Lieutenant. Twenty to thirty in the Federal cooler."

"Let me see—that'll make you almost fifty when you get out. Fifty's not a bad age, Douglas. There's still some time left to beat the world." Haggard watches with harsh amusement the notion of lengthy incarceration register behind the boy's eyes.

"In your travels as a bomber, Douglas," he hammers on pitilessly, "ever run into a chap named Klejewski?"

"Who?"

"Klejewski—Janos Klejewski. Some people call him Kunj or Kunje."

The boy ponders the name a moment, then shrugs. "Never heard of him. Who is he?"

"A big monkey. Likes to play around with firecrackers, like you. What about the name Meacham? Ever hear of a young dude called Wally Meacham?"

The boy stares blankly at the detective. And in that blank stare, the detective can read all too clearly the answer to his question. As he turns from the boy, he can feel all the hope he'd been savoring for the past hour or so—since Wershba had called him with something "hot" —running out from him now, running out the way time, too, was running out for him. Suddenly there is a cold sickness in the pit of his stomach.

Fox follows him out the mail-room door, closing it gently behind him. Then in the bank once more, together the two men, heads tilted toward each other, confer for a moment.

"These are not your guys, ay, Lieutenant?"

Haggard nods, stands silently, arms folded, wondering where to go next. What to try. He pushes the battered gray fedora far back on his head and scratches the scalp beneath the white, fleecy, cotton-candy hair. " 'Fraid not. These are just small-town kids come to the big city to make good. See that bomb in there? Junk. Tinny. Lot of mickey mouse. Couldn't blow a note on a trombone with twenty of 'em. Nope—the boys I'm looking for are pretty sophisticated with this kind of stuff. Timing mechanisms. High-powered concentrated explosives. Japanese firing pins. The works. None of this cheap pipe stuff." Haggard sighs. "Well—better be on my way."

He crams the fedora forward on his head and pulls up the collar of the rumpled trench coat.

Fox sees him through the lobby of the Pan Am Building, back out to 45th Street, where the curious crowds are still milling.

"All this got something to do with the ME, don't it?" he asks when they reach the waiting patrol car.

Standing at the open door of the car, Haggard cocks a sharp glance back at him. "Where'd you hear that?"

"Heard something about his daughter."

"Who told you?"

"No one. It's around though—grapevine stuff, that's all."

Haggard regards him silently for a while. Then slowly his index finger rises to the sergeant's lips and remains there momentarily. A hushing gesture. Then he's gone.

≈≈ 49 ≈≈

Call, goddamn you, call. Just tell me what you want and when you want it. I'll get it. I'll be there. Just call. Please call. Give me back my kid.

3:00 P.M. KONIG'S OFFICE.

The Chief sits in the stuffy shadows of his unlighted office. Behind a littered, unattended desk, he waits, staring unblinkingly at his telephone, all his concentration focused upon it, as if invoking some enormous effort of will to make it ring.

He has been sitting there for the past hour or so in those shadows, staring at the small, dark shape, conjuring it. In his head he carries on a series of imaginary dialogues with Wally Meacham. What he will say. How he will say it. What he will concede. He knows, of course, that he will concede everything. Everything is negotiable. But there is, too, buzzing annoyingly at the back of his head, Haggard's stern admonition. "Don't go it alone. Wait for me before you do a thing."

Several times during that afternoon the phone has rung —reporters and the network lice trying to scare up a scandal. Not only do they have the delicious grisliness of a body-snatching scandal, but now it's the Robinson business, and Carslin issuing a new press release every quarter-hour or so from the DA's office. An opportunity for high moral dudgeon on the editorial page.

Konig had declined to speak with any of the media people. But when Benjamin called he had no choice but to speak. There was little doubt in his mind what the call was in regard to, and when the Deputy Mayor reminded him to appear the following morning at the DA's office, he merely mumbled his assent. It occurred to him at that point that he didn't particularly care what they did to him anymore.

Several times during the afternoon he had lumbered

262

down the hall to Haggard's office. There were questions and he was seeking reassurance. Finding no one there each time, he would leave vague, incoherent little notes on scraps of paper on the desk, then lumber back to his own office.

He had not been down to the autopsy rooms once that day. On his desk there were protocols to be read, death certificates to be signed, insurance reports to be filled out, innumerable calls and floods of mail to respond to. He had done nothing. He had let his work slide. He had assiduously avoided seeing any of his colleagues. He knew they had questions for him, as they always did, and that he was holding up their work unpardonably. He knew they sensed something was wrong. Drastically wrong. He knew they were uneasy and that they talked amongst themselves. That Strang, rest assured, was somewhere out there, even now, slandering him, promoting himself among the Mayor's well-paid lackeys at City Hall.

For all that, he cared little. He viewed his dereliction of duties, his almost certain professional decline, with a rather eerie indifference. He dissociated himself from it, as if it were happening to someone else. Anyone seeing him just then, anyone who had known him, that is, known the enormous energy, that inexhaustible intellectual curiosity, would not have recognized him. They would have been struck dumb by the spectacle of this gray, haggard figure slumped untidily over his desk, work neglected, eyes glassy and dazed, jaw slack, the spectacular lassitude of the man.

Still, he sits there in the gathering shadows, staring at the phone and waiting. Then it rings. He jumps as the harsh jingle of the bell rouses him from his torpor. He listens as Carver answers for him, lest it be the press, some prying reporter trying to make a name for himself. He hears the muffled tones of her voice through the closed door. Then a buzzer sounds on his own phone and he snatches it up.

"Flynn," says Carver. "You want to talk to him?"

"Flynn?" For a moment the name doesn't even register. "Flynn—God, no." He starts to fling down the phone, then snatches it back. "Wait a minute—better put him on."

A moment, a click, then Sergeant Edward Flynn talking. At first it's all jokes, mild banter, chatter. All unintelligible. Too fast. His drugged, torpid mind can scarcely keep up.

"—and that's when Browder—"

"Browder?"

"What?"

"You just mentioned Browder."

"I know," says Flynn, puzzlement in his voice. "What about him?"

The name has caused Konig's mind to clear a bit, like a fog beginning to rise. "You just said something about Browder."

"I know I did. Ain'tcha been listenin'? I said we got his prints up from Bragg. They match a set we found all over that shack."

"Oh," Konig says, lapsing once more into indifference. "Nothing else?"

"Nothin' else? Isn't that enough? We got ID's on the two of them now. What the hell's the matter with you, anyway? You sick?"

"I'm fine," Konig mutters. "Just a toothache. Where you been?"

"South Street. Lookin' over some real estate."

"What real estate? What the hell is this real estate you keep babbling about?"

Flynn sighs like a man sorely put upon.

"The real estate I keep babblin' about, my friend, is the old Salvation Army shelter down there."

"Salvation Army?" Konig repeats the words slowly; then something suddenly inquisitive comes into his tone. "Find anything?"

"Nothin'," Flynn snaps. "Pretty much of a dead end. Just the way I think this Salvation Army phantom is gonna be a dead end. Place's been shut up ten years. Lots of old furniture and junk. Rats and leaky faucets. Nothin' much else."

Konig ponders this information for a while. "So where do you go from here?"

"I don't know." Flynn chuckles. "I'm up a tree. We pulled about a dozen different sets of prints out of that shack. We're trackin' every one of them down. We're casin' the neighborhood, pullin' in local derelicts. Anyone who can give us a lead. Even got a couple of guys dressed like winos prowlin' around the area with a few pints of Thunderbird on their hips. So far, nothin'. The only real lead we got is this so-called Salvation Army guy, and I don't think that's gonna pan out."

Even as Flynn's voice drones on, Konig's mind is elsewhere, his eyes roaming restlessly around the office.

"So I don't put too much hope in—"

Suddenly Konig's wandering gaze falls on a shadowy place beneath a long trestle table opposite his desk. It's a table full of reports, books to be read, specimens excised from cadavers, sections of organs enclosed in jars of formalin. He is staring intently at a cheap, shabby suitcase. The kind of vinyl thing purchased in a Whelan's or a Liggett's for about $5.99. This one is old and battered. Scored with mud and old college paper pennants. It is the suitcase in which the two severed heads exhumed from beneath the shack near Coenties Slip arrived at the Medical Examiner's office.

Konig has a sudden sharp memory of opening that case, the trembling, anxious fingers fidgeting at the clasps, the almost breathless sense of expectation as he unwrapped each head from the newspaper coverings— Newspaper coverings.

Suddenly he's on his feet, talking quickly, breaking abruptly into Flynn's chatty conversation. "Listen—where are you?"

"What?"

"I said, where are you? Where the hell are you right now?"

"Where am I?" Flynn goes suddenly peevish. "I'm in a piss-hole phone booth talkin' to you, goddamnit."

"Where? What phone booth?"

"Outside a Howard Johnson's on Eighth Street. What the hell does that—"

"Give me the number."

"The number?"

"Yes, the phone number. Are you thick? Goddamnit, give me the phone number. I'll call you back in five minutes."

The moment after he's hung up Konig is lumbering across the room to the trestle table, stooping and hauling up the battered little suitcase, prying open its rusty clasp, plunging his hands into the smeared, crumpled newssheets.

It's not the sheets of the *Daily News* or the *Post* he's

looking for. These are there in abundance—mud-streaked, bits of clotted gore still clinging here and there, a slight excremental odor rising all about them. All these are dated between March 27 and March 31, all quite consistent with a time of death having been established at approximately April 1.

But these are not what he's looking for. Several days back, when the heads arrived in that small satchel, shortly after he had succeeded in assigning each head to its proper trunk, he recalls coming back to this grisly little carrying case and picking through the papers. Then, oddly enough, he recalls sitting down at a chair by the window and reading them—one in particular.

Riffling now hectically through those same old newspapers, he ransacks his brain, trying to recall exactly what it was he read that sticks so sharply in some dark, inaccessible corner of his mind.

There is a great deal of international and national news that flies past his eyes. Strife in the Middle East. Bombings in London. Mass starvation in Pakistan. Senate investigations of the Chief Executive. On the moldy yellowing pages of the *Daily News*, Konig pauses over the face of a murdered policeman; an East Side madam along with a stable of her hostesses being arraigned in night court; the picture of a small, timid-looking fellow with ferret eyes and a goatee who'd beaten his three-year-old daughter to death.

Still, that's not what he's looking for. He rummages on, tears like a cyclone through this noisome paper, bits of human hair, brain tissue mizzling downward as his feverish eyes search. If he could only recall what it was he'd been reading that night. Or wasn't it early in the morning after having worked through the night? It was that night, after McCloskey had gone home, and he'd finally succeeded, along about four or five in the morning, to assign each head properly to a body. He'd sat down in that straight-backed chair over there by the window. It was warm in the office and so he'd opened the window. The damp night air came in and cooled him. Roused a bit his tired brain. And then he'd started reading. It was something about— Something about—a contest. A beauty contest. That was it, a beauty contest. Feeling a sense of mounting excitement, he mutters the words aloud to himself, "A beauty contest," and in that quiet moment of articulation, the words just off his lips, in his mind's eye he sees a picture. It is a photograph of a tall, angular girl in a bathing suit. She wears a banner across her bosom, and as a man, shorter than she, reaches up to crown her with a cheap rhinestone tiara, she is smiling a wide, toothsome Latin smile.

Then suddenly, even as his mind is conjuring the page, there it is—crumpled, wadded, buried somewhere near the bottom. In the next moment he's holding it in trembling hands, sweeping off debris, smoothing out the creases of the page on the surface of the long trestle table. And there, finally, is the very picture he imagined— the smiling girl; the short gentleman with the tiara. Above it, a headline, partially torn and obliterated, reads:

CARNIVAL QUEEN CROWNED

Then an inverted pyramidal subhead: "Gloria Melendez to Represent Clinton at City-Wide Beauty Finals."

His eyes gloss quickly over the story, all the details suddenly flooding back to him. Then he realizes what it was that had registered in his mind, several days back, but which, at the time, he didn't fully comprehend. It's not the story, which is innocuous and common enough to be completely forgotten moments after it's read. No. Rather it's the page upon which the story appears. Not a page of one of the big city dailies that are crammed into that valise. Instead, it is the front page of a small publication called the *Clintonian*, one of those little community sheets that come out three or four times a year, distributed as a special slip edition with one of the larger tabloids.

Somewhat smaller than a regular tabloid-size page, this one is crammed with news about the Clinton community, that sprawling ghettolike area running north and south through the Forties and Fifties, and east and west from Eighth Avenue all the way to the Hudson River. Once known as Hell's Kitchen, it is now an area in rapid flux. Crumbling old brownstones next to urban-renewal projects. Factories and warehouses side by side with small merchants—Greek butchers, Italian bakers, Puerto Rican *bodegas* and costermongers. Black dudes and their hookers. And the lower-middle classes there fleeing burgeoning crime.

And that's what had stuck in Konig's head. Not the pretty Puerto Rican girl with the cheap tiara crown. No. It was this little neighborhood newspaper, crammed full of homey little items about a famous local community. Mr. Karolides, the butcher, announces the engagement of his daughter, Rosanna, to Nicholas Magos, a local florist. Mr. Joseph Pappalia slashes all prices by half in his small haberdashery. A picture of Miss Lottie Muñoz, proprietor of a local beauty parlor, waving the hair of Miss Flossie Jewel, cashier at the local cinema, and so forth.

Konig rummages about in the valise for other pages of the publication, but this is the only one he finds. The front page. It bears the date, Sunday, March 31, 1974. In the upper right-hand corner is the serial number 3118. On the opposite side of the page is the photograph of Gloria Melendez.

In the next moment, Konig is back on the phone, dialing Flynn at the phone booth on 8th Street.

"Where the hell ya been?" Flynn growls before Konig can get a word out. "There's three people waitin' on line outside this goddamn booth making faces at me."

"Make a face back," snarls Konig. "Now listen to me."

"You said five minutes," Flynn carps. "Instead you keep me waitin'—"

"Listen to me, goddamnit. Where'd you get that paper?"

"What paper?"

"The paper you packed the heads in."

"That's the paper they were wrapped in."

"The paper you found them in?"

"Yeah, for Chrissake— didn't I just say so?"

"Okay, that's all I wanted to know," Konig shouts. "I'm sending you a page of newspaper—"

"What the hell for?"

"Never mind what the hell for. I'm telling you what for."

"Don't you start your goddamn shoutin'—"

"Shouting?" Konig's voice booms into the speaker. "I'll come down there myself and stuff this paper down your throat. Now you listen to me, goddamnit—"

"Now just a min—"

"Don't interrupt me. Just shut your mouth and do exactly as I tell you."

Long after he'd hung up, Konig continues to sit at his desk while the shadows of the dying afternoon creep all about him From downstairs in the street below the sound of children playing stickball and roller-skating wafts upward through his open windows. But Konig hears nothing. He is watching the phone again and waiting.

Now that the Novocaine has worn off, a dull pain has begun to gnaw at his jaw where the dentist drilled that morning It is a pain, he well knows, that will mount steadily during the next few hours.

From out of the wide assortment of phials, tablets, and spansules in his lower drawer, he takes a Demerol, and another amyl nitrite to relieve the growing sense of constriction in his chest.

A short time later the mail boy walks in, dumps a banded packet of new mail on his desk, and walks out. Konig never stirs. In fact, he scarcely notices the boy's coming or going The mail simply sits there along with the rest of his business, untouched, unattended.

An hour later he is still sitting there. Carver has already poked her head in to say good night, just as she has done religiously each work night for the past twelve years She warns him against staying too late and then goes herself.

Still he waits and watches his phone, all alone in the encroaching dusk of an April night in the city.

Shortly after seven o'clock he pushes his chair away from the desk and on stiff legs lurches to his feet. He has decided to go Where, he doesn't know Certainly not home Not back there to all that. Incredibly, he's hungry. It occurs to him that he hasn't had a thing in his stomach but coffee and Scotch for the past three days.

Putting on his jacket, he catches a glimpse of the packet of mail still on his desk, bound with a thick rubber band "Time for that tomorrow," he mutters and starts out. But something there calls him back Some letter of great urgency His University mail Budgetary matters. A decision on his request for Federal grant monies. Internationa correspondence Something—

With a sigh of resignation he removes the rubber band and flips disconsolately through a stack of envelopes and finds nothing of any great moment But in all that package of stern official-looking correspondence, each with its own glossy and portentous imprint, there is one small, strangely anonymous-looking envelope. It is of a pale-lilac color, suggesting female stationery. The name "Paul Konig" is printed on the face of it in a large, wavering, childlike hand, and it is postmarked Grand Central Station. There is no return address. Inside, he can feel something flat, heavy, metallic.

He studies it for a while, hefting it in his hand, turning it about, uncertain why he feels that sharp visceral spasm. His legs wobble beneath him and in the next moment he has to sit. For a long time he holds the little lilac envelope in his hand, eying it warily, reluctant to open it, like a man trying to evade some long-expected bad news. Then slowly he tears the seal.

The first thing that comes out of the envelope is a large brass key with a flat numbered head that reads "2384. Grand Central Station. Property of Baggage Clerk."

Inside, on more lilac stationery, is a note put together from words cut out of newspapers and magazines, then glued to the paper. It reads "Friday. 12:15. $300,000. denominations no higher than $20. deposit locker number 2384. after depositing, leave at once. NO TRICKS PLEASE."

It is not signed, but on the bottom is a small thumbprint pressed in what is unmistakably blood. Beneath that, the word "lolly," as if to suggest it is her blood.

For a while he sits there holding the brass baggage key, cold and clammy to the touch, the crooked, wobbly little letters of the message swimming before his eyes, the thumbprint of his daughter like the bloody spoor of a small hurt animal.

His first instinct is to hide the letter. His next is to run. Get the hell out of there, lest Haggard blunder in and see the letter. And if not see the letter. then see him. See his face and divine everything. Then trouble. The detective would insist upon going himself. Detailing a squad of plain-clothes men. Staking out the baggage pickup. The hell with that. The hell with Haggard. No sir. Not with his daughter's life. "No tricks please," the message said, and there was something ominous, very scary about the quiet tone of civility. "No tricks please." And they meant it. They even signed it with her blood. Goddamn animals. Freaks. Psychopaths. 'No tricks please." Right you are, Wally Meacham. Right you are. You're the boss. We'll do it your way.

But in the next moment he's out the door of his office like a man with his clothing on fire. Streaking down the corridors to the still-lighted office of Lieutenant Francis Haggard.

≈≈ 50 ≈≈

"$299, 940—960—980—and $300,000 even."

"In tens and twenties?"

"Yes, sir. Just as you instructed."

FRIDAY, APRIL 19. 9:15 A.M. CHEMICAL BANK,
FIFTH AVENUE AND 42ND STREET.

"It was a bit thorny putting together that large a sum in such small denominations on such short notice, but we coped." Mr. Whitney Graybard beams radiantly, like a small, eager puppy waiting to be patted. "We had the twenties here, but we had to send out to a half-dozen branch offices for the tens."

"Sorry I put you to such trouble," says Konig.

"Not at all, sir. That's what we're here for. Your lawyer did give us something of a start though, when he called yesterday."

"It was a bit late, wasn't it?"

"About 4:15. I was already gone, but fortunately he caught Peters, my assistant. Frankly, it *is* a great deal of cash to put together on such short notice." Mr. Graybard leans back expansively in his large leather chair behind a commodious leather-topped desk unblemished by so much as a single scrap of paper. "Any special reason for it?"

"For what?"

"The small denominations," Mr. Graybard retorts, and in that instant all the cheery affability of his former manner shifts and in its place is something rather cagey and skeptical. "Bit irregular, you know."

"Oh, is it?" says Konig, trying to sound unruffled. What he needs now least of all is an inquisitive bank official.

He well understands the man's suspicions. Hadn't he had the same difficulty with Barstow, for years the family attorney? Calling him that way late in the afternoon with a highly implausible story about a business venture he wanted to invest in for Lolly. Wanting $300,000 in cash drawn immediately against a trust fund that Ida's family had established for Lolly. Until her twenty-fifth birthday, he was custodian of the fund and had her power of attorney.

Of course Barstow was curious. He knew nothing of Lolly's present situation, and the more evasive Konig became, the more intractable grew the lawyer. Didn't Lolly realize that by withdrawing such a sizable chunk of the fund prematurely she would be losing a considerable amount of income each year from accruing interest?

Yes, she realized that, Konig said, trying to remain calm. What kind of business was it she wanted to invest in? Had they had good solid investment counsel? Why hadn't they consulted him? Why cash and why small denominations?

Of course the man balked. Wanted to put the thing off till he had a chance to look the whole matter over. Of course, Barstow went on begrudgingly, Lolly did have the right to withdraw from the trust before her twenty-fifth birthday, but only with the consent of the custodian, and if there was good and sufficient reason for her doing so.

"Goddamnit, I wouldn't be calling you and asking you for it if there wasn't," Konig, looking at the bloody thumbprint on his desk, bawled into the phone.

The violence of the outburst made Barstow even more wary. He started questioning Konig about his health. Then he asked, "How is Lolly, anyway?"

At that point Konig erupted. They shouted oaths and epithets back and forth at each other for ten minutes. Konig hectored and badgered the man, finally beating him to his knees. The attorney capitulated, making a sound of weariness and disgust. The money would be ready and waiting for him at the Chemical Bank the following morning, he said, and flung the phone down.

"Just a business venture I'm getting into with my daughter," says Konig now, unable to meet the icy but cordial stare of Mr. Graybard, lolling regally behind his desk.

"Yes, Doctor, I know. You said that. But still, it is a bit unusual."

"You mean the amount of money or the small denominations?"

"Both."

"Well, possibly," Konig replies. And beneath his small, crooked smile he's beginning to smolder dangerously. "Still, that's what we need."

Mr. Graybard says not a word. Merely gazes at him with an odd smile. "Well," he says, suddenly rising from his desk, as if to signal that the meeting is at an end, "if that's the way it is, that's the way it is. I wish you and your daughter every good fortune in this new undertaking. You have something you can carry all this in, Doctor?" Mr. Graybard strides across the room to a long console on the far side of his office where the bills have been stacked in tall, neat piles. "Three hundred thousand in tens and twenties has quite a heft to it." He chuckles. "I can let you have one or two of our own transferral cases."

"Thank you. That won't be necessary." Konig, eager to go, waves the suggestion aside. "I've brought this." He lifts to a nearby chair a battered old Gladstone that has been sitting by his feet.

Mr. Graybard's distant inspection of the bag is cursory but thorough. "That ought to do splendidly," he says. "Here, let me give you a hand."

Swiftly and methodically the two men pass huge stacks of bills between them, cramming them into the throat of the bag till it's fairly brimming. In a matter of moments the surface of the long console is cleared of bills and the clasps on the battered old Gladstone are snapped shut.

Graybard sees Konig to the door of his office. Standing there, he extends his hand. "If ever we can be of any further assistance, Doctor—"

"Thank you," Konig mumbles, moving blindly past him. "You've been very kind."

"Nevertheless, don't hesitate." With that oddly enigmatic smile still on his lips, Mr. Graybard watches the rumpled figure lurch across the marble floor of the bank to the street doors. "Would you like one of the guards to see you out, Doctor?" he cries after the receding figure.

"No, thank you," Konig replies without looking back. "I have a patrol car waiting outside for me."

"Deep-grooved, inverted V-shaped abrasions about the neck, caused by mattress ticking; old cut wounds on the front of ulnar aspect of left wrist; recently ingested food particles in the stomach, undigested, intact rice granules and green bean fragments; half-inch-long abrasion above the left eyebrow; ecchymosis, left inner surface of scalp overlying fracture area; fracture of skull, fresh."

10:00 A.M. DISTRICT ATTORNEY'S OFFICE, CRIMINAL COURTS BUILDING, 100 CENTRE STREET.

"Those then, I take it, Dr. Konig, to the best of your knowledge, are the salient features of the Medical Examiner's report?"

"That is correct."

"And the gist then of the ME report, if I understand it correctly, has been that the injuries enumerated here were sustained when the body fell from where it had hung in the cell? That is, after Robinson was already dead?"

"Yes," Konig replies briskly. "That is the main thrust of our report." He gazes sharply about at the three men gathered there—Deputy Mayor Benjamin, Dr. Charles Carslin, District Attorney Clifford Binney.

The District Attorney, a tall, sallow man with a jesuitical manner, reflects inwardly a moment. Then he turns to Carslin. "Now, Doctor, will you present those features of the second autopsy, conducted by you, that either differ from or are totally omitted from the Medical Examiner's report?"

"I'd be happy to." Carslin rises.

"No need to stand, Doctor." Binney gestures him back to his seat. "We're quite informal here."

Looking somewhat miffed, Carslin fumbles back into his chair. Then settling his glasses firmly on the bridge of his nose, he begins to recite aloud from his report.

As Carslin drones on in his most official-sounding voice,

Konig's eyes drift upward and around the District Attorney's musty, cluttered office with its shelves of books, tomes—torts, New York State law, criminal practice—lining each wall from floor to ceiling. There must be thousands of volumes crowding in upon the office, gathering dust, using up all the available air, making the atmosphere of the place close and oppressive.

"—two additional and separate head wounds not reported by the ME." Carslin's voice is strident with accusation. "An area of extensive hemorrhage over the back of the right hand that was not mentioned at all. Dark-red contusion over the right shinbone. And, instead of the superficial abrasion over the left eyebrow described in the ME report, I found a deep, gaping wound reaching to the surface of the skull bone. Also, the injury to the left side of the head was miserably understated. It was twice as large as the one described by the ME." Carslin's eyes seem glowing, almost triumphant, as he delivers this final *coup de grace.*

But the Chief Medical Examiner seems scarcely aware of what is going on around him. He sits listlessly in his chair, his expression vacant and uncaring. At a certain point his straying eyes collide with those of the Deputy Mayor, who is staring at him with a puzzled expression, as if he was waiting for the Chief—expecting him to—make some reply to Carslin's report. But no reply seems forthcoming.

"Can we come to the crux of the matter, please, Dr Carslin?" Clifford Binney's tones are calm and reasonable. "Did the prisoner, Robinson, die as a direct result of injuries inflicted upon him by others or were the injuries self-inflicted during the process of a suicide by hanging?"

"I'm coming back to that now." Carslin throws back his shoulders and straightens his glasses. "During the course of my examination I concluded that at least five separate injuries had been inflicted on the deceased prior to death, and in all probability were sustained during the course of a beating."

Benjamin, fidgeting and twisting in his seat, gapes at Konig, waiting for him to reply. But Konig never stirs. The Deputy Mayor swings around to Carslin. "How can you say that? How can you sit there so smug and self-righteous—"

"Maury—" Binney's voice rises just enough to subdue the Deputy Mayor.

"If you'd just let me finish"—Carslin glowers at Benjamin—"I'd be glad to tell you. Dr. Konig could tell you too."

There's a moment of awkwardness as all their gazes appear to converge upon Konig, still sitting there, eyes lowered, looking listless, disheveled, curiously small.

"In any event," Carslin continues, "the wounds suggest that they were inflicted by a blunt weapon; that they were sufficient enough to have caused considerable pain and suffering. And, as a result of tissue studies I prepared right at the site, tissue studies that the ME had neglected to carry out, I think I can now say without any doubt that the wounds and contusions I found on Robinson were inflicted before he died. Not after, as the ME has reported. And that the most likely explanation of his death was that he was beaten to death or at least into unconsciousness by the prison guards, who then strung him up in order to make his death appear to be a suicide."

"Preposterous." Benjamin leaps to his feet, red in the face, shouting, waving his hands. "Preposterous. I will not sit here and—"

"Maury—" snaps the District Attorney.

"—permit that man to impugn the reputation of an entire penal system just because—"

"Maury—" the District Attorney nearly shouts.

"No—I'm sorry, Cliff. I won't sit here and—"

"Either you sit and keep quiet," Binney says, jaw taut, voice ominously low, "or get out."

There is something now in that quiet, jesuitical manner that brings the Deputy Mayor up sharply, overwhelms and flusters him, so that he falls back to his seat, baffled and puffing.

"Now let me understand this." Binney swivels back to face Carslin. "You're suggesting that the deceased did not hang himself, but was strung up by guards after they'd beaten him senseless, so as to make it appear that he took his own life."

"Don't you see what he's trying to do, Cliff?" Benjamin turns appealingly to the District Attorney. "He's out to make a big name for himself by slandering the entire City Corrections Department."

"Maury, if you don't shut up," Binney suddenly thunders, "I'm going to throw you the hell out of here."

Benjamin is on the verge of shouting back. But thinking better of it, merely gnashes his teeth, folds his arms, and turns away.

Finally unnerved, Binney sighs, pushes his hand hectically through his hair, and turns to Konig. "What do you have to say about all this, Paul?"

Konig sits silent, unmoving, as if he had not heard the question directed at him.

"Paul?" Binney says once more. His voice is once again quiet, and infinitely patient.

Konig sits stonily, his eyes fixed on the floor.

"Paul, have you been following all this?"

"Yes," Konig replies listlessly.

"Is this true, Paul? Did your office omit doing these rather crucial tissue studies?"

"Yes," Konig says, eyes lowered, shoulders slumped wearily. "It's true. And the man responsible for the omission has been reprimanded."

"And," Benajmin interjects, "he refuses to identify the man on his staff who conducted the first autopsy."

"Let's not open that can of beans now," says Binney, sitting back in his chair, the tips of his fingers folded across his vest. He is still looking toward Konig, studying him intently. "And now, Paul, now that you've had an opportunity to examine the tissue studies prepared by Dr. Carslin, what's your opinion of his conclusions?"

"Very plausible," Konig replies at once.

Benjamin's head snaps around. Gaping at the Chief incredulously, he has the hurt, puzzled look of a man betrayed.

Carslin smiles quietly to himself.

Konig's eyes slowly rise from the floor, and he stares around at them. "This sort of thing has certainly happened before in penal institutions. No one has ever suggested that the Tombs is a fresh-air fund for underprivileged boys."

"Let me get this straight, Paul," says Binney. "Are you now repudiating the conclusions of your own office?"

"Yes, sir, I am. But only those aspects of the report that pertain to time of death in relation to the time when the injuries in question were sustained. And I must also concede that Dr. Carslin's excellent tissue studies demonstrate enough leukocytic infiltration at the site of the injuries to leave no doubt in my mind that the injuries were sustained while the deceased was still alive, and undoubtedly were inflicted by guards or other prisoners."

"More like guards, Paul." Carslin's manner, now that he's had substantial concessions, is suddenly full of solicitude and warm regard for his old teacher. "Robinson had been isolated, put in solitary confinement, for at least two weeks before his death."

"That's because he was a goddamned troublemaker," Benjamin snarls. "You know that as well as I do, Carslin. Daily fistfights and quarreling with other prisoners and guards."

"So I've been told." Carslin shrugs. "Be that as it may, however, he was in solitary confinement. Other prisoners simply could not have gotten at him."

"Guards, prisoners, whatever," says Konig with sudden irritability. "The fact remains he was beaten. I concede that. I concede that my office neglected to carry out the requisite tests to determine that he was beaten. I concede that the ME report stating that Robinson's injuries were caused as a result of the body falling to the floor while it was being cut down from where it hung in the cell—that, too, was wrong. Wildly wrong. I concede that." Konig gazes around at the three men gathered there, staring back at him raptly. "But I think also—" his gaze suddenly drops on Carslin like a trap—"that Dr. Carslin would have to concede to me that those same superb tissue preparations of his also reveal that the wounds shown there are at least forty-eight hours old."

"The implication being that"—Binney leans quickly forward on his desk—"Robinson died at least two days after the beating was inflicted?"

"That's right," says Konig.

"And that the wounds, in and of themselves, were not the direct cause of death?"

"That's right." Konig smiles wearily at Carslin. "You neglected to mention that in your excellent report, Charley."

Benjamin laughs out loud, but his hilarity is immediately quashed by a portentous arching of the District Attorney's brow.

"How can you be sure of this, Paul?" Binney asks.

"Ask Dr. Carslin. He'd be glad to tell you."

"Is this true, Dr. Carslin?" Binney turns to face the

young pathologist. "Were these wounds shown here in your photographs and tissue slides really inflicted forty-eight hours before death?"

"Yes, sir," Carslin murmurs a little grimly. He is no longer smiling. "What Dr. Konig so shrewdly points out is the simple, incontrovertible fact that a human body responds to injury by mobilizing thousands of white blood cells—we call them leukocytes—at the site of injury. This is a vital reaction. It can occur only in a living animal. There are several basic types of this white blood cell and they arrive at the wound in fairly regular sequence. It's a process that takes from two to forty-eight hours. Repair cells become abundant about twenty-four hours after the injury has been sustained, and these scar-tissue cells, along with the leukocytes, are spotted quite easily through the microscope. In the tissue specimens we took from Robinson's body, the number and types of cells present suggest not only that the wounds had been inflicted while he was still alive, but also about forty-eight hours before death."

Carslin's voice drops an octave or so in tone as he concedes this last point. Some of the starch has definitely gone out of him.

"Very interesting." The Deputy Mayor beams happily for the first time that morning.

Carslin's face has gone a deep red. "What the hell does that mean? Only that he didn't die directly after the beating. It doesn't say that he didn't die *as a result of the beating*. I defy Dr. Konig to examine the fracture line in this X ray of Robinson's skull and assert that a skull injury of that magnitude could not cause death—even forty-eight hours after having been inflicted."

All eyes now shift back to Konig, who appears to be very carefully weighing his reply. "I've already conceded a number of things here this morning," he sighs wearily in his chair. "That Robinson's injuries were sustained while he was still alive; that they were undoubtedly inflicted during the course of a beating; that the Medical Examiner did not carry out the requisite tests to determine that such a beating took place. I have conceded all that. I have even repudiated the Medical Examiner's conclusions as to the actual cause of death. Now, yes—I will also concede Dr. Carslin's last point. Such injuries as the one shown here in this X ray can, in certain instances, be judged the *direct cause* of death even forty-eight hours after they're inflicted. I concede that to you, Charley, but, unfortunately, that is not the case here."

There's a moment of total silence which the three men struggle to digest the significance of Konig's final point. Then suddenly Carslin is on his feet shouting. "Not the case here?" he bawls across the room. "Not the case here?"

"That's what I said." Konig lifts an X ray from the desk. It shows a skull in profile with a long, dark, clearly verifiable fracture line running along the side of it. "As a matter of fact," he continues, "while this fracture is long, it's trivial."

"Trivial? Trivial?" Carslin splutters, unable to find another word. "You have the colossal gall to sit there and describe that fracture as trivial? I dare say, it might seem trivial to you. I bet it didn't seem very trivial to poor Robinson at the time they bashed his head."

"I object to your use of the word 'bashed,' " snaps Benjamin.

"Well, I assure you it was no love tap that produced that fracture." Carslin flings another X ray down hard on the desktop beneath the Deputy Mayor's nose.

"Who're you kidding, Carslin?" Benjamin sneers. "You're not interested in this Robinson boy. You're just out to make a big name for yourself by portraying the prison system of this city as inhuman, barbaric. Something out of the Dark Ages."

"Well, isn't it?" Carslin is on his feet again, shouting. "Don't these X rays and tissue studies prove just that? And I object to your suggesting—this is the second time now—that I'm trying to make a name for myself just because I'm looking for the truth. Would any of this have come out if I hadn't been looking for the truth? Not if it was up to you. Not if it was up to Paul Konig. This is all too embarrassing, isn't it? Could cause a scandal. So let's keep it quiet. Right? All I can say is, thank heavens for the vigilance of a mortician in Yonkers who had the perspicacity to see great disparities between the Medical Examiner's report and what he could see directly before his eyes."

"You have just suggested," Benjamin says between clenched teeth, "that the Department of Corrections, the Medical Examiner's Office, and the Mayor's Office are in a conspiracy to suppress—"

"By God, yes," Carslin shouts. "That's exactly what I'm suggesting."

"Gentlemen, gentlemen"—Binney pounds the desk with an open palm—"we're straying from the point. We're not here this morning to judge the merits of the City penal system. What we want to determine is the cause of Robinson's death, and whether or not there is sufficient evidence here surrounding the circumstances of the boy's death to convene a grand jury. Paul"—Binney turns back to Konig—"a moment ago you described these skull injuries as 'trivial.'"

"Trivial!" Carslin laughs bitterly.

The District Attorney scowls at Carslin above his glasses, then continues. "What exactly did you mean by 'trivial'?"

Konig pauses, his manner suddenly guarded and uneasy. "I meant," he says at last, "that in all these X rays of the deceased's skull, and in our own examination of the brain at the time of the first autopsy, we found no visible sign of gross injury or hemorrhage to the brain. I don't think Dr. Carslin can refute that."

Struggling between rage and disbelief, Carslin sits down again, struck dumb, shaking his head incredulously. The blood has drained from his face. His lips, clamped tight against each other, have the appearance of rubber bands stretched to the point of breaking. "Would you say that again, please?" His voice as he speaks is barely above a whisper.

"Very well," Konig sighs. "Neither your X rays nor our autopsy reveals any sign whatsoever of either gross injury or hemorrhage in the brain as a result of that fracture. As evidence, those X rays could only be described as circumstantial. So I most definitely do not concede that the fracture shown there is the cause of death."

"You're saying to me then"—Carslin struggles to control the tremor in his voice—"that all blows to the head causing death can be shown to produce either gross injury or hemorrhage to the brain?"

"Now what's all this about?" Benjamin whimpers feebly.

"It's a very significant medical point," Carslin snaps, his eyes still fixed on Konig. "Answer the question, Paul. Yes or no?"

"Yes," Konig replies in a very quiet voice.

"*All* blows to the head, Paul?"

"Yes," Konig whispers. "All."

"And what exactly does this mean?" Binney asks, sensing he has come now to the crux of things.

"Ask Dr. Konig." Carslin seethes with scorn. "Let him tell you what it means."

"What's he suggesting, Paul?" the Deputy Mayor asks, sensing, too, that something is going wrong. Slipping away from them. "What the hell is he trying to pull?"

"I've said all I can say," Konig addresses the floor.

"Well, if he won't tell you," Carslin says, "then I will. There's not a neuropathologist today who has not described well-documented cases of blows to the head resulting in instantaneous death where the most meticulous examination of the brain at autopsy fails to produce a single visible sign of brain damage. Gross, micro, or whatever. I have seen cases like this and so has Dr. Konig."

For a long moment only a large clock ticking on Binney's desk can be heard. When at last he speaks, the District Attorney's voice is very soft. "Paul?"

Another pause, then, "That may be Dr. Carslin's experience," Konig says, his manner grown even more furtive and guarded. "It is not mine."

There is a moment when no one seems able to speak. There is the sense of a point having been passed, a bridge crossed; a sense of irretrievable loss.

Finally Carslin breaks the silence. He seems no longer angry. His expression is full of quiet wonder and amazement. "If I had not been a witness to this, I'd refuse to believe it had ever happened. To see Paul Konig, one of the world's leading forensic authorities, possibly *the* outstanding authority, a great scholar, a great teacher, a scientist, reduced to this contemptible face-saving performance."

Carslin stands and starts to gather his papers. All the while Carslin has been speaking, Konig's eyes have been glued fixedly to the floor, as if he were seeking a sort of sanctuary there. Slumped in his chair, hands folded in his lap, staring resolutely downward, like a child chastised, he has the look of defeat about him. More than that, shame. A defeat born of the loss of self-respect.

"Amen." The Deputy Mayor rises with a sigh of relief. "The skull fracture then was not the direct cause of death."

"That's your version," Carslin snaps, stuffing X rays and

papers into a briefcase, "not mine. And I don't intend to sit around here and permit the Mayor's Office, the District Attorney, the Correction, Department, the Medical Examiner, the whole goddamned kit and caboodle of you to bury the truth of what I—"

Even as Carslin rants on, stuffing papers into the case and glowering, Konig rises slowly to his feet. Looking neither right nor left, eyes hollow, vacant, like a man in a trance, he stoops and lifts from the floor the battered Gladstone bag. Dumbfounded, the others watch him as he turns his back and, without a word, starts walking slowly out of the room.

"You're a liar, Paul," Carslin shouts at the retreating figure. "You know you're a liar."

Konig neither pauses nor turns. No sign whatever to signify that he has heard. Sagging a bit beneath the weight of the bag, he just keeps moving straight ahead, out the door, leaving it open as he goes.

≈ 52 ≈

"Yeah, that's ours. We did that job."

"You did?"

"Sure—come right outta this shop. What about it?"

"Can you tell me somethin' about it?"

Noon. Triangle Printing and Linotype Corp., 22nd Street and Eighth Avenue.

Mr. Murray Bloom bites deeply into a corned beef on rye. Chewing energetically, he waves with almost pontific grandeur at the piece of torn and crumpled newsprint held by Flynn. "Sure. What can I tell you?"

Flynn reaches across the desk and lays the page before him. "Says there you printed this paper on March thirty-first."

"Wrong. It was distributed on March thirty-first." Mr. Bloom bites deeply into a sour pickle, then sucks Coke noisily up through a straw. "Ran it off about a week and a half before." He dabs hectically with a napkin at the pickle juice that has squirted onto his tie.

The phone rings on Mr. Bloom's desk. He snatches it up, listens a moment, making a series of long-suffering, explanatory faces at Flynn. "Listen—can't talk now. I got someone here. Call me back in half an hour." He hangs up, reaches once more for his corned beef on rye, and nods at Flynn to resume.

"Says here." Flynn goes on, "in the upper right-hand corner. number 3118. What's that?"

"Serial number."

"That mean that this here is the three thousand one hundred and eighteenth copy of the paper you printed?"

"Right   Mr Bloom's jaws clamp neatly over a full quarter of his sandwich "That's what that means."

"Every paper you print have a serial number?"

"That's right" Mr. Bloom nods and chews.

"Can you tell me how many you printed?"

"Oh, Jesus—how the hell would I know? You gotta know that?"

Flynn smiles. "It'd help."

Bloom presses a buzzer on his desk and stares impatiently out of the glass wall partition of his office. Beyond the glass can be seen rows of Linotype and huge offset machines making monstrous clanking sounds Men wearing sun visors and elbow garters are seated at each Proofreaders and messengers, galley runners and secretaries, swarm back and forth outside the glass like innumerable small fish in an aquarium.

Shortly an enormous woman of Buddha-like proportions waddles toward the glass door of the office She has a Kewpie-doll face, heavily made up, and she is sweating profusely.

"Come on in, Tessie." Bloom, sucking his Coke, waves her in. "Tessie, this is Sergeant Flynn of the police. Tessie Balbato."

They mumble hellos, and for a moment the heavy girl is flustered overwhelmed with shyness.

"Tessie"- Bloom holds up the sheet of newsprint—"offhand, can you give us the print run on this *Clintonian* job?"

"We pulled seven thousand five hundred copies," the girl replies instantly.

"So that this one was pretty near the middle of the run?" Flynn asks.

"If it says 3118"—Bloom ingests the second half of his pickle— "you know then we pulled some four thousand more—right?"

"Four thousand three hundred and eighty-two more," says the fat girl, instantly supplying the exact number.

Mr. Bloom glances sharply at her. "Right—four thousand three hundred and eighty-two more."

Momentarily baffled, Flynn glances back and forth at both of them.

Mr Bloom bites hard into his corned beef on rye. "So what's next?"

"So," says Flynn, "where do these papers go after they leave here?"

"Jobbers, wholesalers. They then distribute it to the newsstands and cigar stores in the area. That particular paper's only distributed in the Clinton district. Comes out four times a year. Is that through the *News* or the *Post*, Tessie?"

"The *News*," says the big girl. "They slip it right in at the stand."

Flynn nods and makes a note on his pad. "These jobbers—how many of them take care of the Clinton district?"

Bloom's chewing comes to an abrupt halt, a bit of corned beef still sticking out of the corner of his mouth. He glances toward the girl. "Tessie?"

"We deal with four in that area," she replies instantly. "Spiegel Kristofos Wagoner Brothers, and Charles."

"Charles pay that bill yet, Tessie?" Bloom snaps.

"No." The girl looks uneasily at him "Marty went over to see him today They promise for next Friday."

"I'm not holding my breath Bloom inserts the final quarter of the sandwich into his mouth, continuing to speak all the while. "Go right ahead, Sergeant. Sorry to interrupt."

"That's okay." Flynn smiles. "I'm almost finished anyway. Just one more question. You got any way of tellin' me which one of those four distributors handled this particular piece of paper?"

Bloom chews pensively for a moment. "You got the invoice slips for that run, Tessie?"

"I'm pretty sure." She glances nervously at Flynn. "Hold on. I'll be back in a minute."

She waddles quickly from the office with that curious, light-toed grace not uncharacteristic of very fat people. For a few moments the two men chat inanely about the weather while Bloom goes about the business of polishing off the remainder of his lunch. He now has before him a macaroon and a large paper container of tea with lemon.

Shortly the fat girl is back in the office with a thick folder of invoice sheets. Licking her thumb periodically, she flicks swiftly through them. "Okay—here it is," she says, evidently pleased. *"Clintonian*—Spiegel took the first two thousand, Charles took the next two thousand. The Wagoners took the next eight hundred, so that'd start with number 4001 and run through 4800. And Kristofos took all the rest—4801 through 7500. What number were you interested in again, Sergeant?"

"3118."

"That'd have to be Charles," Tessie says, snapping her invoice folder shut.

"Charles—my good friend Charles." Mr. Bloom belches softly.

"Where is this Charles located?" asks Flynn.

The fat girl glances down at her invoice sheet. "452 West 49th."

"Over by Tenth Avenue," Bloom says. "You going over there?"

"Right now," says Flynn.

"If you talk to Stanley, see if you can't get my money." Blooms chuckles. "Tell him you're the police and I sent you over."

Bloom laughs out loud; then, so does the fat girl.

"Say, what's all this about, anyway?" Bloom bites deeply into his macaroon and waves the crumpled page of newssheet at Flynn. "What's all the big fuss about this piece of paper anyway?"

"Nothin' much." Flynn laughs along with him. "We just found a severed head wrapped up in it. We're trying to find out who did the choppin', that's all."

For a moment there's complete silence as the laughter wanes on Mr. Bloom's lips and his jaws cease to chew. Then the page of crumpled newssheet slips from his fingers, wafting languidly downward to his desktop like a snowflake. For a man who only moments before had been hooting with glee, who was even then still savoring the mingled flavors of his lunch, he appears suddenly green and queasy.

"Finish up your macaroon," says Flynn, grinning broadly, "it looks very good. And thanks for everything." He reaches across the desk and snatches up the torn, crumpled page from where it has lighted on the waxed paper and various leavings of Mr. Bloom's lunch.

As he passes the fat girl on his way out, he tips his hat raffishly and winks.

≈≈ 53 ≈≈

12:10 p.m. Grand Central Station, Upper Level.

The noon lunch hour. Crowds streaming out of the arrival gates, bustling through the arcades. Queues formed all about the place. OTB queues, New York State Lottery queues, Merrill Lynch "Big Board" queues, the Friday payday queues at the First National City minibank, at the Ticketron booth, at the Information Booth at the center of the station. Outside the gates of Track 17 there is the weekend queue waiting to board the 12:30 to New Haven and Boston.

Lunch hour crowds are rushing for the Oyster Bar, Charlie Brown's, the Trattoria, Zum Zum, the Liggett's lunch counter, the pizza stands, the frankfurter stands, the Carvel stands. They browse in the Doubleday Book Shops and wait for a chair at the Esquire bootblack stands.

Down an escalator from the mezzanine floor of the Pan Am Building, Paul Konig descends into the strangely muted electric glow of the Grand Central underworld. At the foot of the escalator Konig steps off the moving stair with a small, tentative hop that suggests frailty and old age. In his right hand he carries the Gladstone bag. He knows exactly where he is going, having been carefully instructed by the NYPD as to the exact location of that long bank of gray steel lockers in which baggage locker number 2384 is contained.

At the bottom of the escalator, Konig takes a sharp right, goes past a baggage counter. Then at the Esquire shoeshine stand he takes a sharp left. A few steps from there on his left again is a long wall of baggage lockers, battleship gray and much scarified with graffiti and the like. Directly opposite is a Savarin lunch bar.

At the moment of Konig's appearance, the 12:15 from Stamford arrives, disgorging passengers through Gate 34, who swarm outward from there in all directions. Caught up in the dizzy tidal rush, Konig wends his way through a swarm of humanity. In a matter of moments he reaches the wall of lockers, his eyes streaming up, down, and across, searching for his number, his heart thudding in his chest. Number 2384 is at chest level near the center of the bank of lockers and it's locked. The key, carried in his trembling fingers from the moment he stepped from the cab and into the station, now jabs hectically at the hole. Two, three of those tremulous jabs go wildly awry, one at last connecting—and the key slides in effortlessly. A sharp twist now to the right, the lock disengages, and the door swings open to a stale, rather fetid emptiness.

Without hesitation, Konig hoists the Gladstone into the locker, slams the door shut, twists sharp left, thus locking it, then drops the key back into his pocket.

Now he turns sharply on his heel, and looking neither right nor left, he walks quickly out of the station.

At the Savarin lunch counter across the way, his back to the bar and having a beer, Francis Haggard watches Konig lumber heavily past the glass windows and disappear beyond, leaving in his wake an unimpeded view of wall lockers.

The detective sips his beer slowly. He knows it will be some time before Meacham makes his move, if indeed he makes one at all. Haggard's own guess is that he won't. Not now. This is merely a trial run. A test to see how Konig performs. And just as Haggard has staked out the pick-up location, so he is certain that Meacham's people have done the same. Within those hordes of people swarming past the windows like schools of fish, among the innumerable figures loitering in that area for one reason or another, among them, he is certain, are Meacham's people. They're doing precisely what he is doing—keeping locker 2384 under very close surveillance.

Tilting his beer back, his eyes, above the rim of his

glass, swarm over the area. At the Esquire stand he spies a portly fellow having a shoeshine while his eyes appear to devour a racing form. That is, he recognizes, Detective Sergeant Donnello of the 41st Precinct. A short distance away, at the Nedick's juice stand, wolfing a frankfurter and an orange drink, is Freddie Zabriskie from the 23rd. He wears a trench coat and a peaked checkered cap. With his attaché case and his slightly agitated manner, he gives the impression of a harried commuter grabbing a bite before boarding a train.

Working behind the baggage pick-up counter, in red cap, looking flushed and jovial, is Wershba's very own Morrissey from the 17th; while a little way down the concourse, the thoroughly unsavory-looking creature, complete with foul clothes, and a long, licey beard, is young Sam DeSoto, a man with whom Haggard has never worked. It always makes him uneasy, working with someone he doesn't know. And this DeSoto is young, little more than a novice. But his record is outstanding. Already he has made a quick name for himself at the 41st. Right now he appears to be loitering there for vaguely immoral purposes.

Haggard orders a second beer, nibbles a hard-boiled egg from the free-lunch counter, and prepares for a long siege.

It is a game of watching now. If they come at all, the detective reasons, it will be after the lunch hour, when the crowds thin out. Then people still lingering there will be conspicuous by their presence. For this reason Haggard and his small force have worked out a plan of rotation. If no one shows at locker 2384 within an hour, Haggard will leave the Savarin bar and stroll outside to a waiting unmarked police car where, by means of radio and highly sophisticated transponding equipment, he will maintain contact with the other four men still inside.

Donnello, his shoes now shined, has already left. But he's gone only a short way off—up to the mezzanine by the Ticketron booth that juts out above the main station. He cannot see the bank of lockers from that point. Nor can anyone in that area see him. But he can see Morrissey working behind the baggage counter and Morrissey can see him easily enough to make the most innocuous of hand gestures abundantly clear.

Freddie Zabriskie has now strolled to a magazine stand

and proceeds to thumb through *Playboy* and *Penthouse* beneath the hostile glare of the newsstand attendant. Soon he too will go. And then, finally, DeSoto. That will leave only Morrissey, who, because of his official position behind the baggage counter, can remain indefinitely without raising suspicion. Then, if no one has shown by 1:15 to pick up the bag, a whole new platoon of four will take over. Four new faces, completely unrecognizable to anyone who happens to be somewhere in the vicinity watching.

By 1 P.M. Haggard is still leaning up against the bar at the Savarin. Other than Morrissey, he is the last of his group still there. Though he will wait until 1:15 as planned, he does not seriously think anyone will show. Not this first time anyway. This is merely a test to see how Konig will perform, and that, he is sure, they are closely monitoring. For, if it were to become apparent to Meacham's people that the area around the baggage lockers was staked out, or if, indeed, they did send a pick-up man and it became evident that the man was being followed, Lauren Konig's life wouldn't be worth a plugged nickel. Haggard knows there are two things they must not do. If a pick-up man does show, they must not move in too quickly, before the man can lead them back to Meacham; and if they do follow a pick-up man, under no circumstances may they lose him.

Glancing across at locker 2384, still locked, its contents still untouched, Haggard wipes his mouth with a napkin and picks his change off the bar, leaving a half dollar for the bartender. The big clock above the station says 1:15, and just as the detective moves out through the glass doors of the Savarin bar, a short, stocky fellow with a glabrous dome and enormous mustaches sweeps in. Sergeant Leo Wershba of the 17th Precinct, first man of the second rotation, is now in place.

Out once more in the busy concourse, Haggard pauses to light a cigarette. Another man by the name of DeGarmo, up from the 22nd, is just then climbing up to the chair at the Esquire shoe stand.

Haggard will now stroll at a leisurely pace out of the station and take up his vigil in the unmarked patrol car standing just outside the station at the Vanderbilt Avenue exit. On his way out he passes Morrissey, wrestling a bulky carton up onto the baggage counter beneath the stern glare of a petulant old lady who is loudly rebuking him.

Just then the 1:25 from Hartford pulls in. The track gates open and Haggard is caught up in a swarm of detraining passengers. For some reason he turns, and just as he rounds the corner he sees, or thinks he sees, someone standing before the wall lockers in the immediate vicinity of 2384. Is the person about to insert a key? He can't be sure. The angle of his vision is such that he can't be sure precisely where the person is standing with relation to locker 2384. And besides, there are now two other totally unrelated people in the area about to pick up luggage from the same wall of lockers.

In the momentary flash in which Haggard had seen this figure, he had an impression of a person of average stature, a somewhat seedy, innocuous-looking creature in a raincoat. But he can't be certain. He's tempted to circle and come around again for a second look. Or even just to glance back. But either action would be perilously stupid. Anyone observing that area from a secreted spot, seeing a man of Haggard's large, imposing stature suddenly turn, wheel about, even casually double back on his tracks, would pick that out in a minute. No—he must go directly on now. Straight out of the station to the waiting car.

Just as he is leaving, he glances up, sees Donnello, on the mezzanine, suddenly turn, then leave very quickly. Then, a bit off to his right, his gaze falls on Morrissey, nodding almost imperceptibly at him.

≈≈ 54 ≈≈

"How the hell would I know?"

"You got the serial numbers on the invoice right there in front of you, don't you?"

"So what the hell does that mean?"

"That copy number 3118 of the *Clintonian* passed through here."

"So it passed through here. So big deal. So did nineteen hundred and ninety-nine other copies of the goddamned paper pass through here. You think I know where I sent each one of them?"

"It's just possible?"

Stanley Charles stops short in his tracks and laughs out loud. It's a short, fierce laugh. Flynn comes to a dead halt behind him, almost piling directly into him.

"Just possible?" Charles laughs again. "You gotta be kidding."

They're standing in the middle of a large warehouse crammed full from floor to ceiling with magazines and newspapers. The storage area is divided into rows and aisles made up of towers of publications waiting to be sent somewhere. A half-dozen or so workmen move through these aisles wrestling huge cartons on and off a fork-lift truck.

Mr. Stanley Charles is a short, brusque man of unbridled energy. A lean, ulcerous-looking fellow who seems always to be smoldering inwardly. Standing now in the middle of one of those narrow aisles, made stuffy and airless from the effect of tons of paper pressing inward, Mr. Charles glares at Flynn.

"I must take care of at least forty stands in that area. You think I know where the hell I sent one lousy goddamned newspaper. For Chrissake. Look—I'm busy here—"

Clipboard in hand, Mr. Charles goes barging up the dusty aisle with Flynn in hot pursuit.

"You mean you could've sent that paper to any one of forty outlets?"

"More like a hundred, pal. I didn't mention the cigar stores, the luncheonettes, the drugstores, the markets—"

Another short, fierce laugh. Flynn is momentarily buffaloed.

"Okay—can you at least tell me this—"

"Tell you what?"

"When those papers come in here from Triangle, how do they arrive?"

"On a truck. How the hell else would they arrive? On a goddamned camel?"

Flynn reddens. "I know on a truck. What I mean is —in a carton? In separate packages? How?"

"Separate packages of fifty."

"Packages of fifty." Flynn's face brightens. His slight expression of pleasure is a source of great irritation to Mr. Charles.

"So what the hell does that tell you? Just that you got forty packages of newspapers to distribute. Don't tell you where the hell you sent them."

"How do they come off the truck?" Flynn goes on doggedly.

Mr. Charles screeches to another halt. "If you think they come off in numerical order with serial numbers attached, and then I send them out again in numerical order with serial numbers attached to a hundred separate invoices—"

"Well, don't you?"

Mr. Charles's goitrous eyeballs bulge even more ominously than usual. Unable to speak, he is reduced to a few choked splutters. Flynn recalls Mr. Murray Bloom's parting words to him when he was leaving the Triangle Printing Corporation—the business about telling Charles that he was a cop and there to collect past-due bills. Standing now with bulging eyes and wattles quivering, Mr. Stanley Charles does have the look of a badly harried man with a surfeit of past-due bills on his desk.

"You must be crazier than I thought you were," he snarls. "Look, I got no more time for this. I'm up to my ass in problems here." He jerks his clipboard up and once again starts pedaling madly up the aisle.

"Okay, okay." Flynn scoots after him. "You say you got about a hundred customers in that area?"

"Mister, I got thousands of customers. All over this goddamned city. Thousands of 'em. See?"

"But you said around a hundred in that area."

"If I said that, that's what it is."

Charles halts before a newly delivered crate of girlie magazines with fairly lurid covers and titles—*Black Leather, Satanic Nights, Dears and Rears,* and other such items. Charles glances at the cover of one and shakes his head. "Look at this garbage," he mutters and in the next moment plunges ahead.

"Well, what I wanna know is"—Flynn puffs along behind him—"did every one of these hundred customers of yours take a delivery of this *Clintonian?*"

"Some did. Some didn't."

"Which ones did?"

"Oh—is that all you want to know?" Charles smirks at him. "That's easy, fella. All I gotta do is go into my books and dig out every one of those invoices for March thirtieth and see which ones took the *Clintonian*. Crazy. All crazy," he mutters and moves on.

"Is that hard?"

Charles laughs again. But this one is not short and fierce. Instead it's rather languid, world-weary. Tinged with exhaustion and futility. "You're a lulu, pal. A real lulu."

"Well, what's the big deal?" Flynn scurries after the wiry little man. "I'll dig 'em out. Just show me where your books are."

"Books. Books." Mr. Charles smiles mournfully. "I got books here up to my ears. Books coming out of my ass. I need a whole new warehouse just for books. Books? You couldn't begin to— Look"—he whirls around, suddenly compassionate, a note of pleading in his voice—"you think them hundred names are all in a neat little pile somewhere with a ribbon tied around them? They're in a huge central card index around a block and a half long. All in alphabetical order. Someone would have to go through those files, look at every address and zip code and see which ones are in Clinton. There are thousands of cards in there. You know how long that'd take?"

"Don't you have a billing department that keeps that information right at hand?"

"Sure we got a billing department." Mr. Charles struggles on with even greater tolerance. "We even got all our customers on a computer. Fancy. Modern. Right? But to dig out that information, separating customers by postal zone numbers, that's still gotta take a couple of people at least a couple of days working on the machines. Right? Then, after I get you the names, I gotta pull out every invoice and see who did and who didn't order the paper for that day. That's a lot of time. You understand? A lot of money. I'd like to help you out, pal. Really, I would. You seem like a nice guy. But I can't. I got a lot of troubles of my own, see? What's the big deal about this lousy piece of paper anyway?"

Flynn pauses, regarding the man silently. Then he speaks. "The guy who bought this lousy piece of paper might've murdered two other guys."

"Murdered?" Mr. Charles's eyebrows cock. "When was this?"

"Around three weeks ago. Dug up the pieces down by the East River this week."

"All cut up?"

"That's right. Chopped into little pieces."

"Sure—sure," Mr. Charles says, curiosity mounting. "I read about that. A dog found the hand. Right?"

"That's right."

"Son of a bitch." Mr. Charles is full of sudden wonderment and awe. "And you think one of my customers did it?"

"Maybe—or more probably, one of your customers' customers."

Mr. Charles shakes his head and whistles softly to himself.

"It's a long shot," Flynn goes on, fanning the man's obvious interest, "I admit it, but I can tell you, one of the heads was wrapped in this piece of paper."

Mr. Charles gapes down at the torn and crumpled front page with the picture of the Puerto Rican beauty queen peering out between the creases. "Wrapped in that?" He whistles softly to himself again and shakes his head in quiet awe. "Son of a bitch."

All the fierce tension seems to melt from the man. Suddenly limp, he leans wearily against one of those floor-to-ceiling towers of newsprint. "This used to be such a good city. Beautiful city. Best goddamned city in the world. Now it's a toilet. The goons and freaks have taken over. Had a cousin of my own shot to death a couple of months ago. Over in Flatbush. Couple of freaks—hopheads—come into his shop over there. Shot him to death. For what? For nothing. For thirteen dollars and some change. He was closin' up and they come in and shot him. Just like that. The way you swat a fly. Young guy. Thirty years old. Just startin' out. A couple of kids. Fuckin' creeps."

For a moment both men are silent.

"And you got no leads?" Charles asks suddenly.

"Nothin' great. Just this piece of paper. And even if I find the guy who bought it, that don't necessarily mean he's the one who did it."

"Nope—it don't," Mr. Charles murmurs distantly. "Look—the auditors and the IRS bastards were here yesterday. This morning a U.S. Marshal handed me a subpoena. I got a tax man coming over in a few minutes. I'm up to my ass here right now. See? Gimme a day or two. I'll get back to you."

Going out, Flynn glances back to wave at Charles. But already the fierce little man has turned back to his clipboard. He is standing near the end of one of those endless avenues of paper, between two enormous towers of unsold magazines. Their monumental size diminishes him. They emphasize his smallness. They slope precariously inward, as if they were about to topple down upon him like the crumbling pillars of some ancient temple. Mr. Stanley Charles, standing there at the foot of them, clipboard poised at the ready, gazing up at them, appears finally cowed. Whatever pitiful pose of defiance with which he confronted these towers before is now all gone. Instead, he looks now very much like a man who has lost something and is trying very hard to find it again. And indeed, he has lost a few things—a city, a cousin, and now, so it appears, he is even about to lose a business.

≈≈ 55 ≈≈

3:00 P.M. FOREST PARK, QUEENS.

Young Sam DeSoto sits alone on a park bench in the cool shade of a full-blooming chestnut. The big white blossoms, like great puffs of cotton, hang low from the branches all about him. On the ground, strewn about his feet, are the myriad tiny blossoms that have showered intermittently downward during the past three-quarters of an hour he has been sitting there.

Slightly after three o'clock now, with school out, the park is beginning to swarm with children. They bike past the bench where DeSoto sits reading a *Sports Illustrated* and looking like a hobo; they roll past him on skates; mothers push infants past in carriages. Back up to the left in a concrete playground encircled with a wrought-iron fence, kids swing on swings, slide on slides, soar up and down on seesaws, and stream all over a Junglegym. Out beyond the playground, in a field across the way, there are kite fliers and softball players. Almost directly behind him, in a thick clump of trees, an old circus carousel whirls more squealing children around and around to the tune of Strauss waltzes wheezing out across the park.

Along with the very young there are, of course, the very old. They sit idly on benches, some dozing, some reading —the retired pensioners, the sick and the resigned.

DeSoto glances up now from the glossy pages of the *Sports Illustrated*. His eyes stray fleetingly off to the right, to a bench about one hundred yards down from him. There sits another man, an innocuous-looking fellow with colorless hair and a recessive chin. His dress is shabby but respectable enough—shirt, tie, suit, raincoat, although there is not the slightest sign of rain. The tatty, rather soiled appearance of the man suggests that he hasn't changed his costume for quite some time. He reads a newspaper, and beside him on the bench sits the battered old Gladstone.

Sam DeSoto has followed this man out from the city, out from Grand Central Station. For the first part of the trip he followed him in the gray unmarked radio patrol car along with Haggard, Zabriskie, and DeGarmo; then later he rode with him in the subway, when he'd taken over from Donnello, who'd followed the man out of Grand Central Station onto 42nd Street and west to Sixth Avenue, where they had both descended into the IND.

By means of small, powerful radio transmitters carried by Donnello, his movements in the subway had been quite easily charted from the patrol car riding along above. Just before entering a train, Donnello had been able to radio that he was boarding an eastbound F train. From there it was a relatively simple matter to follow a series of steady, rhythmic beeps along the well-known route of the F train, moving east under the river and out toward Queens.

The chief danger of this technique was that the followers would, in turn, be followed by Meacham's people. Since the trains in the early afternoon are fairly empty, anyone lingering too long in proximity to the man carrying the Gladstone would be conspicuous. In order to minimize that danger, they had worked out yet another fairly simple system of rotation that involved the patrol car's reaching stations along the route shortly before the train itself. This, too, was a fairly simple matter. And so it was that when Donnello got off the train at Lexington and 53rd, Zabriskie got on. He stayed in the small vestibule one car down from the pick-up man, watching him through the glass door all the way under the East River, through 23rd and Ely and on through Long Island City. When Zabriskie got off at Roosevelt Avenue and Jackson Heights, young Sam DeSoto, who'd arrived there seven minutes before, got on.

It had all gone quite smoothly. When the man with the Gladstone got off at 71st and Continental Avenue, so did DeSoto. From there, by lagging quite far behind and moving at a stroller's pace, he had shadowed the man through the quaint, narrow, Tudorish streets of Forest Hills Gardens right on out through to Woodhaven Boulevard and across to the park, where he sits now far enough away from the man to arouse no suspicions.

He has been sitting there now for nearly an hour, ostensibly reading a magazine but actually watching the man with the Gladstone's every move. His orders from Haggard were not to let the man out of his sight, and under *no* circumstances to apprehend him.

DeSoto glances at his watch. It's going on 3:30 now, and it troubles him a bit that no one has yet shown up to rotate him out of there. Surely any of Meacham's people in the area to pick up the money had observed him by now. He has simply been sitting there too long to go unnoticed. Obviously, they wouldn't move until they were absolutely certain about him. DeSoto sits there now with a growing sense of unease.

Still, he's not unduly alarmed. He knows that DeGarmo is to replace him there. True, DeGarmo is now a half-hour late, but the small, powerful radio transponder beneath his shirt continues to beep reassuringly, beaming out sharp, powerful electronic signals that will guide the men in the unmarked patrol car directly to him.

DeSoto puts his magazine aside now and sits back, closing his eyes, pretending to sleep, but watching the man on the bench through the moist cage of his eyelashes. The thudding oom-pah-pah of Strauss waltzes from the carousel continues to roll out, stridulous and tinny, across the park. And in the air, mingled with the scent of hyacinth, jasmine, and the first lush growth of grass, is the smell of frankfurters and sauerkraut wafting from the vendor's refreshment stand near the carousel.

Aside from the tension of his job there, the scene is all very pleasurable to young DeSoto, a weed sprouted on the city streets, sprung from the hot pavements, the airless brown brick tenements sprawling up around the Hunt's Point district of The Bronx. For him, grass and trees, the sound of children rooting at a softball game, squealing on a carousel, are rare pleasures, and despite the urgency of his job, he succumbs to them. He does not know, has no way of knowing, that Haggard, along with his replacement, DeGarmo, and several others, is still somewhere back there in Jackson Heights, where the battery of the unmarked patrol car had given out, cutting all radio communication between him and them. At that very moment, while the battery is being replaced, Haggard has not the slightest idea where young Sam DeSoto has gone.

≋ 56 ≋

"Fifteen old extractions."

"Right."

"Shell gold crown on the mandibular right third molar."

"Right."

"Partial denture."

"Right."

"Including upper left lateral incisor, canine, and first premolar."

"Right. Any scars? Identification marks?"

"Vaccination. Right upper arm."

"No skin on the right upper arm."

"No skin? Well, what about an old bayonet wound, left side of the pelvis?"

"No skin left on the pelvis either. Stripped off clean. Part of the dismemberment."

"Jesus."

3:25 P.M. MEDICAL EXAMINER'S OFFICE.

"Was he on any medication?" Konig asks, and the voice of Colonel Angus McCormick, dry, perfunctory, comes instantly back at him through five hundred miles of wire from a dispensary office of the post hospital, Fort Bragg, North Carolina. Both men have been at it for the past three-quarters of an hour. Trading data. First merely general physical characteristics—age, height, weight, blood type, and so forth. Then on into ever and ever more specialized clinical detail.

"Codeine, cortisone, and steroids," McCormick replies dryly.

"We picked up the cortisone on gas chromatography. Great deal of codeine in the blood. Arthritic, wasn't he?"

"Certainly looked that way. He'd been in and out of the dispensary approximately thirty times during his last year here. Lived on APC's. Pains in the—"

"—hipbone and sacroiliac?" Konig offers, a vision of Haggard flashing through his mind.

"That's right, although nothing very much showed up on his X rays. How'd you catch it?"

"Reassembling the spinal column. Pronounced osteoarthritic changes in the right hipbone, sacroiliac. Lipping changes in the cervical vertebrae. Must've had a helluva lot of pain." Where is Haggard now? he wonders. Has someone picked up the cash?

"Not just physical either. There was a great deal of psychological pain as well. Browder was a bit of an oddity around here."

"So I gather," Konig remarks. Somewhere far back in his head is the sound of a girl shrieking on a street corner, and even farther back, yet another shriek, more terrified, more anguished.

McCormick goes on. The initial reticence past now, he is more eager to talk. "Browder was a man of extraordinary courage. Decorated five times. Citations of valor. Super-patriotic. Gung ho, I guess is what you'd call him. Joined as a kid. Never knew anything else but Airborne. Served in Vietnam. Rose quickly through the ranks. Very proud of being a jumper. But he was getting a little long in the tooth for jumping, and when the arthritic problems worsened, we simply had to ground him. He was reassigned to training cadre. Very cushy job around here. Lot of men love it, but he took it as a setback. Couldn't stand being grounded. Began drinking. Then Ussery entered his platoon. That's when he really fell apart."

Very shortly McCormick and Konig are trading data on Billy Roy Ussery. Konig, armed with X rays and dental charts on his desk, drones wearily into the phone. "No previous extractions."

"Right. He had all his teeth, but they were in pretty poor condition."

"Extensive caries. Marked abrasions due to bruxism."

"Right on both counts."

"All four wisdom teeth unerupted."

"Right."

"Left upper showing signs of impaction."

"Right."

"Many roots not yet fully calcified."

"Right," McCormick drawls. "Wouldn't be, of course. Still just a kid."

Konig shuffles the X rays on his desk, plucks one out of the pile. "Do you happen to have a picture of the lower left central incisor there?"

"Lower left central incisor," McCormick murmurs half aloud to himself.

Konig waiting there can hear the crinkling sound of papers being rummaged on a desk. Then, creeping through the conscious stream of his thought, yet another sound—the voice of a man, soft, infinitely refined, lethally gentle, whispering at him, all around him. "Dr. Konig. Dr. Konig."

"Yop." McCormick's voice drowns out the other. "Got it right here. Lower left central incisor."

"Fine," says Konig. "Now look at the upper third of the outer surface."

"Upper third, outer surface. Oh, yes, little cloudy white patch."

"That's it," Konig says with a surge of mounting excitement. "Yours have a small stain in the center of it?"

"Sure does. What the hell is it?"

"I don't know. I was going to ask you. Our dental people couldn't figure it, either."

For a while the two men are silent, each pondering the mysterious cloudy white patch on the radiographs before them.

"Beats me," McCormick sighs. "Probably just congenital discoloration of the enamel."

"Could be," Konig concedes. "He on any special drugs? Medication?"

"Reserpine."

"Right. We caught that."

"Mild essential hypertension. High-strung boy. Actually, I believe it was just a passing thing with him but we were watching it closely."

"Probably linked to the stress of his situation there."

"Right. All in all, Ussery was a pretty healthy boy. Just minor things."

"Any history of foot problems?" Konig asks.

"Now how the hell did you know that?"

"Reassembling a foot. X-rayed it. Found a hallux valgus."

"In the right or left?"

"The left."

Konig waits while McCormick consults his records.

"Nope" comes the voice at last. "Nothing down here in Ussery's records about a hallux valgus. At least we never diagnosed it. But he did have to wear special shoes."

"What size?"

"Eight and a half, triple E, says here on his clothing requisition. His toes were humped and he had bunions too. Problem no doubt grew out of the hallux valgus."

Konig whistles. "Hallelujah! Our boy had bunions too. Also wore an eight and half triple E sneaker."

For a while they continue to talk, trading additional details, but already Konig's mind has turned off. He has closed the book on Ferde and Rolfe to his own satisfaction. The two cadavers glued together in the morgue below are Browder and Ussery. No doubt of that. Now in the place of coolly dispassionate clinical talk, all he can feel is his own slowly mounting sense of terror. His mind is elsewhere. As the shriekings return, he can no longer fight them down. He can barely sit in his chair, chatting with the colonel. There's a feeling of flush in his face and a suffocating fullness in his chest. His cheeks are burning. He has the feeling he is about to blow apart. The shrieks come again, filling him with a sense of impotence and rage turned inward against himself. Like a man running as hard as he can against a concrete wall. He can barely manage another civility to the colonel.

"Well," McCormick sighs at last, "looks like we can close the books on this."

"Looks like it." Konig fidgets nervously. "Just need the medical records now to tie it all up. Make it official."

"You've already got both sets of fingerprints."

"Right. Browder's came yesterday."

"Good. Sent them directly to your man."

"Flynn?"

"That's the chap. He told me the whole story. Nasty business."

"Yes, it is."

"Knew them both fairly well," McCormick says, a weary note in his voice now. "Nice boys, both of them. Browder was a fixture around here. Ussery I knew only briefly. Came into the dispensary a lot."

"The foot problem?"

"The feet. The teeth. The blood pressure. Lots of other vague complaints. Nothing you could ever put your finger on. Psychosomatic, most of it. He was a kid with a lot of problems. And he knew he had them. Wispy, pretty little thing. Almost girlish. Browder was like a father to him. How the hell a kid like that got into this kind of an outfit—" McCormick chuckles. "Funny though. Airborne is full of that kind of thing. Scared kids trying to act tough. Boys with problems trying to prove they don't have them."

"Common enough," says Konig. "We see a lot of that here on the Force too."

"As for Browder," McCormick goes on, "you wouldn't have thought he had any problems. Big tough son of a bitch. Wouldn't have wanted to tangle with that one." He laughs suddenly. "Should've seen the two of them together. Mutt and Jeff. Thick as flies."

"Got pretty sticky, I imagine," Konig says, so desolate now he can barely speak.

"Sticky? My God—downright embarrassing. Should never have tried to separate them though. Should've discharged them both. Medical discharge. Clean. Easy. Probably both still be alive if they hadn't had to go off and hide out like that."

"Well—" Konig sighs, his voice trailing off, wanting desperately to put down the phone, to go off somewhere himself and hide.

"Sad," McCormick continues his dirge. "Nice boys.

Both of them. Weren't hurting anybody. How'd they get messed up in this thing anyway?"

"Who knows?" says Konig, forcing himself to be civil. "I'm up to my neck here with nice boys and girls who get messed up in this city. It's a big, noisy, scary place. I used to love this city. Now, quite frankly, Colonel"— Konig laughs bitterly—"the place gives me the god-damned creeps. Who knows? Who knows?" His voice trails off, then picks up again. "Do you think you might be able to release those medical and dental records? We'll need copies, affidavits for our own files."

"I'm trying to clear them for release right now. Probably be able to send them up by courier this weekend."

"Thank you," Konig says. "You've been very helpful."

"Not at all, Dr. Konig. I'm glad we've been able to clear this all up. You've done an incredible job up there."

"Not all that incredible," Konig says, his voice husky with fatigue. "Important thing now is to get the bastard who did it."

"Got any leads?"

"Nothing very dramatic, I'm afraid. Oh, by the way—" Konig pauses oddly, as if he were on the verge of saying something, then changed his mind.

"Yes?" McCormick waits.

"Nothing. Nothing really. I was just wondering—"

"Yes?"

"—if you might send me their photographs. I have a picture of each man in my head, and I'm curious to see how close to the real thing my impression is."

McCormick laughs. "No sweat. We'll send you the ID photographs along with the records."

"Thank you," says Konig, "thank you very much."

"Not at all." McCormick sighs. "I've got the really unpleasant job ahead of me now."

"Oh? What's that?"

"Notifying the parents."

4:00 P.M. FOREST PARK, QUEENS.

DeSoto glances at his wristwatch again. He knows now that something is wrong. There's been a hitch somewhere. The man with the Gladstone bag appears restless too. Several times during the past hour he's glanced at his wristwatch, then gazed around impatiently, as if he were waiting for someone. DeSoto's main worry now is what he would do if the man should suddenly rise and start to go. Then he would have to follow suit, thus blowing his cover. That would be very awkward. Very awkward indeed.

Only a few minutes ago the fellow had stood up, turned around, and stared into the deep woods behind the carousel, as if he expected someone to emerge from there. For a moment it appeared he was about to go, and DeSoto held his breath and waited till the man sat down again.

Sitting there, the young cop toys with the idea of moving off to some different spot, out of sight, but where he can still keep his man under surveillance.

A steady stream of traffic drones languidly up and down Woodhaven Boulevard in front of the park. DeSoto glances wistfully toward it, hoping at any moment to see the gray unmarked patrol car roll into sight. But if Haggard is around someplace, there is no sign of it.

Suddenly, the man on the bench rises, muttering, and starts to go. The muscles in DeSoto's legs coil, ready to spring, but he cannot make any precipitate motion, lest he give himself away. Instead, he forces himself to sit there, staring hard at the *Sports Illustrated*, while the man in the raincoat strides swiftly down the lane in the opposite direction.

In his agitation, with his mind racing a mile a minute, all of DeSoto's attention has been riveted on the man.

Only now does he notice that the Gladstone bag, with its $300,000 in unmarked tens and twenties, remains unattended on the bench.

Something like panic overtakes the young cop. Already the man in the raincoat has turned a bend in the lane and is out of sight. If he doesn't go after him, he surely will lose him. Still, he cannot abandon the bag with the money. Perhaps Meacham's people had set it up this way to force any tail to blow his cover. Haggard had provided for a whole set of contingencies. This was not one of them.

Near panic, DeSoto gazes desperately around for some sign of his own people. Seeing none, he bolts. In the next moment he's on his feet, moving quickly toward the bench where the old Gladstone sits, an air of malevolence about it, waiting spitefully for him. Snatching it on the run, he bounds forward down the lane after the raincoated figure receding now into a landscape of trees and shrubbery and people. Having blown his cover, he's committed now. He must take the man.

Rounding the bend of the lane, he has a momentary glimpse of the fellow up ahead nearly two hundred yards off, moving toward one of the park exits on Woodhaven Boulevard. There's a bus stop ahead and several buses are stopped there, their motors idling, disgorging and taking on passengers. It is toward those buses that DeSoto sees his man going.

In the next moment he's loping like a wild man across the green toward the exit, the Gladstone and its sharp buckles banging cruelly at his knee.

The man in the raincoat is waiting in a queue behind three other people. There's no one behind him, and the moment he steps onto the bus the doors close behind him. At that moment, DeSoto bursts through the park exit, gesturing wildly at the driver. For anyone sitting there, he simply looks like a man determined to catch a bus. But the driver doesn't see him, or at least pretends not to, and the bus, with a wheeze and a sigh of its great diesels, starts to swing out onto the boulevard.

It's then that De Soto, gasping like a winded creature, sees a gray blur of motion out of the corner of his eye. There's an awful sound of brakes squealing, the crunch of metal impacting, glass shattering, the blare of horns, people shouting. In the next moment he sees the bus at a dead halt in the middle of the boulevard, traffic starting to back up behind it, and the gray unmarked patrol car, with a smashed right front fender, directly in front and athwart it where it had veered suddenly in front of the bus, blocking any further movement.

DeSoto is already at the bus, banging on its doors, when he sees Francis Haggard bulling toward him through the jammed traffic, his face purple with rage.

In the park, the oom-pah-pah of the "Gold and Silver Waltz" scratches fitfully out through the PA system, while the horses on the old carousel, rising and falling alternately, swing around and around. The children squeal with delight and shout back and forth at one another from horse to horse. On one of those carousel horses, a big gray-white Percheron with beautiful eyes and a pink muzzle, sits a young man. He might be anywhere between eighteen and thirty-five, with one of those perennially boyish faces that will look just as youthful even in old age. It is a refined, intelligent face, with thin, angular patrician features. The rather bookish air about him is heightened by an indoor pallor as well as by a pair of steel-rimmed glasses. The evident pleasure he takes in the carousel ride appears to be no less than that of the squealing children all about him.

He is looking out across the park now to the boulevard, where there appears to be some excitement. Traffic has stopped out there; crowds gather; horns blare. Several patrol cars out of the Queens 53rd Precinct have rolled up into the area, and the place is starting to fill with police. Stepping down out of the commandeered bus, several men —two in uniform, one a tall, white-haired plainclothesman—appear to be escorting the man in the raincoat from the bus.

The young man sitting on the carousel smiles curiously to himself while the music plays and the beautiful old wooden Percheron with the big eyes and the flaring nostrils whirls him round and round.

≈ 58 ≈

"I'm sorry."

"You keep saying that."

"I know. I can't help it. I'm sorry. It was all my fault."

"I don't care whose fault it is, goddamnit. What about her? Where does this leave my kid now?"

5:15 P.M. MEDICAL EXAMINER'S OFFICE.

"I don't know. Believe me, this guy knows nothing." Haggard's voice croaks dismally through the phone. "A small-time drifter from out of town. Served time on a couple of raps. Breaking and entering. Couple of vagrancy raps. Loitering for immoral purposes and so on. Nothing. Believe me, nothing. All he knows is he met a couple of guys in a Village bar."

"And he doesn't know who they are?"

"Never seen 'em before in his life. Don't even know their names. All he knows is they offered him twenty-five dollars to go up to Grand Central, pick up a bag, take it out to Queens."

"And he did it? No questions asked?"

"If you saw the guy," Haggard growls almost pleadingly, "you'd know right away he's not the kind to ask questions. They gave him ten down; the rest was supposed to be on delivery. He needed the bread. He was on the take. Believe me, Paul—the guy knows nothing. He's too stupid."

Konig sits hunched over his desk, a toppling pile of letters before him. There is a throbbing pain at his temples and he struggles to suppress his rage.

"So he was just a set-up?" Konig mutters through clenched teeth.

"'Fraid so. Just using him to test us."

"And they made monkeys out of you."

"Right—we blew it. That goddamned stupid battery,"

Haggard fumes. "All my fault. Should've known enough to have a backup car. And this poor kid, DeSoto—stuck out there like that. Had no choice. Hadda blow his cover. Either that or risk losing the money or the guy."

"Should've just sat there, goddamnit," Konig shouts, his fist pummeling the desk so that papers and pencils fly askew. "Why the hell couldn't he just sit there? If Meacham's people were there, they wouldn't have let that bag sit all by itself on that bench for too long."

"I know, I know." Haggard's voice is full of self-reproach. "The kid was green, inexperienced. I know."

"And you entrust my daughter's life to some klutz rookie—"

"He's not a rookie, Paul. He's—"

"Oh, Christ."

"I'm sorry. I'm sorry."

"Jesus—will you quit saying that? Your sorrow's not going to help her any. What do we do now?"

The silence at the other end is devastating. An admission of defeat. Finally Haggard summons the courage to speak. "I don't know what we do now. Frankly, I've run out of leads. I've got nothing to go on. Zero. Goose eggs. I spoke to the Bureau today. They don't have a helluva lot more. They're still working from the bomb angle. They believe they can tie a number of so-called political bombings in the Northeast to Meacham and some of the people he served time with in Danbury."

"How does that help us?"

"They're trying to track down every one of these guys in the hope that they'll know where Meacham is. I've identified one from this area. Fellow by the name of Klejewski, whose last place of residence, incidentally, was that bomb factory up in The Bronx. Even ran down his old lady out here in Astoria. I'm sure this guy's in contact with Meacham. Couple of bombings in this area recently indicate they're together again and working. If I could lay my hands on him, I'd find Meacham. I'd beat it out of him."

"But the point is," Konig snarls, his manner ugly, full of repudiation, "you can't find him, can you? You can't find anything. And the goddamned Bureau can't find anything either. A handful of fleabag revolutionaries making monkeys of you all."

"Paul—"

"You're a fool. You're all fools."

"Paul, wait—"

"Forget it."

"Listen to me, Paul. Listen—"

"Forget it, I said. Stay out of it now. I did it your way and it's a botch. Now I take over. I'd rather make my own mistakes than yours. The next time will be my way—that is, if we're lucky enough to have a next time."

"Paul, listen to me. Wait a minute—listen—"

But Konig has already hung up. In a cold sweat he sits now in the dusky shadows of his office, a pain like an ax blade buried in his sternum, constricting his chest.

For a long while Konig sits there slumped over his desk, rubbing the pain in his chest, flailing himself with ghastly imaginings of what Meacham and his frends were at that moment doing to Lolly as repayment for the ludicrous episode in the park. He would certainly take it out on her now. Make her pay for her father's treachery.

At any moment now he expects the phone to ring, to pick it up and hear one of those long, ghastly shrieks, then the obscene little snigger in the background. That would be Meacham's idea of paying him back—the anguish and terror of his child. It was all his own fault too. He was responsible for her agony. Had he not mentioned anything to Haggard, had he simply delivered the money, done what they asked, she might be home now, sitting there with him at that very moment.

Then indeed the phone does ring. He freezes there, unable to reach for it. It rings several times more while he stares at it with a mad fixity, waiting for Carver to pick it up. Then he realizes that it's past five and she's gone for the day, and he springs for it.

"Is that you?" comes a familiar voice from the other end.

"Yes. Maury?"

"Figured I'd find you in." The Deputy Mayor's voice is halting, stilted, even mildly self-deprecating. He seems oddly embarrassed as he flounders around with the kind of casual chitchat that is not his stock in trade. Then suddenly, out of the blue, he says, "The Mayor would like to see you tomorrow, Paul."

"Oh?" Konig replies, listless, uncaring. "What time?"

"Any time that's convenient for you."

That in itself, Konig knows, is ominous. He has known the Mayor long enough to know that he doesn't see people at their own convenience in order to pin medals on them.

"Anything special on his mind?" he asks bleakly.

There's a pause and he can hear Benjamin squirming at the other end. "You haven't heard anything up there, have you?"

"About what?"

"Something to the effect that a *Daily News* reporter got ahold of one of the prison guards at the Tombs?"

"No, I haven't. What about it?"

"You haven't heard anything about that?" Benjamin asks again.

"I just said I haven't." Konig slumps a bit lower in his seat and waits.

"Well"—a long, weary sigh issues from the Deputy Mayor—"I suppose it was inevitable. All this business about the body-snatching racket. And then your pal Carslin whooping it up over the Robinson matter. I guess it was inevitable."

"What's inevitable?" Konig gnashes his teeth. "What's all this about the *Daily News?*"

"One of their investigative reporters—"

"Yes—"

"—got ahold of one of the prison guards at the Tombs—"

"I know—you've said all that."

"Well, this guard made a full statement that he'd been witness to the beating of Linnel Robinson. According to this guy, when he came on the scene one guard was already in the cell with Robinson. What he was doing in here I don't know. There's a specific rule, strictly enforced, that under no circumstances does a guard ever enter a prisoner's cell all by himself. If you ask me, this fellow went in there to settle a few old scores with Robinson, then found he'd bitten off more than he could chew. Three more guards rushed in with blackjacks—"

"This is all in the guard's statement?" Konig interrupts.

"Yes. The first guard then held Robinson while the other three proceeded to beat the hell out of him. According to this fellow who spoke to the *News,* after that beating Robinson crawled out of his cell on all fours, bleeding from the face and head. He asked to see a doctor but they refused him. Instead they handcuffed him and tossed him back into solitary confinement where he was found two days later hanging from the bars of a cell window."

"So?" Konig says, the shadows of his office deepening all around him.

"Blaylock has already suspended three guards," the Deputy Mayor continues. "A fourth has left for reasons of 'health.' "

"Blaylock showing the proper moral outrage, is he?"

"You ought to hear the stuff," Benjamin fumes. "Makes you want to puke. All the self-righteous trumpetings. 'This sort of thing will not be tolerated.' 'I will not permit—' So forth and so on. You know the garbage."

Konig's fingers drum idly on his desktop, the sound, percussive and loud, echoing through the shadows. "I fudged it up there at Binney's this morning, Maury," he announces suddenly. "Carslin knew I was fudging and so did Binney. And you, of course, wanted me to fudge it, Maury. Don't deny it. 'Don't make waves' is the gist of everything you've been telling me for the past week."

"Now just a minute—"

"Not exactly in those words. But the essence of what you've been telling me is that the Medical Examiner's Office couldn't stand another scandal. No more bad publicity."

"Well," Benjamin snarls, the old truculence back in his voice, "if that's what I've been telling you, it hasn't helped things very much. As far as more bad publicity goes, you've got it. In spades. The story'll be in every paper tomorrow morning. And what I neglected to tell you is that a couple of U.S. congressmen from Robinson's district, who just happen to be running for re-election this year, are now demanding a full grand jury investigation. Binney has no choice other than to call the grand jury into session."

"Good."

"Good?" the Deputy Mayor splutters.

"I deserve everything I get." Konig laughs, a long harsh, mordant laugh.

"I don't see what the hell's so funny."

"Everything. Everything's funny. You and me, Maury.
We're funny. And the Mayor's funny, too. Everybody's
funny. There is a justice, isn't there? Oh, I don't mean the
whorehouse justice of a courtroom with a lot of sons of
bitches dancing through a charade. I mean something beyond that. Far beyond that." He laughs again, cackling almost gleefully. "And the funniest thing of all is me. All
my life I've been fighting this sort of thing. These hypo-
crites. These trimmers and bastards. These son-of-a-bitch
liars trying to cover their tracks in the slime. And now,
Maury, the funniest thing of all is that I'm one of them.
Tell His Honor I'll be there at ten A.M."

When Konig hangs up it is almost dark in his office.
A comforting darkness to cover his desolation.

≈≈≈ 59 ≈≈≈

"Dr. Konig."

"Yes."

"Go to your front door."

"What?"

"Open it, but don't step out the door or make any
false move."

"What? What the hell is—"

7:00 P.M. KONIG'S HOME.

A click, then silence.

"Hello—hello—hello." Konig stands holding the phone,
peering hard into its mouth, a feeling as if he'd been
kicked in the stomach. "Who's this?" he shouts but hears
only the sound of silence roaring back at him through
the wires. "Who's this?" he mutters again, dumb with
fright. But he knew who it was. That voice, quiet, infinitely refined, was unmistakable.

Turning now he stares wildly at the window. Then in
the next moment he is striding, lurching, tripping across
the dining room, through the library, the living room,

plunging headlong through the front hall, and standing, finally, shirt-sleeved at the open door.

The soft April dusk is poised quiveringly on the verge of becoming dark. Framed in the orange glow of antique coach lanterns hung on either side of the door, Konig squints through the thickening shadows down his front walk. He can see nothing. It's the supper hour. Lights flicker from the windows of surrounding homes, but the streets are strangely deserted.

His eyes suddenly adjusting to the dark, Konig sees at the foot of his front walk the squat silhouette of a small foreign-built car. It's almost directly on a line with the front door and pointed up the street. In that light he can discern neither the color nor the model of the car, but he can hear its motor idling there in neutral.

In the next moment he hears the click of a door opening. The dim illumination of a dome light suddenly floods the car's interior. It is quite easy to see four distinct heads in the car.

Craning his neck, he squints harder. There's movement going on within the car. Then from one of the rear doors he sees a figure emerging, or being pushed out.

Remembering the order not to step outside the door, he waits breathlessly. Someone is now standing by an open rear door. Not really standing so much as leaning, or being propped up from behind. The figure appears to wobble drunkenly, and in the dim illumination of the dome light he can see hands reaching up from behind, gripping the upper arms of the wobbly figure, supporting it.

The figure standing there at the foot of the walk has a rag-doll quality. Its legs won't support it. Its head lolls like a puppet's to the side. Slowly now the head rises and as if with great effort appears to be gazing directly at him. In that light he cannot see the face, but he knows it is a female's, and he knows the outline of the head, the stature—

Lolly Konig is standing at the foot of the walk, perhaps fifteen yards off in the dusk, so close he might almost reach out and touch her. Because she totters and wavers so, he has an impression she's drunk. Or more probably under heavy sedation. If it weren't for the two hands supporting her from behind, she'd crumble right there where she stood. She appears to be holding her head up with tremendous effort, trying to see him. He can hear voices muted and conversant behind her. He stares back hard, struggling to see her face.

Suddenly she slumps. A cry strangles in his throat. He starts down the front steps. The moment he moves, however, there's a scramble in the area of the car. He hears more voices. The rag-doll figure is yanked back into the car. There's the sound of several doors slamming and a motor being gunned.

At the foot of the walk, paralyzed and grieving, Konig watches the two red taillights recede into the darkness, turn the corner at the end of the block, then disappear. For several moments, however, even with the car out of sight, he can hear the mocking roar of its motor.

He stands there for some time, riveted to the spot, staring at the point where the car had disappeared, as if willing it to come back. The air is heavy with the languid scent of honeysuckle and lilac. Permanence and serenity appear to be everywbere this night. How many such nights had he sat outside with Ida and Lolly, barbecuing steak, having a drink, laughing, chattering over the day's work. The soft glow of lights from the windows of neighboring homes flicker prettily all about him. Beyond those windows, families are gathered for the evening meal. People talk and chatter and laugh over the day's events, lulled by the illusion of a benign universe.

Konig turns now, hearing the ringing of a phone coming harsh and insistent from within the house. In a matter of moments he's back up the stone walk, up the stairs, through the front door, and into the hall where the phone is shrieking at him.

"Dr. Konig."

"Speaking."

"That was awfully stupid what you did today."

"Yes, I know. I'm sorry."

"By all rights I should have killed her immediately."

"Please don't hurt her. It was my fault—I—"

"Never trust yourself to the police. The police are bunglers. And the Bureau agents are even worse. They're retarded."

"I'm very sorry about all that. It wasn't any—"

"My associates are infuriated. They know you tried to screw us today. Now they insist I execute your daughter at once. As retaliation."

"Please don't hurt her," Konig can hear himself pleading.

"I don't want to hurt Lolly. I'm actually quite fond of her. She's a lovely girl. Sensitive. Artistic. I've enjoyed having her. If this were a different sort of world, if circumstances were different—" Wallace Meacham's voice trails off into wistfulness, then shifts back into its gentle but insistent tones. "I brought Lolly around tonight so you could see her. See she's alive and well. I didn't want you to worry. We're not barbarians. We're quite human. I know how a devoted father worries about an only daughter—"

"Bring her back." Konig struggles to control the emotion in his voice. "I have the money right here. Bring her back now and—"

"I'm afraid that's impossible, Dr. Konig," Meacham goes on quietly, persuasively. His voice has an almost hypnotic effect. "You see, I'm a very trusting fellow. Very naïve. I like to believe the best about people. If someone strikes a bargain with me, I assume he's honest. That he'll play straight." He chuckles warmly. "My associates call me a fool. They say, 'Don't trust this guy. He tried to screw you once and he'll try it again.' I'm afraid that in the light of today's events, I must now believe them. Wouldn't it be foolish for me to walk into your house now with Lolly? Very easy, very tempting, but foolish. For all I know you've got a half dozen of your stooge cops sitting in there with you."

"There are no cops here now, I swear to you. Just bring her—"

Suddenly an operator's voice cuts in asking for an additional twenty-five cents. Beads of sweat glisten on Konig's forehead while he stands there waiting for the conversation to resume. Shortly he hears a coin drop in a slot on the other side, then a bong.

"Dr. Konig?"

"Yes—I'm here."

"This is Friday night."

"Yes."

"Sunday morning, three A.M., I want you to be at the Brooklyn end of the Brooklyn Bridge."

"All right."

"You'll see a white Chevrolet, '74 convertible, black top."

"Yes."

"You follow it."

"Yes. I understand."

"Follow it wherever it goes."

"Yes. I will."

"When it stops, you stop. When it goes, you go."

"I understand."

"At a certain point the car will signal you to stop and then pull alongside. You do that."

"Yes."

"Someone in the car will roll down his window. Don't attempt to talk with him or communicate with him in any way."

"Yes. I see."

"Just hand him the money."

"I understand."

"Is that clear?"

"Yes. Yes, it is."

"I want to warn you—there's very little traffic on a Sunday morning at three A.M. in Brooklyn. Particularly the areas you'll be driving in. Consequently, if a number of cars, or even one car, should just happen to be following you and the white Chevrolet, your daughter's life is over. You understand that, Doctor?"

"Yes. I understand."

"Very good. Because I must tell you. As a result of today's treachery, my associates are in an extremely ugly mood. If something untoward were to happen this time, I don't believe I could restrain them any longer."

"Nothing will happen," Konig says a little breathlessly, his heart smashing in his chest. "I understand perfectly. Please don't hurt her."

"That all depends upon you now, Doctor. Sunday morning. Three A.M. Brooklyn end of the Brooklyn Bridge."

"Yes—three A.M.—white '74 Chevrolet convertible. I'll be there. After I turn over the money, when do I get her back?"

"If everything goes well on Sunday morning, you can look for her twenty-four hours later."

"All right," Konig stammers. "I'll be there. I'll be there. Just please don't hurt her anymore."

"Don't worry, Doctor," Wallace Meacham murmurs

soothingly. "Trust in me, so I can trust in you. Oh, and Doctor?"

"Yes?"

"That bugging device I hear on your phone. Awfully noisy. You ought to change it."

≈ 60 ≈

"Personally I don't believe half of it."

"Half of it is true."

"Then it's the other half that's important."

"I'm afraid that half won't sell newspapers."

SATURDAY, APRIL 20. 10:00 A.M. THE MAYOR'S STUDY, GRACIE MANSION.

"And the figure of a million dollars a year is greatly exaggerated." The Mayor strides up and down the length of the study. He is a short, burly man with unremarkable features that nevertheless convey a sense of inner strength. It is Saturday morning, not normally a working day, and so he is not yet dressed, but simply attired in a silk paisley bathrobe. There's a pot of coffee on his desk. "When the auditors finish going through the books, I think we're going to find the amount of money paid out to these chiseling morticians considerably less—"

"Nevertheless," Konig says bitterly, "money was paid out. The situation was there. I was aware of it and I did nothing about it." From where he sits, stony and resigned, in a capacious leather wing chair beside a large picture window, Konig has an unimpeded view of the East River flowing swiftly past.

"But I'm not worried about that." The Mayor marches truculently forward, waving a copy of the morning's *Times* before him. "We can get past all that. There's not an agency or department on the City payroll that doesn't have its share of chiselers and grafters. A certain amount of that is unavoidable. For Chrissake, Paul—you're not a god. Why should your office be different from any other office? It's not that I'm worried about."

"You're worried about the Robinson business."

Something apprehensive and troubled clouds the Mayor's features as he sits down at his desk. "If it were just your office, Paul. But it's not. It involves several other departments. Even the DA's office. Binney's very upset. This other chap— What's his name?"

"Carslin."

"Right, Carslin. This bastard had the gall to suggest to me that even the DA's office is in collusion with innumerable City agencies to cover up this thing. Have you seen the papers yet?"

"I saw the *Times* this morning. I gather a grand jury is unavoidable."

"Binney thinks so. And of course you've heard about the two congressmen?"

"Yes." Konig stares resolutely out at the river.

"Both up for re-election this year, and this, of course, is the cheapest form of campaign advertising."

"I understand," Konig says, watching a tug beat its way upriver against the current. Looking south he can see the towers of the Queensboro Bridge wavering phantom-like through a yellow morning haze. "What would you like me to do?"

The Mayor folds his hands before him on the desk and stares fixedly at Konig. "I'd like you to think about taking early retirement."

Konig sits unmoving, his gaze still riveted on the gauzy spires of the distant bridge. "Do you want me to just think about it or do it?"

"Oh, for Chrissake, Paul," the Mayor fumes. "Don't make this thing any harder on me than it is now. I don't want you to do anything for the time being. For the next few weeks the newspapers are going to be beating their chests, clamoring for a public execution. There are men in this Administration I'd gladly consign to the scaffold in a minute. You're not one of them. You've served six Administrations loyally. Your career has been distinguished throughout. You've built up one of the finest forensic departments in the world. You've run it with integrity and guts. I will not permit these self-righteous media bastards to make hay out of one foolish, ill-considered slip. Why in hell have you been protecting Strang?"

Konig's head snaps quickly about, his burning gaze locking with the Mayor's. "Who told you that?"

"Oh, come on, Paul." The Mayor yanks a cigarette from his pocket. "I've known that for weeks. Just as Strang was so eager to inform on you in this mortician scandal, there are others just as eager to inform on him. You've got some very ambitious boys down there on your staff." The Mayor grins slyly. "But I really didn't need anyone to tell me. The minute Strang walked in here, I had him pegged. Show me a selfless, dedicated public servant, and I'll show you a very ambitious man."

"Who told you?" Konig asks again.

"That Strang had done the Robinson autopsy?"

"Yes—who told you that?"

Once again the sly smile spreads across the Mayor's features. "You keep your secrets, Paul, I keep mine."

"Probably Bonertz. Or Delaney—he's unhappy enough."

The Mayor shrugs, smiles, touching his fingers to his lips to show they are sealed. "In any event," he goes on, "I don't want you to leave immediately. That would give it the look of a public hanging, and I will not permit that to happen."

Konig stares grimly back out the window. "Then what do you propose?"

"I want you to slowly reduce your responsibilities over the next three months."

"Phase myself out?"

"In a manner of speaking."

"It's only a matter of two more years, George," Konig suddenly pleads. "Couldn't you possibly—"

"No." The finality of the Mayor's word has the effect of a great gate closing. Konig's hurt eyes linger for a moment on the Mayor's stern but not unkindly features. Then they wander back out the window and south to the bridge. "It's not only this Robinson business either, is it, George?"

"No," the Mayor replies flatly. "It's your health too."

Konig shakes his head and laughs bitterly. "They tell you everything around here, don't they, George?"

The Mayor laughs out loud. "I've got an office full of selfless, dedicated public servants. But seriously, Paul. You've got to quit. You're killing yourself. If you don't leave soon, you'll be carried out in a box."

"I'd prefer that to this slow but discreet retreat you've got planned for me."

"Skip the self-pity, Paul," the Mayor snaps irritably. "It doesn't become you. The minute you leave the City, a dozen foundations, universities, hospitals, will be banging at your door. You've still got a great deal of living ahead of you. Why the hell aren't you under a doctor's care?"

"I'm under my own care," Konig's voice rises harshly. "Who's to be my successor?"

"Up to you entirely. I presume it won't be Strang."

"Pearsall's your man," Konig goes on matter-of-factly. "First-rate pathologist, and a good administrator. I trust him."

The Mayor scratches the name on a pad. "Then so do I."

"And just for future notice," Konig continues, "I've got a man down there now, a kid, actually, but worth while watching."

"How old?"

"Late twenties. Just out of school a few years but definitely a comer."

"Name?"

"McCloskey—Tom McCloskey."

Once again the Mayor scribbles hastily on his pad. The discussion ended, Konig now rises to go. The Mayor rises, too, and for a moment the two of them stand there awkwardly searching for a graceful way to end their talk. Suddenly the Mayor is laughing. "Thirty years I've known you, Paul, and you haven't changed a bit. Not in all that time. You're still the same surly, tough old son of a bitch you were then."

Still laughing, the Mayor comes around his desk and throws an arm warmly about Konig's shoulders. "Only Ida could take the bite out of you. Take the wind right out of your sails. God, how well I remember Ida, bless her soul. Remember the picnics and all the kids?" His arm still about Konig's shouder, they move slowly toward the door. "Your little girl—"

"Lauren? She's a big girl now. Twenty-two."

"Twenty-two." The Mayor repeats the number wistfully, the march of all these years passing suddenly before his eyes. "Twenty-two, is it? I'm a grandfather three times over. What's she doing with herself?"

"She's an artist."

"An artist?"

"They're showing her paintings right now," Konig says, swelling a bit with pride. "Some fancy gallery over on the East Side. Charging very fancy prices for them too. She's coming home tomorrow," he blurts out irrepressibly, not having intended to mention anything about Lolly. But the moment he says it, the moment the words are out, a great weight lifts from him, as if the saying of it actually makes it so. Suddenly he feels giddy and happy. "Yes, she's coming home."

"She been away?" the Mayor asks.

"Oh, just for a while," Konig says, a kind of shy evasiveness in his eyes. "Little misunderstanding. But that's all behind us now."

"Good—very good, Paul." The Mayor clasps his hand warmly. "All the better. Then the free time in the months ahead will be a good time for the both of you to get to know each other again."

"Yes—I think so." Konig's face is glowing. "I think the first thing we'll do is open up the place in Montauk. We can go out and stay for the whole summer. Lolly loves the ocean, you know."

"Can't say I blame her," the Mayor booms. "Say hello to her for me. Tell her my Joanie is the mother of two now."

Konig stands there by the door smiling rather idiotically, the Mayor still clasping him warmly by the hand but all the while jostling him gently out the door, a political liability now to be quietly, but swiftly, dispatched. "And, Paul," he adds, lowering his voice a litte conspiratorially, "don't worry about all the trash you read in the papers. You're still the best."

A short time later Konig is back downtown at his desk trying to tunnel through more of the unfinished paperwork. The unanswered letters sit there, a quiet reproach, awaiting him.

It is Saturday morning and so the place is empty. He has it to himself and he relishes the quiet of it. His mind still harks back to his conference with the Mayor. The forced retirement had disheartened him, but he knew, of course, that it was coming. The fact that their conversation took place in the informality of the Mayor's home rather than at City Hall, as well as the fact that Konig was permitted to pick the time, was the tip-off to what the purpose of the meeting was. So it came as no shock. That he was disheartened was quite true. But walking out of there this morning, he'd also felt a curious exhilaration, as if a great weight had been lifted from him. It had all to do, he knew, with Lolly. The fact that she was coming home now, and that thing the Mayor had said (quite inadvertently, because he knew nothing of Lauren Konig's situation) about their having "time to get to know each other again." It was that that had set him off, buoyed him so, had him whistling all the way down from 89th Street to the Medical Examiner's Office on 30th. In slightly more than twenty-four hours now they'd be together again. After a separation of five months, they'd be a family once more.

Then, too, when he'd walked in that morning around 11:30, made his coffee on the Bunsen burner, watered his plants, lit his first cigar of the day, he'd seen a plain white envelope on his desk with his own name typed across the face of it. It was Carl Strang's resignation. Curt, succinct, devoid of acrimony, it simply declared he was leaving. It asked for nothing in the way of favors or references. Konig was relieved. It even added to his exhilaration.

Then he turned to his correspondence.

DEAR DR. GRISWALD:
    I have studied your reports and protocols with considerable interest and it occurs to me—

And so it went for several hours until he'd actually come within striking distance of the bottom of the pile. He'd typed his own replies, fully enjoying the afternoon's work. The old communication with colleagues, the reaching out, so to speak, across the land, across the sea, to perfect strangers who'd reached out to him, sought his advice. The common bonds that joined them. That pleased him mightily. His concentration had been deep. His mind keen. He'd even felt a touch of the old vigor surging through him.

Glancing at his watch now, he is astonished to see that it is nearly 3 P.M. He rises instantly, anxious to get home. There are several errands to run before nightfall. Before his rendezvous at the bridge. There had to be food in the larder if Lolly was coming home. He had to stock up. The girl had probably been starved, or at least minimally fed, during the course of her ordeal. Then, of course, there were the paintings. Her paintings. The ones he'd bought at the Fenimore Gallery. He would hang them on the walls as a kind of surprise for her homecoming. Gleefully, he imagines her reaction when first she'd see them there, hanging throughout the house. He can barely contain himself at the thought of it.

When he'd rinsed out the beaker of coffee, extinguished the Bunsen burner, stubbed out his smoldering cigar, then put out the lights, he was at last ready to go.

Striding out the door of his office, he suddenly catches sight of a small white calling card that had been slipped beneath the outer door. On one side it read "Francis Haggard. NYPD." On the other, in a rather bold, untidy scrawl, it said merely: "Please don't try to go it alone."

≋ 61 ≋

"No—we got no Salvation Army customers, pal. The way my customers pay bills, I'm the only Salvation Army around here."

"Know what you mean. Thanks a lot."

"My pleasure, pal."

5:15 P.M. TENTH AVENUE AND 50TH STREET.

Sergeant Edward Flynn stands outside a small neighborhood grocery that happens to sell newspapers and magazines. "QUINONES Bodega" it says in faded yellow letters on the window. Then the word "Grocery" printed in smaller letters beneath it.

Flynn stands there in the bright April sunlight scanning a list of seventy names of which Mr. Quinones was the forty-third. Incredibly, at 9:30 this morning, Mr. Stanley Charles had furnished him with a list of names. In alphabetical order, it had been scaled down from the intial hundred-odd retailers who on March 31 might have sold

issue number 3118 of the *Clintonian* to a man who may or
may not have been a Salvation Army officer.

"Don't thank me," snarled Stanley Charles, much be-
leaguered and fuming, muttering intermittently about the
"lawyer leeches" and the "tax bastards." "Thank the little
fourteen-year-old black kid who works for me on the
trucks. He's better than all the goddamned computers put
together."

"You mean he actually worked out a system with those
serial numbers?" Flynn asks incredulously.

"Yeah, but don't ask me to explain it. He tried to explain it to me but I'll be damned if I can understand it.
Something about the order he stacks them on the truck for
delivery. Anyway, he narrowed down the list of 100 or so
to the bare possibilities. That's seventy names. They're
in alphabetical order. That's all I can do. The rest is up
to you."

And so it was. Since ten o'clock that morning he'd seen
forty-three people. He'd walked up and down Eighth
and Ninth Avenues between 40th and 59th Streets. Then
he'd trudged as far west as Eleventh Avenue, where he
could see the river and smell the warm, bilgy odors of
it. He'd been to newsstands, luncheonettes, drugstores,
supermarkets, groceries, subway vendors—any place
where newspapers were sold. Asking the same questions
and getting the same unsatisfying answers. Certainly no
one recognized the serial number, which was never listed
on their invoices from the distributor. And so far no one
had a customer who walked around in the uniform of a
Salvation Army officer.

It is quite warm now, and from where Flynn stands he
can see way down to the piers on the river and the big
white smokestacks of a docked Italian liner, its gaily
colored pennants flapping listlessly in the breeze, and gulls
screeching overhead. It makes him think of travel; foreign
lands; long, white sandy beaches; palm trees waving;
beautiful, accessible women—many things he's never had.

The gentle breeze is soughing eastward off the river,
bringing with it the smell of low tide. Flynn is hot and
tired. His feet hurt and his underwear, sticking to his seat,
has chafed a raw welt on his inner thigh.

There are twenty-seven names left on his list. He is
physically incapable, he knows, of finishing the list today.
But before quitting, he will see just a few more.

Next on the list is a newsstand vendor by the name of Resnikoff—Tenth and 49th. After that, Siegel's candy store—Eleventh and 49th. After that, a grocer by the name of Salerno—Eleventh and 46th.

At that very moment, Francis Haggard is leaving the New York offices of the Federal Bureau of Investigation on East 69th Street. He'd spent the afternoon there going through mug shots, comparing prints and data with the Federal agents assigned to the Lauren Konig case.

Because of a number of remarkably similar incidents involving the bombing of public buildings in the greater Boston area, the Bureau has a theory that both Wally Meacham and Janos Klejewski are somewhere in that vicinity with a number of their cohorts, as well as with Lauren Konig. For that reason they have concentrated their search in the Boston area, going as far north as Concord, as far south as Walpole.

They had presented to Haggard that day a lot of solid evidence to substantiate their beliefs, the most impressive being a recent sighting of Janos Klejewski, positively identified on closed-circuit television during the course of a bank robbery in Boston nearly a week ago. The second link in that theory is substantiated by the Bureau's contacts with paid informers who insist that Meacham and Klejewski, old friends from Danbury days, are back working together again.

Finally, the Bureau's agents concluded on a somewhat more ominous note. The body of a young girl had been exhumed from a peat bog outside of Worcester three days ago. She'd been beaten, strangled, put in a sack, then submerged in the bog. She'd been part of Meacham's coterie—in fact, his girl friend.

The force of the first two facts is impressive. The third is something the detective doesn't even wish to contemplate. But Haggard is still dubious. He cannot refute videotape or privileged information bought at high cost from reliable sources. But all his instincts tell him that Meacham is right here in the city. It's not merely yesterday's fiasco in Forest Park that makes him feel that. That could have simply been a few of Meacham's people doing business for him down in the city while he remains far north, up in New England, out of harm's way. In fact, that would be the most sensible thing for Meacham to have done, Haggard reasons, with so much heat on for him in the city.

Still, the detective cannot let go of the idea that Wally Meacham is somewhere right around him. Under his nose, so to speak. Within spitting distance. Most important, however, and to his distinct disadvantage, he could not possibly know that both Meacham and Lolly had been at Konig's house the night before. How could he? Konig hadn't told him. Nor did he intend to. And had Haggard known that Konig was keeping such crucial information from him, he probably would not have blamed him. Not after the colossal blunder of the day before.

More perplexed than ever, and with a slow but relent-less, nagging sense of panic, of time slipping through his fingers, the detective starts for home.

In Riverdale, Paul Konig has just finished hanging the portrait of Ida. He's hung it in a commanding position, directly above the marble mantel, having removed from that spot a fine old Hudson River painting. The effect of it has been to brighten the room immeasurably. The brilliant seaside light of Montauk seems to be shimmering off the canvas. It pierces the musty, tenebrous shadows of the room like a shaft of sunlight, and Ida's smile, glowing there above him, has a salubrious effect. So much so that for those brief moments he feels very close to her. Once again her spirit is back with him in the house.

He checks his watch now. He has been checking it all day. It is nearly 6 P.M. and the countdown to 3 A.M. is already well under way. Moving about the house now, his feet have almost a spring to them. He has stocked the refrigerator with food, the first of any substance that has been in there in months. On the walls of the stairway he has hung Lolly's three small paintings. Going up the stairs he chuckles gleefully as he views them. And upstairs in his den his fishing rods and tackle box are out, bright, gaily colored plugs lie scattered all about, oil and rags all waiting there for him to apply to the reels that he's brought down from the attic.

Once more he glances quickly at his watch.

≈ 62 ≈

"But how would I remember the number?"

"I didn't expect you to."

"The paper, yes. I certainly sold issues of the paper, but whether or not the particular one you're holding in your hand—"

"Uh-huh?"

"—that I have no way of knowing."

5:55 P.M. A SMALL CANDY STORE,
49TH STREET BETWEEN TENTH AND ELEVENTH AVENUES.

Flynn stuffs the dog-eared, much-thumbed sheet of the *Clintonian* back into his pocket. Sighing, he slides wearily onto one of the red Leatherette stools before the soda fountain. "How about a lemon and lime?" he says. "Plenty of ice."

"Would be a pleasure, Sergeant."

Mr. Saul Siegel is a big, powerfully built man of seventy some years. He is a splendid, barrel-chested specimen with flowing white hair and somewhat Biblical mien. On the back of his head he wears a black skullcap. Flynn watches him scoop crushed ice into one of those old Coca-Cola glasses held in a steel zarf. Then the old man punches the button of a big glass syrup dispenser and proceeds to make cold green, bubbly soda.

The vision of the skullcap, the cold green soda effervescing in a zarfed glass, the smell of the old zinc bar, and suddenly Sergeant Edward Flynn is back again, forty years or so, a little boy in Kastle's candy store on Hester Street, stealing penny candy, while old Mr. Kastle, sorely put upon by young hooligans, cordially looks away.

Yes, Mr. Siegel's establishment touches a nostalgic chord in Edward Flynn. It is a kind of warm, shabby hole in the wall (no bigger actually than a couple of good-sized closets) with a sliding-window counter that faces out on to the street. Having never been in there before, nevertheless the detective knows it perfectly. There in the back of the store are the same two little phone booths that Mr. Kastle had. And on the back wall is the same floor-

328

to-ceiling magazine rack. On another wall is a glass display case crammed full with cheap toys—kites, model
planes, model clay, plastic dolls, toy soldiers, jacks, pen-
knives, packets of foreign postage stamps, and little girls'
tea sets.

By far the biggest allotment of space is given over to the
bright old zinc bar with the Breyer's ice cream signs and
the faded posters depicting hamburgers and Coca-Cola.
Directly above it, hanging from a long, black string,
are innumerable cards of key chains, nail clippers, pipe
cleaners, Zippo lighters, pencil sharpeners, rubber bands.

But it is the zinc bar itself that really captures Flynn's
heart, the splendid old bar with its shiny soda spigots, the
huge inverted apothecary jars full of vividly colored
syrups—the bright-red cherry, the cool green lime, the
sunny yellow pineapple, the gorgeous black root beer. And
there, too, a big glass cake saver full of cheese and prune
Danish. And, wonder of wonders, a counter full of penny
candy at the far end—boxes of jawbreakers, jelly slices,
red-hots, banana candies, coconut-covered marshmallows,
halavah; they're all there. Even a bubble-gum machine—
a colored ball of gum and a tiny plastic toy, all for a
penny.

For a man who's been plodding about all day, badger-
ing a lot of irascible people, it all has a very pleasant
nostalgia about it. And old Siegel there, with his skullcap
and his flowing white hair, looks exactly like the old rebs
on Hester Street, with their tall beaver hats, their long,
black frock coats, the braided forelocks streaming out
from beneath the wide-brimmed hats.

Edward Flynn, as a boy, had a strange awe, a fascination, for these old men, always reading, studying day and
night in the synagogue.

Sipping his lemon-lime slowly, he studies Mr. Siegel,
hunched over the zinc bar, bifocals perched on the tip of
his nose, and reading.

"Know the neighborhood well?" he calls to him.

Mr. Siegel glances over the rim of his bifocals, a question on his face.

"I asked if you knew the neighborhood well."

"Been here thirty years."

"Then you should know it."

"I do—but it's changing."

"So is everything." Flynn smiles. "Trouble?"

"Sure. But at my age, who's running? Besides, everyone's got trouble. Right?" Mr. Seigel smiles, and out of that craggy, patriarchal face, something like peace shines.

"Right." Flynn nods. "What are you readin', may I ask?"

"The Bible. Sabbath night I read the Bible."

"What book?"

"Book of Numbers. An acient book. Old Hebrew laws."

Flynn ponders a moment, then says, "Will you read some to me?"

There is a look of gentle amusement on the old man's face. "You want me to read you the Bible?"

"Sure—I could use some Bible tonight."

Mr. Siegel considers that a moment. "Well, if you could use it, who am I to deny it. Any particular passage?"

"Just where you left off will be good enough."

Mr. Siegel is still smiling. It is an inward smile, as if something had pleased him vastly. Then, propping the bifocals on his nose, he proceeds in a quiet but curiously powerful voice.

" 'And if he smite him with an instrument of iron—' "

"Not in English, please," Flynn interrupts.

Mr. Siegel looks up again. This time the smile of amusement has turned to one of mild perplexity. "You understand Hebrew?"

"No—I just like the sound. Brings back memories."

Mr. Siegel shrugs, nods his head, and in the next moment his soft but resonant bass rises and spreads like a shawl over the little store.

אם בכלי ברזל: ואם באבן יד אשר־ימות
בה הכהו ומיתו רצח הוא מות יומת הרצח
גאל הדם הוא ימית את־הרצח בפגעו־בו
הוא ימיתנו: ואם־בשנאה יהדפנו או־השליך
עליו בצדיה וימת: או באיבה הכהו

Mr. Siegel looks up, that most kindly of smiles beaming upon Flynn.

"Very pretty." The detective nods appreciatively. "Very pretty indeed. What does it mean?"

"It's a passage on the Cities of Refuge. The places where a criminal may or may not seek sanctuary. Would you like me to translate it for you?"

"Yes—I'd like that."

The old man adjusts the glasses on his nose and peers back into his book:

And if he smite him with an instrument of iron,
so that he die, he is a murderer: the murderer
shall surely be put to death.

And if he smite him with a stone in the hand,
and he die, he is a murderer: the murderer shall
surely be put to death.

Or if he smite him with a hand weapon of wood,
and he die, he is a murderer: the murderer shall
surely be put to death.

The revenger of blood himself shall slay the
murderer: when he meeteth him, he shall slay him.

Mr. Siegel closes his book. Outside there is a flash of heat lightning and a distant rumble of thunder. "Rain," he murmurs quietly.

"Looks like it," Flynn agrees. "Tell me something. Of all your customers here in the neighborhood, you don't by chance happen to have a Salvation Army officer?"

"Salvation Army officer?" Mr. Siegel's eyes narrow and he ponders a bit. "Those fellows in the black uniform with the red collar, the peaked hat?"

"That's right."

Mr. Siegel smiles brightly. "I got one of them."

Flynn's heart leaps in his chest. "You do?"

"Sure—that'd be the colonel."

"The colonel?" There's a moment of silence. "Colonel who?"

The old man stares up at the ceiling trying to recall. "Let me see—takes a *Post* weekdays, *Daily News* Sunday mornings. Has it delivered."

"You don't know his name?"

"Hold on a minute." Mr. Siegel goes to the back of the store, disappearing into a back room, only to reappear the next moment bearing a small gray ledger book. It is one of those cheap paperbound ledgers, full of pink-ruled lines and smudgy inked entries. The old man thumbs through hectically, licking a finger every now and then to make the pages fly more swiftly.

"Ah, here," he says, halting finally at a page and adjusting his glasses, which keep slipping down his nose. "Colonel Divine," he announces triumphantly. "Colonel Joseph Divine. That's the fellow—610 West 49th. Just a few doors down the block here."

Flynn feels something like butterflies flutter in his stomach, a slow but inexorably mounting sense of excitement. "Can I see that a minute?"

"Sure." Mr. Siegel hands the detective the ledger book.

Flynn scribbles the name and address from it onto his pad. "Just down the block you say?"

"Sure. Old brownstone near the corner. He do something wrong?"

"Who knows?" Flynn shrugs, his face a little flushed. "Can I use your phone?"

"Sure. It's in the back. Help yourself."

At the rear of the store Flynn dials the precinct house, arranging to have a squad car meet him at the brownstone on 49th Street. Then he is out front again with Mr. Siegel.

"How much I owe you?"

"For what?"

"The lemon-lime."

Mr. Siegel, looking more patriarchal than ever, shakes his hoary, white-maned head and dismisses the offer of money with a broad, regal motion of his arm.

After the glass door has closed behind him, with the sound of little entry bells tinkling out after him into the street, Flynn glances back to wave farewell to Mr. Siegel. But the old man is already hunched over the counter again, elbows on the bar, cheeks resting in either palm, back deep in his Bible.

Outside in the street it is now thick dusk. The street lamps have just gone on. Children are playing tag around some trash cans on the pavement and young Puerto Rican couples stroll eastward, arm in arm, toward the great Saturday-evening glow of white lights shimmering above the Times Square area. The old sit in the windows and merely watch.

Another long gash of heat lightning turns the sky momentarily white above the river, and in the close, balmy air there is an imminence of rain.

Six ten West 49th Street is a three-story brownstone near the end of the block, quite close to Eleventh Avenue

It is one of those houses built around the turn of the century, in the gaslight era of the city. Once an elegant town house for a banker or a wealthy merchant, now it has been partitioned into a number of small dwelling units (efficiency apartments, they're called) and has fallen upon hard times.

In the small tiled vestibule downstairs is a narrow wall into which are set eight badly defaced mailboxes. The dim light flickering above them provides scarcely enough illumination for reading the names: Moody—Grayson—Donnelly—Terhune—Horwitz—two more scarcely legible—then, on a neat, elegantly printed little card, the name Divine, apartment 3B.

There is no buzzer so Flynn cannot ring to announce himself. The glass door between vestibule and hallway stands open, its lock having been removed *in toto* and never replaced. So the detective merely walks in.

Standing in the hallway, he can hear voices behind doors, footsteps, a hi-fi blaring the *Eroica*, kitchen sounds, people going about supper and life.

Before starting up the narrow, rickety stairs, Flynn's hand grazes lightly the area where the pistol in its holster rests snugly just beneath his armpit. Outside he can hear the rain starting to drill heavily on the pavements.

Mounting those stairs now, the steps creaking beneath his shoes, he has a strange sense of exhilaration, like a man who's been climbing a long time, who can see the summit now just a few feet ahead. And there is that heady buoyancy of the second wind. It all has a kind of inevitability about it. Particularly since the name Divine, which appeared on Stanley Charles's paper-route list, also appeared on General Pierce's ten-year-old duty roster, the one from the old South Street Salvation Army shelter.

Number 3B is in the far corner of the hall, looking out, Flynn surmises, over the back of the building. The name plate on the door says "J. Divine." Before ringing, the detective stands quietly outside the door listening for sounds from within. But there are no sounds. Nor does any light appear from beneath the door. He smiles oddly there in the shadows, shaking his head. Then he presses the small white buzzer to the side of the door.

He can hear the sound of the buzzer ringing within, and then a cat meows. Then silence. After a moment he rings again. This time he hears—or thinks he hears—the squeal of springs. Possibly a person rising from a couch or sitting up in bed. Then he hears something like the sound of a throat being cleared of phlegm, followed by the words "Just a minute" pouring muffled through the plaster walls. In the next minute he hears footsteps, then a crack of light glares beneath the door.

He is staring up now at a tall, strikingly handsome man with a shock of iron-gray hair. The rimless glasses from out of which gaze two greatly magnified eyes give him a parsonical look—faintly disapproving.

"Colonel Divine?" Flynn hears his voice coming back at him over great distances.

"Yes."

"Sergeant Flynn—New York Police, Sixth Homicide Division. I wonder if I might have a few words with you."

≈≈ 63 ≈≈

6:15 P.M. THE HAGGARD APARTMENT, PARKCHESTER, THE BRONX.

Shirt-sleeved, a small, pink dotted-swiss apron tied around his middle, Francis Haggard hovers over a sink full of supper dishes. While the water runs and suds rise about his elbows, he broods on the events of the day. Facts gathered at the Bureau that afternoon shuttle and flash through his head, and he toys with the idea of a quick run up to Boston.

Greatly troubled and perplexed, his chief worry now is that Konig, given any chance, will act alone, without the police. And given the disaster of the day before, he could scarcely blame him if he did.

The shrill whistle of a boiling teakettle jars him from his ruminations. Shortly he's steeping tea leaves in a small china pot, then pouring that into a rich mixture of cream and honey.

Looking ludicrous in the pink apron, he carries a tray,

its contents rattling slightly, out through the living room, down a short hall, and into a bedroom.

Mary Haggard sits in bed there, in a blue silk lounging robe, watching television. She is a small, pretty woman with vivacious eyes and blond hair going prematurely gray. On the bed table beside her is a stack of books, novels and histories, plus a tray of medications. On the big plaid comforter covering the bed are a nearly completed jigsaw puzzle depicting the Botticelli *Primavera* and a chessboard with a game half completed and waiting there for Frank Haggard to resume.

In the corner near the bed is Mary Haggard's wheelchair. The victim of a slowly worsening neuromuscular disease, she has used that chair for nearly the full twenty years of her marriage.

Displacing the books from their spot on the table, Haggard carefully sets the tray down beside the large double bed. Next he spreads a napkin across his wife's lap, then pours her tea.

"Isn't it beautiful, Frank?" she says, taking the tea from him, her eyes still focused on the TV. There on the large color screen is a spectacular view of the Grand Tetons.

"Wyoming?" he asks.

"Yes. It's a travelogue. Sit down and watch a while." She makes room for him beside her on the bed, but he will not discomfort her. "I'll stand. I've been sitting all day."

And so, arms folded, leaning against the wall in his apron, the detective hovers above his wife, watching the screen and still thinking about Boston. Gone is the surly, growling manner he reserves for the office and the precinct houses. With Mary Haggard he becomes uxorious, attentive, almost courtly.

"Can't get over how lovely it is," she says. On the screen a great six-point stag saunters majestically down to the shore of one of those tiny gemlike lakes sequestered, still and timeless, high in the mountain forests of the Yellowstone. Suddenly she looks up at him, smiling. "Wish we could go."

"Someday, maybe." He smiles quietly down at her, knowing she would never be able to make the trip.

Suddenly the phone rings out in the kitchen. Haggard's legs are moving instantly. "I'll be right back."

"Who?"

A hoarse, gruff voice, thick with sibilants and a heavy accent, jabbers frantically at him.

"Who?"

"Guzman—Guzman. Antonio Guzman."

"Oh, yes—Mr. Guzman."

"Das right. You remember? Da superintendent. You come up here. We spoke a couple days ago."

"That's right. I remember."

Mr. Guzman proceeds to jabber more frantically. He speaks in a whisper, as if he feared being overheard. His sibilants crackle and hiss so sharply through the phone that Haggard has to hold the receiver away from his ear. Intelligible words come to him only in snatches. "Dem guys—"

"Who?"

"Dem guys. Dem guys. Wit' the bombs—"

"They're there?"

"Yeah—das what I'm sayin'. They come back again. Just like you say. They here now." His voice cracks and he coughs violently into the phone. "Movin' out stuff. Loadin' up a car. You told me to call, remember?"

"I remember," Haggard nearly shouts, tearing off his apron. "Can you stall them there awhile?"

"No, man. I ain't gonna mess wit' dem. No way. Dey're bad. Bad."

"How many?"

"Four. You betta hurry. They ain't gonna stay aroun' all night."

"All right. I'm coming right over."

Haggard flings the phone back into the cradle, starts out, comes back, makes two fast phone calls. Then he strides back to the bedroom, composing himself so as not to alarm his wife.

"Gotta go out," he says, rolling down his sleeves. Mary Haggard watches him strap on his shoulder holster.

"Trouble?" she asks, unruffled by the haste in which he must leave. She has lived with Frank Haggard long enough to understand and accept the irregular pattern and rhythm of his life.

He shrugs. "Maybe. Anyway, I called Mrs. Grogin. She's coming right over to sit with you. Don't touch that chess game. Figure I got you checkmated the next three moves." He slips into his jacket, then, holding her chin in his great raw, red paddle of a hand, he stoops to kiss her.

"Be careful, dear."

"No sweat," he growls happily. "Don't wait up. Dream of the Tetons. I got a couple of weeks coming to me. Who knows? Maybe we'll go this spring."

It's no distance from Parkchester in the east Bronx to Fox Street in the south Bronx. In fifteen minutes' time Haggard has pulled his Pontiac Le Mans convertible out of the garage, pointed it west on Tremont Avenue, blazing through West Farms to Southern Boulevard, then south on into the no man's land the police call Fort Apache. It is a grim landscape strewn with sprawling tenements and abandoned buildings crawling with rats and junkies. There is the look of a bombed-out city about it, a place of undeclared war where the grim battle of survival, even at the basest level, is perpetually waged. Finally Haggard turns west, into Fox Street.

Full darkness has descended over the scene and only the dim orange glow of a solitary street lamp, the rest having been stoned out by marauding gangs of teenagers, illuminates the night.

Fox Street is narrow. The crowded tenement buildings huddling there appear to arch inward above the street, blacking out any view of the sky. Cars are parked on either side of the street, but there are no people in the street. People don't walk on Fox Street after dark.

The moment Haggard turns the corner into Fox Street he sees what he's looking for. There, double-parked in the street up ahead, beneath the single street lamp, is a black late-model station wagon. Its doors are open, its tailgate down. Several people are scurrying around it in the dim light.

The detective cruises slowly to within twenty feet of it and watches for a while unnoticed. Finally he withdraws the .38-caliber police special from its holster and steps out into the night. Crossing casually to the station wagon he is aware of his own accelerated heartbeat and the sound of his footsteps ringing on the empty pavements.

He reaches the station wagon just as a burly, panting figure lumbers from the building, hauling a large table-model TV to the car. There's a great deal of noise and activity from within the station wagon, where several people, unaware of the detective standing there, are busy packing clothing, luggage, odds and ends of furniture. Just

as the burly figure, grunting with his burden, is about to
shove the TV in over the tailgate, he glances up and notices
the tall, white-haired figure waiting patiently there beside
the car.

Haggard stands silently, peering into the startled face.
It's a face the detective knows well, having seen it dozens
of times in the last few days on mug shots, wanted posters,
police files, FBI dossiers. In the hazy glow of the street
lamp, the big, thick acromegalic features, the abnormally
large head, are even more apelike, more grotesque than
in the photographs.

Still holding the TV, Janos Klejewski stares blankly
at the tall man with the white fleecy hair, then down at the
.38-caliber police special pointed squarely at his belly. In
the next moment his head snaps sharply, first right, then
left, his eyes sweeping the street just in time to see the two
16th Precinct patrol cars Haggard had called for from
home turn the corners and wheel slowly toward them from
each end of the street.

"Hello, Kunj." The detective smiles warmly and points
to the TV. "Can I give you a hand with that?"

$$\approx 64 \approx$$

SUNDAY, APRIL 21. 2:55 A.M. CANAL STREET.

Paul Konig sits alone in his car on the edge of Chinatown. He is parked on the south side of Canal Street close
to its extreme east end. The nose of the car is facing the
huge illuminated towers of the Brooklyn Bridge. On the
seat beside him is the Gladstone bag.

He has been sitting there now for well over a half-hour,
having set out at approximately 1:30 from Riverdale. It
is drizzly outside after a heavy April drenching and from
time to time Konig wipes his windshield with a wad of
Kleenex to keep it clear. The wide-arc street lamps poised
like rows of sentinels along the street are all circled with
white gauzy halations.

Once again Konig checks his wristwatch, following closely the progress of the minute hand creeping across the face of the dial.

If it was privacy Meacham wanted in order to negotiate their transaction, he certainly had it. At that hour of the morning there is no traffic, and except for the occasional Bowery wino huddling in a doorway or a Chinese waiter scurrying homeward, there is virtually no one in the street. Most of the restaurants have already dimmed their lights and closed. Only where Konig sits does a solitary red neon dragon, with lights that run up and down its silhouette, blink hypnotically in the mist-hung night.

At exactly 2:58 Konig turns the key in his ignition. The engine turns over and he slips the car into drive. Before edging out onto the causeway leading to the bridge, he glances back over his shoulder to make certain that he himself is not being followed by the police. Once he has satisfied himself on that score, he proceeds to roll out.

The cobbled road over the bridge is slick from the rain and he moves slowly, not so much as a matter of precaution, but as a matter of timing. He wants to arrive precisely at 3 A.M. With the exception of the big subway cars rattling along beside him on the bridge, there is nothing in sight.

Somewhere just past the midpoint of the bridge it occurs to Konig that his mouth is very dry, his palms moist. But aside from a few vague, unarticulated misgivings, he is sanguine about the outcome of events.

Approaching the Brooklyn end of the bridge, he wipes the misted windshield again with the balled Kleenex and squints through the glass. Up ahead he can see nothing, and at the prospect of that, his heart begins to sink.

Glancing quickly at the illuminated dial of his watch, he sees that it is now exactly 3 A.M. Konig rolls to a stop at the far end of the bridge, shuts down the ignition, turns off the lights, and waits. The cold drizzle drums forlornly on the roof and hood. There is nothing in sight and he is profoundly alone. It's unthinkable that they would drag him out here at three in the morning and then, as a kind of test, or possibly just out of revenge, not show. Unthinkable. Or is it?

By 3:20 still no one has shown, and he has almost concluded that no one will. With a sense of sick, almost nauseous, grief, he is about to start up his car and drive away forever from that gray, cold, forsaken place. But just at that moment, almost spitefully, as if it had been watching all the while with a kind of vicious glee, a car rolls placidly around the corner, its headlights bearing down upon him, and moves like a white, phantomy object toward him out of the mist.

At a certain point, perhaps ten yards off, the car executes a graceful, unhurried U-turn, then backs around into the spot directly before him. Its motor and lights go off at once.

Scarcely breathing, Konig sits, frozen rigid, and waits. There is enough light from the bridge for him to see that the rear license plate of the car ahead has been covered over with a piece of burlap. He sits waiting there, watching the car, wondering if someone will get out, if he is to be given new instructions, if he should approach their car. Nothing seems to be happening—and still he waits.

Suddenly the lights of the white convertible switch on. He hears the engine turning over up ahead. Then the red blinker signals him right, and slowly, at last, they move out into the night.

It is a curious ride, aimless, meandering. Intentionally so. They turn here and there at random, stop and start for no discernible reason, all of it conducted at a speed of no more than twenty miles an hour. Clearly they are watching, and very closely, to see if any car attempts to follow Konig.

At that hour and in those narrow, huddled streets it would be impossible for anyone to follow without its becoming quickly apparent to the people in the car ahead. There is simply no one else out and driving at that hour. The cold, drizzly rain has even eliminated the occasional cruising cab.

From the bridge they move down Flatbush Avenue and out through Prospect Park. Somewhere in the middle of the park, on a road lined with woods, the white convertible stops. Konig rolls slowly up behind it and he too stops. Sitting there with his window open, listening to the rain dripping in the trees and his heart thumping in his chest, he waits.

In the next moment the white convertible moves out again, this time driving out of the park and onto Ocean Parkway. The stopping and starting business goes on exasperatingly—once at Ditmas Avenue and several times on Kings Highway.

At least a half-dozen times the white convertible swerves sharply, inexplicably, into residential blocks, winding slowly down them between large apartment buildings where people sleep unknowing and uncaring. Thus, traveling a bewildering route, the car ahead winds, turns, spins around on itself, while Konig is obliged to follow.

Several times during those interminable pauses, while the car up ahead merely sits there, its taillights glowing, malevolent and taunting, Konig is certain that this is the place. Now is the time. Any moment now they'll signal him to pull alongside and pass the money. But no. Instead they start up again, driving back onto Ocean Parkway, moving toward Shore Parkway, the awful winding, zigzagging, spinning about, resuming itself. Are they moving toward the water? They don't get on the Shore Parkway. Instead they go under the parkway, past Emmons Avenue, and out toward Coney Island.

It's approaching 4 A.M. now and still they've made no signal to him, no gesture. It is still this exasperating stop-and-start business, then sit and wait in the red taillight glow a few feet behind.

It's too early in the season for the amusement park to have opened, and they ride now parallel to the boardwalk in the shadow of those huge, unearthly, unattended structures—the Roller Coaster, the Whip, the Cyclone, the Parachute Jump, past the weirdly baroque architecture of the Steeplechase. All seem to be waiting there for some cosmic ringmaster to throw the switch. And then the lights going up, the music starting, and once again all the wild tumult of motion—swaying, dipping, lurching, whirling, rattling, roaring through the gaudy night.

The white convertible turns slowly into one of the fairground's parking lots. It is deserted, and all around it are the boarded-up windows of concessionaires—frankfurter and pizza stands, custard and corn-on-the-cob joints. The convertible rolls to a stop now, motor off, lights out, and waits. They're right at the water's edge. The mist is thicker here. Foghorns boom dolefully far out to sea. The air is redolent of salt and rotting seaweed. Sitting by the open window, the chill night air on his face, Konig can hear the tolling of a buoy not far off shore.

In the dim light of his dashboard, he checks his clock

—4:15 A.M. He pats the Gladstone bag beside him and waits.

Shortly he hears the motor of the convertible start up again, and with a sinking heart, he prepares to roll out once more. But this time something is different—a white-gloved hand protruding from the front right-hand window is waving him forward.

Eager to comply, Konig jerks and lurches his car forward, the white hand signaling him to stop directly parallel to it. He does so, shuddering to a halt directly opposite an open window.

It is pitch-dark in the parking lot, and in that mist-thick darkness he cannot see the occupants of the car, or even tell how many there are. He knows there are several, but all there is between him and them is that disembodied white-gloved hand thrust out toward him, waiting patiently and immobile.

Clumsily but without hesitation, he tugs the Gladstone bag across the seat, hoists it through the window and passes it anxiously to that waiting white hand. In all of that transaction not a word passes.

In the next moment the bag and the hand withdraw into the pitchy darkness of the convertible, the car's motor guns, and it roars off into the night, its headlights still extinguished. Far up ahead, Konig can hear its tires squeal around a corner, then nothing more.

He is all alone now in the parking lot, by himself there at the water's edge, the mist licking his windshield and the foghorns booming and the harbor buoys tolling like poor lost, stricken creatures far out to sea.

Somewhere near 5 A.M. Konig is driving back to Manhattan over the Brooklyn Bridge. The sky is still dark and a pale moon hangs low in the west, just above the jagged skyline of the sleeping city.

The car slides easily now between the tall, mist-hung towers, the tires singing on the slick cobbles. Spent, but curiously exhilarated, Konig drives. He has no way of knowing that only five minutes before, Frank Haggard had passed over that same bridge at a high speed, a crumpled sheet of paper with the scribbled address he'd finally extracted from Klejewski in his pocket, and two patrol cars from the 23rd Precinct winging along behind him.

Going home now to Riverdale is unthinkable. And, a

Meacham said, Lolly would not be released until twenty-four hours after the payoff, presumably giving him plenty of time to get far out of the state. The only place Konig could go now, even at 5 A.M. on a Sunday morning, is his office. After all, it is the only refuge, the only solace, he's known for nearly forty years.

Ten minutes or so up the FDR Drive, exiting at 23rd Street, driving up First Avenue to 30th Street, and he's there. Parking his car in the private lot in the back, he walks around the building and through the front gate, past the startled, drowsy night man still on duty there.

Shortly he's at his desk, coffee boiling in a beaker over the Bunsen burner, and a cigar already smoking in the littered ashtray on his desk. He busies himself there, making a concentrated effort to think neither of the night he's just spent nor of the past five months. Only the future and Lolly and getting "to know each other again." Isn't that what the Mayor said? Well, he would make up now for lost time. He would make up for a lot of things.

Whistling softly to himself, he goes about watering his plants, which have been sadly ignored—the poor drooping Dracaenas and the philodendrons, the spider plants and various succulents, looking ragged and parched. Only the glorious wandering Jew flourishes there in the window.

Then, with a sense of relief, he is once again settled at his desk, the good familiar feel of wood and old, cracked leather, the not unpleasant smell of cigar smoke and formalin wafting all about him.

There, on top if everything, lies a large, brown manila envelope with a Fort Bragg imprint. In it he finds the complete medical and dental records of Browder and Ussery. Included with the records and clipped to each are two standard military ID photographs. He leans back in his chair now and studies them.

Browder is precisely as Konig imagined him from his skull conformation—a tough, craggy face with a rather brutal Slavic cast to it. The closely cropped hair, worn GI fashion, and the heavy, prognathic jaw that he'd seen in the skull all tend to heighten the rather brutal mien. But the eyes are not brutal at all; indeed, there's something even shy and rather vulnerable in them.

Ussery, on the other hand, comes as a complete surprise to him. Even something of a shock. Recalling the hand with the luridly lacquered nails, Konig had naturally expected something fey and effeminate. But what he sees before him now takes his breath away. It is a strikingly beautiful face—small, delicate bones, large, oddly haunted eyes—a kind of male Nefertiti. A rare orchid, exquisite, ephemeral, will-o'-the-wispish. There is, too, something about it unspeakably sad. Perhaps it is the sense of doom that it conveys.

Included is a letter from Colonel McCormick saying that the Army had notified the next of kin. Browder had a wife from whom he was separated. She had already instructed them that the remains were to be sent to her for burial. Ussery's people, however, were Southern Baptist farmers—pious, hardworking, churchgoing. They were mortified at the scandal and wanted no part of the boy's remains.

Putting the records aside, Konig is now ready to turn to the stack of unopened mail before him. Letters from clinics, foundations, universities, and hospitals; correspondence from colleagues, old classmates practicing all over the world. Each seeking some favor, petitioning advice, questioning him on aspects of cardiovascular diseases, central nervous system injuries, narcotic deaths, sudden unexplained natural death.

A Chief of Police in Philadelphia wanted ballistics advice in the murder of an old grocer there. A coroner in Cincinnati queried him on a complex toxicological problem. A district attorney in Coos County, New Hampshire, petitioned his services as an expert witness in a crime of passion. A physician in Rangoon, Burma, sought his guidance in establishing a department of forensic medicine at the university there.

Then came the letters of a more personal nature— a grieving mother, a bereft father. These letters, though the details differ widely, are always the same. The same strain of grief and puzzlement runs through them. Written by good, often simple, people who'd been hurt and wanted to know why. Often he couldn't tell them. The mystery was as deep to him as it was to them. But when he had answers, or solace, he gave them. A woman in Topeka had just lost her infant child as a result of crib death. She had read somewhere that he was doing re search in the subject and wanted to know why this had happened to her child and if somehow she was responsi ble. A father in Wilmington thanked him for concluding that the death of his daughter was due to natural causes and not suicide. He and his wife were Catholics, he explained, and the question of suicide was unbearable to them.

"Dear Paul," wrote an old classmate practicing in Spokane, "Here's a lulu for you—"

Konig laughs out loud, recalling suddenly a bright, boyish face belonging to a young man who used to sit behind him in Bahnhoff's pathology lectures.

When he looks up again it is half-past six and the first gray, sooty fingers of dawn streak the sky outside his office windows. He is just about to resume his reading when the phone rings. He sits watching it impassively, as if he'd never seen such a thing before. It rings again, and in the large, empty building, at that hour, it has a ghostly and foreboding sound.

First he's annoyed, then apprehensive. Who could be calling him there at such an hour? Who would even know he was there? Someone who'd tried to reach him in Riverdale and found him not at home.

The phone rings again, shrill, insistent, echoing through the empty corridors of the building. Reaching for it, he pulls his hand back. It rings once more. Suddenly he's aware of sweat on his forehead. His body feels clammy beneath his clothing.

Finally he picks up the receiver, but he doesn't bring it immediately to his ear. Instead he holds it at arm's length, only a few inches off the cradle, hearing then a man's voice, very far off, repeating the word "Hello" over and over again.

"Hello," Konig murmurs hesitantly into the phone.

"Hello."

A pause follows, portentous and clumsy, in which both parties sit there listening to each other breath.

"Paul, it's me."

"Where are you?" Konig snaps, his heart starting to sink.

"Sheepshead Bay," Haggard says gruffly. "I got Meacham—" Another interminable pause. "But I'm afraid—"

Konig doesn't actually hear the rest of it but he knows what the detective is saying.

For a long time, it seems, neither man speaks. Konig merely sits there looking at the pile of opened letters on his desk, feeling nothing. It's as if someone had just spoken to him in some old, lost tongue. It is information he cannot begin to comprehend. Then finally, clearing his throat, he speaks. "When?"

"Just before we got there. They waited for your bag of cash to arrive. Then they did it. Had no intention of ever freeing her. They were getting ready to dump her in the bay when we busted in."

Nodding his head ever so slightly, Konig hunches over his desk while Haggard waits wordless at the other end for him to react. But there's no reaction. No shrieks. No groans. Not even a choice obscenity hurled at the gods. "Bring her in" is all he can say. "Bring her in now."

≈≈ 65 ≈≈

AT 6:45 A.M. ON A SUNDAY MORNING THE CITY HAS A soiled, spent look. The revelry and carnage of the night are over and soon the ragpickers and sweepers will come to clean up the mess. The big, buglike sanitation trucks will double-park in the side streets, grinding up the debris of today to make room for that of tomorrow.

Standing at a window now, Konig gazes over to the west. The sky is glowing neon pink and crimson above the Times Square area where some of the night lights have not yet gone out. It has the look of a city in flames.

Down below on the street the stray cats are picking among the overflowing trash cans. A few dirty pigeons wamble in the gutter and an old tart in a rumpled dress weaves precariously down 30th Street. Her hair is hennaed; she has a Kewpie-doll face heavily made up like a mask, a hideous *maquillage*. At a certain point she bumps into one of the trash cans, nearly knocking it over, but only dislodging the lid, sending it clattering to the pavement with a loud crash.

A few early risers are already out there too, walking the dogs, picking up the milk and *The New York Times*

Soon all the bells of the churches will be pealing. The great cathedral bells—St. Patrick's, St. Bartholomew's, St. Clement's, St. Mark's—all the church bells of the great Empire City calling the faithful to worship. Great gorgeous bells tolling diapasons, their huge bronze throats sending great lead circles of sound skyward.

From somewhere far to the south Konig can hear the sound of a distant siren screaming northward up the FDR Drive. He gazes toward the river now. The water has a choppy, sullen look. A tugboat and a sand barge are out there plying upriver.

It had never occurred to him before how close the morgue was to the river. And then quite suddenly it dawns on him that its placement there was not merely fortuitous, that most of the morgues of the great cities of the world had been built either on the banks of or in close proximity to mighty rivers. Similarly, all the great necropolises of antiquity. All had been built on or near water. Some ancient superstition, no doubt, he thought, trying to recall some passage in Herodotus about that. Something about facilitating the voyage of the soul back into the great ocean of time. Suddenly, as if in a flash, he has a vision of all the great rivers of the world flowing at that moment into the East River: the mighty Nile and the Tiber, the Tigris and the Euphrates, the Danube and the Ganges, the Rhine and the Volga, and the Father of Waters, the Mississippi, all flowing past his window, bearing their cargoes of dead souls out to sea. Then suddenly, in another flash, he sees all the great necropolises of the world rising below him on the banks of the river —Memphis, Thebes, Carthage, Tyre, Persepolis. There, King Djoser's mighty tomb, Saqqara, with its huge pentagons of marble columns. And there, the great mortuary temples all along the Nile—Luxor, Karnak, Birket Habu. He sees the Roman catacombs—St. Calixtus and St. Sebastian—those intestinal tunnels winding along beneath the Via Appia, and then, the funerary pyres, the burning ghats, beside the muddy Ganges. And there, the great efficient incinerators of Buchenwald and Auschwitz. Then, that even greater marvel of technological efficiency— Hiroshima, and its thousands incinerated in a flash. All those burial grounds, he sees. All those graves suddenly open and yawning. All those souls suddenly flowing past him on the river below his window.

Then, in another blink of an eye, the vision has boiled past, sinking slowly beneath the brown, sullen waters of the East River, leaving in its place only a view of the Queens skyline sprawling gray and squalid beyond it.

The sound of wailing sirens has grown louder and closer. Dozens of them appear to be converging on the spot where Konig stands, looking down into the street. Shortly several patrol cars turn into 30th Street, followed by a large black police van, swaying and tilting as it rounds the corner. Then come several more patrol cars and another van, causing a small crowd to collect outside the courtyard at the rear entrance.

Half a dozen night men from the morgue stream out into the courtyard, wheeling their steel gurney carts up to the vans. The doors of the patrol cars are opening and slamming, their dome lights still rotating slowly. Police pour out from them into the street, many of them sooty, unhatted, their eyes bleared, their uniforms strewn with ashes. The drivers of the big Black Marias are out now too, moving around in the courtyard, swinging open the big rear doors of the vans.

Then from both vans, simultaneously, a grisly cargo is unloaded. Nearly twenty cadavers, burned and charred beyond recognition, victims of a ghetto fire in Bed-Stuy. One sack after the next—women, children, the old, the young—all unloaded onto the shiny carts, then swiftly, efficiently wheeled through the big basement portal gates to the mortuary beyond.

There are more sirens and Konig watches a 41st Precinct patrol car turn the corner, leading another van. Yet another complement of the shot, the slashed, the bludgeoned and garroted. No more than a typical assortment of a no more than typical Saturday night.

At last another patrol car wheels slowly into the street. No van follows this. It rolls slowly down the street with a kind of bleak majesty, weaving through the gathering congestion, and turns into the courtyard just below the window. In the next moment, Konig sees Haggard's fleecy white hair through the car window, then his tall, stooping figure climbing out from the front seat. His hat is off, his rumpled raincoat open, his tie loose at the collar. Two uniformed patrolmen get out of the car and come around the back.

Standing there in the sour dawn, in the slight, mizzling

rain, Haggard glances upward and sees Konig standing two stories above him at the open window looking down. They stand there for a moment merely staring at each other.

Shortly, Konig himself is down in the courtyard, limping through the noise and confusion, past the chatter of police and porters, canvas sacks and rolling carts, past the gaping crowds gathered just outside a makeshift police cordon. He is moving directly toward the place where Haggard and the two patrolmen are struggling to remove a large canvas sack from the rear seat of the car.

Haggard glances up as Konig joins them, and without a word they gently lift the sack out of the back of the car. One of the porters, without knowing what is contained in the sack, rushes over with a cart and starts to take the sack from them. Instantly Konig's face flushes, his eyes bulge. He flings the man roughly aside. It is the diener—the little Albanian with the furtive eyes.

"Don't touch her," Konig booms. "You keep your goddamned hands off her."

Cringing, the little man gapes at him, then turns and slithers off into the milling confusion around the vans.

Haggard and the two patrolmen start to lift the sack onto the cart.

"Leave her alone," Konig shouts, pushing them aside, prizing their hands from the canvas. "I'll take her. I'll take her now. Don't touch her."

They watch silently as he eases the sack onto the cart, then proceeds to push it, all by himself, down the ramp and through the large open gates leading to the mortuary.

Inside, the place is jumping. A blur of motion. Carts rolling in and out. People shouting. Phones ringing. The doors of the cold lockers banging open and closed.

Konig is scarcely noticed as he rolls his cart into one of the empty autopsy rooms. He looks like anyone else there, hard at work, going about his business. No one knows anything of his grief.

Unloading his burden onto one of the examination tables, the top of the sack comes undone and a coil of soft honey-brown hair spills up over the top of it.

Now he stands there over the half-opened sack, his legs wobbling beneath him, thinking that he's about to throw up. But nothing happens. The worst of it is that nothing really happens. He feels nothing. Forty years in the business have made a zombie of him, and after the wobbly legs and the slight nausea, he is once again the dispassionate professional, that highly skilled, carefully calibrated instrument, measuring, recording, deducing.

Finally Lolly Konig is out of the canvas and lying there on the table. He can see where they'd beaten her, the blackened eyes, the large contusions about the face and head, the ugly weals on her shoulders and ribs, the black-and-blue marks circling like dark planets about her temples. He can see nail marks and the dull yellow-violet abrasions across her throat where she'd been strangled. Palpating the area gently, he can feel the fracture of the thyroid cartilage, and quickly suspects the cause of death to be an avulsion of the hyoid membrane with fractures to the great horn of the hyoid bone.

Her tongue protrudes slightly and is bruised where she'd bitten deeply during the process of being throttled. He tucks the tongue gently back in, reducing somewhat the harsh effect of rictus on her features. Her eyes are still half open and with a thumb he carefully rolls the lids up, revealing the widespread petechial hemorrhage beneath the conjunctivae and the unmistakable signs of *tache noire* just beginning to radiate out from the pupils.

There is little sign of rigor and, as of yet, no lividity. She is still warm, her body temperature, he estimates, only a few degrees below the norm. Very soon it will start to take its dip.

With his thumb he gently presses the lids closed. She seems now almost to be sleeping, an oddly peaceful expression about her features. Just as she used to look as a child when he'd come in late from work and poke his head through her door to have a look at her. She looks just like that now, an innocent little girl sleeping, her face wreathed in tousled honey hair, dreaming of toys and dresses and birthday parties. He has a sudden image of her pedaling toward him on a tricycle. Poor bird. Poor pretty bird. This little torn, crumpled sleeping thing was his child. He might just nudge her now and she would stir in the sweet warmth of her bed. Then turn and yawn, glance up at him through drowsy eyes and smile.

Why should a dog, a horse, a rat, have life,
And thou no breath at all?

For a moment he's the old mad king again, lurching
across the stage in an ill-fitting costume in a laughably inept college production. "Howl, howl, howl."

Gazing down at her now he pushes the tumbled hair
from off her face and smoothes it. Suddenly, looking down
at her, he sees the lineaments of his own face staring up
at him. To him she'd always looked like Ida. Now in
death he could see his own face in her reposeful features.

"*Looks exactly like you, Ida.*" He laughs and it's more
than twenty years ago in a maternity ward on Long Island. "*The spitting image.*"

"*No—I've seen her too. That's your daughter, Paul Konig. Your chin. All your—*"

"*Don't push the child so, Paul.*"
"*Who's pushing her? Hell, she's got to learn.*"

"*Hurry, Lolly, hurry. The bus is coming. If you miss
that damn thing, don't expect me to drive you way the
hell up to camp—*"

Suddenly the door of the autopsy room bursts open.
"Chief?" It's the night doorman from upstairs. "Phone
call for you."

"Who is it?"

"Sergeant Flynn."

"Tell him I'm not here."

The attendant gawks at him helplessly.

"I don't want to talk to him," Konig says quietly. "I
don't want to talk to anyone."

The man shrugs. The door closes and once more Konig
is alone. For a while he merely sits there, holding the
cold, stiffening hand of his child, waiting for her to
awaken, calling up in his mind old, lost memories—holi-
days, picnics, long vacations at the shore. Ida is there and
so is Lolly. Always Lolly—a bright, funny little girl, ani-
mated, irrepressible, so invulnerable to harm. They're all
there. All together again.

Again the door opens, and once more the attendant is
standing there, shamefaced and stammering. "Sorry,

Chief. It's Flynn again. Says he's gotta talk to you. Says it's an emergency."

"Tell him I don't care." Konig stares listlessly at his child. "Tell him to go away."

"I did, but he says he's just gotta talk to you."

"Tell him—" Konig sighs, still gazing at Lolly. Then, knowing he can do nothing more there, he covers her gently and turns to follow the night man upstairs, up the green spiral steps of Stairway D and out of the under-world of 30th Street.

"You were right. Goddamn it, you were right."

"Right? Right about what?"

"That newspaper with the serial number—"

"Oh," Konig murmurs disconsolately.

"What a brainstorm," Flynn roars into the phone. "What a goddamn brainstorm."

"You get the guy?"

"Get him? Did I get him? You bet your sweet ass I did. Don't ask me all the details. I'll show you the blis-ters on my feet when I see you. But I got him. Walked right in on the son of a bitch. No sooner than I laid it on him than the poor bastard broke down, started to bawl. Confessed the whole thing. Said he was glad I found him 'cause he was gettin' all set to do it again. Had the guys all picked out too. Another pair of queens. Live down the block from him. Got a thing about fags, this guy, and if you ask me, he walks a little tippytoes himself." Flynn howls gleefully. "I tell you—"

Konig sits at his desk, his hand covering his eyes to block out the glare of sunrise streaming through his win-dow. "Was it the Salvation Army guy?"

"Sure it was. Knew it all along. Had a hunch," Flynn roars, full of the exhilaration of victory. "When I come in, the son of a bitch was still in his collars. Colonel Divine he calls himself. *Divine*. Can you beat that? Guy was a missionary in Africa."

"A doctor?"

"No, but he had medical training. Worked in a hospital out in the bush somewhere. Knew a lot about medicine. Used to assist the doctors in the surgery. Pull teeth. Sew up holes. Stuff like that. Place was full of old medical journals. Had a whole drawer full of medical instruments. Forceps, sutures, the works."

"That figures," Konig murmurs listlessly. "How come he left the church?"

"Did I say he left the church?"

"You said he *was* a medical missionary."

"Oh—right. So I did." Flynn laughs. "You're some smart guy for a sawbones. He didn't actually leave the church. The way he tells it he had a crisis of faith. But what actually happened was that he got busted."

"Defrocked?"

"What?"

"Never mind. Go on."

"Sure," Flynn says, momentarily puzzled, the wind out of his sails. "Anyway, I contacted the church organization that sent him out there, and they refused to discuss the case. Just said he was asked to leave. Turn in his collar, so to speak." Flynn giggles meanly. "So he come back to the States and joined the Salvation Army. They canned him too. Around seven years ago. I just got off the phone with the commander of the New York Division. Chap by the name of Pierce. He wasn't too anxious to talk about it either. Just said Divine was asked to leave for conduct unbecomin' and so forth and so on. A lot of fancy argle-bargle, but you get the picture."

"Yeah, I get it. And he's been running around loose in that uniform all this time?"

"Sure. Like I told you—found his name on a ten-year-old Salvation Army duty roster. He had a key to the old shelter down on South Street. Been lettin' himself in and out of the place for years; operatin' on his own. Ministerin' to the flock. Savin' all the lost souls, God help us." Flynn howls merrily. "Department's got at least half a dozen unsolved homicides on the books involvin' derelicts in that South Street area. And they're pretty sure now this is the guy that did 'em. Actually, I kinda like the guy. He was very nice. A real gent."

"Sounds like a sweetheart," says Konig, desolation heavy in his voice. "Glad you got him. Listen—I can't—"

"Hey. Wait a minute. Don't hang up. I got a job."

"What?"

"I got a mess down here."

"What?"

"Town house. Gramercy Park. It's a slaughterhouse."

"Oh, come on, Flynn."

"What d'ya mean 'come on'?"

"I can't come now."

"What d'ya mean you can't come now? You gotta come. I can't handle this alone."

"Well, you're going to have to. I'm finished. I'm all done here."

"Done? What d'ya mean 'done'? Day's just started. Sunday's the best day for work."

"No—I mean I'm finished here for good."

"For good?"

There's a pause in which Konig can hear the detective's puzzlement. "Forever," he goes on. "No more for me. Never again."

"What d'ya mean 'never again'? What the hell is all this about?"

"Just that. Never again. Goodbye," Konig murmurs quietly and hangs up.

For a time he sits there slumped over his desk, numb and scarcely hearing the shouting and hurrying footsteps, the banging doors, the noise and excitement outside his window as more canvas sacks are brought in from the fire in Bed-Stuy. The building has collapsed now and dozens of charred and broken bodies have been dug out of the rubble and rushed here for identification.

Once again the phone rings. Konig reaches for it. Lifts it to his ear.

"I get it. I get it now," Flynn jeers at him through the wires. "It's the goddamned morning papers. Right?"

"What morning papers?"

"The *Times*. The *News*." Flynn laughs harshly, tauntingly. "Listen. I read them too. I know all about it. The Robinson case. The body-snatching thing. The grand jury investigation. They really put it to you." Flynn howls gleefully. "They really shafted you this time."

"Shut up, Flynn."

The detective's glee grows even more shrill. "They scared you, didn't they? First time I ever seen you scared. You gonna go run and hide someplace now just 'cause they gave you the business? Screw them holier-than-thou bastards. Sittin' on their asses all day with a